Other books by Randy V

COVEN OF CELSUS – HEATHER
another erotic horror

COVEN OF CELSUS – NONA
Tears of the Sorceress
(Co-written with Ellie Ravencroft)

COVEN OF CELSUS – TRILOGY
The complete collection

Coven of Celsus
Elizabeth

an erotic horror

(6th edition)

Randy V

Coven of Celsus - Elizabeth

*Published under the pseudonym Shauna Tully, Coven of Celsus —
Elizabeth was first released in 2007 through iUniverse.*

Published by White Choker Publishing, LLC

Sturgis, South Dakota

Available exclusively through Amazon

ISBN: 979-8-9889543-1-6

Dedicated to Justine & Juliette,
the ones who freed me.

𝍸/𝍸/𝍪𝍪𝍸 𝍪𝍸

Coven of Celsus - Elizabeth

CONTENTS

O Jews and Christians, no God or son of a God either came or will come down to earth. But if you mean that certain angels did so, then what do you call them? Are they gods, or some other race of beings? Some other race of beings doubtless, and in all probability demons. They assert that the angels who come down from heaven to confer benefits on mankind are a different race from the gods; in all probability, they would be called demons.

Celsus (*c.* A.D. 178)

Lions shall meet with hyenas; a wolf-demon shall call to them;
There too Lilith shall repose, and find a place to rest.
There shall the owl nest and lay and hatch and brood in its shadow.

Isaiah 34:14

CONTACT

Her mind went blank as she fought through the brutal icy wind. It was only two blocks to the university's coffee shop, yet it seemed much longer in the bitter cold. This particular December evening seemed heavy with an inevitable snowstorm. She could smell it…and then *He* appeared.

Dressed entirely in black, his long wool trench openly flapping toward her like two great wings, he seemed immune to the cold. A weird, fleeting fantasy left her imagining the cold radiating from him. As their paths converged, their eyes met.

I know you.

For a timeless moment, she held his stare as they passed each other. The biting wind then forced her head down for protection. She kept up her tenacious march without looking back and arrived at the little shop a few minutes later. Two blocks had passed in an instant as she tried to figure out where she'd seen him before.

Oh well, she thought as she shook off the cold. She found her favorite spot, ordered an espresso, settled in with her books, and prepared for her final exam in cultural anthropology. She had two hours and was determined to get a perfect score.

27-year-old Elizabeth Marie Larochelle has equal parts French, German, Irish, and Ojibwa blood. She has lengthy, shimmering, dark-brown hair with large curls that bounce when she walks. With a glance from her doe-like brown eyes, she can make any man's heart skip a beat. At five feet two inches in height, she is voluptuous and soft but proportionate to her stature.

She was born and raised in Toledo, Ohio, known as the Glass City for its greatly diminished glass industry. She lived there her entire life until she moved to Ann Arbor, Michigan, to pursue higher education at the nontraditional age of 25. Her teachers and peers described her as intelligent, moody, and unapproachable.

She was a loner throughout high school and never fit in with typical cliques. She didn't even have a real friend until she started college and met Carrie, a fellow student and next-door neighbor at her apartment complex.

She rarely had problems getting boyfriends; she just couldn't keep them. Her life's small list of exes chalked this up to her subtly strange nature. She was not physically intimidating, but something in her eyes was disturbing and challenging to deal with for any length of time.

Nothing ever came easy for her, especially her admission into a Big Ten university. She fought hard for every milestone and saved enough money to pay for one school semester while her parents covered another. Unfortunately, it would take maxing out on student loans to accomplish her academic goals.

She was just finishing up her third semester and had already changed her major three times, once at the end of each semester. She started in education and history when she first arrived. Hearing about all the opportunities in business administration, she switched. After finding out how boring those classes were, and with every possible elective used up, she finally settled into anthropology. At the end of her first semester in the new discipline, Elizabeth was sure she had found her home.

The study of other cultures and beliefs had always intrigued Elizabeth. However, she openly rebelled against some of the elitist Western interpretations, especially when it came to Native American culture. She never used the word

Ojibwa when someone had the intelligence to ask which tribe ran through her veins. For her, *Anishinabe* was the correct and only nomenclature.

She was never satisfied with anything in her life, often depressed and discontented, constantly feeling like she was born in the wrong place at the wrong time, and continually questioning those feelings.

As a child, she suffered night terrors regularly. When they came upon her, she would cry or speak in what her Native American grandmother would call the 'spirit voice'—and sometimes, she would scream hysterically. The worst episodes occurred when she would sit up silently, eyes glaring wide, rotating her head from side to side disturbingly slowly. This behavior frightened her parents more than the screaming. The terrors simply stopped when she reached puberty.

Although she had always been somewhat moody, she was in perfect health otherwise. In fact, she had never been sick. As her parents recalled, Elizabeth hadn't had so much as a cold or a fever the entire time she lived with them. They attributed it to good nutrition and genes, which was clearly extraordinary. Her mental state was another matter.

She had fought depression nearly every day of her life. She had seen two therapists, but neither could pinpoint the source of her despair. The sadness she felt was relentless and unforgiving. Her own literal description of the way she felt was that it was like having a vast sucking black void in the middle of her chest. She said when the sadness came upon her, it was like her heart was cut open and breaking. This was her life before the devil came for her.

Just before their fated meeting, she had contemplated suicide. Hard depression had set upon her again, and she wrote the following poem the night before their paths crossed.

The darkness grips me
Grips me tightly
A vice-like embrace,
Draining life force and will
Too blind to care about the future
Too distant to reach into the past
The present, a longing for the suffering to end
No love, no touch,
Only the cold embrace of darkness
While the heart reluctantly beats

Elizabeth was used to crushing depression, but nothing could prepare her for what would come. As she would soon learn, suicide was never an option.

After an hour of studying, the darkness had come. Elizabeth felt she was being watched, and looking up from her notes, she realized that the young man in the black wool trench had followed her into the shop. He sat no more than 20 feet away, sipping a cup of Earl Grey tea and watching her intently. He made no secret of it, either. It was an unsettling stare, and her initial reaction was apprehension.

A slow and confident smile emerged from his lips as if he could sense her angst. He took a sip from his cup and narrowed his eyes upon her.

Come to me.

Elizabeth could see and feel his intensity. Although she was reluctant to do so, she rose from her seat as if compelled. She wasn't comfortable being drawn to something against her will. The first year of college had accustomed her to making her own decisions, especially regarding men. So she decided to try a little power trip of her own. She walked toward him, held her head slightly higher than usual, and began a toe-to-head scrutiny from across the fairly crowded shop.

Shiny black dress shoes with wingtips? His feet must be frozen. Nice pleated black slacks. Is he a professor? No, too young. Black button-up shirt, perfect starched collar, a diamond in the left ear, large silver ring with an onyx stone, deep blue eyes, shoulder-length blond hair—his eyes—I have seen him before—somewhere.

He was enticing. Cautiously approaching without betraying her emotions, she sat across the table from him. His eyes never left hers. It was disturbing to her that he did not blink or flinch. Most men couldn't handle direct eye contact with her for very long. She thought he was trying to play her and sensed he was good at this game. She decided to speak first, in her mind getting the upper hand immediately.

"Did you follow me here?"

"I did," he responded confidently. "What are you studying?"

"Cultural anthropology," she replied, struggling to contain her curiosity.

"One of my favorite subjects."

"Do you teach here?"

"No," he said, looking right through her again.

"Have we met before?"

"Not in this lifetime."

Elizabeth was not amused, yet she was fascinated in the oldest sense of the word. Her brain came to a screeching halt as he fixed her with a penetrating stare. Finally, when the silence became uncomfortable, he spoke.

"I'm here—for you."

Typically, Elizabeth would respond to this type of line with a cutting retort. But she stopped just as the dagger was about to leave her lips. Something was commanding about him. It wasn't arrogance he exuded but the sheer force of will. This excited her, and she tried to respond flirtatiously but still revealed her fear with a slight quiver in her voice.

"Oh yeah? Why me?"

He did not answer but instead took another sip of tea. She didn't know what was happening, nor could she understand why she was getting so excited. Her world sensuously melted away before him. There was an incredible animal attraction about him and a weird familiarity.

"Come visit me when it's warmer," he said.

He spoke with a calmer voice, and the tonal change was so abrupt that it left an echo of longing within her. The content of his words upset her. There was something very intense—in the middle of winter, in the middle of her depression—and now she was being blown off with *when it's warmer*. Her mouth dropped open from the mild shock as he held out his hand and introduced himself.

"Celsus."

She took his hand, which felt hot. She barely responded.

"Elizabeth."

"Enchanted," he said before kissing her hand. "When will you be here again?"

"I have another final Friday. I always come here to study before a test. I'll be in at two in the afternoon this Friday."

She was trying not to sound so enthusiastic. Still, her mind seemed detached from her voice, and the words sounded uncontrollably desperate. Celsus grinned and responded.

"Since you are an anthropology student, you must understand what a cultural barrier is, right?"

"Of course," she answered, somewhat perplexed.

"Well, we must bridge that barrier before we meet again."

She cocked her heels outward so that her toes pointed inward.

"Whatever do you mean, sir?"

She acted childish, flirting to retain his presence. But the mysterious Celsus had already slipped into his long, black trench.

"You will understand soon enough. Wear this ribbon around your neck Friday when you come back."

He produced what looked like curled sheets of old paper from his coat, secured with a dark purple, satin choker. The choker was half an inch wide, and the color was vibrant.

"Why?"

"You'll know soon enough. Pouvez-vous lire français?"

She found the entire encounter very creepy. She could not think clearly nor shut off the uncharacteristic lust that had utterly engulfed her.

"I know you spoke French to me, but I can't... My great-grandfather came from France. I just never learned it," she muttered.

Celsus gave her a warm smile, exited the front door, and disappeared into the swirling snow and dark of night, all in one seemingly flawless movement.

Elizabeth suddenly felt she had just encountered something unnatural. Her knees felt weak, and her head was spinning. The fear of this man was still there, but so was the sexual tension. She was soaking wet.

Dazed and unable to think clearly, she pulled the ribbon off and exposed four old sheets of paper. The pages were so old that she assumed they would crumble to dust if not handled with the utmost care. They appeared authentic, and she quickly looked to see if anyone had noticed. No one noticed, and no one cared. It was finals week.

She did not speak French but recognized immediately that the text was elegantly written in French, probably with a quill pen. The paper seemed made of parchment and looked ancient and fragile, its edges broken and decayed. One item was decipherable immediately—the date at the top of the first page.

She examined the fascinating documents and fought for some rational explanation, contemplating their authenticity and monetary value. She returned to her seat in a complete daze and carefully placed them in the back of her giant textbook. They would be protected until she could have someone look at them.

She gazed at the exit again—into the night—stunned. Her thoughts were disjointed, and she could not process anything. Trying hard to ground herself, she thought of her upcoming test. It was the life-saving rope to reality she desperately needed.

It took enormous discipline, but she was able to study for her test and scored 108 out of a possible 110. That night, lying alone in bed, she thought of his lips, warm blue eyes, confidence, and absolute command over her. She imagined him taking control of her body, taking control of her life, giving herself totally and absolutely to his every desire. She brought herself to a devastating climax, imagining him thrusting into her. She dreamed of him, was possessed by him, and Friday could not come soon enough.

Celsus was born in Portland, Oregon, in January 1980. He is half Norwegian and half German. His pale skin, shoulder-length dirty blonde hair, and deep blue eyes reveal his Norse-Teutonic bloodlines. Except for his sister Sophia, he has not seen his family in years, nor does he care to. Celsus is not his given birth name. Only two women know this surname and have sworn never to speak it out loud.

Standing five-foot-nine, he is not someone you would notice in a crowd, and he likes it that way. While not imposing nor remarkably handsome, he is unsuspectingly strong. He has an unlimited reservoir of charm, charisma, and something akin to animal magnetism. He is a master of seduction.

Erratic, moody, and control-obsessed in the extreme, he can be generous, benevolent, loving, or brutally sadistic. He is a despot but reveals a paradox concerning the women in his life. The women refer to him as 'the master,' and when addressing him directly, they end most of their sentences with 'my lord.'

Of these women, he is consistently kind to his younger sister, Sophia, regardless of his mood. There are rumors of an incestuous relationship between them. When seen together, they are very intimate, like lovers rather than siblings.

During childhood and adolescence, he had only one friend, a Brazilian immigrant girl named Nona. The two were inseparable and attended school together from kindergarten through high school. It is well known that the other children feared both of them immensely. Even their teachers were unnerved by their superior intelligence, apathy toward fun and games, and refusal to socialize with other children.

He still laughs when he remembers homework, which consisted of creating mistakes so as not to draw attention to his abnormal intelligence. It was all a ruse to bide time until he could leave without being pursued.

At 18, he took a trip to Boston for what he explained to his parents as "a unique opportunity." He returned with enormous sums of money and hid this from everyone, including his parents. After turning 20, he told them he was on a spiritual quest, and they should forget about him. At the turn of the century, he left his home in Oregon for good. His then 18-year-old sister Sophia and his best friend Nona departed with him.

Getting ready for this second meeting was a nerve-racking task. After trying on several different outfits, Elizabeth's thoughts revealed her frustration.

If he doesn't like what I'm wearing, fuck him.

She paused for a moment.

I think I'll go with the low-cut white blouse.

Slipping into it, she took a deep breath, pulled on her tight black corduroy jeans, looked into the mirror, and admired herself.

Yeah, he'll like this.

It was frigid that Friday, but thankfully, there was not even a breeze between her and the coffee shop. The sun created countless shining diamonds from the freshly fallen snow, and the anticipation silently killed her. The shop was not so crowded this afternoon as most finals had passed throughout the week. Her last torture—biology.

She reached her usual spot while glancing in all directions for Celsus. Disappointed by his absence, she reluctantly sat down, dragged out her enormous textbook, and began watching the front door. Like a teenager with a crush, she flipped her hair back over her shoulder to ensure the purple satin choker was completely visible.

It's a little early yet, she thought.

Then, a sweet female voice surprised her from behind her left ear.

"You must be Elizabeth."

She turned, and there stood a cute and seemingly happy young woman—a woman of short stature who looked around sixteen, with thick, wild blond hair in tight ringlets that barely touched her shoulders and a fierce sexuality that seemed to radiate from her.

This girl displayed the same discomforting fixed gaze that Celsus had. She wore white snow boots, tight faded jeans, and a baby blue shirt with a big red heart in the middle, all under a white oversized winter parka. The sleeves were so long that only her fingertips peeking out were visible. Her eyes were a brilliant light blue and exuded a completely deceiving vulnerability. Elizabeth immediately and irrationally felt this woman was highly sexual and deviant. A white satin choker adorned her neck.

"I'm Linzie," she said, holding out her hand exactly as her predecessor had.

Again, Elizabeth felt compelled to comply with another perfect stranger. As soon as they touched, Elizabeth's world fell away once more. Time stopped, and it seemed she would faint for a moment if she didn't regain her composure. Pulling her hand back, she inquired calmly.

"What's with the chokers?"

Elizabeth surprised herself with this question and how she asked as if this were some ordinary conversation. In fact, it was a subconscious defensive tactic to hold onto her reality. Strangely, this unusual meeting became a new power struggle that toyed with her memories and sanity. She felt she had met or seen this girl before. Linzie responded, completely ignoring Elizabeth's question with one of her own.

"You have a final today?"

"At five," Elizabeth said as she attempted to ground herself.

"The master loves to play with us. It's just the way he is. He can't help it."

"What are you talking about? Do you go to school here?"

"I can't say the chokers constitute rank except for Megan's. Her choker is white like mine but has a ruby in the middle. She definitely holds rank. Nona's choker has a stone, too—lapis lazuli."

Linzie's eyes sparkled with mischief. She twirled a pair of sunglasses in her hand and giggled in an exceedingly cute and strangely hypnotic manner. Elizabeth found her world slowing down and thought to herself, *the master*? As if Linzie had read her thoughts, she politely explained.

"I am from the House of Lord Celsus."

It finally struck Elizabeth where she had heard the unusual name. There was talk on campus of some cultish playboy's mansion north of the city and out of the public eye. The name was mentioned. She never got the whole story, nor had she met anyone who had actually been there.

"What is the House of Lord Celsus?" Elizabeth condescendingly asked.

Linzie's disposition immediately changed. The quickness of this transformation took Elizabeth by surprise. Linzie leaned within inches of her lips and spoke softly.

"How about your place—tonight?"

The sound of her voice and the intensity of her eyes pulled Elizabeth's mind into some kind of vortex. Nothing seemed natural at that moment, and all her thoughts stopped cold. She was absolutely zombified when the intrusive question came into her head.

Where do you live?

"The Briar Cove, apartment 207," she responded from her trance.

"Great, I'll see you at nine, then."

When Elizabeth finally came to her senses, Linzie was gone. She struggled internally to determine if Linzie had verbally asked where she lived.

I just blurted out my address to a total stranger. Fuck.

FRENCH MEMORIES

Completely distracted by the witchery of young Linzie, Elizabeth didn't do nearly as well on the biology test as she'd hoped, nor did she care at this point. She cleaned up her apartment while strange thoughts relentlessly tore at her.

How do I know them?

Illuminating her apartment with several fresh blue linen-scented candles, she selected *Vivaldi's Four Seasons* for music. She placed two glasses of Pinot Grigio on the coffee table in front of her couch. It was an intimate setting with no rationale behind it. She just did it and had grave concerns flooding her mind. She glanced at her DVD player.

Nine o'clock on the dot.

In the middle of her internal dialogue, the knock came. It was not on cue but rather an interruption of her thoughts. She paused a moment before answering, secretly hoping it was Celsus. Resigning to whatever the universe had in store for her, she unlocked the door and swung it open a little faster than she would have liked. Her anxiety was swelling.

Linzie stood with her back to Elizabeth. She wore a white wool trench coat with the belt hanging casually from two loops in the back. With arms stretched out over the metal railing, hands flat upon the frozen surface, and only a quarter of her profile showing, Elizabeth could see this was a woman of substance, regardless of age. With little clouds of white mist that softly ascended before her, Linzie appeared as a statue—an interpretation of a modern Aphrodite.

Elizabeth's eyes traveled down to the bottom hem of Linzie's snow-white trench, which gently lapped at the curves of her exposed calves; below that, a pair of old, torn, brown mukluks protected her feet from the subzero cold. Elizabeth cocked an eyebrow as she gathered her courage.

"So, what do you do during the winter, run a dog sled team?"

The only response from the woman was a subtle grin.

"Well, don't just stand there. Come on inside before we both freeze to death!"

Without moving in the slightest, Linzie casually responded while looking up into the black winter sky.

"You're inviting me in?"

Her voice sent a shiver down Elizabeth's spine, and she realized this woman had been feigning her innocence. Her excitement compelled her forward. The cold was wicked, and she wanted her inside immediately.

"Yes, please come in."

Elizabeth backed away from the door as Linzie closed her trench, turned around, and entered like Celsus when he departed the coffee shop—unnatural—too smooth.

Linzie Van Arnam was born and raised on the hard streets of Dayton, Ohio. Half Dutch, half German, and independent in the extreme, she dropped out of high school at 15. Her parents had no control over her. During her time in Dayton, she spent several months in and out of juvenile detention centers for vandalism, petty theft, and assault. By 18, she was making nearly a grand a week selling drugs to her dealers in and around her neighborhood.

Like Elizabeth, Linzie never gets sick. Unlike Elizabeth, she has never been depressed. She is known for having three major characteristics: a clever and shrewd mind for business, a superiority complex, especially concerning men, and an unpredictable, violent nature. One of her greatest loves is to be underestimated.

Standing only five feet tall, she is cute and seemingly harmless. For street thugs who don't know her, she appears to be easy for the taking. The first time she got burned, she told one of her friends she'd been "waiting for this moment." She explained the dreariness of Dayton vanished in the face of getting to "teach this motherfucker a lesson."

History showed the result of that drug burn—the dealer convulsing out in the street after being tased by one of her loyal soldiers, followed by her beating him severely about the head and genitals with a baseball bat until blood ran from his eyes and ears.

He spent several weeks in the hospital and ended up having a ruptured testicle surgically removed. The police tried repeatedly to get a statement from him, but he refused to talk. Linzie said it was one of the most satisfying experiences of her life. Respect was given immediately, and to this day, she has a ghetto pass in the nasty neighborhoods of Dayton, where they still refer to her as "Lil' Linz."

With Celsus, her sociopathic and sexually deviant nature is encouraged. One of his favorite pastimes is sitting by the fireplace, listening to her stories of supremacy over what she describes as "testosterone-driven retards" who have tried to impress her, snare her, or fuck her over. He chose her to connect with Elizabeth for no other reason than his love of watching her work.

Linzie removed the mukluks and exposed her bare feet, which Elizabeth found exquisitely petite and beautiful. When Elizabeth attempted to take her coat, she clenched at it tightly.

"I'd like to keep it on. I'm a bit chilled."

"Suit yourself. Would you like a glass of Pinot?"

"Yes, please," she said as she sat on the couch.

Elizabeth took note that Linzie had yet to look directly at her. She thought maybe some genuine shyness might be revealing itself. She could not have been farther from the

15

truth. Linzie was merely trying to conceal her eyes, her purpose.

Not ready for a direct confrontation, Elizabeth went straight to her desk, opened her textbook, and carefully pulled out the old papers.

"Do you know anything about these?"

"May I see them?" Linzie asked, with only a peripheral view of the items in hand.

Elizabeth handed her the papers and sat down on the opposite end of the couch. She looked curiously at the white satin choker around Linzie's neck.

"Do you need more light?"

"I'm fine, thanks."

Every time Linzie spoke, Elizabeth felt an intense heat flash throughout her body. She wondered if it might be the glass of Pinot she'd downed a few minutes earlier but quickly put the thought out of her mind as she realized it was only an insignificant amount of wine. She tried to get a grip and stay focused on the extraordinary papers that were now in the hands of this *Linzie*.

"Do you recognize the handwriting?" Linzie asked softly.

"Is there a reason I should recognize the handwriting? I don't read, write, or speak French at all. I can read the date. They look authentic, but I wouldn't know."

Linzie smiled and began to recite the document word for word in perfect French. Her tone was deliciously sensual, and Elizabeth was aroused immediately. She was completely turned on by this woman, something that had never happened in her life—the desire for another woman.

As Linzie continued her sensual verbal assault, Elizabeth could feel herself perspiring, her anxiety growing, and her thought processes faltering. The arousal intensified when Linzie placed the papers on the table but continued reciting the content in flawless French, dripping with sex. Elizabeth's mouth parted open in amazement, her eyes wide in disbelief. When Linzie finished, Elizabeth forced out the obvious question.

"You know this by heart?"

"Oui, mon bel amant," she said, her eyes hungry with desire. Elizabeth found it increasingly difficult to communicate with this woman.

"Would you please reread it in English?"

"I would love to," she replied mischievously.

With no consideration whatsoever about the papers on the table, Linzie continued to look deep into Elizabeth's soul. She spoke slowly and sensuously, word for word, her English burning with the same heat as her French.

December 2, 1813 – Asylum of Charenton

My master's financial persuasions finally secured my long-awaited dinner at the asylum. It is a tragedy he could not join us this evening. Apparently, this was meant solely for me. I shall express my undying gratitude when I see him later.

After everything I thought I knew about Donatien, I really expected him to make an advance on me. Perhaps he could sense what I am, or maybe he just wanted an interesting conversation with an intelligent woman for a change. In either case, he was a perfect gentleman.

In our discourse over wine and cake, Lilith and her place in Judeo-Christian mythology was brought to the center of attention. He wanted to know about her origins, and so I obliged him. I first told him to entertain me and set aside his rabid atheism for our conversation. I explained the discussion could only continue if he could, for this one moment, attach an actual intelligence to what he always defends in his writings as 'Nature.' He seemed sincere and genuinely interested and agreed to a middle ground where we could communicate with some understanding.

I explained that all gods and goddesses are simply different faces of the same god and goddess: the true power of the base male and female elements in nature, not some grandiose human-looking couple walking around in robes deciding the fate of mortals. I said to him that pagan gods are nothing more than expansionistic ideas of the human condition. When enough people put their energy into thought, that thought can be tapped for those supposed attributes.

For example, I used something he would love and readily accept, Bacchus, the Roman god of wine and pleasure. When enough Bacchanalia festivals had occurred, there was a collective energy that could now be tapped into to secure the love of a man or woman, make the rod painfully hard, and incur explosions of intense pleasure. I paused momentarily, fondly remembering the many festivals I had attended in ancient Rome.

I told him there are gods and goddesses for every facet of human thought and emotion. In this, he agreed wholeheartedly. I added that these "emotional collectives" are like balls of energy circling around the earth and readily tapped into with serious concentration. In this, he was skeptical.

Every once-born capturing our attention usually turns into a complete idiot, removed from consciousness, eyes wide open, ready for the slaughter. With the Marquis, it was different. He just smiled, listened intently, and looked like he wanted to fuck me. But there was great reverence in that look, almost worship for me. He is the first and only once-born I've known to remain unaffected by my true nature. Did he really see, or is he just insane, I wonder?

I stated that while "Lilith" is known to the Jews as Adam's first wife, she was known thousands of years earlier as "Lili" to the ancient Sumerians. I told him with all sincerity that she is before humanity itself. I explained that "Lili," as I know her, falls outside the parameters of human thought and universal consciousness. She has nothing whatsoever to do with the human condition. I told him that Lili is a being of original ancient intelligence, before humanity and far beyond human understanding, but most assuredly part of the natural world.

I had a vision of her then. I saw that she would visit him precisely one year from this night and told him of it. I told him she would be there for his death, to devour his very soul, which she would find quite palatable and enjoyable. He laughed. It was genuine laughter. His response was thus, "I respect the myth dearly, and if what you say is true, so be it. Let the luscious serpent of the ancient world take me with herbs and salt." He reminds me so much of my master. They have much in common.

While I did not desire a sexual encounter with him, feeding on his blood was a different matter. I had to have that, unquestionably. He stayed perfectly still as I produced a small knife and made an incision through a vein in his arm. With no intention of killing him, I fed softly, my greater self held in check.

As his blood filled me, my eyes rolled back into my head. His genius and rot intoxicated me. I connected with him, and an unprovoked biblical verse from Isaiah resonated within my dark soul. Some have seen us. Some know...

The information went beyond what Elizabeth's mind could process. Nothing registered as she stared blankly at Linzie, the translation immediately forgotten as if it had never been spoken. Linzie looked at her and spoke tenderly.

"May I have a glass of water?"

"Sure, I'll be right back."

"Thank you."

"Yeah, no problem."

Elizabeth mindlessly walked into her kitchen, grabbed a glass, and filled it with water from the sink when the hairs on her neck stood up. She dropped the glass and spun around to see Linzie only inches from her face, her bright blue eyes revealing her wanton nature. Elizabeth was paralyzed with fear and desire.

Linzie gently grabbed Elizabeth's right hand, pulled it under her trench coat, around her waist, and placed it on the upper curve of her naked bottom. Elizabeth felt compelled to protest, but Linzie closed the last few inches of space between them and kissed her with great hunger. Elizabeth felt her knees grow weak as she ultimately succumbed to the passions of the strange young woman.

Without asking, Linzie led her into the bedroom as if she had been there many times already. Elizabeth followed like an obedient child, and all resistance was destroyed. The two women made love for hours. Elizabeth felt things she had never experienced with any man and never would again save one.

During those precious winter months that followed, her time with Linzie seemed like a dream. Nothing seemed natural, yet everything seemed inexplicably right. She grappled with internal conflicts; was this really what she wanted, was it a turning point in her life, was she gay? She often wondered why she felt so lethargic when Linzie was not around.

On the other hand, Linzie had no conflicts. Her sole mission was to hook, educate, and prime Elizabeth for the coven. With single-minded focus, she indoctrinated her, explaining the rules, the courtesies, and the general ways of the *House*. She also brought her to a state of extreme submission. She did this methodically, using various skillful pleasure and pain techniques. Finally, she said that Elizabeth was *chosen* and would be sponsored as an initiate with the coming of spring.

Even in the blissful state Elizabeth found herself in, she managed to demand answers from her new lover. At this point in time, Linzie was permitted by Celsus to impart only the following information:

1.) The *House* of Celsus was a small but growing group of submissive men and women who swore absolute allegiance and subservience to the *Coven* of Celsus.

2.) Membership in the *House* had the potential for astonishing benefits and/or disastrous consequences.

3.) The *Coven* was an exclusive internal family of eight extraordinary women led by Celsus.

4.) Membership in the coven meant unlimited riches and unimaginable power.

5.) Disrespect or disobedience concerning the master or the coven could be hazardous to one's health.

As bizarre as it all sounded, Elizabeth committed her heart and soul to whatever Linzie said. As the winter wore on, she fell madly in love and would have done anything for her "little girl."

Randy V

THE FIRST VISIT

Gazing out the enormous ivy-encircled window, he watched the sun descend from the world. Spring had come, and as the master inhaled the fresh air, he felt his bond with the earth. Nature had a way of making him swell with lust, especially in the spring. He thought of the stag-horned god and the old grand rite. He thought of nature as the most irresistible woman. No matter how much he wanted control, he couldn't help but get hard in her presence.

Megan handed him a glass of red wine and began to go over the daily business of the house. Without looking at her, he listened intently, especially when she reminded him that Elizabeth would finally have the first of her visits that night. He smiled and savored his drink in anticipation.

Elizabeth found the property with some difficulty. Linzie had left specific instructions on how to get there, but the roads were winding and unmarked as she got closer. Arriving before the massive iron gates, she reached for the intercom button. Just before her finger made contact, the gate opened. She noticed little cameras atop the stone gateposts rotating and following her as she drove through.

Even after passing through the gates, the winding road continued for another quarter mile. The trees were mature birch, red and white pine, and weeping willows. When the house finally came into view, it was nearly dark. Still, she could make out the heavy block stone and the enormity. Extremely intimidated, she thought to herself.

Money—lots and lots of money.

The drive led her to the side of the massive structure, where precisely ten carports were buried into the very hillside. Only two spaces were empty, and she felt embarrassed parking her battered, rusted 1987 Ford Taurus between a brand-new Jaguar and a Mustang Shelby. She was careful to back her car in as Linzie had instructed and noticed all the other vehicles were also backed in. The cars were lit up from the ground with deep-blue flood lights, and it reminded her of the Detroit Auto Show her father had always taken her to when she was small. For a brief moment, she fantasized about her own dream car, a Mercedes Benz SLK 350 convertible.

Exiting her car, she noticed other high-end machines: Lexus SC430, Dodge Viper, Audi A8, BWM 750Li, and, closest to the house, a black Rolls-Royce Limousine. She could make out a silhouette in the driver's seat and briefly wondered how long the driver had been sitting in the calm dark of night.

She followed the little stone path leading to the front of the house and noticed another open parking lot adjacent to the carports. The massive lot was completely empty. The high-end cars and the vacant lot freaked her out, but the house really got into the core of her psyche.

She could tell it wasn't that old. Yet, it was covered with ivy and exuded a European medieval flavor. Standing three stories high, she guessed it had between fifteen and twenty bedrooms. While the outside looked a bit threatening, the inside looked warm and inviting. As she passed the windows leading up to the massive front porch, supported by equally gigantic colonial-style pillars, she saw dozens and dozens of candles lighting the inside. The large double-entry oak doors, engraved with intricate Celtic knots, intimidated her and gave reason for pause. An actual battle shield bearing a menacing coat of arms graced the top of the frame.

When she finally found the courage to ring the doorbell, she was startled to hear what sounded like the single strike of a massive church bell. It all seemed larger than life to her.

When the two libertines heard the ring, they grinned at each other. Lady Megan, known as the XO, curtsied before her master to take leave. Celsus merely took a sip of wine and gazed out the window as he waived her off to greet the new initiate. She turned around, glanced over her shoulder, and sashayed toward the foyer. She knew he stole a gaze at her, and she loved it.

Megan opened the door, and her eyes immediately traveled the length of Elizabeth's form, taking in every curve, every nuance. She then looked into her eyes with admiration and a piercing desire that made Elizabeth quiver.

Elizabeth was dressed precisely as Linzie had instructed. She wore a black silk dress that revealed her neck and shoulders, complimented her cleavage, and ended just below her knees. The simple accessories included black pumps, the purple choker, and subdued pink lipstick. Her long hair was tied up in a bun with several loose curls resting upon her breasts. Megan noticed everything and did not attempt to hide her visual explorations of Elizabeth's body.

"I see Linzie was modest when she described you. Elizabeth, you may enter the House of Lord Celsus."

With a long, slender finger, Megan indicated the way to what was known as the great coven room. As Elizabeth passed, she suddenly felt dizzy with an irrational, wanton hunger. She wanted to kiss Megan and felt a nearly uncontrollable animal-like attraction toward her.

Linzie had told Elizabeth several stories about Megan, but she had no idea how enticing she was in the flesh. A white see-through gown framed her tall, lean body. Her nipples seemed painfully erect, creating two little vertical ridges in the silk fabric. Wild red hair cascaded over her shoulders like a blood-soaked waterfall, while beauty freckles sprinkled her face and arms. At five-foot-nine, she looked intimidating yet soft. Her bare feet were adorned with anklets and toe rings, and her lips displayed the most beautiful pout. She wore a thin, white satin choker with a large ruby in the center, just as Linzie had described. *Irish goddess,* Elizabeth thought.

Megan's eyes were a brilliant shade of green, and her intense stare made Elizabeth feel weak in the knees. She quickly looked down at the floor to avoid it. Megan sensed her angst, reached for her hand, and began to soothe her.

"My lord, the Lady Elizabeth has arrived."

Elizabeth felt a strange, new feeling as Megan led her into the great coven room. Something between fear and comfortable familiarity possessed her as she examined the priceless historical relics that graced the enormous, antique-looking family room. There were weapons of all ages hanging on the oak-paneled walls: sabers from the civil war, court swords from Renaissance France, poleaxes from medieval times, and gladiator short-swords from the Roman Empire. She looked down and was impressed by the expensive Persian rugs that covered the gorgeous wooden floor.

A crystal chandelier hung from the 16-foot-high ceiling; directly beneath that, a solid oak table stood as the centerpiece. This table was round and exactly nine feet in diameter. Surrounding it were eight beautiful antique chairs and one throne with a wolf's snarling face embroidered into the royal-blue backrest. The throne was hundreds of years old and considerably worn. Two four-foot stone griffins guarded a massive marble fireplace along the southern wall, with lounging sofas and chairs in a large half-circle around it. Numerous ropes and pulleys hung from the ceiling close to the fireplace, which Elizabeth found very strange. Books and erotic sculptures filled the eastern wall.

Elizabeth noticed the sculptures' dancing shadows, created by all the tapers, and became mesmerized. She watched the strange shadows for a moment and was startled when Celsus rose from one of the high-backed chairs in front of the fireplace. No one could have guessed he was sitting there so motionless. Smiling, he spoke warmly.

"Elizabeth."

"My lord," she responded.

She quickly remembered all the rules Linzie had imparted before the crucial first visit: *Avert your eyes down unless he tells you otherwise. Always address him as "my lord." Do not speak unless his words require a response. Don't do anything unless he gives you permission. Most of all, don't ever disobey him.* He seemed delighted by her presence.

"You look absolutely ravishing."

"Thank you, my lord."

"You may look at me."

She lifted her eyes to meet his and gasped when she caught sight of his steely manhood along the way. He was barefoot, aroused, and donned what looked like a king's robe. The royal-blue velvet housecoat was open, touched the back of his heels, and looked heavy but comfortable. Elizabeth's mouth parted open in mild shock as she felt a new wave of lust overtake her. He ignored her momentarily and held out his hand to Megan, beckoning her.

He took Megan in his arms and nibbled on her ear while looking directly into Elizabeth's eyes, his intent obvious and revealingly wicked. She felt a shiver travel up her spine as he softly caressed Megan's neck with his lips.

Megan responded by massaging him between the legs. Though Elizabeth's view was blocked, she found Megan's arm movements smooth and determined. Elizabeth's voyeurism was forced, but she could not look away as Megan's stroking was intensely sensual and hypnotic. Time seemed to slow and become meaningless. The master broke Elizabeth's fixation with total indifference to what Megan was doing to him.

"Do you think it's better to live your life in relative comfort, even if it means being ignorant of your true station in the world?"

"My lord, there is no comfort in not knowing who I am."

"What if *not* knowing was the lesser of two evils? What if knowing your true self reveals something horrific beyond belief? Would you still want to know?"

"Yes, because *not* knowing has only led me to despair. I already know that path intimately. I find as I get older, it only gets worse. There is no comfort in not knowing—at least not for me, my lord."

"You are right, Elizabeth—not for you. Looking into your eyes, I see that you will succumb to madness or suicide if you do not find your true self. I will help you, but I must warn you: the price for knowing is very high."

"My lord, I would rather be in pain for knowing who I really am than walk through life wanting to die because I don't know."

Elizabeth wondered where her blind faith was coming from. She had no reason to trust him, yet he seemed as familiar as the earth and sky. From some hidden place within her, she knew the answers would be unconventional. Intuitively, she knew the answers would be nightmarish.

Celsus smiled at Megan and gently stopped her operations.

"Megan, your touch never ceases to amaze me, even after all this time. Come with us, Elizabeth."

The three ascended a hand-crafted wooden spiral staircase to the second floor. They proceeded down a long hallway where a young woman greeted them. She wore a white cotton dress, which betrayed her broad shoulders, curvaceous thighs, and hourglass body. She wore a thin white choker like the others, but it was unique in that a lapis lazuli gemstone graced the center.

"Is everything ready, Nona?" Megan asked.

"Yes, my lady."

Elizabeth admired Nona's physique and exotic beauty. She thought she might be Hispanic and guessed her to be about five-foot-eight, physically powerful and very thick, but devoid of fat. Nona looked like she could handle her own. Still, her gentle light blue eyes and warm smile made Elizabeth feel less nervous among her intimidating hosts.

"Is she part of the coven, my lord?" Elizabeth asked.

Immediately, she regretted saying anything. She knew she was not supposed to speak unless he spoke to her directly. He did not respond but slid a hand down her back, cupped her butt cheek, and whispered.

"Your scent is maddening, and you are creating a terrible hunger."

"Shall we, my lord," Megan said, grinning over her shoulder as she led Elizabeth into the room on the left.

Elizabeth was shocked at the scene before her. Eight white, tautly corded ropes descended from the ceiling. At the end of those ropes, bound by their wrists, were four beautiful young women in superior physical condition, gagged and naked except for their white satin chokers.

They were of different races; one white, one black, one Asian, and another who looked Middle Eastern. Their feet were bound with matching white corded ropes to iron rings bolted on the hardwood floor. Celsus appeared slightly mischievous as he addressed her obvious distress.

"Introductions are unimportant; you'll meet them all soon enough."

But as he spoke, she realized with a chill that Linzie was one of the women. She knew not to acknowledge her lover. She had been warned that until she was a full coven member, direct exchange without permission, even with Linzie, was forbidden.

Upon the wall, an assortment of cat o'nine tails, whips, metal clothespins, and paddles gave Elizabeth pause for concern. Megan sensed her apprehension and tried to calm her.

"It's alright, Elizabeth. These women are here for you."

Elizabeth unexpectedly and irrationally felt alright about the bizarre scene before her. Somewhere in her mind, there was a justification. Her body tingled as she looked at her lover, tied up and helpless.

"Pick one," he said. "See how you torment the others. Their divine envy shall drip down their silky, delicious thighs."

Elizabeth pointed to Linzie. Celsus laughed and responded with supreme confidence.

"An excellent choice, though I am not surprised."

She held her breath as he walked around Linzie and continued.

"Come now, Elizabeth, I sent her to you. This little witch is amazingly gifted, is she not?"

Before Elizabeth could respond, he gave Linzie a hard slap on her rear. The sound reverberated around the room, and Elizabeth trembled with anticipation. She could sense that Linzie was trying to ready herself. Megan moved before Linzie and gazed into her eyes while Celsus began surveying which instruments he would use.

"I love you, angel," Megan said as she caressed Linzie's face.

Celsus picked up a long rectangular paddle wrapped in black leather and secured with metal studs. He pointed it toward a throne-like chair.

"Sit down, Elizabeth. The chair is for you. You may please yourself as you wish, but you must not move from the chair."

"Yes, my lord."

She had a perfect view of everything as Megan began to suck one of Linzie's nipples while pinching the other. Linzie could only close her eyes and moan as, from behind, the master caressed and kissed what he called her "ripe and perfect peach."

Elizabeth felt another shiver as she watched a tear roll down Linzie's cheek. Megan's mouth caused the flood of emotions to issue forth from her bound-up young lover. Megan kissed her way down between Linzie's legs, giving her oral devotions that bordered on worship. This caressing and kissing lasted several minutes before the master finally used the paddle. She cried out from the gag, and her breathing became very rapid. The muffled whine aroused Elizabeth greatly, and the sound of the paddle shook her to the core. Celsus stared intensely at Elizabeth and held his palm about a half-inch from Linzie's fresh welt.

"Instant heat," he seethed. "It takes so much effort to find the excitement in things. As we get older, everything just becomes so boring. Wouldn't you agree, Elizabeth?"

"It does seem so, my lord. I am only 27 and have lost the ability to enjoy even a single day. This room has given me more excitement than anything in my life, my lord."

Celsus grinned at her, flipped the paddle vertically, and gently slid it between Linzie's legs. Its edge barely touched Megan's chin with each sawing movement.

Elizabeth could not resist the urge any longer. An unseen force seemed to motivate her actions as she began working her clitoris with one hand while sliding two fingers into herself from underneath her leg with the other. The disposition of Celsus blossomed as he spoke.

"I could just eat all of you—so sweet and delicious—my mouth waters."

Another hard whack landed on Linzie's behind, followed by more muffled screams and moans as Megan gave her ever-so-proficient mouth to Linzie's little blond mound.

Linzie had told Elizabeth many times that Megan's lips were the most talented in the house and that the experience of her mouth was always a spiritual matter. She said Megan had "the mouth of an angel." Still, she repeatedly retracted her statement, saying, "No *angel* could produce such hot pleasure."

Clearly, Linzie was deep in the throes of bliss. The stinging hits from the master's leather paddle and Megan's expert tongue were causing a terrible frenzy in her. Celsus wound up and struck her again. The sound carried a distinct echo throughout the room. Linzie's moans possessed Elizabeth to no end, as did her growing envy over Megan's aggressive oral delights. The master smiled and took another hard crack at Linzie's now cherry-colored bottom while observing the others.

"The other women are now soaking wet, to be sure."

At this point, beads of sweat began appearing on everyone. Celsus abruptly dropped the paddle on the floor and walked around to inspect the other three women.

"See how juicy my poor darlings have become."

He grabbed the Asian girl by the hair, pulled her head back, and let his ridged staff ascend between her legs.

"How enchanting," he said, revealing his glistening organ. "See how they suffer for you."

The master moved before Linzie, now impaled on Megan's talented tongue. A muffled scream signaled Linzie's release. He continued.

"Not our Linzie, though. She will not suffer this night."

He moved behind her and bit the back of her neck. Linzie breathed heavily through her nose as he spoke softly in her ear.

"Would you like me to remove the gag?"

Linzie nodded, and Celsus pulled the panties from her mouth.

"My angel, how are you this night?"

"My lord, I worship you."

"And how is our XO treating you?"

"A living goddess tends to me, my lord. Her mouth is divine."

Linzie was about to say something else when she had another shuddering climax. Her moans were animal-like as Celsus then turned his attention to Elizabeth.

"Notice how Linzie does not look at you?"

"Yes, my lord."

He grabbed Linzie roughly by the hair and jerked her head back while maintaining eye contact with Elizabeth.

"Her punishment will be most severe if she does."

Elizabeth was nearing her orgasm and began to increase the pace of her fingers as he playfully demanded her attention.

"See what all this does to me?"

He let his saliva drip off his lower lip, which perfectly landed on the head of his cock, now sticking nearly straight up in the air, the veins pulsing with blood. He licked two of his fingers and began working them into Linzie's anus while biting the back of her neck. After a few minutes of preparing the subordinate, he slowly pushed himself deep inside her.

Megan, her perfect lips still locked on Linzie's womanhood, wrapped her arms around them and dug her fingernails into her master's hips. She kept up an ideal methodical rhythm, systematically pulling and pushing her master into Linzie's rear while tongue-fucking her simultaneously. Within minutes, between the sodomy and the oral pleasures, Linzie fainted from a third and most powerful orgasm.

Elizabeth watched Linzie with half-opened eyes. The visual of her lover held unconscious between her two wicked masters produced her own shuddering, mind-blowing orgasm. She could see and somehow *feel* the other three women who were left bound up and ignored. She sensed they actually suffered greatly from their deprivation. Celsus seemed to savor his moment of glory, and she found it impossible that a man could endure this without an end. She sensed his resolve for the right moment to let go.

After swooning in the afterglow, Megan rose to her feet, her lips glistening with Linzie's nectar, and approached the new initiate. She pulled Elizabeth to her feet and kissed her deeply, pressing their sweat-covered bodies together.

Elizabeth kissed and licked the familiar juices from Megan's face. At the same time, Megan slid her hands down Elizabeth's back and cupped her beautiful rear.

After a few minutes, Celsus led the two women out of the room. They descended the winding staircase two levels until they reached the mansion's basement. He spoke to Elizabeth with a more serious tone.

"To truly feel alive again, we must resort to drastic measures. As you get older and trapped by the mundane, things strangle and ultimately kill your spirit. When you embrace only the everyday grind as your entire existence, your life becomes no longer worth living. Add a lot of age to that situation, and suddenly, you have a serious problem."

Megan sensed Elizabeth's apprehension and tried to calm her.

"Don't worry, Elizabeth, we will not hurt you."

Elizabeth felt Megan was telling her a lie. It was a strong gut feeling, but she had no real willpower to deal with it—not since she had entered this house.

They walked into a small dark room, and Megan lit four white candles, one on each wall. The candles revealed an unremarkable cinder block interior with no ornamentation. It reminded Elizabeth of a prison cell. Celsus spoke reverently.

"Let me introduce you to *the machine*. You may have a woman placed upon it and observe the effects or sit on it yourself. But, if you choose another, you shall never be allowed to experience it."

"Why is that, my lord?" Elizabeth asked.

"My sweet, I would love nothing better than to see you in torment for not having had such an experience that you passed on because of fear."

Elizabeth was more than a little afraid of the monstrous 'machine.' The whole scene looked like something straight out of the Inquisition. A rusted iron pillar, at least a foot in diameter, rose five feet high from a large circular hole in the floor. The part she assumed one would sit on looked like a saddle, except for two strategically placed holes in the center.

Celsus laughed at Elizabeth's anxiety. He held out an industrial-looking control box attached to a large cable and pressed one of the buttons. This started what sounded like a generator, though she could not see it to be sure. The actual motor that drove the machine was hidden under the floor. It was somewhat loud, and Celsus had to raise his voice a little.

"What say you, Lady Elizabeth? You or another?"

"I choose the machine, my lord. My curiosity overpowers my fear. I think I would be a fool not to, my lord."

"We shall see," he said with a grin.

"Megan, prepare our initiate for the machine."

"Yes, my lord."

He then took his place at another voyeur throne, exactly nine feet from the machine.

"Spread your legs," Megan ordered as she stood behind Elizabeth.

"She is already prepared because of our previous operations, my lord," she said as she slid her fingers in and out of Elizabeth's womanhood.

Megan then picked up an old crock pot from the floor. She opened it, took out a good portion of lubricant, and carefully worked it into Elizabeth's rear.

Celsus was fixated on the task, which lasted a mesmerizing nine minutes. Megan knew her master's desires and stared into his eyes as she performed the task. She purposely worked slowly because of his nature.

"Enough," Celsus commanded as he stroked himself.

"Place her upon the machine."

Megan led her up a small stepladder and helped her onto the machine. She then fastened leather wrist and ankle restraints to Elizabeth's four limbs, securing her from the ceiling to the floor. The restraints were secured by heavy chains that allowed no movement of her outstretched arms. In contrast, the ankle restraints allowed only slight movement of her legs. The reality was that she was spread eagle, upright on the machine, and totally helpless.

"Come," he said to Megan. "Sit on me while facing her."

Megan obediently did an about-face, smiled at Elizabeth, and slowly slid herself down his thick, ridged cock. She started to grind and gyrate on him while he pressed another button.

Elizabeth moaned as two hydraulic-powered dildos slowly emerged from the two holes, simultaneously entering her front and rear. She resisted at first, but because of the ankle restraints and the knowledge that fighting it would be more painful, she resigned her body to the massive instruments.

The one in her front was nine inches long and four inches in diameter. The one in her rear was six inches long and three inches in diameter. Even though she was sufficiently lubricated, the later instrument slightly tore her anus. She was twice impaled, and the sensations took her breath away.

Megan moaned out loud as she wiggled on her master's engorged shaft. She gazed into Elizabeth's now tearful eyes with a wicked smile as Celsus raised the remote and pressed another button. This started a gentle rocking of the saddle, back and forth. The new sensation made Elizabeth's eyes roll back white.

"Give me your ass," he said to Megan.

Megan rose up, lubricated the master's staff with her own lust, and, squirming with some difficulty, popped him inside her rear. She then placed both her feet on the master's muscular thighs and slowly clenched and unclenched her cheeks while sliding up and down the length of his organ. He kept his head tilted around Megan's torso to observe Elizabeth.

"Lady Elizabeth, how are you coping?" he asked.

Slowly rocking, she replied, "My lord, the instruments are very thick, but I am doing well."

"Ah, so you are ready for more?"

"That depends, my lord. I'm not sure how much *more* I can take."

"Perhaps a hundredfold of what you are experiencing now?"

He pushed another button that sent the two dildos into subtle gyrations that made Elizabeth whimper.

"How now, Lady Elizabeth?" he inquired.

"My lord, I cannot …"

She could not finish as the gyrations started taking a more expansive course.

"Nonsense, of course you can," he said, pushing the next button.

Like those of a jackhammer, severe vibrations went through the dildos with such force that everything rattled considerably. The sound was quickly joined by Elizabeth's screams. Linzie had once told her about the machine. She said the master referred to it as a "reality breaker." Elizabeth was now certainly having a break from ordinary reality.

The screams set off both Celsus and Megan. Megan clenched him hard as little rivers of her love ran down the inside of his thighs. He, in turn, shot himself deep into Megan's rear. There were so many stars as Elizabeth fell into total darkness.

Elizabeth woke up in an unfamiliar room. She looked around and was drawn to a cozy little fireplace several feet away from the queen-sized bed she found herself in. It was burning nicely and provided the only light for her new surroundings. She had no idea how long she had been there. Clocks, watches, or timepieces were forbidden in the House of Celsus.

Her body trembled as she slowly rose and looked around the room for something to clothe herself. A purple cotton robe had been placed at the foot of the bed. She quickly slipped into it, cinching the belt tightly, and hesitated momentarily to listen for movement. Hearing nothing, she opened the door and entered the quiet, dark hallway. She immediately recognized the second floor of the house.

Her attention was drawn to a capital 'C' carved in old English on a door at the end of the hall. The door was slightly open, and she saw a lit candle on a nightstand beside the bed.

She thought *this has to be his room,* as she boldly decided to enter.

The room was massive, and the wooden walls were sparsely carved with ancient Celtic knots, as if the artist had been interrupted and unable to finish the work. There were bladed weapons everywhere and mirrors galore. Most impressive was the king-sized bed that graced the center of the room. It was a four-poster bed, but unusual in that the four posts were four great medieval poleaxes welded to the iron cage of the frame.

She had no doubt about the sharpness of the blades, the points, or the authenticity. The rich velvet bedspread was too alluring to resist. She crawled on top, face down, and let her hands roam over the fabric that was an exact match in color to her royal purple choker. She was so engrossed with the texture of the velvet that she didn't notice Celsus silently observing her from the doorway.

He watched her make snow angels on his bed and especially liked how she arched her back naturally from the exquisite moment.

"Elizabeth," he said softly.

The sound of his voice startled and aroused her.

"You did not have my permission to come in here."

Elizabeth panicked.

"My lord, I'm sorry. I woke up, and no one was there…"

"Come with me," he said firmly.

His expression revealed nothing as he exited the room, Elizabeth obediently following behind. Soon, they were standing in front of a door Elizabeth somehow knew was the one leading to Megan's bed chamber.

He opened the door, quickly crossed the room, and entered the bathroom. Megan was reclining in a large black claw-footed tub. Though it appeared she was sleeping, her eyes opened once Celsus entered.

"Yes, my lord?" she asked.

"Lady Elizabeth has erred and must be punished, as have you. It was your duty to be there when she woke, yet you were not. Come with me."

He turned and walked out of the room. Lady Megan rose from her bath, dripping with oil and water, and immediately followed.

"I'm sorry, Elizabeth. I didn't expect you to wake so soon."

Celsus moved quickly down the hall until he reached what was known as the Adjustment Room. Megan had a solid grip on Elizabeth's hand as they hurriedly entered behind him. His voice was reprimanding as he addressed the two women.

"Disrobe, Elizabeth. Stand with your backs to each other in the center of the room, and do not speak or move until I return. If you do, it shall be the worse for both of you."

"Yes, my lord," they both said meekly.

He walked out, and Elizabeth could faintly hear him issuing orders. The room was obviously built for the fine-tuning of subordination. Ropes hung from the ceiling, and "tools of the trade" were strewn everywhere. A large circular bed with a black and blood-red velvet canopy occupied the center of the room.

It seemed like forever, but the two women did as they were told. Elizabeth began trembling uncontrollably while Megan, sworn to obedience, could do nothing for her. They could hear footsteps approaching, but only Elizabeth could see who was coming in. With a sudden awareness of her injured anus, her fear was magnified.

Celsus and Nona entered and wouldn't acknowledge either of the women as they stood only a few feet away. Nona manipulated the two naked women to face each other. She bound them to the ceiling and floor with leather wrist and ankle restraints like Elizabeth had witnessed earlier. Now completely nude, Celsus had an altogether different demeanor about him as he announced his verdict.

"Both of you have acted recklessly, and now you shall receive your punishments."

Linzie then entered the room carrying a cat o'nine tails. Only Megan was in a position to see it. It looked terrible, and the nine long leather whips dripped with olive oil. Clad only in black leather thigh-high boots, hair drawn back tight in a ponytail, and with perfect obedience, she addressed her master.

"You requested my presence as an adjuster, my lord?"

"Yes, my wicked angel."

He walked behind Elizabeth and spoke in her ear.

"Let's see how you handle this."

Then he whispered in Linzie's ear.

"I need you on your hands and knees, on the floor, facing the rear of our ignorant little initiate. You are to give Elizabeth the very best of your talented mouth. Do you understand?"

"As you wish, my lord," she replied.

"When it appears she is close to coming, I want you to stop. With all your strength, you will stand and let loose with nine lashes upon her backside. You will allow the space of nine counts to occur before each lash. Do not miss the count, and do not hold back. If I think t that you showed mercy in even one of these blows, your fate will be nine times worse."

"I shall carry out your wishes to the letter as always. What about the XO, my lord?"

"Ignore her. For the time being, pretend she doesn't exist."

With that, the master kissed Linzie passionately, probing her mouth with his tongue, and sat on the bed to observe. Linzie knelt down behind Elizabeth as directed.

Megan had not been forgotten. On the contrary, his orchestrated punishment for Megan was one of deprivation. Deprivation was the worst within the coven, far worse than any physical punishment. She was to be ignored, untouched, and left only to witness the pain, not experience it. She stared into Elizabeth's eyes and could *feel* the intensity of Linzie's mouth. At the same time, Elizabeth gave verbal confirmations through moaning admirations.

41

"She is divine, and I miss her so. I am quivering, my Lady Megan."

Megan protested.

"My lord, how can you do this to me? The offense does not warrant such deprivation."

He did not respond but began to stoke himself as the scene unfolded.

"Don't stop!" Elizabeth cried, on the edge of an orgasm. "Goddess, I love you so much!"

Linzie sensed the oncoming orgasm, slowly disengaged herself, and rose. Megan screamed out a pointless order when she realized what was happening.

"Wait!"

There was a loud crack followed by a scream. Megan was connected and empathetic to Elizabeth. She felt the hot breath of her devastating scream, born of nine oil-soaked whips, shocking and unexpected, unleashed by a woman Elizabeth was madly in love with.

It was brutal, and it ripped at Elizabeth's flesh and soul. Her eyes were closed tightly from the pain washing over her burning backside. Megan tried to comfort her.

"It's going to be alright. Try to think of something else."

CRACK!

"Fuck!" Elizabeth screamed out again as a single tear dropped from the corner of her right eye. She began to sob.

Celsus was lost in the moment. He was slowly pumping himself and savoring the moment with every strike. With his other hand, he massaged his swelling balls. With each scream from the new initiate, the master came closer to coming.

Upon the sixth terrible lash, the XO loudly addressed the situation.

"Linzie, your lashes are too fierce. You are hurting her!"

"How dare you, Megan!" Celsus shot back. "Linzie, remember my words, and do not falter!"

CRACK!

More screaming—more wounds.

"Please!" Elizabeth cried. "Please stop!"

CRACK!

More screaming as blood trickled from four fresh cuts on her back above her left buttock.

"Ah yes, le petit mort," seethed Celsus.

Linzie was in a trance as she stepped like a batter, throwing her total weight into the final brutal lash.

CRACK!

Elizabeth let loose a final desperate scream and then fainted. At that exact moment, the master, leg muscles ripped from the exquisite pleasure and perfect timing, squirted his semen all over his chest.

Sweating, exhausted, and traumatized, Linzie dropped the whip on the floor and spoke to her lover.

"I'm sorry, Elizabeth."

Elizabeth, tears streaming down her reddened face, could only whimper as she painfully—and tenaciously—faded back into consciousness.

"Nona, untie them," Celsus said.

He looked strangely peaceful and slowly walked behind Elizabeth to inspect the damage. Eighty-one scarlet ribbons told of Linzie's strength, ferocity, and absolute obedience. He examined the welts and cuts, some superficial, a few reasonably deep. Little droplets of blood and oil trailed down the back of her legs. He spoke with no detectable remorse.

"My poor, innocent Elizabeth. I have chills from your wounds."

He knelt down, gently licked up, and swallowed every drop of blood and oil. He did it slowly, deliberately, and with great reverence. When the task was complete, he closed his eyes and spoke to her.

"My goddess Elizabeth, your blood feeds my very soul. I can feel my heart beating. I feel alive."

When Megan was freed, she turned toward him in reluctant servitude. She helped Nona free Elizabeth from her bonds and cradled the initiate's weary head.

"My sweet, I am so sorry."

Celsus licked the remaining blood from his lips with a look of contentment, then addressed Nona and Megan.

"Our new initiate has been wounded. Help her and be gentle. She deserves the greatest of our affections."

The master then spoke directly to Megan.

"Are you pretending to be empathetic? Perhaps you are hiding jealousy regarding how and to who the punishment was administered?"

He then cupped Elizabeth's face and licked the remaining tears from her cheeks, savoring the salty taste.

"My darling," he said as he stared into her eyes. "You are perfect. You always have been."

Before departing, he gave her a delicate and lingering kiss. Although the throbbing pain was mercilessly stinging her backside, she melted into his arms.

When Elizabeth woke, she was lying face down on the same bed she was in after her experience on the machine. Megan was lying beside her, massaging an herbal balm into her wounded backside. She felt no pain, only the warm sensation of Megan's expert hands and a numbness in her bottom.

Megan was engrossed in her healing touch, unaware that a weary Elizabeth was gazing at her.

"You are so beautiful, my Lady Megan."

Never taking her eyes from Elizabeth's wounds, she replied, "As are you. How do you feel?"

"Like I've been whipped severely. Why did he do it?"

Megan paused for a moment before answering.

"A hunger grips everyone under this roof, including him. We all have different names for the satisfaction of this hunger, 'the spark of life,' 'the awareness,' and even 'true love'—our version of love. This hunger overtakes him, and he is addicted to the feelings it produces when he is gratified. He is a libertine of the highest order, which is a curse. As time passes, the satisfaction of this hunger becomes more extreme. You will learn this as you get to know us."

"Must I endure this at every visit?"

"You should rest now."

"Kiss me, Megan," she said, straining her neck to fully see her.

Megan got close, stroked Elizabeth's hair, and gently kissed her face and lips.

"It has been decided," Megan said softly, mere inches from Elizabeth's face.

Elizabeth looked puzzled as Megan reached over to grab something from the nightstand.

"While you were sleeping, the master wanted me to give you this."

Megan opened her hand, revealing a scarlet satin choker. Instinctively, Elizabeth felt her neck and realized her purple choker was gone.

"Have I been accepted?" she asked, surprised by its beauty.

"Of course—I had a feeling he was going to accept you on the first visit."

"Where is he now?" she asked, still admiring the color of her new choker.

"He is with Linzie. She is terribly distraught over her role in your punishment, and he is easing her pain. You will not see him until your next visit."

"Can you tell me some things?"

"Maybe."

"Tell me about the chokers."

"The chokers symbolize our allegiance and obedience to him. Black is the lowest level. Those chokers are only worn by *members* of the house and never by the women of the coven. Each member is led by the master or a woman of the coven.

"How does one become a member?"

"A person is required to have nine visits, just like you. A covener must sponsor one seeking membership. The sponsor must present the pledge at a prearranged dinner attended by the master. After the function, the master may or may not grant status. If the master grants immediate status, the function shall be considered the first of the nine required visits. On the other hand, further visits may be necessary if he has not decided. Status may be terminated at any time through misconduct or actions that are not in line with the principles of the house."

"And the other chokers?"

"Well, my poor Elizabeth," she said, working the herbal salve deeper into her wounds, "you already know the next two. Purple and red."

"Yes, but I like the clarity of your explanations. And I like the sound of your voice. It makes me feel better."

"Alright, Elizabeth. A coven initiate is one who has been selected by the master to undergo a rigorous examination for full coven membership. A coven member is then chosen to sponsor the new initiate. In your case, it was Linzie. Upon the initial visit or visits, the pledge dons a purple choker. Upon acceptance, a scarlet choker is awarded. The point of time in which the initiate is given the scarlet choker shall be considered the first of the nine required visits. So, in your case, you received the red choker on the first visit, so this visit counts toward the nine."

"Have all the women made it on the first visit?"

"You are the first. It took Sakura three terrible visits before he would award her the red choker. He is always picky when it concerns a man or woman trying to become a house member. When it concerns a potential *coven* member, he is tyrannical."

"And the white chokers?"

"The master grants the initiate a formal place in the coven after the ninth visit, after which the new coven member is awarded the white satin choker. As you know, a white choker distinguishes coven members from lesser house members. All members of the lesser houses are subservient to the coven members. And all of us are subservient to the master."

"Why does yours have a ruby?"

"When the master takes leave, I oversee the house and coven. I am also his counselor. He says the ruby symbolizes this designation."

"It seems unlikely that he would want anyone's counsel."

"You would be surprised. He always listens. He may not agree or take heed, but he always listens."

"What about Nona? Her choker has a stone."

"That designation came about solely because of who Nona is."

"What do you mean?"

"She is not like us. Her designation is special. She is also his counselor."

"What do you mean she is not like us?"

"It is time for you to rest."

There was silence as Elizabeth slipped out of consciousness, her brain reeling from the strange new world she found herself in. Her dreams were fantastic, and she spent the remainder of the night on her belly, watched over by Megan.

It took a week before Elizabeth could sit down without pain. It took several more weeks for the wounds to completely heal. She had survived her first visit, and as the days passed, she experienced a maddening desire to return.

HEATHER'S REVENGE

Elizabeth's every waking thought revolved around the coven. Two months had passed since her first visit, and she longed to hear from them. Before leaving the visit, which forever changed her life, Megan told her she was forbidden to contact the house for anything. This rule was absolute and another test of obedience. If she attempted to contact any of them, especially Linzie, the initiate status would be null and void. She would have to start all over from scratch as well as wait nine months to do it. Megan assured her the new tests would be far worse under those conditions. Elizabeth thought they had forgotten her and exploded with gratitude when Linzie finally called.

"How do you feel?" Linzie asked in her girlish voice, which made Elizabeth electrified with desire.

"Like I've lost my mind," she replied. "I miss you so much it hurts worse than the wounds I left with."

"I bawled my eyes out that night. I had no choice. He would have whipped me a hundred times worse, and I wouldn't have been able to see you for a very long time. Anyway, it's totally normal for you to feel this way."

"What do you mean?"

"Your desire will only get stronger."

"Well, I won't lie. I am desperate for another visit."

"That's why I'm calling. We have another coven candidate having the first of her visits this Friday, and your presence has been requested."

"Really? What's going on?"

"Her name is Heather. She has been a friend of the coven for nearly a year, and the master is finally letting her in. He wanted to wait to make the occasion special."

"What time?"

"Be there by eight. The ceremony starts at nine."

As Elizabeth rounded the corner of the coven's massive stone house, a bare-footed Linzie was already running toward her, wearing a pleated white tennis skirt and a pink tank top. With her wild hair in pigtails bouncing high atop her head, she embodied adolescent sexuality. No one would have ever guessed her actual age of twenty-seven. Linzie looked more like a sixteen-year-old. When Elizabeth's eyes met those of her long-lost lover, she felt ghost pains along her backside. She shivered.

Linzie had wanted to make up for the whipping ever since that dreadful night. She jumped on Elizabeth, wrapped her arms and legs around her, and stole her soul with a deep kiss. Elizabeth held her effortlessly, tightly gripped her rear, and became lost in the moment.

"I missed you so much," Elizabeth confessed.

Linzie jumped down, grabbed Elizabeth by the hand, and led her through the giant front doors. As they entered, Elizabeth was overwhelmed by the lights of hundreds of white candles. It was a sight to behold once again. Linzie ran up the stairs, still leading Elizabeth by the hand. When they arrived at the top, Linzie kissed her again and whispered to her.

"You must be prepared," she said as she led her into Megan's bed chamber, where dozens of white candles illuminated this room.

The next sight stopped Elizabeth's thoughts completely. Megan and three other women were completely naked except for their snow-white chokers - the same three tied to the ceiling with Linzie during her last visit. They sat obediently, with damp hair, legs together, and hands upon their laps. Without moving, they greeted both women with warm smiles.

Megan pointed to a place on the floor and signaled Elizabeth to stand upon it. Meanwhile, Nona pulled off Linzie's clothes and led her to Megan's bathtub. Elizabeth fleetingly remembered when the master had disturbed Megan's bath because of their insubordinations.

Around the tub, beautiful black velvet drapes were tied back with rich crimson corded rope. Elizabeth clearly saw that Nona was washing Linzie thoroughly from head to toe. It was gentle and magical. The sight fascinated her, and she felt her reality slipping away again.

She watched as Linzie hooked the toes of her left foot on the edge of the tub while Nona inserted two long plastic tubes into her anus and vagina. Obscured by the angle of her observation, Elizabeth could only hear the sound of liquid pouring into a container that filled the tubes.

After Linzie's purification, the water was drained from the tub, wiped clean, and refilled with sachets of hyssop and fresh rose petals. As the tub was filled with steaming hot water, Nona carefully towel-dried Linzie's body and sprinkled her with baby powder.

Linzie and the other women had undergone a ghostly appearance, and the powdered scent made Elizabeth delirious. Time became meaningless, internal questioning stopped, and she looked at her lover curiously. The supernatural beauty of these women put her in a trance-like state.

Nona stepped before Elizabeth and disrupted her fixation with a gentle kiss. Goosebumps ran the length of her spine as Nona undressed her, led her to the claw-footed tub, and guided her to step inside.

The scent of the hyssop was strong, and the water held a dark green hue, the surface laden with dozens of rose petals. Nona made her dip her head in the water. This was done without words, only little tugs and pushes. She washed every inch of Elizabeth's body. It was efficient, sensual, and accomplished in total silence.

When the time came for Elizabeth to wash her feet, Nona turned her around and placed Elizabeth's hands on the wall. She then curled her hand under Elizabeth's shin, pulled her foot out of the water, and methodically cleaned it with absolute reverence, religiously repeating the process on the other foot. Finally, Nona gently inserted the tubes as she had done with the others. The liquid was uncomfortably warm as it went in and flooded back out. The scent possessed her completely. *Lavender*, she thought.

After the washing, she was led out of the tub, dried off, dusted with baby powder, and led to the only open chair between Linzie and Megan.

Nona, the only woman fully clothed, quietly left the room. Elizabeth was electrified with anticipation and felt as if she were floating. After what seemed like forever, Nona returned and addressed the XO as if addressing a vital dignitary.

"My Lady Megan, the master is ready to receive the coven."

Nona quietly left the room again, and Elizabeth believed something extraordinary was about to happen. Megan grabbed her hand, instinctively knowing to hold Linzie's hand until a chain of six beautiful naked women moved gracefully down the stairs to greet the master in the great coven room.

Torches and hundreds of white tapers bathed the room in warm splendor. Celsus, dressed in black tails with an open white collared shirt, occupied the tallest throne of the great round table. He eyed Elizabeth as the chain of naked women circled to greet him.

Megan knelt before him with her head bowed, lovingly kissed the top of his left hand, and took the seat directly to the left of him. Linzie followed in the same fashion, taking the seat to the left of Megan. Elizabeth could only imitate the others and felt uneasy about her status as an initiate. She felt isolated and kept her eyes down as the other women took their seats.

Without warning, a young woman exuding great confidence strode into the coven room, paid her respects to the master, and took the seat directly to the left of Elizabeth. This was Heather, a bouncy, hazel-eyed, auburn-haired beauty.

Two long pig-tails stuck out above a royal-purple bow crowning the top of her head. It perfectly matched the familiar choker around her neck. Below that, she wore a one-piece lavender flower-print sundress with nothing on underneath. She was five feet four inches tall and in apparent superior health. Her build was hard and thick with all the muscles of a dedicated gymnast. She was gorgeous and had a confident and mischievous look about her.

Heather Ostertag was born in Toledo, Ohio, and raised in the suburb of Perrysburg, not more than ten miles from Elizabeth. Her parents were upper-middle-class socialites, so she was blessed with some privilege. She has an outstanding intellect and extraordinary natural abilities for foreign languages, sports, music, and theater.

Seemingly the perfect daughter, her life was not one without flaws and oddities. From four to 11, she suffered strange "blank-outs," where she would go into an open-eyed trance and not come out for hours. When she did, there appeared to be no lapse in her perception of time. She saw two different neurologists and three child psychiatrists, none of whom could find anything wrong with her. Around puberty, the trances stopped, never to occur again.

Her greatest strength is her intuition, a relatively mild way of describing her true-to-life psychic ability. Early on, she realized that secrecy was an absolute necessity because, most of the time, she was disturbingly right about what would happen next. She had the foresight to see that she was different. Starting at five, she kept this ability secret as a defense against unwanted attention.

Academically, her forte was always history. Her teachers praised her extraordinary powers of memory. When it came to history, she could close her eyes and transport herself to a place with such vivid imagination that, to this day, she believes time travel to be a real possibility. In her mind, there was no doubt or question regarding her sanity. Still, she could never synthesize her thoughts about why these visions of the past were so crystal clear.

As an alumnus of the University of Toledo, she will be the first to tell anyone that it is not history that moves her but rather the stage, drama, and the art of acting. She cherishes her BFA and appears regularly at her old stomping grounds, the UT Theater and the Toledo Repertoire Theater, also known as The Rep. Many agents tried to persuade her to leave the wretched city, but she diligently maintained that there was someone she was waiting for. She was so sure of this belief that she suffered severe losses by declining several career-changing roles that would have required her to travel extensively.

Her only apparent weakness was a young Arab attorney, Abdul Ghaazi, who practiced criminal defense in Ohio and Michigan. His parents were respected second-generation attorneys in the greater Detroit metropolitan area. His quest for her started shortly after watching her performance as Abigail Williams in *The Crucible*.

This relationship lasted only two years before it dive-bombed into oblivion because of an incident of vicious domestic violence. She used her pain over the loss to continue performing superb performances, never once believing he was the reason why she stayed in Toledo. One night, a beautiful freckle-faced woman with fiery red hair presented her with a rose after one of her excellent performances. Not surprisingly, her contact with Megan was predicted, and the young actress was satisfied that she had found what she was waiting for. She knew her fate had finally embraced her.

Celsus, Heather, and Nona were the only ones who were fully clothed at this point. Nona poured wine into all nine silver chalices before taking her seat directly to the right of Celsus.

When everything was completely still, Celsus stood up and addressed the coven with the soft, seductive voice Elizabeth remembered from the coffee shop where they first met.

"Beautiful women, goddesses of my home, tonight we are celebrating the long-awaited arrival of our beautiful Heather. She has waited nearly a year for the opportunity to don the scarlet choker. Her exploits are wonderful, and tonight, we shall witness the power of this young libertine. But first, allow me to introduce everyone to our newest initiate, Lady Elizabeth. Elizabeth, you already know these faces, but I believe proper introductions are now in order."

"Yes, my lord," she softly replied, eyes lowered.

"This is our Executive Officer, the Lady Megan. Her station is one of absolute trust. Although this is my domain, Megan takes care of everything I hate—all the mundane garbage—and is, in my absence, the only one who carries my full authority. She is my advisor. I decide everything, but her opinions are always carefully considered. If she chooses you for some task while on coven time, you must obey her without question or suffer consequences. She is my left hand, figuratively and sometimes literally."

Some women giggled as a smiling Lord Celsus spun a light and sensuous atmosphere around the group. He continued speaking as he walked counterclockwise around the table.

"The ever-so-sweet Lady Linzie is our sustenance minister, who selects our drink, food, and other nonconventional nourishments. Her role in the coven is similar to that of her previous life: supply the coven with awareness enhancers such as peyote, psilocybin, and the exotic Ayahuasca from South America to augment a visionary state of mind and a heightened sense of feeling during sex. You do not harbor any ill will toward her for what happened, do you?"

Elizabeth trembled as she responded.

"No, my lord. Linzie was only doing her duty. I was the one who erred by trespassing, and I was punished accordingly."

"And do you harbor any ill will toward me?"

"No, my lord, and if you give me a chance, I would love to show my gratitude for making me an initiate of such a fine and perfect coven."

"My dear, you will have the chance soon enough. The other three women are Lady Sakura, Lady Sanem, and Lady Tara, the three women you saw tied with Linzie during your first visit. Sakura is the coven's treasurer and takes care of all the finances. No money comes in or out without her knowledge. She is a gifted accountant and a supernatural investment guru. Christ, our money has tripled since she took over the finances last year. She is gifted in so many other ways as well."

Elizabeth gazed at Sakura. Of Japanese descent, only five feet tall, with a perfect porcelain complexion, waist-length jet-black hair, cat-like eyes, and a beautiful, gentle demeanor, she was another exotic woman of the coven. Her sensual brown eyes gave a timeless feel, yet she looked so young. For a moment, Elizabeth was transfixed until Sakura met her eyes.

Elizabeth took a deep breath and could feel the power of this woman stirring her soul. Sakura was expressionless but assuredly knew the effect she was having on her. Celsus broke her trance.

"Lady Sanem is our physical guardian. She is from Turkey, a martial arts master, and quite versed with countless weapons and security systems. It is she who designed our perimeter and internal security, and it is she who will eject anyone from my house who is not behaving properly. My dear coveners, did she not remove a 300-pound, drunken, belligerent idiot from our presence with one hand?" All the women nodded in affirmation.

As Celsus spoke, Elizabeth's eyes shifted to Sanem. Indeed, the most physically intimidating woman in the room, her six-foot frame carried 180 pounds of ripped muscle, yet her regal, feminine loveliness was undeniable. Elizabeth was sitting close enough to see the incredible shape of her legs, the rips of her abdominal muscles, and the cut of her triceps. She was so taken by the physical power of this woman that she didn't notice Sanem smiling at her until she looked up. It startled her, yet the smile was one of compassion and love.

Sanem seemed an icon of Turkish beauty and mystery. Her black, spiky hair, cropped short around the ears, took nothing away from her elegant face, graced with a prominent, aquiline nose. Her body, Elizabeth thought, was one to die for. The voice of Celsus faded back into her consciousness.

"Lady Tara is our attorney general. She knows every law of this land that could ever pertain to this coven's mischief. Tara never loses and will vigorously defend any house member in court. She wears many hats and leads other lives, to be sure, but she has sworn her absolute dedication to this coven countless times. Ah, my goddess, what a mind, what a body, what lips," he said as he leaned down and slipped his tongue into Tara's mouth.

Elizabeth immediately equated Tara's beauty with the Egyptian goddess Isis. Her majestic height, large brown eyes, and mischievous smile made Elizabeth dizzy with desire. Early on, Linzie had confessed that Celsus felt Lady Tara's derriere deserved deep worship and contemplation. He would always say that Tara's rear was the absolute and indisputable truth that the goddess existed. He said outlandishly playfully things like that about all the women of the coven. Lady Tara looked like a natural queen, and Elizabeth imagined what it would be like to kiss her. Celsus then spoke about Nona.

"None of us could ever forget our beautiful Nona. Her family came here from Brazil 24 years ago, and fate brought us together. We were little kids, so to speak. The laws of this coven do not bind Nona, yet she is completely subservient to it. Once you are a full member, you may ask her to do things for you, within reason. However, never mistreat her. If you do, you shall find yourself on the street and out of my house permanently."

Elizabeth admired Nona's confidence as she bowed her head toward Celsus. She looked powerful, and Elizabeth was getting the strange sense that somehow she had *always* known every one of these women. It was a peculiar feeling that grew as he continued.

"Our darling newcomers are Elizabeth and Heather. One cold evening last winter, I needed to visit Ann Arbor and walk around the campus. You know how it is. I just had the feeling someone of substance would be there. Elizabeth created great heat where there was none. Girlish, submissive, beautiful—I knew immediately you were one of us. You feigned attitude at first, but I saw you tremble—and I sensed your subconscious recognition of me. It was not hard to assess that Linzie would be your mistress and seduce you as she did. You all know how Elizabeth had the fortitude to ride the machine and endure a wicked lashing within the same night. You are adorable, and we are grateful for your presence tonight."

Elizabeth bowed her head in gratitude as Celsus shifted his attention to Heather.

"Heather is known by every single one of you except Elizabeth, though ironically, they grew up in the same city. I know you have all been dying to get your teeth into her and have her under our roof. The thought of drinking from her has driven me absolutely insane. Megan arranged for Heather and me to finally meet a few months ago, and we had a most interesting conversation."

Celsus paused momentarily, allowing Heather to bow her head in silent acknowledgment. He then addressed the coven with much ceremony in his voice.

"And I am Lord Celsus—your master. I will give you the secrets of your souls, Elizabeth and Heather, but that is not tonight's focus. Let us turn our attention to our guest of honor," he said, turning to Heather. "Megan, tell us how you know this sweet thing."

Megan took a deep breath and gazed lovingly upon Heather while answering her master.

"It was you, my lord. You clipped a fresh rose from our garden and told me I would be attending a theater in Ohio that night. I did as I was told and recognized my sister immediately. *Dial M for Murder*. Heather played Margot and was brilliant. I knew her right then and there. She emerged from her dressing room wearing torn, faded jeans and a plain white t-shirt. She was devastating and beautiful, and my hunger for her was vicious, though she never knew, not then anyway. We became lovers, and never once did she experience the questioning anxiety that plagued the rest of us when we joined you, my lord. She is my sister, my friend, and my lover. She always has been."

"Delicious," Celsus said, looking at Heather. "You are so perfect."

Elizabeth had always wanted to see a play at the Rep and even remembered when *Dial M* was there. She had come so close to seeing that play and talked herself out of it for whatever reason. She remembered the strangeness of the memory because she had a robust and irrational desire to see that particular play, even though she had no idea what it was about. Celsus was grinning at her as if he knew her internal debate. He stood up, took a drink, and addressed the coven.

"Though my affections for Heather are deep—and she knows they are—she must go through what everyone else has gone through. She must prove herself, and I am confident she will. Tonight, the test is one of impression and domination. As usual, I set the rules. The main event of the evening will require the introduction of a house prospect by the name of Abdul Ghaazi, sponsored by Tara. I will turn absolute power over to Heather for this event. You may orchestrate whatever you like, but you must ensure that everyone in the coven is involved somehow. Understood?"

"Yes, my lord," Heather replied.

"But first, let's talk about Abdul."

Celsus walked silently around the table before drawing a deep breath, commanding Heather to speak.

"Heather, you must tell us everything about Abdul-- your feelings, passions, and pain."

"Yes, my lord," Heather said as she stood up.

Elizabeth detected the first sign of vulnerability in the young woman. With a sullen expression, Heather told the story.

"He saw me at that very same theater in 2002. It was the way he looked. You know the old cliché—tall, dark, and handsome. That's the illusion, anyway. After my performance, he handed me a rose. This in and of itself was meaningless, as

I am used to roses from both men and women. But this single rose and the look in his eyes captured me. Yes, my lord. I was fascinated, and it was all surface, like a huldra."

Celsus raised an eyebrow and commanded her softly.

"You test me when using such a word. Show respect at all times and pick another culture for your analogies."

"I am sorry, my lord. Please forgive me."

"Continue."

"Within two months, we were living together. His parents hated me. He was successful, beautiful, rich, intelligent, and charming but had no heart. He was as deep as tracing paper. I was his white trophy girlfriend, and his sole intention was to make me his slave."

"And yet you stayed with this man for two years?"

"Yes, my lord."

"Why?"

"I don't know. Perhaps it was fate, my lord—hard lessons to be sure."

"How did you separate?"

"Throughout our two-year relationship, he became less and less of a gentleman and lover. He started acting like he owned me. He insisted that I leave the theater and hurled ridiculous, chauvinistic insults at me. He would say, "the theater is no place for a woman,' or 'the theater is for whores.' Then, I could see right through him into my own disgusting emotional dependency. I decided then to move back into my parents' house. My mom was waiting for me with open arms. I closed my last suitcase when he told me I was forbidden to leave. I told him to fuck off and started to march out when he grabbed me and threw me down the stairs. The fall broke my left wrist. He ran down the stairs, picked me up, and punched me in the stomach. I could taste my own bile as I fought for air. And then he just kept punching me in the face, over and over. Then he raped and sodomized me. Somehow, I managed to get to the hospital after he fell asleep."

Celsus walked in front of Heather and cupped her chin in his hand, lifting her eyes to his.

"I saw the photographs. He beat you bloody."

At this point, Elizabeth noticed Sanem's muscular arms tensing and a cold expression on her previously benevolent face. Celsus continued.

"Yet here you are, with not so much a blemish on your angelic face. You are beautiful."

"Thank you, my lord."

"So what happened after that?"

"My father wanted him dead. Abdul's father actually showed up at the hospital to see me. He suggested I forget about what happened—that it wasn't that bad—our son's career—blah blah fucking blah. Unbelievable. He started screaming at me when I told him I was pressing charges. He told me that in his country, his son would have the right to kill me for the embarrassment I caused him. He told me he had always thought I was too independent, too brash, too loud, too whorish, and then he stormed out. My family went to bat for me and ensured the prosecutor was up to the challenge. We lost! Can you believe it? We lost. His bigot father represented him."

Elizabeth now noticed Tara looking down at her wine, immersed in thought. Somewhere, it came to her that Tara felt guilty for not helping the prosecutor with the charge of Heather's horrendous beating. Celsus inquired.

"How in the world did you lose?"

"He actually put forth the argument of self-defense. He made the jury believe that he was throwing me out of his home, that I was violently hysterical, and that I had attempted to stab him. He told them my injuries were sustained when I *accidentally* fell down the stairs during the confrontation. The prosecution submitted photos taken right after I drove myself to the emergency room at St. Vincent's. My face was broken, which is how they won the case. When we went to trial, the doctor who had treated me could not testify as a witness because he was dead. The defense picked up the ball and killed us with it. Abdul's asshole father asked the judge and jury to look at my face from every angle. He asked if I was wearing face makeup. I said no, and then he asked the jury if they had ever seen a more beautiful face—hardly the broken jaw, fractured eye socket, and deep lacerations depicted in the x-rays and photographs. After the defense revealed that *all* intake documents, photographs, and treatment records were signed by the now-deceased physician, they fortified their premise that the entire medical portion of the trial was faked to harm the good name of an outstanding Middle Eastern family that had been in Michigan for three generations. all in the legal field. In his closing statement, Abdul's father called the entire accusation of assault and rape fraudulent and insisted that the State of Ohio was wasting good money over nothing more than a woman with a grudge. Abdul is about to find out how bad my grudge really is."

The voice of Lord Celsus now took on a serious tone.

"Be seated, Heather. You will prove your point tonight, and how you prove that point will determine whether or not you wear the scarlet choker. I'm sure all of you are wondering how Abdul came to us. For the sake of our great hedonistic ways, I commanded Megan and Tara to be silent. As you all know, Tara is an outstanding lawyer. She felt responsible—a step too late to serve justice and send an imbecile to jail. Tara wanted desperately to make it up to her. Tara, tell your story."

Tara Peterson was the youngest of six children, four boys and two girls. She was born and raised in Calumet City,

Illinois, a hardcore suburb of Chicago's southeast side. This precocious African American girl was a perfect child, always keeping her nose to the grindstone despite the violence, drugs, and hopelessness that encumbered her daily life.

At five feet ten inches tall and aesthetically beautiful by any standard, she was consistently solicited by people from the entire spectrum of life—from athletic coaches, modeling scouts, and college recruiters to gangbangers, businessmen, pimps, and some of the city's most brutal lesbians. She was respectful but firm in her refusal to give up any part of herself, admitting early on that her absolute freedom was necessary for her future. She politely declined all offers and broke many hearts.

She is undeniably irresistible but has never consciously taken advantage of her charms or looks. She was obsessed with her future and reasoned at an early age that good grades and a good education could lift her out of what she saw as a mass grave. By the time she turned 16, she had one goal: to be an attorney.

Tara's parents and high school teachers recognized her extraordinary talents and zeal to learn the legal system. Earning perfect grades, spending her summer vacations observing Chicago's courtrooms, and cozying up to some of the best attorneys in the city, she made herself known as a young aspiring lawyer before she had even graduated high school. By her senior year, her brilliant mind and tenacity won her a scholarship at the Chicago-Kent College of Law.

In early 2001, she was awarded a free trip with five other classmates to attend a prestigious conference at the University of California, Berkeley. It was at this conference that she met the mysterious Celsus. It was also the only time she seriously dropped the ball on a mandatory report on the conference's topics and discussions.

Her family, friends, and colleagues noticed a marked difference in her personality upon her return from California. She began studying for the Michigan Bar Exam. She snapped at her mother and siblings when they inquired about it, telling them it was none of their business. Her peers were equally perplexed when they noticed her new obsession with the psychological dynamics of polygamy—and criminal forensic science. By the age of 24, she had earned her Juris Doctor and Legum Magistra and passed the Illinois and Michigan Bar Exams.

Two years later, she began working exclusively for Celsus and purchased several houses in Michigan on his behalf. She also closed the deal on the multi-million dollar estate in the northern part of the Lower Peninsula where the coven resided.

Tara handles all legal matters regarding the coven. She has broken off all contact with her family and refuses to see any of them.

Elizabeth's heart beat faster as Tara gracefully stood up, towering above the table, and spoke with great dignity.

"I started to follow his cases, watch him work, learn his strengths and weaknesses, and assess for retribution. I befriended him. It was all business, but it was also sorcery, my lord. Abdul explained that his father and grandfather were attorneys, and he was expected to follow in their footsteps. Once I realized what kind of man he was, I began to spin my web around him. In all fairness to Heather, I believe she could have done the same thing, but her emotions and pride got in the way. The state of being *obsessed* can diminish or even kill one's personal power."

"Well said, Tara," Celsus stated. "Please continue."

"Abdul was fascinated by me, and I knew it would be easy to work a spell. He is as weak in his repressive convictions as he is physically strong. I apologized for having to cut lunch short and asked him if he would meet with an associate of mine later at the Trash Bar. I lured him with city politics and insider information, making him believe I could advance his career greatly. He agreed to meet us there. When I returned to the house, I told Megan about it, and she was more than willing to help me. Megan and I dressed in business casual attire, creating subtle eye traps. Megan left enough of her blouse open so he could see her tits, which were crushed together by a push-up bra. I wore extra tight slacks to show off my better assets."

"Of course," Celsus chimed in.

"Abdul was clearly intimidated by our dress and mannerisms. We had all of our charms on display, subtle and effective. He forgot why he was there in the first place, and that's when Megan and I noticed we were having the desired effect on him. His hand was trembling when before it was steady. That's when I decided to test his faith. I asked him if he was a religious man. He said that he was a progressive Muslim. Megan laughed and asked him if there was such a thing. He was not amused and glared at her for the crass comment. I asked him what his thoughts were on female attorneys. He told us that in a perfect world, under the direction of Allah, women would not work outside the home. He said they would be happy and content to serve their husbands and children from inside the home. Megan sarcastically said his response sounded *very* progressive to her. This time, he warned her that he would not suffer another insult. Megan apologized, though I knew she was not sincere. It was all I could do to keep from laughing. He never stood a chance."

Heather did not respond but maintained a cold, neutral expression as Tara continued.

"That's when I decided to reel him in. While he was using the restroom, Megan proceeded to pour about three teaspoons of pure liquid Yohimbe extract into his drink. When he got back, he drank the entire glass. We sat and talked about nothing for a while longer. Megan feigned that Abdul had some lint in his hair. He kept brushing his hair with his hand until Megan finally told him she would get it. She plucked a strand of hair from him and told him it was gone. We were laughing, touching his shoulders, and rubbing up against him. I knew he was high from the aphrodisiac, and I winked at Megan to depart. She said goodbye, gave Abdul one of her sweet kisses on the cheek, and walked out of the Trash Bar with a strand of Abdul's hair wrapped around her pinky. I could tell he didn't want to get up. I knew his cock was killing him, and little beads of sweat started appearing on his brow. I told him I had to leave and asked if he would walk me to my car. He acquiesced and made it a point to let me walk in front of him. I knew the soul of this coven was reaching into his very being, possessing him. I told him to get in when we got to the car. I said I had something for him. He stuttered and looked around to see if anyone was watching. As soon as he got in the car, I was all over him. He made a feeble attempt to push me away, but I had him totally under control. I shoved my tongue in his mouth and started massaging his crotch simultaneously. No resistance then, none. Once I had him out of touch with any sense of reason, I unzipped his pants and freed him. He was ridged and just stared at me with this pleading look as I went down on him in the parking lot. I treated him to slow and sloppy deep sucking. He came in only five strokes. I took every drop from him, and he cried like a woman on the machine. He will forever belong to us, my lord."

"Fucking Voodoo woman," Celsus declared with a wild look in his eyes as he slammed his chalice down on the table.

"Come!"

Tara obediently walked to him as he slid his throne away from the table and unzipped his pants.

"Show me how you sucked him."

"As you wish, my lord."

With the entire coven watching, Tara knelt, gripped her master's steely organ, and sucked him precisely as she had described. Celsus clenched his teeth together and seethed.

"Goddess fuck!"

The coven watched silently as Celsus allowed this to go on for a few minutes before guiding Tara back to her feet.

"Return to your seat, Tara. You would take from me what I have pledged to Heather this night."

Tara smiled and returned to her chair as Celsus again started his slow, methodical walk, speaking reflectively.

"Megan and Tara returned to the house with the entire tale. I knew nothing of it until that time. After a night of contemplation, I decided Abdul's great internal convictions regarding a woman's place in the world would be tested this night. I summoned Lady Tara and gave her a nine-inch wax figurine of a man. I told her to instruct Heather to take one of her own pubic hairs and twirl it together with the strand of Abdul's hair, then split the combined strand into three equal parts. After that, heat a nail and melt three small areas, one in the figurine's head, one in the heart, and one in the groin. Place the hairs into the small puddles of wax and let it dry. Get sexually stimulated, masturbate with the doll, shoving the head and as much of it as you can into yourself, and chant with vigor the following: *You are mine, trapped forever by the fountain of my pleasure. There is no rest for you, no thoughts of your own. Forever, you are possessed by me. Forever, you are haunted by me. Only my voice and touch can soothe you. You belong to me now, forever.'*

At the point of your climax, you will force the outcome. You will make it a reality. Have faith, and it shall always be done— a simple but powerful spell."

As he spoke, he walked up behind Heather. Elizabeth was visibly trembling, and she didn't dare look up. He put his hands on Heather's shoulders and softly asked her.

"Have you performed this operation, my sweet little witch?"

"To the letter, my lord," she replied as she turned to look up at him.

"Very good. Now, you must prepare yourself for your role as high priestess. Nona, please show her to her bedroom and then bring Abdul. Heather, when you are ready, we shall obey your every wish until the sun rises. Go now."

Elizabeth tried to take it all in as Nona and Heather left the room. It was certainly bizarre, yet somehow it all seemed normal, even familiar. When Celsus returned to his throne, Elizabeth noticed her perception of things was different. It was as if the real world had disappeared, and she was amid supernatural beings. She wondered if she looked as they did, if her eyes shimmered. She jumped when Celsus addressed her.

"Of course, they shimmer," he said. "You are one of us. You always have been."

My God, he can read my thoughts.

"We all can, and the thoughts of each other when we permit it. You'll be able to do the same soon enough. For now, be content that you are home. You are exquisite, my love."

As Elizabeth struggled with the concept, a female voice came into her mind.

It's all right, darling. We'll stay out of your head for now.

Elizabeth never knew whose voice it was. Nona then opened the door with some drama and addressed the coven.

"My lord and esteemed women of the coven, I present to you Abdul Ghaazi."

Abdul walked in, blindfolded and completely naked. He was six feet tall, dark-skinned, with short, curly black hair and a lean, athletic build. His hands covered his penis, and he was clearly uncomfortable.

"Why have you come here?" Celsus asked.

"I am petitioning my admittance into the House of Celsus to wear the black choker," he replied with as much confidence as he could muster.

"Who is your prospective mistress?"

"Lady Tara—my lord. She never leaves my thoughts, and I am unable to function in my life without her."

Abdul spoke with desperation, while Celsus spoke with contempt.

"What about Allah?"

"I will surely pay for what has transpired with Lady Tara and my thoughts of her every night since. Allah may not forgive me, but I must have her. She told me that she belongs to you—my lord."

Celsus looked at Tara and raised an eyebrow. Tara merely smiled and shrugged her shoulders. Celsus then addressed Abdul in a commanding voice.

"Islamic and Judeo-Christian beliefs disgust me. I find these religions as useless today as they have been throughout history. On the other hand, these beliefs can easily turn my disgust into humor. Has Tara explained what you must endure to be a member of my house? I see already you are having a problem addressing me as your lord."

"For her, nothing is a problem—*my lord*. First, I must be accepted as an initiate of the House. The number of visits to get to that level is unknown. It may be tonight, it may be after a hundred visits, or it may not happen at all."

Abdul's voice revealed both his fear and his courage. Celsus clarified.

"And that's just to become a house initiate. After that title, you must endure nine more visits. Do you understand that you must obey my commands along with the commands of every single woman in my coven, no matter what the order?"

"Yes! I am prepared to do anything for Tara."

"How romantic," Celsus said sarcastically as he took a healthy drink of wine. "We shall see if you still feel the same in the morning. And by the way—is there no one else you think of? No one else who sets your mind on fire like Tara?"

"There is, my lord, but I have no idea what happened to her. We used to live together."

Celsus leaned forward with a devilish grin and inquired.

"Who do you think of most? Which one drives you more insane, Lady Tara or this woman you used to live with?"

Abdul shuddered but maintained composure.

"Your question is difficult, my lord. Lady Tara has possessed me to no end, but recently, this other woman has been creeping into my thoughts more and more. I fear I am cursed, but I can't seem to get away from any of it. May Allah have mercy on my soul."

Celsus shot back with a laugh.

"Please, your piousness is killing me. Are you trying to spoil the party before it gets started?"

"No, my lord, I am not. I shall refrain from voicing my torments."

Celsus signaled Nona as he addressed Abdul further.

"Silence now, Abdul. Your test is about to begin."

Nona left the room, and a strange silence followed. Elizabeth felt apprehension and sexual excitement. She knew this night would be as life-altering as her first visit.

The sound of hard shoes hitting the stairs became almost threatening as Elizabeth stared at the entrance in disbelief. Celsus broke out in boisterous laughter as Heather gracefully entered the coven room, dressed as a nun. She carried a large, black shoulder bag and marched into the room like a soldier on a mission. She walked by Abdul and whispered in her master's ear.

Elizabeth could make out the master responding with, "Bravo." Then Heather walked over to Lady Tara and whispered something in her ear. Tara smiled at her with evident love and kissed her. Everyone else continued their obedient silence. Celsus held his palm toward the great round table, signaling Heather to its center. Tara helped her up as he spoke.

"Abdul, the great love of your life, has taken her place at our great round table and bids you to come forward to receive her kiss. Proceed."

Abdul kept one trembling hand around his groin as he felt with the other to arrive at the table's edge. Heather knelt down, cupped his face in her hands, and kissed him softly upon his lips. Everyone could hear Abdul sigh as Heather stood on the table and glanced back at Celsus, who smiled and addressed the room.

"Ladies, without further ado, I give the reign of power to the chosen one. This is a coven event, and she, until the sun rises, is the absolute high priestess and ruler of the coven, ruler of Abdul, and even the ruler of me. Whatever her command, you must obey without hesitation. Does everyone fully understand?"

Except for Abdul, the entire group responded: "Yes, my lord."

Celsus noticed and addressed him with a raised eyebrow, "Abdul?"

Abdul, clearly thinking Lady Tara was the high priestess, responded.

"I will do whatever she commands, my lord."

"Very well," Celsus replied. "Let us proceed."

Elizabeth watched as Heather's face became very stern. She convincingly personified a strict, mean-spirited nun. Her voice was commanding, emotionless, and steady.

"Remove your blindfold, Abdul, and behold your goddess!"

Abdul's expression turned from puzzled as he struggled with the blindfold to absolute shock when he realized he was standing before his ex, dressed as a nun.

"Heather?"

"Close your mouth! You will not speak unless I tell you to! Understood?"

Abdul nodded with his mouth open.

"So, you are in love with Lady Tara, are you? You may answer, but answer truthfully, or the punishment will be most severe."

Clearly shaken, Abdul responded, "I will not lie to you, Heather…"

Even more angered, Heather screamed.

"You will not use that name tonight or ever! From now on, you shall respond at the end of every commanded utterance with 'my goddess!' Do you understand?"

Abdul paused for a few moments and answered.

"Yes, my goddess."

"Good. Now answer my question."

Elizabeth was spellbound, and her fear was genuine. Celsus and the women of the coven seemed strangely indifferent, almost cold. Abdul's voice quivered as he replied.

"I would not call it love. I believe I am possessed. I can think of nothing but her—and you, my goddess."

"Me? Why do you think of me? You never obsessed over me that way."

Abdul looked down at the floor. He was at a loss for words.

"Look at me, you fool!" she commanded. "You dared to lay your filthy hands on *me*? I am the goddess incarnate, and you are a disgusting son-of-a-pig fucker! Where were your so-called principles when you were beating me or raping me?"

"I don't know, my goddess," he meekly replied. "It just happened."

"It just happened," Heather replied, pacing around the top of the table before stopping in front of Lady Tara.

"Well," Heather said softly, "I am insulted and demand a contest. I will choose the two combatants. It's me against Abdul's justifiable principles, me against his pretentious assessment of women, me against his ridiculous God. I challenge your God, Abdul. You will be Allah's champion. Perhaps you can justify the despicable action of spewing your seed in Tara's mouth right in front of a nightclub or—infinitely worse—beating and raping a goddess. You now have the opportunity to prove that you were in the right all along. If you win the contest, you may do as you please with any of us tonight. If that gets you off, you could beat us all to your heart's content. However, suppose my champion defeats you and your precious Allah. In that case, you will immediately endure my punishments for your crimes against nature."

Heather jumped down, walked close to Celsus, took a long drink from his chalice, and spoke to him.

"You have no idea how much I love my power over you as well, my lord."

Celsus smiled at her as she continued on about the contest.

"Abdul was a wrestling champion back in high school, so I have decided to let him fight the best way he knows how to fight. Yes, a wrestling match."

Abdul quickly glanced at Celsus, confident he could beat him but worried about the consequences. The expression of Celsus was cold and unchanging as he easily read Abdul's thoughts. Heather took a deep breath and spoke with increasing conviction and authority.

"So it is you, fighting for your God and your principles against me, the goddess, and a champion of my choosing. You may have the upper hand Abdul, but we shall see."

Elizabeth became aware that Abdul's confidence was returning to him. He was standing taller, and she sensed some self-assuredness. She could *feel* that Abdul was thinking of his strength and masculinity. Heather continued.

"For my champion, I choose—the Lady Sanem!"

Sanem Demir was born and raised in the ancient city of Antalya, Turkey. By all accounts, she was an average healthy child except for one terrible burden—her father.

Due to complications during her birth, her mother's reproductive organs had been damaged beyond repair. As such, Sanem was the only child the couple would ever have together. In retrospect, she believed her father resented her for not being born a male.

She tried to appease him by excelling in sports and besting the boys every chance she could at whatever challenge was offered. He remained unimpressed, regardless of her accomplishments—first-place medals in track and field, swimming, and martial arts. He was openly disappointed that she was female, and nothing she did could change his disappointment. Her father was the key to shaping her life, and not in a healthy way.

One summer day, while her parents were outside gardening, nine-year-old Sanem and a neighborhood boy began to wrestle in her backyard. Her tomboyish behavior received no reaction from her father until she made the boy cry out for mercy. Before any training in martial arts, she had the boy in a perfect arm-bar submission between her legs. Yelling out to her father to take notice of her win, he responded by demanding the boy's release.

After ensuring the boy was not injured, he dragged Sanem into the house by her hair and beat her legs severely with a wooden spoon. The brutality went on for minutes, yet she never cried out. When he was finished, he told her he would kill her if he ever so much as heard of her doing anything like that again, disgracing their family. She had no doubt he would keep his word.

The incident did not deter her from pursuing excellence in combat but strengthened her resolve. From that moment on, it was a secret undertaking and an obsession synonymous with worship. Despite the consequences of that day, it was the interaction of her parents that locked in her absolute and total hatred toward her father.

He was a conservative Muslim, though not devoted in any way. He believed that a man's worth was above a woman's. For him, it was the natural order of things.

One frightful night, a teenage Sanem witnessed the horrific beating of her mother. Her father had been drinking all day in misery over losing his construction job. In a drunken rage, he thought his wife had insulted him. The first blow was a direct, closed-fisted punch square in her face. Her nose shattered, and blood spurted out freely. As Sanem's mother ran out into the street to escape his wrath, Sanem grabbed her father's leg, begging him to stop. He kicked free of her, chased her mother down the road, and stomped on her face until she lost consciousness.

Her mother lay in a coma for three weeks before she woke with severe facial disfigurements and moderate brain damage as the final sum of his wrath. The perceived insult was simply bringing up the subject of an athletic scholarship for Sanem at the dinner table. Mysteriously, her father died from natural causes only a week later.

Her mother's sister immediately moved in to help care for Sanem's mother. Though Sanem loved her mother and aunt dearly, her independence and wanderlust motivated her to a higher calling, the Khazar University in Baku, Azerbaijan.

After this incident, she was totally possessed with all concepts of martial combat, all forms of weapons, and even the tactics and strategies of war and defense. Along with this came another, albeit irrational, obsession with North America. There was no rhyme or reason to it. She had to find a way there and did it through the Khazar University/University of Winnipeg exchange program.

She knew English well enough to get through school, but martial arts took precedence in her life as usual. She wasn't interested in social integration with the Canadians and politely refused all advances. During her first brutal Manitoba winter, she alleviated her boredom with constant sparring, weight lifting, and training at her favorite dojo. She frequently questioned herself about her strange obsession with North America. She felt she could have done all this in Turkey, with much more hospitable weather. Deep down in her soul, she knew there was a reason. That reason would soon reveal itself in a life-altering way.

After claiming absolute victory at an open Judo competition in Winnipeg, she was approached by the charismatic Celsus. Like all the other women, she followed him obediently with total trust and faith. Until now, she had held herself above the male gender in every way, yet she immediately fell in love with the eccentric young man. Unlike the other women of the coven, she stays in close contact with her mother. Celsus provides a generous monthly stipend for her mother's care, with no requirement to repay the money.

Sanem's eyes met Heather's, and she bowed her head with calm affirmation, thankfulness, and obedience. Abdul was clearly in shock, and again, his mouth fell wide open as Heather continued.

"You must fight this woman. She is my champion, the champion of the goddess, and the champion of Nature. How do you feel about that?"

Abdul regained his composure and carefully replied.

"My goddess, I hardly think it is fair for me to wrestle with this woman, and I'm surprised it was not the master you chose for your champion."

"I must confess: the idea of you and the master wrestling with each other makes me very hot. It would be a sight to see, but I have chosen. The champion whose faith involves the greater truth shall win the contest. Lady Sanem is a woman, and a woman should represent nature in this battle for the truth. What say you, Abdul?"

"My goddess, I accept the challenge if you put it that way. It will be my redemption. Perhaps I can break the spell that you women seem to have cast over me and the spell Lord Celsus has over you."

"Then here are the rules. I want everyone to push all the furniture away from the fireplace. The center of the room shall be the battleground. There will be no hitting, kicking, biting, or eye-gouging. It's a wrestling match. The fight is over when one is pinned or begs for mercy, and the truth will be known. Abdul, is there anything you want to say before the match begins?"

"Yes, my goddess. I believe Allah will prevail."

Heather responded with contempt.

"Why am I not surprised? Your God could never break the spell. I can sense your body pleading for Tara and me now. You have false courage fueled by an impotent religion. Lady Sanem, is there anything you want to say, my beautiful champion?"

Sanem looked hotly into Heather's eyes.

"I thank you for choosing me, my goddess."

Heather looked at her passionately, licked her lips, and addressed Abdul again.

"You may take two minutes to ready yourself. Everyone else should form a circle around the center of the room. Lady Sanem, a word, please."

Heather took Sanem by the bookshelves and whispered to her.

"Do not win too quickly. Feign that you are the weaker and less skilled, and let him think he can beat you. Draw it out. When the time comes, make it a submission. Make him beg for mercy, then humiliate him. You will do this at my command and to the letter. Understand?"

"Yes, my goddess," Sanem said as she bowed her head. "It shall be as you desire."

Abdul looked up at the sky from the great window. He was by himself and obviously praying. Elizabeth could hear fragments of his prayer and tried hard to see if he was speaking or thinking. She was lost in a seemingly strange new ability and was beginning to reel from the oncoming power—or insanity. At this point, she wasn't sure which held the grip on her mind.

"It is time," Heather said. "Champions, take your places."

The entire coven formed a large circle around the two naked fighters. Elizabeth found Abdul and Sanem beautiful as they squared off for the match. The coven appeared to her as both angels and devils.

"Begin!" Heather shouted.

The two fighters circled each other. It looked primitive and ritualistic, the fire behind them and the tribe around them. The stalking became tighter and tighter until Abdul made a sudden lunge for Sanem's right leg. She allowed the closure. Abdul's momentum forced her down on her butt, which caused a loud thud and shook the room. He hooked one arm under her right leg and tried quickly to get his other arm around her neck, but Sanem would have none of it. She trapped his free arm and kicked off with her free leg as he tried to make his move, spinning them into a ground skirmish.

She fought him precisely as she was told. Whenever it looked like Abdul had her locked up or pinned, Sanem would initiate a brilliant move out of it. After nearly five exhausting minutes, one could see fatigue and frustration on Abdul's face.

They were both breathing heavily when Sanem glanced at Heather for a sign. Heather gave it with a nod. The speed with which Sanem subdued Abdul was beyond comprehension, and the hold she put him in was magnificent.

When Abdul looked like he was about to pin her, Sanem reversed the predicament, putting Abdul flat on his back. Sanem had Abdul's head locked between her powerful thighs, so he was forced to stare at her exposed sex. She was sitting on his chest with her feet hooked around his elbows so that his entire upper body was pinned and unable to move. She also gripped the middle and index fingers of both of Abdul's hands. She had them painfully bent the wrong way and could have easily broken them. Naturally, with his legs free, Abdul tried to buck Sanem off. He screamed in agony.

"Don't!" Sanem shouted, looking down at him between her breasts.

His face displayed obvious pain. Sanem was crushing Abdul's skull and stressing the bones and ligaments in his hands.

"That's it," Heather started with a giggle. "That's all you've got? Are you still certain that women are a weaker subhuman species?"

Abdul tried again to kick and turn out of Sanem's leg-lock, but she was too strong. Again, he screamed from the vices that tightened. Elizabeth watched in amazement and was utterly without thought as she gazed upon Sanem's legs, crushing Abdul into total submission. Heather's ever-waxing confidence and leadership made Elizabeth weak with desire when she spoke.

"Your God is no match for Mother Nature, is he? Repeat after me, and I shall have Sanem release you. The goddess is much older and stronger than my God. The goddess is my Mother and my *only* salvation. Say it!"

Abdul looked on the verge of passing out but managed to reply.

"No. I would never say that because it's not true."

Heather stepped back and commanded Sanem.

"Piss on him!"

Sanem looked down at Abdul's contorted face and spoke coldly to him.

"You remind me of my father."

Elizabeth was shocked at Heather's command and even more so when Sanem complied. Abdul was coughing and choking on the steady stream of urine that Sanem unleashed upon his face. When he closed his mouth, it went up his nose. When it went into his mouth, it sounded like he was drowning. Abdul could not turn as Sanem maintained the death grip on his head. Her urine rolled out over her thighs and knees. Elizabeth cooed at the scene of this proud young man, reduced to nothing by a local theater vixen and the cunning fighting skills of a beautiful Turkish woman. The members of the coven exuded apparent satisfaction at Abdul's expense. His face and hair were soaked with urine.

"Renounce your God or suffer the consequences," Heather said. "The choice is yours."

"Never!" Abdul managed to scream out.

Sanem looked up, and Heather gave the nod. Abdul's scream was brief as Sanem squeezed her legs together so tight that he immediately lost consciousness. She released her leg hold and let Abdul's head hit the floor with a thud. She stood proudly over her vanquished opponent as her piss ran down her beautifully sculpted legs. Elizabeth found the entire scene disturbing yet highly erotic. Heather spoke.

"The night has just begun. Nona, I need you to grab two large bowls of warm water and soap. Bring them back here with clean towels. You will clean Sanem, then Abdul, and finally, the mess on the floor. Make sure everything is immaculate. Tara, Sakura, and Megan, fetch me ropes and tie Abdul to the great table. Tie his feet to the floor rings and spread them far apart. Tie him face down on the table so we all can see his humiliation perfectly. Secure his wrists tightly and far apart. Make sure he can't move. Hurry now before he wakes."

But Abdul was already turning his head and coughing as he rolled into a semi-fetal position.

"Sanem!" Heather shouted.

"Worry not, my goddess," Sanem said calmly as she helped the stunned man to his feet. While keeping a submission hold on his wrist, she led him to the table and gently pushed his torso over it.

"I need the ropes," Sanem said.

Megan hurried out of the room to fetch the bonds as Heather bent down close to Abdul's face and looked at him inquisitively.

"How do you feel?"

"Not so good," he said in a pitiful voice.

"Well, it's going to get a lot worse-- let me assure you," she said, smiling as she stood up and looked at Celsus. "It certainly is ladies' night, wouldn't you agree, *Wolfie*?"

Elizabeth waited for some kind of reproach for the informality, but he only bowed respectfully and responded.

"Absolutely, my goddess."

"Alright then," Heather said, brimming. "Linzie, I will take the master's throne. Stand behind me, massage my breasts, pinch my nipples, and whisper wickedness in my ears. And while she is kneading my tits, my naughty wolf shall get down on his knees and cunt-suck me. I have waited forever to feel those lips. Do your very best, both of you, understand?"

Linzie and Celsus responded in perfect unison, "Yes, my goddess."

"Proceed then," Heather said.

Linzie pulled the large throne away from the table to allow Celsus to sit on his heels in front of it. Heather lifted her nun's skirt high to her waist as she sat down and unbuttoned her blouse. Elizabeth took a deep breath when she saw Heather's precious little tuft of soft fur. The others waited patiently for their commands as Megan returned with giant loops of black velvet rope and a long, serrated knife.

The woman began working frantically until they had a stark naked Abdul, wholly bound, facedown over the table. Four ropes secured his four limbs while a fifth curved tightly and diagonally across the back of his skull. He was completely immobilized. Nona knelt down before Sanem and gently washed her legs and sex. She then cleaned the urine from the floor and washed Abdul's face, neck, and hair. She had to physically turn his head with Sanem's assistance to wash the other side because he was so tightly bound. After Nona tried unsuccessfully to wash Abdul's hair, his head was again secured and forced in Heather's direction.

Elizabeth watched in excitement at Heather's wicked resolve. Heather was utterly lost in bliss, still donning the nun's flowing headdress. Elizabeth could feel the deprivation from the other coveners who waited patiently for Heather's commands. She swooned with her toes hooked over the table's edge while Linzie pinched her nipples and whispered into her ear. Elizabeth could hear this perfectly, though her rational mind told her this was impossible.

"Pretty little slut, how does it feel, the master sucking on your sweet little thing? Can I suck you too, my pretty little slut?"

Elizabeth squeezed her legs together and could simultaneously *see* from Linzie's eyes and *feel* the master's hunger. Celsus had one hand hooked under and around Heather's left thigh. He spread her vaginal lips as wide as they would go with his thumb and forefinger, exposing the little love nub to his ravenous tongue. His other hand was splayed; the first two fingers probed her womanhood while his little finger tickled her anus. Heather could feel the climax coming when Abdul made the awful mistake of nearly interrupting her powerful orgasm.

"Why are you doing this to me?"

Heather's focus was undeterred. Her curled toes rose a few inches above the table, and the muscles in her thighs and calves tensed hard as wave after wave of her elixir was released into the mouth of the master. Linzie only added to the climax by pinching her nipples and whispering what Elizabeth could somehow still hear.

"That's it, my goddess. Cum for us. Make us yours with rivers of your divine love."

It seemed the entire coven could feel her release. Heather looked positively dreamy and frightening with renewed power as she caught her breath and started anew.

"Stand, Lord Celsus. You have the tongue of a devil, as good as any woman's, save that of Lady Megan. Linzie, I shall require more of your talents later. I like it very much the way you speak to me. I am quivering, but I am ready again. You may take your place with the others. Abdul, I warned you about such informalities. And your timing is as idiotic as your prejudices."

Heather stood up, her nun's gown falling naturally into place and her nipples proudly peeking out from the opening of her snowy white blouse. She gave Abdul a fierce look while speaking to everyone.

"It is time for grand rewards and grand punishments. Everyone in this room except Abdul shall be rewarded for loving me. You, my ignorant pig, shall be punished for what you did to me."

Abdul closed his eyes while Heather removed everything but her nun's hood. She walked around the table to the black bag she had brought. Abdul opened his eyes and tried vainly to see but could not turn his head.

Elizabeth watched in wonder as Heather pulled out a four-inch thick, twelve-inch long, strap-on dildo that she casually donned. It was monstrous, and instant heat circulated throughout the room. Elizabeth could feel the anticipation of the entire coven.

Heather spoke in a commanding voice to a poor, helpless Abdul, a man about to come face-to-face with his female side in a most vicious manner.

"I am the goddess incarnate, your true redeemer, and tonight, you will be purified from the twisted falsehoods that spew from your ignorance."

As Heather slowly walked into Abdul's view, he showed little hesitation about voicing the horror of what he saw.

"No! No!"

Elizabeth felt goose bumps over her body as Heather laughed sinisterly.

"You disapprove, my little angel? You should thank me, for I am about to release, teach, and purify you. Lady Sanem, my bag carries the means to quiet our insolent boy here. Please make use of it now."

The light of the fire seemed to swirl around Heather. She took on the personification of some ancient and exotic hermaphrodite. Her nun's hood, her pure look of innocence, her beautiful, porcelain white, athletic body, and the massive abomination, the tool of justice swinging in front of her, made her out to be more than human at that moment.

Heather stretched like a feline, reached high in the air, closed her eyes, and took a deep breath while Sanem crushed a sizeable black rubber ball into Abdul's mouth. He groaned in futile resistance, but surprisingly, Elizabeth did not feel sorry for him. Heather interrupted her dilemma, looked straight into her eyes, and spoke from an unknown memory.

"Tonight is not the first night for us. In time, we will both remember. You are as old and familiar to me as the air itself. So the first order shall be yours, my sweet. In my black magic bag, there is a jar. Retrieve it now."

Elizabeth immediately went to the bag and found the jar among various dildos, whips, restraints, and paddles. She held it up, and Heather continued.

"Go to Abdul and work the lubricant into his ass. Be thorough. We wouldn't want to stop the party to rush our poor boy to the hospital now, would we?"

"As you wish, my goddess,"

Elizabeth went straight to Abdul's backside, took out three fingers of the gooey substance, and worked it into his anus. The coven tried desperately not to laugh, but Heather heard Megan giggle.

"Lady Megan, my sweet lover, I can sense your wetness from here. Lie next to Abdul and spread your legs wide for me. Gaze into his eyes."

"Yes, my goddess," Megan said as she playfully bounced up on the table, opened her legs wide, draped her left leg over Abdul's back, and smiled seductively at him.

"He cries, my goddess," Megan said.

"He is afraid," replied Heather. "We shall make him a new man—or a new woman. Tara, I want you on the table, squatting over our beloved XO. I want you facing sideways, away from Abdul, so that our foolish boy can see the perfect ass he longs for and your chocolate sweetness penetrated by Megan's glorious tongue."

"Yes, my goddess," Tara said.

Tara stepped up on the table as if it were merely a stair and placed her womanhood within an inch of Megan's lips. Heather then turned back to Elizabeth.

"That's enough, Elizabeth. Go under the table and massage his cock. When and *only* when I give the command, you will administer the best oral sex you've given any man. You will milk the very life essence from his balls. Until I give that command, you will keep him hard and not permit an orgasm. You will be held accountable if Abdul loses control, and the punishments shall be transferred to you. Do you understand?"

"Yes, my goddess," Elizabeth said as she withdrew her fingers from Abdul's ass and disappeared under the table. Surprisingly, she found that he was already half-erect. She cupped his balls with one hand and began working his staff with the other.

Heather then addressed Linzie and Sakura. "I want you two directly next to Megan and Tara, but in a way that should

Abdul's eyes glance upward, he may see you. Sixty-nine each other until I say stop. Proceed."

"Yes, my goddess," the two women replied excitedly as they jumped up on the table.

Sakura lay on the table, allowing her legs to dangle over the edge a couple of feet from Megan and Tara. At the same time, Linzie climbed up and straddled Sakura's face. The sucking commenced immediately and was heard loud and clear.

Abdul's nose-breathing became quicker as Heather stood directly before Megan, lifted her lover's legs upon her shoulders, and touched her sex with the tip of the massive strap-on. Before penetrating her, she continued the orchestration of her debauchery.

"Sanem, since you won the duel, you shall be the adjuster. Retrieve a weapon of your choice from my bag of goodies. If Abdul blinks, closes his eyes, or looks at anything other than what lies next to him, lay on hard, with no mercy, as often as necessary. Make it good."

"Yes, my goddess," Sanem said as she grabbed a horse-riding crop and stood to Heather's right.

Elizabeth continued tugging on Abdul and was surprised at how solid he was, considering his predicament. She could feel his fear and slowed her massaging as he reached critical mass. His legs were trembling. Heather addressed the master as she worked the tip of the enormous dildo into Megan's soaking slit.

"Sweet wolf, I have not forgotten you. There in my bag is a nice wooden paddle for you. Stand to my left and let Linzie take care of that delicious cock of yours. She can suck on you or Sakura, whatever she wants. You will administer the paddle to Linzie as you see fit. You too, Tara! Whenever your heart desires to redden Linzie's rear, you do so. She is much like me and desires a heavy hand. Sanem, fetch Tara a paddle from my bag."

"Yes, my goddess," Sanem said.

Heather firmly worked the head of the massive tool in Megan as Sanem handed Tara a ping-pong paddle.

"We are ready, my Turkish lover. Elizabeth, how is our ignorant boy?"

"He is hard, my goddess. Very hard," Elizabeth said as she yanked on him.

Heather reached under Abdul's thighs and gripped his balls roughly. She then commanded all of them.

"You will commence at the sound of Sanem's crop across Abdul's backside! Whenever you are ready, Sanem."

A crack followed by a muffled scream began the wicked orgy. Elizabeth started to suck him as an unusual trance of nothingness took over her mind.

Heather asked Abdul, "Did that hurt?"

Abdul closed his eyes and whimpered while Sanem laid on three more brutal hits. On the third strike, Heather drove half the length of her wicked toy deep into Megan. A primal moan could be heard as she arched her back in response, her lips touching Tara's sex.

Tara began to randomly strike Linzie with the paddle. Linzie moaned as she was deep in the bliss of drinking Sakura's nectar while violently pulling on the master's cock. Celsus was displeased at the callous way she yanked on him and so leaned over and bit Linzie hard on her rear before Tara got her next hit in. Linzie released her mouthlock on Sakura and yelped in pain. Heather seethed.

"I wish this cock was real just for tonight. Megan's little red pussy would be well worth the knowledge!"

Three more cracks from the riding crop reverberated around the room. Abdul's breathing became quick and loud, as did his muffled crying. Heather screamed at him.

"What a coward you are!"

Elizabeth sucked slowly and deeply. She made both her hands extensions of her lips, and it became a battle to keep him hard. Whenever Sanem struck him with the crop, he would go slightly limp. Still, she could taste his pre-cum.

Meanwhile, Megan detached her mouth from Tara as she experienced a powerful climax from Heather's monstrous tool. Tara's love ran freely down both sides of Megan's face as she cried out in ecstasy.

Tara and Celsus continued paddling Linzie's rear. Now, Linzie was sucking as hard on the master as Sakura was sucking on her. She would suck him and then push his steely cock into Sakura, only to put it back in her mouth again. While Linzie could not see who was striking her, she could easily feel the difference. Tara had a touch of mercy, whereas Celsus made sure it hurt.

This orchestration went on for half an hour. Elizabeth had to pinch off the end of Abdul's penis several times to avoid his climaxing. She worried he could not go much farther. Celsus maintained his integrity, but Tara, Sakura, Megan, and Linzie had multiple orgasms. Nona merely stood at the ready, causally watching the debauchery as Heather continued her torments. She went deep into Abdul's subconscious.

"You're about to become a woman. What do you think? Can you handle it? How does your ass feel? Does it hurt? If you think it hurts now, just wait until I finish it. Everyone, stop! Sanem, I want you to lie down on the other side of Linzie and Sakura. Lord Celsus, stand in front of her and wait for my signal. Treat her well, as she deserves to be treated like the goddess warrior she is. Sakura, Linzie, Tara, and Megan, grab toys from my bag and get on the floor. Form a circle lying down on your sides and have at it on my signal. Elizabeth, how is our prisoner doing?"

"Good," she replied. "He has gone to both extremes but is stable and hard again, my goddess."

"Bravo," Heather said as she worked a considerable portion of lubricant around her massive rubber appendage. "On my signal, you will commence sucking him again. Tap my ankle once when he is close and twice when he is about to come."

"Yes, my goddess," Elizabeth said while gripping Abdul's penis.

"Begin!" Heather shouted.

Celsus stood before Lady Sanem, who was now spread-eagle on the table. He positioned her powerful legs on his shoulders and slowly worked deep into her wetness. She used her fingers to pleasure herself while the master fucked her deeply—deliciously.

Sakura, Linzie, Tara, and Megan worked each other with vibrators until they were all senseless. The smell of their sex permeated the room. It was one giant continuous orgasm, and the flowing magic was fabulous. Elizabeth began to suck Abdul more vigorously and could feel him swelling.

Heather continued to lubricate the massive strap-on as she watched the operations of the coven. She leaned over and spoke softly into Abdul's ear.

"This thing is huge, and I will rip you with it."

Elizabeth's oral vigor was bringing Abdul close. Suddenly, without altering her rhythm, she detached from her operations and fell into a brief analytical state. She started to ponder Heather's character and resolve. The answers were elusive, and the questions were many.

How does she do it? How is she so comfortable? My first visit overwhelmed me, leaving me fearful, depressed, and crazy. It's like she's already been with them for years. Her first visit, and she's calling him Wolfie?

Elizabeth cupped Abdul's balls with her free hand and could feel his sack tightening. She let go and tapped Heather once on the ankle as instructed.

Heather placed the tip of the weapon on Abdul's anus. He instinctively tried to get away. His cheeks tightened, but he was unable to do anything else. Heather spoke to him with maddening coldness.

"Remember when you beat the fuck out of me? Remember when you raped me and left me lying there broken and bloody? Well, it is payback time, you little bitch."

Heather then gripped the base of her weapon and readied it to administer destruction upon his soul. Elizabeth worked him hard, keeping a free hand close to Heather's foot. Heather was distracted for a brief moment when Sanem screamed out.

Celsus was deep in Sanem, pumping her hard while gripping her ankles far apart. He was in the same stance as Heather, and the muscles of his legs were ripped with pleasure. He pulled out at the exact moment of bliss and spurted semen over her. Heather smiled and questioned him.

"Master Wolf, how are you?"

Celsus caught his breath, squeezed the remaining drops of his silver rain upon the inside of Sanem's muscular left thigh, and responded.

"My goddess, Sanem has a divine vice. My balls are deliciously drained."

Sanem looked at him sweetly as she massaged his semen over her breasts.

"We shall see about that," Heather said as she focused on her revenge, which twitched and puckered before her.

The four women on the floor continued to suck and masturbate each other in the powerful ring, their scents and sounds dominating everything in the room.

Elizabeth sucked wildly, and everyone in the room could hear this as Abdul closed his eyes and shook. She could feel the volcano erupting, quickly tapped Heather twice on the ankle and squeezed his balls. Heather yelled out as she grabbed a handful of Abdul's hair and drove the obscene instrument deep inside him.

Elizabeth gagged at the force of Abdul's sperm hitting the back of her throat but quickly recovered to swallow every drop. Abdul's body was going into spasms from the unnatural and violent intrusion. There was no sound from him as the shock of Heather's assault took his breath and then his consciousness. Heather proceeded to pound him mercilessly, and, despite the preparatory lubrication, his anus was torn open. His blood covered Heather's horrifying toy while drops spattered on Elizabeth's face, chest, and legs.

As Abdul's body went limp, Elizabeth noticed a change in taste as she sucked the final drops from him. She closed her eyes and realized blood was flowing under his penis, through her fingers, and into her mouth. Rather than feel revulsion, she savored the new taste and began to drink the blood zealously. It was a primal urge bordering on cannibalism, and any internal dialogue or rational thought vanished from her mind. The scene had attained a dimension of horror. Heather screamed.

"Everyone stop! I can't believe he passed out! Nona, can you wake him?

"Yes, my goddess."

"Do it now," Heather commanded. "Elizabeth, you can come out now."

Elizabeth emerged from under the table and was unsure of her surroundings. She felt intoxicated but knew she had not a single drop of liquor in her. Looking down at Abdul's motionless body, she wondered if he was dead. There was so much blood. She was surprised at how indifferent she felt staring at his gaping asshole and the blood that ran down his legs, pooling at his feet. Heather spoke to her.

"Look at yourself in the mirror. You're a cute little blood-sucking vampire."

Celsus yelled out.

"Heather!"

The master was out of his role. Something profound had transpired.

Elizabeth turned and walked mindlessly toward the giant mirror. What she saw at once mystified her—the vision, timeless and extraordinary. White, dreamy, and dead, she looked like a ghost. In great contrast to the almost supernatural whiteness, her mouth, chin, neck, and hands were covered in blood. In fact, there was blood all over her. Everything became very dark as the room spun into oblivion. Her mind was shutting down. The last thing she heard was the voice of Celsus.

"Catch her!"

When Elizabeth woke, she had a terrible headache. The right side of her skull was pounding as if someone were kicking her in the head. She moaned and could not figure out where she was. She tried to raise herself to look around, but her body would not allow it. She managed to roll to her left side and found Linzie sound asleep and looking angelic with her locks of blond curls partially draped over her peaceful face. It was morning as sunlight beams broke through the sides of the heavy black drapes. Unable to move, she snuggled up to Linzie and drifted back into the darkness.

Elizabeth had a vivid dream. It was a nightmare, but upon waking the second time, she could not recall anything except being very afraid. The second time she woke, the headache was not as severe, and Linzie caressed her face. Nona knocked on the door, and Linzie responded.

"Enter."

Nona came in with a stocked food tray of milk, freshly squeezed orange juice, eggs, smoked turkey, and fresh bread, with various jellies adorning the delicious buffet.

"You're a darling. Thank you so much," Linzie said as she climbed out of bed.

"At your service always, my lady," Nona said as she backed out of Linzie's room and quietly closed the door.

Elizabeth finally found the strength to speak to Linzie, whose silhouette was now framed by a single ray of sun bleeding through the drapes.

"You are an angel, a sweet, beautiful angel."

"No, I have horns," Linzie said as she stretched out her naked body.

Elizabeth didn't reply right away. Linzie's statement suddenly triggered memories of the preceding night. She tried her best to recount everything, but the last thing she remembered was giving fellatio to Abdul during a coven orgy. Trying desperately to remember, she blurted out the first thing that came to mind.

"Did Heather get her scarlet choker?"

"She did not."

"Why not?" Elizabeth asked, desperately trying to remember what happened.

"Heather broke a vow of secrecy, and the master was not pleased."

"What secrecy? What do you mean?"

Linzie slid back into the bed beside her.

"We can't talk about this right now," she said, planting light candy kisses all over her face. "In time, you'll know everything—you will remember."

Elizabeth succumbed immediately to the onslaught of kisses, caresses, and little love bites. She was helpless in Linzie's grasp, and her lover's eyes had turned completely black.

Randy V

A LITTLE TASTE

Elizabeth's life had taken on a terrible dependency. Her separation from the coven was far more depressing this time and nearly impossible to deal with. Without the coven in her life, she fell into a severe depression.

She was completely unaware of the summer heat wave, sweating in front of her living room window and staring at the other tenants enjoying the swimming pool. Devoid of thought and miles away from the kind of willpower it would take to enjoy the midsummer sun, she no longer cared about anything.

The packet for fall semester registration remained unopened along with the rest of her mail, now a small mountain on her dining room table. Money problems were not an issue as Linzie had handed her three grand in cash before turning her loose a few weeks earlier. Yet the money remained untouched, and the bills remained unpaid.

One sweltering and humid night, it seemed she would crack as her thoughts turned to panic. She tossed around on her bed, slick with sweat and angst. She was desperate.

"Why am I left here in misery if I am one of you? Get me, or let me die. Let me die," she cried out in anguish.

As she began to weep, a familiar voice entered her mind. *Don't cry, precious. It'll be all right. We're coming for you.*

"Megan!" Elizabeth yelled out. "Where are you?"

Here, in your mind—eating you.

"Come get me, please!"

There was no answer. Strangely and suddenly, she felt a calmness wash over her. Within seconds, she fell sound asleep.

The following day, she felt more alive than she had in weeks. The only residual negative feeling was a nagging desire to remember her dreams. They were scary and sexual, but that was all she knew. As she went into the kitchen to brew a pot of coffee, she noticed the mail was gone from her table and replaced by a single white envelope fixed with a blood-red wax seal. She knew it was from the coven, yet she hesitated before picking it up. There was fear with good reason.

The seal carried the head of a snarling wolf, making her smile. Excitedly, she broke it and pulled out a single folded piece of parchment. It read like an ancient poetic script:

> *For years I have waited for you*
> *This life, like all the rest*
> *Eternal desire waits for you*
> *To enslave one, the new test*
>
> *Be quick now and bring to me*
> *A man to give his blood freely*
> *Possession and control the key*
> *As you fell by the witch Linzie*
>
> *This one, a lost soul*
> *Not one would miss*
> *Come the next full moon*
> *Your third trial blessed*

She knew at once what was being asked. The coded prose revealed itself quite naturally to her. She was being called upon to seduce a man, a loner that no one cared about, and bring him to the coven completely bewitched and under her control. Her depression abruptly ceased at that moment.

She started a hot bath and went to the sink to brush her teeth. The mirror held a cruel reflection, and she reeled at what she saw. It was almost as if she were looking at herself dead. She felt detached, yet she knew everything was falling into place. Her appearance didn't matter. This night, Elizabeth would hunt.

Soaking in the bath, she could feel herself transforming as she carefully washed her body and hair. She shaved her legs slowly and caressed them with lavender-scented bath oil. Letting her head rest against the back of the tub, she slid a finger into herself and fantasized about Megan, whose voice had rescued her from the darkness.

Yes, lover, that's it ...

Elizabeth smiled and knew Megan was linked to her mind, body, and soul.

The coven watches, and we hunger for you.

Elizabeth gave herself a shuddering climax, splashing water over the tub's edge. She licked her lips, rose slowly from the water, and became a living goddess. Ignoring the towel, and with water dripping everywhere, she walked into her bedroom and stood before the full-length mirror. The image revealed something very different from the nasty portrait she'd seen earlier. Dark dripping curls framed her perfect nipples, now hard from the temperature change. She fancied herself a beautiful mermaid. She cocked her head and got close to the mirror. There was something new in her eyes—the glimmer of the coven. Elizabeth smiled and wondered what else she might have.

She took scissors and carefully cut away a pair of old jeans until she produced denim short-shorts. She wiggled into them and dug out a black tank top with blood-red horizontal pinstripes. She tied the shirt into a knot right below her breasts and topped off the wicked look with a pair of black leather high-heeled boots ending just below her knees. Turning toward the mirror again, she felt her confidence and purpose growing.

She drove straight to the Trash Bar, a famous nightclub near the stadium where Tara had seduced Abdul. Sitting in the upper balcony, Elizabeth watched and waited like a great hunter. Not a single thought entered her mind as she experienced an actual present—instinctual, primal, and predatory. Within an hour, some poor fool, emboldened by drink, approached her.

"I noticed you don't have a drink. Can I get you one?"

Elizabeth looked up at the man and was annoyed at the interruption of her nirvana and the fact that he was not the one. Without a word, she began surveying the lower floor again.

"Hey! You don't have to be a rude fucking bitch! A simple 'no thank you' would suffice," he yelled as he slammed his drink on the table and leaned into her face.

With incredible speed, she grabbed his crotch in a vicious death grip. Softly, she seethed.

"Leave me alone, and don't come back. Nod if you understand, or I'll crush your nuts."

He could not respond verbally, though his mouth was open, and his contorted face displayed obvious pain. He nodded, and she shoved him back with one arm, surprised at what seemed to be a significant increase in her physical strength. The man looked around to make sure no one had seen the incident. He hobbled down the stairs, his ego injured along with his testicles. Heather would have been proud.

She returned to scanning the floor level, her mind focused without thought, and found the prey. At the farthest table from the bar sat a 30-year-old man with long, disheveled auburn hair, torn jeans, and glasses so thick the sun would've burned his eyes out if he gazed upon it. He was a pure social outcast. She rose from her table and slowly descended the stairs to the lower level, her eyes never leaving the target.

As she closed in, she was careful to avoid detection. She noticed he was fixated on three women spoon-grinding each other on the dance floor. She bounced down on the empty seat beside him, threw her face into her hands, and whined.

"God, I hate men. All I did was turn down a fucking drink."

The man was shocked at her beauty and the blessing that she had decided to sit next to him, yet he was too afraid to respond. She pulled her face from her hands and looked into his eyes.

"I don't get it. Whatever happened to being polite? Whatever happened to being a gentleman? What an asshole."

Compelled to speak, he finally found the nerve to do so.

"What happened?"

"Nothing I want to talk about. I'm Elizabeth. What's your name?"

She quickly shifted gears, becoming an enthusiastic and vibrant young woman. She realized the rapid change of emotions startled him.

"Raymond," he replied sheepishly.

"Well, Raymond, I've about had it with the Trash Bar. You got anything to smoke?"

"I've got half a blunt. That's pretty much it, but it's excellent," he said, now perking up a little.

Elizabeth noticed a change in Raymond. She knew she'd thrown her talons into him, and there was no escape. She also noticed a difference in herself as a new and unusual hunger embraced her. She didn't have time for analysis and decided to deal with it later. Right now, it was time to secure the catch.

"Let's go. Did you drive?" she asked.

"I don't have a car," he replied, embarrassed.

"I do," she said as she grabbed Raymond's hand.

She marched out of the club, her brown curls bouncing playfully as she dragged him behind her. He focused on the area below the length of her hair, compelled by her denim shorts.

As the two exited the club, she acutely felt this new sensation, a hunger tearing at her. It was an unfamiliar longing, and it was painful. At first, she thought it might be the need for the coven, but then she realized the pain came from her body, not her heart.

She pulled up in the back of an empty church parking lot and shut the engine off. In silence, she turned and looked at him. He did not have the courage to look back. She was mentally and emotionally linked to him and could feel his desire. She could also feel his fear of not being good enough for her and of the possibility of being rejected. It had been a few years since he had been with a woman. She knew that. She *knew* it. She tried to relax him a little by touching his shoulder.

"How about that smoke, Ray?"

He reached into his shirt pocket, pulled out a half-smoked joint, and handed it to her while stealing a look at her legs.

"Aren't you going to light it for me," she asked seductively.

"Sorry," he said meekly as he lit up and inhaled deeply.

"You're too tense," she said, taking the joint and scooting close to him. She also took in a deep hit and let her head fall to his shoulder. As she exhaled, she caressed the top of his thigh.

He carefully put his arm around her shoulder. He still couldn't believe he was sitting with this gorgeous woman and certainly didn't want to make any sudden movements. If there were any movements to be made, *she* would have to be the one to make them.

With the oncoming rush, she let the full strength of the coven fill her entire being. She had never felt more powerful, yet the strange and unknown hunger was killing her. She was keenly aware of Raymond's heartbeat, fear, and longing. This awareness was tied to her hunger. Strangely, she thought eating him would feel pretty good. Her body tingled at the thought.

They smoked in silence, and he began to relax a little. She let her voice get very sensual. Without looking up, she asked him innocently.

"Do you have a girlfriend?"

Raymond laughed a little nervously.

"No."

"Wife?"

"No."

"Boyfriend?"

"I'm not gay," he said defensively.

She raised her head and whispered in his ear.

"I'm curious about you, Ray."

He felt the hair stand up on his neck and a surge between his legs.

"Why?"

"You're not like those assholes from the Trash Bar. You seem pretty cool," she said as she removed his glasses. "Your eyes are beautiful. Look at me," she commanded softly

He looked, and the world as he knew it changed forever. He was fascinated the same way she had been fascinated by Celsus and Linzie the first time she met them. As she slid her hand up to grope him, she could see his life in her mind's eye.

He was a loner. His parents had died years ago in a car accident, and he had no family or friends. He had no job and lived off welfare checks in a one-room studio apartment. The room was filled with rodents, roaches, and bad-tempered neighbors with whom he had to share a bathroom. He masturbated daily, and the Trash Bar was purely a place to imprint new fantasies on his brain. He never even considered the chance that someone might be interested in him—he just couldn't fathom it. He had fallen hard for Elizabeth, the first interested female in over nine years. His only girlfriend had dumped him nearly a decade ago, and he had never recovered.

She digressed from her focus and began to contemplate her telepathic powers while massaging his crotch. What was happening? Why did it all seem so natural? She let her tongue touch the inside of his ear. Ever so slightly, she sucked on his earlobe and then whispered to him again.

"You are mine. I am the end of your misery. Obey my wishes, and happiness shall be yours. I will show you things you can't imagine. You will serve me from this moment on."

"Yes," he said mindlessly as his legs began to quiver.

Elizabeth cradled his face between both hands and slowly probed his mouth with her tongue when a hidden urge suddenly possessed her. She bit down hard and felt the bite crunch into his lower lip.

Raymond hardly noticed the bite as he ascended the heights of Elizabeth's spell. Blood seeped out as she turned her oral delights to his blood. This was the cause of the hunger she was possessed by. Only blood would quench this awful pain.

Control! I need him! The master wants him!

She touched his chest and gently pushed him away while licking the blood from her lips. He tried to kiss her, but she kept him at bay. From that moment on, he was wholly devoted to her. He worshiped her.

As for Elizabeth, the sight of blood running down his chin was nearly more than she could bear. She felt intoxicated and wanted more. It seemed nothing had ever been more challenging in her life than not tearing into this man and drinking him dry. She wanted his blood, his tears, his semen, his life, and—his soul.

"I'm so sorry about that," she said, wiping his chin with a napkin and then holding it to the wound. "Hold it there until it stops bleeding."

He didn't care. She could have eaten him, and he would have accepted it joyfully. She started the car and smiled at him. He was staring at her like a lost puppy.

"You know it's not nice to stare," she said as she pulled away from the church.

"Sorry," he said, mildly confused now that they were moving.

Her hunger was under control for the moment, and she started analyzing what he was experiencing, that strange timelessness she always felt around the coven. She knew he could not recall being bitten or why he was holding a napkin to his lip.

Without asking him where he lived, she pulled right up to his dingy building. She put the car in park but left the engine running. Raymond's desperation irrationally revealed itself, as he hadn't even considered how she knew where he lived.

"I haven't really cleaned up. It's not the nicest place. Why don't we..." His excuses were cut off by her finger over his wounded lip.

"Shhhh," she whispered, coming up close and burning his soul with her eyes. "I promise I will come for you. We shall be together forever by the light of the next full moon. Think of nothing but me until I come for you. It will be the defining moment of your life."

She reached across him and opened the passenger door, letting the hardness of her right nipple scrape his thigh. A dazed Raymond obeyed as if hypnotized and obediently walked back into his ugly, one-room world. She smiled proudly and sped off toward the coven house. Just as she was about to leave the city, she realized the enormous mistake she was making.

"What the fuck am I doing? I can't go there without him. I can't go until the moon is full. Fuck!"

Frustrated at the situation, she burned rubber at the intersection and did a violent U-turn. She went toward her apartment but drove right by it. The terrible hunger had set upon her again, and she began thinking about how good Raymond tasted. She needed someone desperately and fought her thoughts of the coven with all her might.

"Why do I have to go through this? You know I belong, you fucking witches!"

And then his voice came to her, chilling and sweet.

You have come so far - through the endless ocean of time. Think of these desires as growing pains, my love. The hunger will become impossible for you. I'm dying to see how you handle it.

"My lord!" Elizabeth yelled out.

But there was no response. The only thing she could hear was the wind whipping through her hair and the purr of her car engine. She turned around and went back to her apartment, the glimmer departing and depression setting in once again.

Raymond's mind was tormented beyond measure. Everything was meaningless to him at this point. If his life had been pathetic before, now it was pure torture with the unnatural longings for Elizabeth. He had rubbed his penis raw, sometimes masturbating violently eight to ten times a day thinking of her. He would have dry orgasms and unknowingly starve because of his terrible obsession.

The night of the full moon was only a few hours away. Today, he would not have an orgasm. Today, he would wait on the steps, saving himself for her. He knew with all his being that she would come. And somewhere deep in his soul, he knew he would not be coming back.

Elizabeth could not grasp the painful and worsening hunger that overpowered her thoughts. Every time she invoked the coven's power, the hunger would come. When she pulled up to a waiting, exuberant Raymond, it was killing her again. Her eyes became extra sensitive to the oncoming power, and she wore sunglasses to hide them. The sun set, and the full moon rose as Raymond ran to her car. She did not look at him but commanded him coolly.

"Get in."

The two of them sped off to the coven house. She could feel his anticipation and anxiety. Her midsection cramped from the pain that was ripping at her. He noticed her discomfort and asked if she was all right.

"I'm fine, baby," Elizabeth replied. "How are you?"

"It feels like I waited forever. I can't tell you how I feel. I don't know how to tell you. I'm just happy you came back."

"Me too," she said, trying desperately to hide her gnawing problem.

Night had fallen by the time they reached the coven house. She tried using telepathy to get to them, but all was hidden. The moon lit the forest with an eerie, silvery glow. Walking toward the house, they saw the inside illuminated with candles. Nona waited patiently by the door.

"Nona," Elizabeth said softly.

"This way, my lady," she said as she led the couple straight through the house, out the back, and down a long, dark path. There was a large circular clearing in the estate's pine forest, and the coven stood majestically around a large fire. The women wore nothing but their white chokers and braided leather cords around their waists while the master donned a long black hooded cape. At the north end of the clearing stood a large wooden inverted 'Y' with a metal hook near the top. In the east stood a waist-high stone altar with various candles and instruments. The master broke his silence.

"Elizabeth, you enchant us with your presence."

"My lord," Elizabeth said as she took a knee while pulling Raymond into the same respectful position.

Celsus moved close to the couple with a silent grace that was truly unnerving. He reached down and signaled them to rise. Raymond was speechless and terrified. His body felt like running, but as long as Elizabeth was there, he was bound to her movements. Celsus cupped Elizabeth's face in his hands and spoke softly.

"You've done well. How goes your hunger?"

"It pains me greatly, my lord," she said, almost whimpering. Even in her heightened awareness, she realized that Celsus was not himself. His voice was too silky, too inviting. There was an element of fear with every unnatural action he took. At the same time, the overpowering sexuality and hunger compelled her beyond reason. She was standing on the edge of insanity once more. Celsus confirmed her fears.

"Tonight, you will learn, my angel. You will learn."

As he moved his hands away from her face, she could feel a single fingernail slice open a small wound under her jawline. It was so sharp and subtle that she did not feel the injury. She glanced down and noticed Celsus's fingernails were like an animal's razor-sharp claws.

He leaned down, turned her head toward the moon, and licked the blood from her neck. Then he turned to Raymond and looked directly into his eyes. Raymond passed out immediately, and Celsus caught him before he fell to the ground.

"Megan, Sanem," he called out.

The two women helped Celsus bring Raymond to the massive inverted 'Y.' It looked like it had been built from railroad ties and buried deep in the ground. They undressed him completely. Megan tied his wrists with a single black velvet rope, allowing a foot of space between his hands. Celsus and Sanem hung the cord evenly on the massive hook protruding from the top of the fixture. Then, the two women tied Raymond's ankles to the foundational beams. With the binding complete, Raymond found himself immobile, facing the beam of the upside down 'Y,' hanging by his hands from the rope over the hook, his toes barely touching the ground and his legs tied far apart. Elizabeth noticed how his hips and genitals fell just below where the three beams intersected, giving unobstructed access to his front and rear.

"My sweet darling angels," Celsus started elegantly. "We have a new slave in our house. What a wretch this poor soul is. Without us, what would his life be? Simply waiting and longing for death. Elizabeth's body understands, but I keep her memory shrouded in mystery. Tonight, we shall tend to the needs of our new initiate. We aim to satiate her and make a proper glutton out of her. Eat in excess, drink in excess, and fuck in excess. Gluttony above everything. So be it."

"So be it!" the coven responded emphatically.

"Come, Elizabeth," Celsus stated.

"Yes, my lord," she replied.

She felt the intense power emanating from him as he turned her head again and licked the fresh blood from her neck. She felt goosebumps as he gently caressed her face with his hands. Then, without warning, he crossed his arms in front of her, grabbed her by the waist, and flipped her upside down like a rag doll with her legs dangling in the air. He held her tight with one arm around the waist, while with the other arm, he cut away her shorts with a sharp dagger. He threw the knife into the ground, using his fingernail again to make a clean incision between the soft white flesh of Elizabeth's left thigh and her vaginal lip. Then, as he held her effortlessly with one arm, he parted the cape to reveal his throbbing manhood. The tip touched her lips. She attempted to suck him but stopped when Celsus fiercely slapped her butt several times. The pain was most severe, and she cried out.

Her hair brushed the top of his feet, and she sensed his body tensing up. He reached down and made another fingernail cut on the head of his steely sex. Blood began dripping immediately as he pushed her by the back of her head until she gripped his staff with both her hands and mouth. He, in turn, began drinking from her while simultaneously pumping two fingers into her womanhood and a little finger in her rear.

She sensed nothing around her, not the coven, Raymond, or even the master. There were no thoughts as she quenched her thirst for the exquisite elixir flowing freely down her throat. Her body shook in what seemed like a relentless orgasm. She let one hand caress his balls and didn't know how long the incredible lovelock lasted before the master's sack tightened. Briefly, through eyes barely open, she could see the master's calves flex as he rose up on his toes and shot his blood-mixed semen down her throat. He moaned with pleasure as she took every last drop with great hunger, lost in her own bliss.

She let go of her master's steel, gripped him by his powerful glutes, and cried out. She could not help it. Her legs shook violently from the wicked orgasm, and she pleaded with him to stop, but he would not. Within seconds, she was out. A vision came upon her, solid and real.

So beautiful. Silk white drapes descending from an old thatch ceiling and my young friend tied to the bed. He looks so young. "Think of something else, my angel," I say in the ancient language. Torches upon the wall. I am happy to have such an important task.

When she came to, she looked up at the full moon from a bed of soft pine needles. Her vision lingered for a moment before being involuntarily stored away. As her senses returned, she felt someone crouched between her legs, tonguing the wound and her womanhood. It was soothing and gentle—it was Sakura.

Sakura Saito was born in Nagoya, Japan, but grew up in Farmington Hills, Michigan. Her father, an automotive engineer, landed a high six-figure income as the design team leader for one of Japan's leading auto companies in 1986. Sakura and her family—father, mother, aunt, and two brothers—emigrated from a tiny two-bedroom house in Nagoya to an elaborate eight-bedroom Victorian mansion on the outskirts of the Motor City. Every expense, including the house, was paid for by the company.

She quickly picked up English and was an absolute prodigy at math. Her academic skills were considered far above average, but her math skills were exceptional. By the time she entered high school, she was solidly versed in the most complex levels of financial accounting.

By age 22, she was given a prestigious position overseeing her father's company's entire financial accounting for North America. She calculated the overhead and profits, did their taxes and was perfect at the highest accounting and report writing levels. She saved them millions in the first quarter of her new position.

Because of her girlish physical appearance and soft demeanor, the company did not feel comfortable allowing her to give statements to their board of directors. The same consensus was reached regarding news conferences. They hired a spokesman to speak for her and to take credit for her work. It was old-fashioned Japanese chauvinism.

She was paid serious money for her work, surpassing her father's salary, but could never take credit for the position. The CEO had his own ideas about how the company would present facts to shareholders and the rest of the world. No matter how excellent she was or how much money she saved, her face was too young-looking to display before the Americans as the head of finance.

The curse of her appearance, which she would later use to her advantage within the coven, was annoying because no one ever took her seriously. All would acknowledge her brilliance, but none would respect her. She looked like a delicate adolescent girl, not the intelligent, calculating woman she was.

There were no men in her life. Up until her interactions with the coven, she had never experienced so much as a kiss, let alone sexual intimacy. At 26, she was still a virgin. She lived alone and spoke of madness to her younger brother several times. Her biggest fear was that of losing her mind. That fear was obliterated one night while dining alone at her favorite restaurant. She met the man of her dreams, and he would not be denied.

Sakura had just ordered her dinner when Celsus sat at the same table across from her. At first, she found his audacity insulting, but then she melted into his soft voice and warm propositions.

He asked her if she would work for him as his accountant. She responded with a giggle, stating that he obviously knew who she was and that she worked with millions of dollars daily.

He conceded that her employer had staggering wealth but told her she would have unlimited access to the coven's vast wealth, more than she could ever earn with her current employer.

She was unconvinced, right up to the point when he stated, with absolute conviction, that he knew her true purpose in life. Something about the way he said this put a hook in her. She wanted to believe, but she wanted proof of his claim and wanted it immediately.

With apparent but polite skepticism, she asked Celsus how he could prove himself with one token on both claims of wealth and wisdom. He looked at her with a cold grin and replied.

"Someday, you will pay for that insult, but I assure you, Sakura, you will love every stroke."

She was possessed on the spot and found her world spinning out of control, just as every other woman did when crossing his path. He closed the conversation by leaving the keys and title to a brand-new silver Lexus SC 430. She looked up at him in disbelief, barely managing to ask how he knew that was her favorite car. With no response to her question, he spoke comically.

"You would be shot on sight if you drove that into your company's parking garage."

Sakura looked down at the keys and wondered if it was all just a coincidence. She had never told anyone about her obsession with this car. When she looked up, he was gone. She was hooked, and her life would never be the same. Like the others, she disowned her family, quit her job, and joined the coven.

Without moving her body or disrupting Sakura's drink, Elizabeth looked around. She saw the coven engaged in various acts of sex. With his legs spread wide apart, Celsus sat naked upon the stone altar as Tara sucked him. There were wounds all over his body.

She remembered his first self-inflicted wound and trembled with renewed blood lust. Then she saw Linzie kneeling under the 'Y' giving a helpless Raymond her best fellatio. Megan was on her back next to the fire with her legs propped over Sanem's shoulders. Sanem was aggressively fingering her. The silhouette of these two, framed in fire, mesmerized Elizabeth. She couldn't determine what Nona was doing but noticed she sat before the altar preparing something.

Her attention was quickly returned to Sakura, who was now lapping zealously. Sakura's moaning gently vibrated her most sensitive regions, and she could feel another release coming. She looked down at Sakura and became lost in her beautiful dark Japanese eyes—eyes that now looked almost silver with the shining glimmer of the coven. She shuddered as that look sent her over the edge.

The orgasm was powerful. She saw stars in her head but did not lose consciousness this time. Instead, she rocked her hips forward and closed her thighs around Sakura's pretty doll-like face. The coven's power was beyond measure, and Sakura spoke to her without words.

You taste so sweet, and I have missed you so much.

Elizabeth loved her. It was an ancient and unexplainable love. Her legs fell apart, allowing Sakura to crawl up and softly kiss her eyes, nose, cheeks, and mouth before whispering in her ear.

"I love you. I have always loved you."

Elizabeth knew she was on the verge of *remembering* but knew she had a long way to go. Instinctively, she wrapped her arms around Sakura and rolled so that she now occupied the top position. The two smiled at each other as Elizabeth reached out and pulled the master's dagger from the earth.

There was no thinking about what would happen next. She was glowing with heat and made a slight cut just behind Sakura's left ear. Immediately her mouth went to work sucking the blood.

Never in her life had she tasted anything so sweet. Her eyes closed as she felt the warm intoxication flood her body. The two women smashed their clits together and began to grind one another. A frenzy was happening, and everything outside this drink and grind seemed nonexistent. This time, there was a blackout.

The jealous enemy has taken the best of us. My tears cannot bring her back. The master will be the end of us all. Goddess, help us!

She came out of the vision crying uncontrollably. Sakura propped herself up on one elbow, and a trickle of blood slowly moved down her neck. She cradled Elizabeth like a wounded child as the coven formed a circle around them. Megan knelt down close to Elizabeth and spoke.

"Your memories are returning, and you are not strong enough to face them. Not yet, anyway. Understand that what we do now, we do out of love."

As Megan backed away, a fiery Celsus brought down a riding crop hard upon the front of Elizabeth's thighs.

"You constantly complain about how we abandoned you, and you act so desperate when you are with us! On your hands and knees now, spoiled child!"

She obeyed immediately. Still sobbing, she addressed the master.

"My lord, I do not understand."

"Silence!"

Another blow, an uppercut, perfectly placed so that the little leather loop struck her between the thighs and perfectly smacked the full of her sex. She cried out in pain as Celsus admonished her.

"You will learn discipline, Elizabeth. True discipline. You will not speak until I tell you to. You will not look until I tell you to. I will tell you everything, and henceforth, you will obey or find yourself starving outside this family. Do you understand?"

"Yes, my lord," she said, shaking uncontrollably now.

"Nod, for fuck's sake! And stop your crying," he yelled, letting loose with another horrendous blow, this time squarely upon her buttocks. She bit her lip and moaned. She now had matching welts on her front and rear. The tears streamed down her cheeks, and her womanhood throbbed in agony and burning desire. He continued.

"The situation is thus. You are a goddess among the rest of the once-born in this world. Make no mistake, Elizabeth. A goddess. That means all the meat in this world is here for your pleasure and sustenance. I am helping you understand things, my sweet, innocent neophyte. I know what you're thinking. How could I do this to you if I really cared about you? It's not a paradox, I promise. You are learning in two different modes of thought. When you have the *glimmer,* as you call it, you are powerful, knowledgeable, and certainly fine in mind and body. In this mode, you learn through intellect, gluttony, blood-letting, blood-drinking, and administering punishment. All these endeavors make the pain go away, right? You learn through punishment, humiliation, and deprivation when you are mundane. Nod if you understand."

She nodded, and Celsus again brought the crop down hard on her rear. She folded her arms in front of her, leaned into her forearms, and screamed in agony.

"How quickly you forget I can read your thoughts, Elizabeth. You understand nothing. Don't even think of lying to me again—and now for your first lesson."

He roughly grabbed her by the hair and dragged her to where Raymond was bound.

"Look at him. Do you feel sorry for him?"

She saw a naked, humiliated, scared man, unmercifully bound, awaiting an unknown fate. He trembled in fear as she dropped her head down and nodded in agreement.

"And yet you led him here without a second thought, didn't you?"

She nodded, and new tears began to well in her eyes.

Celsus knelt down and presented Elizabeth with the dagger she had used to cut Sakura.

"Take it. The femoral artery is here," he said as he pointed to the inside of Raymond's left thigh. "Drive it in deep."

"I cannot, my lord," she said as the next blow was already cutting through the air.

This one landed on the back of her legs with shocking ferocity. She instinctively jerked up, and several more vicious blows hit her on her hindquarters. Her natural reaction was to run, but suddenly, she felt the powerful arms of Sanem holding her down. Celsus spoke in a deep, serious tone.

"Don't disobey me again, or you will be very sorry."

Elizabeth nodded as tears streamed down her face. Her fresh welts throbbed as Sanem released her grip and stood beside her.

"Stab him!" Celsus commanded.

Suspending both her morals and her revulsion, she gripped the dagger. With a swift uppercut, she stabbed the captive man in the leg. His scream echoed throughout the forest as she let go of the knife, now buried deep in his leg. She was mortified and felt her stomach churn. The world began to spin as she vomited up Sakura's blood, the master's blood, and his semen. Celsus knelt down and spoke gently to her.

"You are hanging on to a weak and insignificant life. You must let this go now. Drink and rule."

Celsus grabbed Elizabeth by the hair, ripped the dagger from Raymond's leg, and pushed her face into the gushing wound. Raymond's second scream and nausea nearly made her faint, but the bloodlust overtook her again. There was a moment of clarity inside the madness as she separated from her body.

She floated in the air above the coven, detached and wraith-like. In the center of the circle, a formless red presence surrounded them. Elizabeth knew it was ancient and female.

Celsus knelt before it and offered a silver chalice filled with blood. The women danced around the circle, chanting and singing loudly. A man hung from the inverted 'Y' and looked dead. Below him was a woman's body—peaceful, unconscious, with blood on her face. Elizabeth felt no emotion as she had become pure thought and energy. A soft voice revealed the truth of the red presence.

I am the eternal Mother. There is no beginning. There is no end. I am forever and shall always be.

She woke up around noon and struggled to remember the preceding night. Turning in her bed, she realized she was not alone. Sakura looked so innocent, so sweet, and so unreal.

"Hi," Sakura whispered.

Elizabeth could not reply. She was too weak. She looked into Sakura's eyes for any answers to her confusion. Sakura read her thoughts like an open book.

"What do you remember?"

Elizabeth's voice was harsh and dry as she responded.

"I remember going to pick up Raymond."

"That's it?"

"I remember driving over to pick him up, and now I'm in bed with you."

Sakura slid her arm over Elizabeth's waist and caressed her lower back, but before she could kiss, Elizabeth jerked back.

"Ouch!" she cried out.

"I'm sorry. I forgot about your wounds."

"What wounds? What happened last night?"

"The master whipped you. It was beautiful."

"Is he mad at me?"

"Not at all."

"Well, I'm a little freaked. I can't remember anything."

"It's okay. You did fine. Your third visit is over, and you were fantastic."

"What happened?"

Elizabeth tried to get up but noticed her muscles ached intensely. There were welts on her buttocks, legs, and back. She was very nauseous and felt stinging sensations on the outside of her vagina and jaw. Sakura responded.

"I cannot tell you; my punishment would be far greater than anything you have experienced. You'll know everything soon enough. It has to be this way. We all went through it."

Sakura guided Elizabeth's hand between her legs. The soft fur between Sakura's thighs took Elizabeth's mind off her aches and pains. She tried to close her eyes, but Sakura curled her finger under her chin and forced her attention. It was like looking into the abyss; one glance was all it took. All of Elizabeth's physical, mental, or emotional concerns became meaningless instantly. She slid a finger into Sakura and became lost in her cat-like eyes. Sakura clenched her womanhood in approval and bit down on Elizabeth's lower lip. It did not take long before the two were grinding each other in the same manner they had done the previous night. It was divine, and it was love—an old love that went beyond comprehension. The orgasms were powerful as the two women continued to make love throughout the day and night. Elizabeth drifted in and out of consciousness.

When she woke again, she felt invigorated. Her Japanese lover was no longer there. Slowly getting out of bed, she wondered what day it was, rubbed her eyes, and thought for a minute.

Come the next full moon, your third trial blessed.

She got up and went to the calendar hanging next to her refrigerator. The full moon was August 16th.

Last night?

Confusion seeped into her head. She was frustrated at her inability to remember anything other than leaving to pick up Raymond.

She thought about Sakura for a minute, and her body tingled. She felt between her legs and her back.

No pain.

She remembered Sakura telling her the master had taken the lash to her, but there were no wounds. She quickly opened the front door and stepped onto the second-floor walkway. The sun blinded and tormented her eyes. Her neighbor Carrie was watering her flowers that hung from the handrail.

"Hey, Carrie," she said in a sleepy voice.

"What's up, Liz?" Carrie asked informally.

"Not much. What's the date today?"

"It's the 19th. Got your classes picked out yet?"

"Not yet."

"What are you waiting for?"

"I'm such a procrastinator. I need to take a shower. Maybe we can hit the Trash Bar sometime this week?"

"Sounds like a plan. Don't be such a stranger."

"Sorry, Carrie. I'll call you later."

Elizabeth closed the door and went straight to the calendar.

"Tuesday? It's fucking Tuesday!"

She was shocked, and panic followed.

What happened? What the fuck have I been doing for the last three days?

She threw on some clothes, grabbed her car keys, and exited her apartment. When she flung open her car door, she stopped cold. On the driver's seat, a fresh red rose greeted her. The heat coming from inside the car was over 130 degrees. The flower should have been wilted, yet it was as if someone had just put it there. When she picked it up, it withered instantly, as if her touch had drained the life out of it.

She drove straight to Raymond's place, marched up the stairs, and pounded on the door urgently. No one answered. She tried again, but there was nothing. As she looked in his window, an old woman walked around the side of the stairs.

"Lookin' for Raymond?"

"Yeah, have you seen him?"

"Saturday was the last time I saw him. He was sittin' out on the stairs all day waitin' for someone."

Elizabeth felt apprehensive. She thanked the old woman, got in her car, and started driving aimlessly. She spoke out loud regarding her weird situation.

"Okay, what's going on now? I know you can hear me."

Her mind began to drift. She remembered Sakura blissfully draining her life force over the last three days, but she could remember nothing before that.

I'm going insane.

Then, the memories of her dreams started hitting her— the fantastic visions in an unknown language, an ancient kingdom, a boy, and some profound loss.

I am definitely going insane. Please don't do this to me. I cannot live, nor do I wish to live, without you.

The tears welled so much that she had to pull off the road to let the flood come. The coven did not answer, yet she knew they felt her longings. She loved them more than she loved anything in her life, and she hated them too—especially Celsus, who seemed so caring and loving one minute and so detached and brutal the next.

She felt sick and opened her car door to vomit, but nothing would come out. She was hanging out of her car, violently dry heaving by the roadside, when Megan's sweet voice slithered into her throbbing head.

Don't beg, Elizabeth. It doesn't suit you. We miss you too, and you will not have to wait long this time.

"You tell me how much I belong. You read my thoughts, strip my memory, and deprive me of your knowledge and love. I'm sick of it. I want to die. Don't you see how much I need you? Help me, Megan. Help me!"

You are so dramatic. When you go home, there will be a treat for you. I guarantee it will make you feel better.

"Where is Raymond? What happened Friday night?"

I'll be in touch soon.

"Wait! Don't leave me, Megan! Please!"

So dramatic...

When she arrived at her apartment, she was weak and nauseous and had to use both hands on the rail to pull herself up the stairs. Upon entering, she landed face-first on the couch in her living room. After about an hour of laying there, wallowing in misery, she crawled into the kitchen. This was worse than any college hangover she had ever experienced, and she had been through a few. When she opened her refrigerator, she was horrified.

Forty-five plastic bags of blood were neatly stacked upon one another. Except for the blood bags, the entire refrigerator had been cleaned out. Her mouth dropped open when she read the note taped to one of the bags.

eternal love

Below this cryptic note, someone had taped a small metal tube. She nearly fainted before the spectacle when the smell hit her—the distinctive scent of iron. It was as if someone had vacuumed the nausea out of her and replaced it with a terrible thirst.

She trembled as she reached for one of the bags. Ripping the tube from the note, she examined it closer. Someone had cleverly cut the end of it into a sharp point. She jammed it in the bag and began sucking.

Her eyes rolled up into her head as she sucked wildly. She could not take it in fast enough and, after draining the first bag, tore a hole in the second with her teeth and drank heartily, blood spilling everywhere. Her thirst was quenched only after downing five bags. She found herself on the cool kitchen floor, looking up at the ceiling, her face and hair covered in blood. A warm contentment engulfed her, and she laughed uncontrollably. Her gluttony, for the time being, was satisfied. She wondered what would happen next. With a bloody grin, she dreamed of the possibilities.

Randy V

PARTY FOR SOPHIA

Elizabeth's reality was a nightly dilemma, but the waiting was painless this time as she had acquired profound patience and supreme confidence. She thought this was why they contacted her within two weeks of the full moon visit. Still, she had no idea what happened that night, nor did she care. Everything seemed perfectly normal—from drinking blood to extraordinary powers of telepathy to sleeping all day and being active all night. It was as if she had always been this way.

As the sun descended, creating steady orange flames inside the cirrus clouds, she closed her eyes and let her mind wander. She felt a gentle breeze kiss her face as her body rose within the deep amber twilight. In the distance, she could make out a shadowy cluster of trees, a lone farmhouse, and a small village beyond. Strangely, there was nothing odd about the vision or the feeling. It was exhilarating, exceptional, and so familiar that it was second nature to her. Where or how she knew this place was irrelevant. This moment—this sky, tonight and forever—was hers. She knew she belonged here. Total emersion was denied as her phone rang and jolted her back to the present.

"Hello," Elizabeth answered with a raspy voice.

"I love it when you sound like that," Linzie said.

Elizabeth smiled and playfully responded.

"You're using a phone to contact me? What's wrong, Supergirl? Kryptonite in your panties?"

Linzie giggled, and Elizabeth's body and soul were immediately set on fire. The intense longing started right up again.

"Liz, you need to come over tonight."

"What's up?"

"A house party. Mistress Sophia is the guest of honor."

"Who is Mistress Sophia?"

"The master's sister and the XO of his lesser house."

"The master's sister?"

"No later than nine, okay?"

"I'll be there with bells on."

"Wear a white sundress and white panties."

"I don't have a white sundress."

"Yes, you do."

Click.

Elizabeth began her ritual transformation process, but no matter how much she wanted the glimmer, it would not come. Apprehension set in, and a foggy memory of the master's voice played out in her mind.

You learn through punishment, humiliation, and deprivation when you are mundane.

Her demeanor was passive and frightened. She slipped on a pair of white cotton panties and went to her closet. Sure enough, as if she had any doubt, the white sundress hung by itself, the other clothes being pushed to one side or the other. Megan's voice came into her head.

You are so beautiful when you are vulnerable. I would comfort you in a heartbeat, but I couldn't bear losing the frightened girl—so delicate, Elizabeth—so delicious.

Elizabeth felt her sex throb and nervously spoke out loud.

"You are a devil, Megan."

She examined herself in the mirror and tied her hair high atop her head into a ponytail. She did look innocent, but still no glimmer and no power. Elizabeth thought to herself.

They are going to hurt me.

It was around nine in the evening when she arrived at the iron gates—gates that formed a massive perimeter around the

400-acre estate and appeared to be created from thousands of medieval spears.

The gates opened, and she had no doubt that Sanem watched her through the mounted cameras. She noticed the night was unusually black as she drove through the twisted, heavily forested drive. The moon was new, and at least three dozen cars were parked in the open lot.

The house looked alive, with well-dressed guests on the lawn, the front porch, and throughout. There were dozens of torches outside, while hundreds of candles illuminated the inside. The coven women were all wearing white sundresses. Only the blood-red ribbon around Elizabeth's neck differentiated her from those she loved dearly. Celsus looked stunning in his black tails tuxedo. He indulged in lively conversation on the front lawn with two other gentlemen. He looked exquisite.

One thing did seem unnatural. Everyone behaved like ordinary people do at an elite social gathering. She looked around from the security of her car and could not find one lewd act before her. This comforted her as she checked herself in the rear-view mirror one last time before getting out. As soon as she had shut her door, two lavender-scented hands came around her head and over her eyes.

"Guess who?" came the barely audible whisper.

"Linzie?" replied Elizabeth.

As the hands fell away, Elizabeth closed her eyes, turned, and let herself melt into the blissful and talented kiss. Opening her eyes, she felt a pleasant shock as Sakura gave her an innocent grin.

"I'm surprised you can't tell us apart by now," Sakura said as she caressed Elizabeth's shoulders.

"I would think so, too," said Linzie, who had secretly maneuvered behind her and kissed the back of her neck.

Elizabeth swooned between the two women, and her voice quivered.

"I am afraid this night. I don't have the power I'm getting used to."

"Perfect," Linzie said, still behind her. "Everything will be fine. It's all part of the process."

Sakura said nothing. She just continued gazing into Elizabeth's eyes with all the coven's power. It was the glimmer fueled by a maddening hunger. To Elizabeth, it now represented love at its highest possible evolution.

"Isn't Sakura beautiful tonight?" asked a teasing Linzie as she slid a hand between Elizabeth's legs and rubbed her from behind.

"Yes," Elizabeth replied with a shiver.

The master's booming voice sounded over the crowd and echoed throughout the forest.

"Members and prospects of my house, Mistress Sophia, will be here in a few minutes. Please come inside so that we may greet her formally. Thank you."

Linzie stopped teasing, and the glow slowly faded from Sakura's eyes.

"Fuck," Elizabeth said softly, followed by a sigh.

"Don't worry," Linzie said.

Sakura and Linzie led her into the house, where she was showered with kisses from the rest of the coven and the guests. They were all so beautiful. The women were spectacular, and the men were stunningly handsome. Besides their aesthetic beauty, they had something else in common. Most of the guests wore black silk chokers, men and women alike.

She could barely contain her excitement and was suddenly dizzy from the magnitude of it all. Megan was dazzling with her long red, bouncing curls that perfectly framed her freckled face. The contrast of her flaming hair, her white dress, and her milky white skin was absolutely perfect. Megan towered above Elizabeth, wearing white stiletto heels, and the *glimmer* was unmistakable.

"Stand with me," Megan said to her.

Elizabeth said nothing as she allowed Megan to lead her by the hand toward the far wall of the great coven room. Everything looked exotic, from the long royal purple drapes descending from the ceiling to the hundreds of candles and torches illuminating the massive living room. The guests were drinking wine from silver chalices, and a sensual energy made it seem like the air was alive.

Nona stood out among the crowd and looked radiant in a black silk gown that framed her curvaceous body. She walked to the main entrance with old-world charm, a perfect model of grace and elegance. She spoke with authority.

"Ladies and gentlemen, Mistress Sophia," she said as she swung open the two great doors of the coven room.

Sophia Almeida was born in Portland, Oregon, in 1982, two years after her blood brother Celsus. They share the same birth month, and their birthdays are nine days apart. Like her brother, she is five-foot-nine, has deep blue eyes, and dark blond hair. You would never know it, though, as her current hair color is pitch-black, like Nona, Sanem, and Sakura.

After embarking on their cross-country journey, Celsus ordered her to dye her hair black. She complied without question. It has been black for years, and she wouldn't have it any other way—unless her brother asked her to change it again. He also ordered her to change her last name. She chose the last name of Almeida in honor of the other idol in her life, Nona Almeida. Sophia tells others that she is Nona's sister, and her brother is most pleased with this.

She misses her family but keeps this to herself, knowing she cannot hide anything from her brother. She has sworn allegiance to him and has promised never to bring up their history in Oregon or their family name. Her romantic love for her brother is beyond reason, and she would kill for him without question.

She still remembers how chilling he was when they were growing up together. Throughout their childhood, he treated her with indifference, or worse, as an annoyance. Unlike the other women in the coven, she grew up with an unremarkable childhood.

Some children stayed away from her simply because of her brother's reputation as the creepy kid who never smiled and could bore a hole through you with one look. Despite his apathy toward her, she loved him more than anything, particularly his strength and resolve. Nothing seemed to bother him, and he appeared to know everything, though he never helped her with homework. He was always plotting his future and never had time for his little sister. All that changed during her freshman year in high school when she was 14.

As the story goes, Sophia tried hard to insert herself into a prestigious social clique with other freshman girls from affluent neighborhoods. She was envious of the special attention they were getting from everyone, especially the heartthrobs of the school. Sadly and superficially, they rejected her based on the clothes she wore. She really had nothing to be ashamed of. Still, her family could not afford the clothes and accessories that adorned this elite snotty group of girls. She was psychologically destroyed by this. Of all the people she knew, including her parents and best friends, Celsus came to her rescue—her cold, calculating, apathetic brother.

He overheard her crying one night, which stirred his curiosity enough to make him investigate. She was so shocked at the spectacle of her brother standing in the doorway and asking her what was wrong that she ceased crying immediately. After all those years of indifference, it was monumental that he sincerely wanted to know what troubled her. As she related her story, Celsus closed his eyes and empathized with his sister's pain of rejection based on their socio-economic status. He opened his eyes and saw her soul and her innocence. He fell in love with her then and there.

All secrets were revealed to Sophia that night. She was admitted into the circle of secrecy between her brother and his beloved friend Nona. Sophia was not privy to everything but understood that when she turned 18, she would want for nothing and would be included in what her brother described as the most elite family in the world.

He loved her so much that he put his plans on hold for two more years. He waited for Sophia to be of legal age and left the day after her birthday. It was an added buffer to keep the family off track as they made their way across the land, picking up the other extraordinary women. Interestingly, every girl who was a part of the clique that rejected Sophia disappeared within six years, never to be heard from again.

When the group finally settled in Michigan, he bought her a beautiful Victorian mansion in the university district of Ann Arbor. He gave her unlimited access to his wealth. His only requirement for his sister is and has always been, absolute loyalty and obedience.

The first to enter was an enormous black man who went by the name Ra. He was Sophia's bodyguard and personal assistant. Bald, with dark sunglasses, standing a towering six-foot-six, and weighing nearly 300 pounds, he was naturally intimidating. Sophia never went anywhere without him. As the female entourage entered, he stood to the right of the great doors.

Four naked young women entered the room in two pairs and split apart as they entered. Entering next were two naked men, crawling on their hands and knees, their faces wrapped tightly in leather bondage hoods, sporting dog collars hooked to chains.

Elizabeth took a deep breath when she realized that each man's penis had been pulled back between his legs with duct tape. Holding the reins of these two specimens was the illustrious mistress Sophia.

Sporting six-inch spike-heeled black fetish shoes, she towered over most of the guests. The shoes had spaghetti straps that crisscrossed along her taunt calves. She wore a black, one-piece silk dress with no sleeves or back, the length ending just above the knees, and cinched by a thin strip of brown leather tied casually around her waist. Her shoulder-length black hair revealed huge curls that bounced when she walked. She also wore a black choker, which was unique in that a teardrop-shaped diamond graced the center. There was no doubt about her status with the coven. Her brother made sure of that. She had a cute, mischievous look about her, and yet she exuded absolute authority. The room went silent when she stopped to survey her surroundings. She held the reins of the two men tightly around her left hand.

"Darling," Celsus said as the guests parted to let him approach her. "You look absolutely stunning." He grabbed her hands in his own.

"As do you, my brother," she said as she bowed.

"Ra," Celsus acknowledged.

"My Lord Celsus," the giant said, bowing his head.

"Sister, it has been far too long since our last meeting. When we last spoke, I gave you leave to assemble my lesser house any way you wanted. Who are these delicious prospects you bring before me?"

"The females are Stephanie, Madison, Gwen, and Tasha. And the two dogs are Troy and Aaron."

"Splendid, my lady."

He led Sophia to the north wall of the room, where two elevated thrones had been stationed for their voyeuristic pleasures. The two men crawled as fast as they could to keep up, but Aaron fell forward on the floor. Sophia stopped and addressed her brother.

"My lord, I apologize profusely. May I have your permission to discipline this prospect for his stupidity?"

"He is yours, my precious. By all means, do what you deem necessary."

"Thank you, my lord."

Sophia dropped the leashes and undid the strip of leather around her waist. Elizabeth felt uncomfortable at the sudden quiet of the room. The only prominent sound was Aaron beginning to breathe heavily through his leather mask. The rest of the room was utterly silent.

Sophia walked behind Aaron and told him to present himself. Aaron folded his arms in front of him and put his head down. He remained on his knees, so his ass stuck straight up in the air.

Elizabeth was still in shock at the cruel way their private parts were bound. She was momentarily hypnotized by the scene, but her trance was broken when Sophia began scolding and lashing him.

"I told you not to embarrass me!"

She whipped him mercilessly. The lashes were brutal and excessive. Sophia seemed to exert little effort for maximum results. He started showing welts immediately. His penis was slightly lacerated near the head because it was directly in the line of her fury.

Elizabeth was terrified of this woman and suddenly became acutely aware of Linzie because of their history. Aaron could be heard sobbing into his arms as Sophia tied the leather back around her waist like an old-school disciplinarian. Troy was trembling as Celsus broke the silence.

"Well, I've never seen such a display, and look at the state you've put my coven in."

Sophia surveyed the room. The house members were mortified to some degree, but the women of the coven were clearly in some sort of controlled frenzy. She spied Tara and noticed a single drop of saliva rolling off her lower lip. She then locked eyes with Elizabeth and smiled. Without breaking her gaze, she spoke to Celsus.

"A red choker? And just what is this deliciousness?"

Sophia marched with purpose as her hard shoes echoed throughout the great room. She came within an inch of Elizabeth's face as Celsus introduced her.

"My sister, this is Lady Elizabeth, and this is her fourth visit," he stated proudly.

"She is trembling, my lord. May I sample a kiss?"

"You absolutely must," he replied in earnest.

She roughly grabbed a handful of Elizabeth's hair from the back of her head, held her still for a moment, and drove her tongue into Elizabeth's mouth. Elizabeth began shaking uncontrollably.

The power Elizabeth sensed from this woman differed from that of the other women in the coven. She felt that Sophia's temperament was taught—created, no doubt, by her brother. She also felt that Sophia was *trying* to be like her brother. She knew this was impossible. Her assessment was in stark contrast to that of the candidate Heather, who, Elizabeth felt, naturally belonged. Then, during that rough, dominating kiss, a female voice broke into Elizabeth's mind.

I knew you'd see right through her. That bitch doesn't deserve her station. She certainly doesn't warrant the time and devotion the master gives her.

Sophia released her lip-lock and pronounced her opinion loudly, "She seems too timid for you and yours, my lord. She is delicious, but are you sure she is one of us?"

"Absolutely," he answered. "However, this night, she has been rendered powerless so that she may take on a submissive role. But we are getting ahead of ourselves. Come, sister. Join me, and we shall discuss tonight's proceedings."

Elizabeth looked around the room, trying to determine the source of Sophia's adversary. She looked at every woman's face and received naught. Her internal debate ended when Celsus addressed the party.

"Coveners, house members, and guests, drink freely. When the time comes, I shall announce the rules of tonight's tribute to my dear sister. Friends, a goddess walks amongst us this evening. Drink and be merry!"

He extended his hand to Sophia, beckoning her to the high thrones. Before she sat down, she gave him a hug and a lingering kiss and casually tied the two leashes to her armrest.

Elizabeth watched the two siblings as the party blossomed. She tried to read their thoughts but received nothing. In fact, for the next two hours, the House of Celsus seemed every bit a typical social gathering among friends. Everyone seemed light and happy. No one was terribly intoxicated, and there was nothing unusual about anything. Even the coven women were on their best behavior. Sophia's four female slaves walked around naked while meekly socializing with the other guests. Celsus and Sophia were involved in deep discussion. At the same time, Aaron and Troy curled in front of Sophia's feet. Ra stood like a massive sentinel by the door, surveying everything. Nona seemed unchallenged by the continual requests for wine refills, and the coven women were helping her anyway.

For the next two hours, Elizabeth fell into a light trance when, just after 11, she realized something strange was happening. No one had approached her. No one had even acknowledged that she was there. At her realization, Nona struck a little handheld bell. At this exact moment, Elizabeth realized Sophia was smiling at her. It was not the glimmer, but it created great apprehension, nonetheless. She knew the experience would be intense. Celsus spoke.

"Ladies and gentlemen, we have agreed on tonight's agenda. My dear sister has agreed to give me the six new prospects who desire a place at her table and the award of the black choker. These slaves will be at my disposal for my entertainment until the sun rises. In return, I am allowing Sophia to rule the women of my coven for whatever her heart desires. You *will* obey her as you obey me."

The female voice came back into Elizabeth's mind with amplified rage.

Absolute blasphemy! The coven taking orders from Sophia? A fucking diamond on her black choker? Oh, my sweet sister, if only I were there.

Celsus continued, "As for the house members, you know the protocol. You can do as you like this evening, but when you are needed, you will come. Nona is off-limits. She is at your service for wine, toys, and anything else you need. I expect everyone to treat her with the utmost respect. Finally, our lady Elizabeth shall be at the mercy of everyone, including Ra and Nona, all the way down to the lowliest ranking prospect of my house. Sophia and I will not intrude upon anyone's command, provided Elizabeth receives an appropriate education. Deal with her as you will and in whatever fashion you will. Stephanie, Madison, Gwen, and Tasha, come before me now. Give me the reins, my sister."

Sophia untied the reins and transferred them to the armrest of her brother as the four naked women surrounded his throne in a half circle on their knees. Celsus looked pleased.

"You have trained them well."

Elizabeth was horrified. She knew the present company would tear her to pieces. All she could do was nod obediently. Any insubordination would bring down the wrath of the master. He was looking at her coldly now, awaiting any sign of retreat. Satisfied, he turned toward Sophia.

"You first, sister."

Sophia took a sip from her chalice and spoke like a seasoned libertine.

"Powerful women of the coven, I adore you. I demand the XO cunt-suck me now. On your hands and knees, Megan. To this day, your divine lips still possess me. Sanem and Tara, get on your knees and administer your talents to my feet. Wash my toes with your tongues, and do it with reverence and love. Linzie and Sakura, my two angelic lovers, I want you on each ear. Use your words, lips, and tongues as if you were challenged to seduce me. Use your hands on me as well. Yes, all this magnifies Megan's goddess-given talents. Take me beyond this world—a continuous release to propel me from my body. Make me yours. Give me what I desire most. Possess me, beautiful bewitching devils!"

Celsus smiled and addressed Elizabeth.

"My sister creates art, does she not?"

"Without question, my lord," Elizabeth replied, trying to mask her fear.

"Strip the tape from Aaron and Troy," he commanded.

"Yes, my lord," she said as she carefully tried to pull the tape off Aaron. The nasty welts on his backside gave her cause for concern. Celsus became impatient.

"Stop fucking around and do it!"

"Yes, my lord."

Elizabeth ripped the tape off, and they both yelped like wounded animals. Celsus was displeased at her empathy.

"Madison, would you slap Elizabeth for me?"

The response was immediate. Madison stood up and slapped her hard in the face. Elizabeth nearly fell to the floor as Celsus apathetically issued an order to her.

"Suck me."

Dazed from the blow, she stepped forward, unzipped his pants, and went to work immediately while he continued.

"Aaron, ready that weapon of yours. When sufficiently hard, I want you to lubricate it with Gwen's mouth and stuff it into Elizabeth's slit from behind."

The operation went off without hesitation, and when Aaron pushed himself into Elizabeth, she moaned. Celsus voiced his pleasure to her.

"Sweet innocent thing, the night is so young."

Meanwhile, Sophia's choreography had taken on a life of its own. Sophia was taken to the heights of delirium in less than a minute. She was completely unaware of anything beyond the supernatural pleasure she was experiencing.

The rest of the room engaged in a massive display of debauchery. Any person standing in the middle of the room could slowly turn 360 degrees and see some sexual act occurring from every point of view. Sophia, spread-eagle and quivering with pleasure, devoured by the five beautiful women, found her voice.

"My god, brother, Jesus, fuck, oh my God!"

But Celsus was all too engaged himself.

"Sloppy Elizabeth, let your saliva drip freely from your lips. Madison and Tasha, present your asses to me. Troy, get behind Aaron and lick his asshole as he pumps her. Aaron, you shall not come, or your punishment will be nine times what my sister gave you. Gwen, spank Troy's bottom while he tastes his friend. Stephanie, I want you to kiss me."

As the slaves carried out their tasks without hesitation, Sophia had an earth-shattering orgasm heard above the orgy. It took several minutes for her to catch her breath and recover, but she spoke with genuine satisfaction when she did.

"My brother, I envy you for having the best tongue I have ever known. Megan, you are a rare jewel, indeed "

With his right index finger in Madison's anus, his left in Tasha's, Elizabeth loudly sucking away, and the sound of Troy's rear being slapped repeatedly, Celsus addressed his sister.

"I am fully aware, my sweet. I know all their talents."

Sophia voiced her desire to continue with her sexual adventure.

"I am in dire need of some cock. What do you recommend, since you are so preoccupied?"

"I have just the man for you," he said, slightly flexing his hips to meet Elizabeth's mouth. "Nona, go fetch the one with the bigger tool, and bring some leather paddles, dildos, and clamps."

"As you wish, my lord," Nona said, departing from the room.

Though she was being fucked by a man she had no interest in, Elizabeth's only genuine concern was the pleasure of her master. She would do anything to gain his approval and was determined to prove herself no matter what. Her sincere desire revealed itself in her operations as she could feel his sack tighten. It made her pursue the matter more vigorously—her saliva dripping generously from her chin. She loved him and wanted more than anything to know his secrets. Suddenly, Aaron cried out.

"Stop!"

But he was too late. He pulled out of Elizabeth and tried to grip the head of his penis to prevent it from exploding. Semen spurted out all over Elizabeth's back and, as he turned around, landed on Troy's leather-covered face. The master was not happy. He grabbed Elizabeth roughly by the hair and held her head back while he addressed Aaron.

"I see you are a fool. No discipline or respect in my house?"

Aaron quickly glanced at Sophia, who had stopped kissing Sakura, to see what happened. She screamed at him.

"You embarrass me! He is the master, and this is his house! I fully support whatever punishment my brother deems appropriate!"

Celsus chimed in, "Sophia's slave has disrespected me by ignoring my commands! I want Sophia's other five slaves to assist Nona when she returns. You will tie his elbows to his knees and hang him from the ceiling pulleys so that he is suspended in a most vulnerable position."

Elizabeth felt the pain in her scalp as Celsus held her by the hair with an iron grip. She was terrified of his anger and noticed everyone had stopped their excesses in anticipation of what would happen next. He twisted her head toward his face and spoke through clenched teeth.

"You've been naughty."

"But, my lord, what have I done?" she inquired without thinking.

"You dare reproach me? How dare you even speak without my permission?"

Elizabeth could only close her eyes as he stood up with his raging, unsatisfied erection in one hand and a handful of Elizabeth's hair in the other.

"Ladies and gentlemen, I apologize profusely for interrupting your pleasure. However, you know that discipline is always part of the entertainment. My precious slaves, when you are done with Aaron, you may string up our insolent Elizabeth the same way, right next to him."

Nona entered the room holding the hand of a tall, weary young man who trudged beside her. At once, Elizabeth recognized Heather's ex. His physical condition shocked her. He was naked, pasty, and appeared famished and weak.

What have they done to him?

Nona interrupted the master's tantrum, "Lady Sophia, I present to you Abdul Ghaazi."

Sophia turned to Celsus and said, "Forgive me, brother. I can see this poor soul is endowed well enough for me, but he looks like he can barely raise his eyes, much less anything else."

Celsus let go of Elizabeth. She immediately dropped to the floor, clutched his ankles, and cried. Her tears rolled off the top of his feet, but he ignored her and addressed his sister's concern.

"Any of my women can make him fully aroused, especially Tara. They do it every single night. My sweet sister, why do you think he looks this way?"

"Come forward, Abdul," Sophia said. "Tara, work your magic on Abdul and make him hard."

The rest of the women watched as Tara gracefully knelt down and put the whole of Abdul's soft penis in her mouth. She gripped his rear and sucked him hard with her voluptuous lips. Abdul moaned in response, his eyes rolled up white, and the orgy started again.

Celsus looked at Nona. No words were spoken as Nona smiled and untied the numerous ropes and pulleys that hung from the wall and ceiling by the grand fireplace. The slaves worked diligently, and within a few minutes, Elizabeth and Aaron found themselves suspended from the ceiling, about three feet off the ground, their elbows and knees tightly cinched together and their private parts totally exposed. They were precisely nine feet from one another. Celsus walked over to Aaron and pushed him so that he swung like a pendulum.

"I want the other dog to sodomize you without lubrication. I think it's the least that can be done, seeing as how you came on his face, not to mention on my new initiate's back."

Sophia seemed pleased by all this. She ran her fingers through Sanem's spiky black hair and addressed him.

"My lord, it seems only you understand my heart. Abdul, come fuck me. Tara, position yourself so that I may taste you, and do it so that your splendid ass is right in Abdul's face. Sakura?"

"Yes, Mistress," Sakura said, bowing her head in subordination.

"Abdul is going to fuck me. I don't want him touching anything. If his hand touches anything, you will slap him as hard as you can, understand?"

"Yes, Mistress, of course," Sakura said obediently.

"You may commence," Sophia said, glowing with a smile.

Without instructions, Megan, Linzie, and Sanem could only watch silently as Tara straddled the throne in front of Sophia's face, placed her hands upon the back of the chair, and slightly bent her knees to give access to Sophia's waiting mouth.

Sophia gripped Tara's muscular rear and sucked her womanhood hungrily. As Abdul entered Sophia, he instinctively touched Tara's flexing glutes. His obsession, his curse, was evident.

As dainty and charming as any woman could be, Sakura let loose a haymaker with an open left hand, catching the right side of Abdul's face. He pulled back quickly and appeared stunned.

Meanwhile, Celsus went to a trembling and helpless Elizabeth, who cried uncontrollably. She wondered what she had done to warrant such fierceness, wondered how and why her life had gotten so out of control. She tried desperately to hold onto the memories of soft moments shared with Linzie in the dark of winter, opposite the base and brutal scene she now experienced.

As if Linzie had heard Elizabeth's thoughts, she turned to her and smiled. Her eyes betrayed the glow of the coven, the hunger in all its intensity, and a monstrous nature. Standing between Megan and Sanem, Linzie slid her hands down their bellies and fingered them simultaneously. Celsus asked Elizabeth a question with genuine curiosity.

"What do you see?"

Unable to see him because of her bondage, she choked out a response.

"My lord, why is she looking at me that way? What's wrong with her eyes?"

"Is that any way to speak about someone who loves you more than anything?"

"My lord, please make her stop." She could no longer look at Linzie, and the master was pleased.

"Now I see why we've always been so enamored with your vulnerability. You are so beautiful. Your tears …" He left off as he bent down and licked the tears from her face. She was terrified as he continued on.

"I will not wait any longer. I will have your gifts now. Madison and Tasha, come. Interlock your arms under Elizabeth and swing her back and forth on my cock. I will not move. You will fuck me with her body, and you had better do it right. Stephanie, you will get on your knees and lick my balls. Gwen, stand behind me. Caress my ass, pinch my nipples, and bite my ears. Do it right, or it will be the worse for all of you!"

Just then, everyone in the room heard another tremendous slap reverberating over the spankings that seemed everywhere now. Sakura had dealt another vicious slap to Abdul's face and opened a cut on his lower lip. A droplet of blood slowly went down his chin, but he was oblivious. His focus and obsession was Tara's rear, which gyrated slowly on Sophia's face. He pumped Sophia hard as he fantasized about Tara, her ass directly before him but untouchable without physical retribution from Sakura.

Elizabeth was thankful for the small mercy of not being able to see the eyes of the monster that was her friend and lover. Her trial was about to begin as Sophia's girls formed an arm cradle under her swinging body. She looked around her own thighs into the unnatural gaze of the master. He was hard as steel and purple with desire, but she could not fathom his eyes. They were black—black like an abyss.

He stepped forward to let the tip of his cock brush her slickness. She caught a glimpse of Stephanie's innocent face before she disappeared under the master. Then Madison and Tasha started to swing her back and forth. Her insides were burning as they rocked her on his thick shaft. He reached around her legs and roughly twisted her nipples but purposely would not move his hips. She somehow *knew* his excitement and pleasure that Sophia's slaves were creating the only movement. Desire washed over her like a great wave, and her mind darkened. *He burns me.* It was the last internal dialogue before she blacked out from an explosive orgasm. Old thoughts from long ago resurfaced uncontrollably.

What makes him think he can control She who is before everything, She who is the Mother of everything? A suicidal goal! Why can't he see that She will kill us all! He brings Her wrath upon us.

Elizabeth struggled for consciousness. The language was unfamiliar, yet she understood every word. Celsus brought her back.

"Ah, god's fuck! What a glorious vice—bewitching!"

When Elizabeth had fully regained consciousness, she saw Abdul lying face down on the floor. Linzie and Sakura were upon him—doing what, she could not tell. Abdul's right foot twitched as if he were having convulsions.

Sophia was on her hands and knees with Sanem directly behind her, fucking her with a strap-on dildo. Tara and Megan were kneeling before Sophia's dark giant Ra. They took turns hungrily sucking his enormous cock. Ra had braced himself against the wall and seemed lost in bliss while Nona sat in the corner, gently masturbating. Her hair was disheveled, and she looked beautiful and wild with desire. Elizabeth found herself surrounded by acts of passion.

She caught her breath as Linzie turned to face her. Linzie revealed a horror beyond Elizabeth's comprehension, ramming her left hand inside Abdul's bloody anus. At the same time, Sakura slurped at an open wound on his back. There was blood everywhere. Sakura stopped momentarily as if she could sense Elizabeth looking at her. She looked up with an inhuman bloody grin, her eyes demonic, causing Elizabeth to scream. Celsus covered her mouth and ordered Stephanie to stuff a rubber ball into it. He spoke to Elizabeth, and the voice was not quite human. Without rational thought, she *knew* it was not human.

"Such weakness. If you were not one of us, I would tear you to shreds, enjoying every scream. Your fear must be punished. Poor Elizabeth," he said as he spun her around.

She was having difficulty breathing through her nose, and how she was tied up was very painful. He stopped her spin so that she could view Troy's act of sodomy on his fellow prospect, Aaron. There were droplets of blood on the floor beneath his suspended body. He had been gagged with a rubber ball as well.

Celsus spun her again and stopped her to face Nona, who seemed angelic, surreal, and so beautiful that Elizabeth began to cry, her fear turning to infinite sadness. Celsus pushed her away hard so that she became a spinning pendulum. Scenes flashed before her, and she felt that her life was over. She truly believed he would kill her. Celsus responded, obviously reading her thoughts.

"Death is no release for us, only an alternate version of the same shit."

Elizabeth felt nauseous and helpless, and the master responded to her feelings.

"Nonsense, you have a constitution of iron! Let's step things up. Nona!"

Nona slowly rose to her feet, her dress falling naturally around her. Elizabeth could only catch glimpses of her approaching as he addressed her.

"I need four bullwhips and a small cauldron of olive oil."

Elizabeth began screaming behind her gag as Celsus admonished her.

"Don't be such a baby. You must go down to the absolute bottom. Then, you will have the openness to truly face yourself. Elizabeth, you are so special, so perfect. You speak about how much you need us, yet I cannot live without you. Understand that what I do now is out of my undying love for you. I will take the gag now. No screaming. No hysterics. You may address me."

She spoke with great fear in her voice.

"My lord, please. Megan told me that none of the women had to endure such brutality. Why must you hurt me?"

"Goddess, you make me hard with your fear. The trembling of your voice is too sweet for me to endure. All the women went through some kind of trial to return to me. Megan lied so that you would not succumb to the foolishness of your fear. You would only delay the inevitable, and eventually, you would try to take your life. We cannot have that."

"It seems you all take great pleasure in my misery anyway. Please don't do this! Why does it have to be this way?"

"You have a flair for drama, and I love it. I take pleasure in your growth, not your misery. You are in the cocoon and transforming. You cannot escape this. This is the way, and you must endure. The chains of your false reality shall be broken. It is the only way."

"My lord, please."

She sobbed as Celsus replaced the gag and took several steps back. She looked at him and screamed a muffled scream. Breathing hard through her nose, she realized he was not human, not at this moment anyway. There was no compassion, only an icy contemplation of what would happen next. And his eyes—so black. She looked around as best she could for someone to help her, but there was nothing but a bizarre orgy and what appeared to be the macabre death of a once healthy Abdul Ghaazi, an apparent murder by two women who had touched her so lovingly just a few hours earlier. It was then that a strange calm replaced her fear. She resigned to her fate.

I thought you all loved me.

Nona was so graceful. In one hand, she carried a small silver cauldron, and in the other, four bullwhips, each only four feet long. Even with the impending doom, she found Nona's beauty hypnotic. For a brief moment, she felt alright about things. Then, complete silence as Celsus drew everyone's attention. His voice was slow, sinister, and contemplative.

"One, two, three, four—time to beat this pathetic whore."

Elizabeth found the twisted rhyme grotesque as he issued new orders.

"I want Aaron taken down now. Troy, I see you are more disciplined than your friend here, so I will reward you. When

Aaron is untied, he will sit under Elizabeth. You will position yourself in front of her as you were before Aaron. In fact, you will sodomize her wonderful ass in the same manner, though a little more aggressively, but with Aaron's saliva to assist you. Aaron, you will suck his cock to keep it ready for her. I want each of Sophia's girls to grab a whip from Nona, dip the end into the oil, and whip her as hard as you can, wherever your heart desires. You will do this one at a time, in sequence, starting with Stephanie, in a counterclockwise rotation. If I see even the slightest hesitation or mercy, I will whip you myself. Believe me—you do not want that."

At that moment, Sophia screamed out while in the throes of another blissful orgasm, compliments of Lady Sanem.

"Goddess, yes, fuck me! I love you! I love you!"

Elizabeth stole a quick glance as best she could. Sanem held Sophia upside-down by her ankles in an assisted handstand. She still donned the strap-on and maneuvered herself to lift Sophia's entire body into her thrusts. Even with the oncoming lashing Elizabeth was faced with, she found Sophia's predicament highly erotic.

After untying Aaron, Sophia's six slaves made their way to Elizabeth. Aaron seemed to have a difficult time just walking and proceeded gingerly. Obediently, he sat underneath her and waited. Troy took up his position while each of the girls took a whip. They soaked the tips in Nona's silver cauldron and formed a circle around Elizabeth. Madison made a hand gesture toward Celsus.

"Speak," he said impatiently.

The young woman expressed her concern.

"If we are to whip her with total abandon, will we not strike Aaron and Troy, my lord?"

Celsus laughed.

"I see why Sophia likes you. I don't care if the whips draw strange blood, only that Troy remains hard and thrusts hard. If he fails, they shall both be punished for it."

Madison nodded in acknowledgment, and the girls seemed ready. Celsus looked positively evil, and Elizabeth took note of this. She thought it was the kind of look that could come about only through extreme deprivation. Her emotions took a new direction. Though her elbows and knees were painfully bound together, her hands were completely free. She let the middle finger of her left hand rise slowly in defiance toward Celsus. He seemed pleased.

"Perfect—Aaron, lubricate your friend."

Aaron began sucking Troy. He did it well enough for Celsus to take notice.

"I believe you've done this before. That's enough. I said lubricate, not suck him off. As much as I can see your enjoyment Troy, I want you to stick that in Elizabeth's ass."

Troy complied, and Elizabeth, humiliated and hopeless, gave up. Celsus then ordered the whipping.

"Starting with Stephanie and moving counterclockwise, you may commence."

The girls repositioned themselves with enough distance to avoid hitting each other. Once they were comfortable, Stephanie laid on the first lash. There was no direction to it, no planning, only as much strength as she could muster. It wrapped around Elizabeth's back and struck her right breast with an awful crack. A muffled scream followed as Tasha delivered the second lash. Their timing was perfect.

Celsus slowly walked backward until he found himself comfortable on his throne again. Sophia was now on the throne beside him, cradling Sanem's head affectionately. She lavished kisses upon her as she watched the drama unfold.

Tasha's hit landed diagonally across Elizabeth's back, and everyone heard it. More muffled screaming, more crying.

Each girl would take the most vigorous possible swing, and the next would wait until the full effect had taken place. Elizabeth closed her teary eyes.

After 18 complete rotations totaling 72 strikes, Elizabeth passed out. Her agony was too great, and her body completely shut down. She looked flayed, a bloody mess. Celsus walked toward her, signaling Sophia's slaves to back away. The bullwhips had done much more significant damage than the cat-o-nine. She suffered multiple lacerations, some fairly deep. Her face had taken several hard lashes that had torn her lips and cheeks.

The master stroked her hair and gently licked the wounds on her face. The room fell silent as everyone watched, mesmerized by his sudden gentleness. All over her body, he licked, and the fresh wounds mysteriously coagulated. He stepped back and addressed Nona without removing his eyes from Elizabeth.

"Bring her back."

"As you wish, my lord."

Nona gracefully placed her hands upon Elizabeth's blood-soaked head. Elizabeth shook in protest, signaling she did not want to return to consciousness, let alone endure anything else. Celsus whispered his adoration to her.

"You are a jewel. You have no idea how great you truly are. I adore and worship you, Owl-Goddess."

She could only moan, and her pain was evident to everyone as she blinked her eyes and looked around the room as best as she could. She was the center of their universe. The brutal pain crawled around her flesh, and she could not believe she was still alive. Her agony took on a throbbing strength, and she longed for death.

Just get it over with, you fucker.

"I would never dream of such a thing," he said, reading her thoughts again. "Take your places, same as before. This time, I want to see the enthusiasm in your thrashings. No more tentativeness. Lay on, or I swear …"

Gwen interrupted him before he could finish his threat.

"I cannot do this! She is really hurt, can't you see that? We need to get her to a hospital!"

No one dared say anything as the master responded, eyes blazing.

"You are speaking without permission *and* refusing me?" Sophia yelled from her throne.

"Do as you are told!"

"I will not! I will not hurt her anymore!"

Celsus grabbed Gwen by the arm and spun her around so she could meet him face-to-face.

"So be it, Gwen Lynn Wagner. You were warned."

Gwen felt herself give in to him. She suddenly felt weak and wondered how he knew her full name when she had not even revealed it to Sophia. She fainted and fell to the floor.

Celsus grabbed the ropes and pulleys used on Aaron and fastened one strap to Gwen's right wrist. He then pulled the system tight until she was on the balls of her feet. He looked at her closed eyes and spoke.

"By all means, be totally aware."

Gwen struggled, but it was no use. She wasn't going anywhere and protested.

"I don't want this anymore! Do you hear me? Let me go!"

"Nona, gag this impertinent bitch," he coldly ordered.

Nona complied immediately by stuffing a rubber ball in Gwen's mouth as he continued.

"Hold her free arm straight. Keep pressure on the elbow. Keep it straight for me, and keep your distance."

Nona straightened Gwen's arm as he picked up the discarded bullwhip and dipped it into the cauldron. She began screaming the same way Elizabeth had only moments earlier. He then spoke to a weary, beaten Elizabeth.

"When I have to do something myself, I can't enjoy it as much. I love being the voyeur, like now, for instance. When I want to watch and then I am forced to participate when I only wanted to watch, I get angry because I can't fully enjoy the visual of the thing."

As he continued his insane rant, he walked behind Gwen, twirled the whip with noticeable expertise, and swung a vicious uppercut between her legs. She tightened, convulsed, and passed out immediately from the shock. He again spoke to Elizabeth with disturbing apathy.

"You see, she has no constitution. She is once-born. No offense, sister."

"None taken, my lord," Sophia responded with obvious delight.

A thick rivulet of dark blood slowly trickled down the inside of Gwen's left thigh. Sophia's other slaves were paralyzed with fear. The master addressed them.

"You five, what are you waiting for? Continue!"

It appeared this was his show now. Sophia, the coven, and the other guests didn't seem to mind either, as they were all captivated. Some of the house affiliates and prospects had gone to various rooms for little private horrors of their own. Everyone heard Elizabeth's muffled, weary pleas as the three remaining women dipped their whips into the silver cauldron again. Aaron got Troy hard again, Troy impaled her rear a second time, the whipping started again, and the vicious lashes took their toll. She suffered an additional 12 rotations for a total of 108 lashes. Elizabeth was mutilated and left for dead.

Satisfied with Elizabeth, a cold, indifferent Celsus knelt between Gwen's legs and licked every drop of visible blood from his perfectly placed wound. He was intoxicated while Elizabeth was lost in yet another vision.

I am sorry for this boy. What terrible misfortune, falling into such evil. He trusts me and looks to me for hope. He loves me. I cannot reciprocate. I am madly in love with my master, a sorcerer of the highest order who will bring us to the king's palace very soon.

Elizabeth had no sense of time when she woke up. Disoriented, she examined her unfamiliar surroundings. A few candles were lit, and the room had a warm feeling. As her eyes came into focus, she saw thousands of books lining two of the four walls. She sat up and found herself on an exquisite black leather couch. A beautifully embroidered quilt fell off her body as she stretched, and a swivel chair slowly turned around, revealing a serene Lord Celsus.

"How do you feel?"

Elizabeth took stock of her naked body and felt around for wounds. There were none. She looked to the master for answers. He smiled warmly and asked her a question.

"Amazing, isn't it?"

"Why are you doing this to me? I thought you loved me."

"I do. Why do you think you have no wounds?"

"I couldn't guess. Perhaps you enjoy my misery. Perhaps you like it very much."

"Be careful how you address me. You will show me courtesy and respect at all times. Now you needed to have everything taken from you—your pride, your dignity, and especially your false self."

"I am sorry, my lord, but why am I not dead?"

"You are extraordinary and would've recovered on your own, but my inclination after your fourth trial was merciful, so Nona and I assisted in speeding up the healing process. Have you ever been seriously hurt in your life?"

Elizabeth searched her memories for the answer.

"I was in a car accident when I was very young. I bashed my head pretty bad. The doctors said it was a miracle I lived. The tests went on forever, but the end result was that I was as good as new. My parents still tell people about it."

"Last night, you were whipped within an inch of your life. It would have killed a once-born a quarter of the way through. If someone had the misfortune of surviving this, they would have needed several major surgeries to repair the unbelievable damage you suffered. It appears Madison turned out to be quite sadistic. I like her. Bravo, sister," he said, closing his eyes with a grin.

Elizabeth took a deep breath and felt her face. It seemed soft and undamaged as he sat down next to her. She did not sense any evil in him. His eyes were comforting, warm, and serene.

"Don't worry. Your face is as angelic as ever."

Elizabeth welled with emotion, and a single tear rolled down her cheek.

"My lord, what is all this? Am I insane?"

He kissed away the tear and held her tightly. His voice was both soft and masculine.

"The worst is over. You are an immortal, a goddess."

"May I speak freely, my lord?"

"Yes."

"I do not trust this. I do not trust you or your women. Last night, I experienced unimaginable pain, horror, and inhumanity, yet I can't live without you. I have incredible clarity when I am with you. But it doesn't work—the love and the horror."

Celsus looked at his books without focus and replied, "It's been three nights since Sophia's party. Every time you leave, we miss you as much as you miss us. In fact, it's time for you to go now."

"Three nights? What time is it?"

"I couldn't tell you because I don't know. It is daylight, of that you can be sure. You know we don't deal in clocks. I know when it's day or night. I know what season it is. I know when the moon is growing and dying. I know what year it is. As for hours and days of the week—well—it's a folly I rarely indulge in."

"I am terrified of losing my mind. Why won't you explain things to me? If I am to go on, can I at least know what's happening? What happened to Sophia and her slaves? What happened to Abdul? What happened to Raymond? What the fuck is happening?"

A gentle knock on the door interrupted Elizabeth's growing panic attack.

"Come," Celsus commanded.

Nona entered, and for a brief moment, Elizabeth forgot everything. Nona's mystical beauty captivated her completely. Celsus did not acknowledge Nona immediately but instead answered Elizabeth's questions.

"My sister and her slaves departed the morning after the party. Sophia is a rarity among the once-born. I love her so much that I made her the XO of my lesser house and allow her to rule it as she sees fit. Her slaves provided sufficient entertainment. Gwen will be fine. She has a nasty gash that will need professional care, but she will be tighter after she heals," he said with a grin. "Needless to say, she will not be a member. As to Abdul and Raymond, you need to forget about them."

"Why? What does *once-born* mean? What is a *lesser house*?"

"Nona, take our princess home. Try not to worry so much, Elizabeth."

"Are you kidding? I'm losing my fucking mind."

He interrupted her with a kiss. It was determined but not rough. He let his tongue roll into her mouth, and Elizabeth found it so sweet. When he backed away, inches from her face, he looked deep into her eyes. His thoughts overpowered her growing fear.

Calm like the lake. Warm like the sun. Infinite like the sky.

"Yes, my lord," she said as Nona gently grabbed her hand and led her out of the great study.

She thought to tell him about the voice that expressed intense dislike toward Sophia. She checked herself, as the master was unusually pleasant—and she was leaving. She didn't want to depart on a sour note, so she quickly shut down her thoughts and obediently followed Nona down the stairs.

The house was strangely empty as Elizabeth made her way out. The sunlight was difficult for her, and she let out a whimper in response—a small protest because the sun seemed to hurt her eyes.

WHEN IN ROME

Four weeks had gone by without contact—no telepathy, no phone calls, no blood drinking, and no word. Elizabeth could not care less. The leaves were starting to turn, the air was cool, and she was blessed with melancholy. Her neighbor Carrie took notice.

Carrie thought Elizabeth might be bipolar and suffering from depression. She didn't ask her about missing the fall semester. She figured Elizabeth was taking a needed break. Carrie was good like that. When a knock on the door came late on a Friday night, Elizabeth knew it was Carrie. It made her giggle, and she thought momentarily before opening the door.

Residual effects from the Celsus freak show.

"Hey, Liz, Trash Bar tonight?" Carrie enthusiastically asked.

"No, thanks. I'm not up for it. Want to come in?"

"Sure."

"I have wine. It's cheap, but it does the trick. Want some?"

"That would be great."

Elizabeth poured a couple of glasses of Pinot Grigio, and the two women sat on the couch in front of the television. The nightly news was barely audible, but neither woman cared. At first, there was an awkward silence as Elizabeth stared at the TV in a mindless trance. Carrie looked at her, hesitated, and then revealed her concern.

"Look, Liz, I don't know you that well, but you seem sad. Is there anything I can do?"

"Not really. I'm in a funk. Wondering about life, why I'm here, and all that crap. I'm just a little down right now."

That was the beginning of a solid connection between the two women. Carrie and Elizabeth found they had a lot in common. The two women sat up for hours drinking wine and talking about their lives, ex-boyfriends, college, and everything shared between two friends. Not once did Elizabeth talk about or even think about the coven. The longer the two women talked, the better Elizabeth felt. It was the first time in many months she actually felt normal. At three in the morning, Carrie decided to call it a night.

"Liz, if you need anything, I'm right next door, anytime."

"Thanks, Carrie. I appreciate it."

As soon as Carrie left, the phone rang. Wholly taken away from all things unusual, Elizabeth unconsciously picked up the phone and frowned when she heard his voice.

"Those things you talked about with Carrie—it's all an illusion."

She was immediately overwhelmed with emotion and began to weep. He tried to explain.

"You only feel better because you are safe with what is familiar to you. But I know who you are, Elizabeth. I know *what* you are. You feel safe with your mundane past because it makes sense, yet you know deep down that until you met us, you were a loner, a misfit to the entire world."

Elizabeth sobbed and then asked him the grand question.

"You're not going to let me go, are you?"

"How could I? I love you so much."

"Then why are you doing this to me?"

She was close to hysterics. She hated him for disturbing her when she had found some peace. She hated him and loved him at the same time.

"Be at the airport in Romulus tomorrow, no later than five. Look for me on the departure level of the McNamara terminal inside the center doors. Pack light and bring your passport."

"Where are we going?"

"It's a surprise."

She cried at his hard-to-swallow truth. He was right about her not fitting in anywhere except with the coven. Still, this insight offered no resolution from her doubts. At that moment, she longed for the innocence of her mundane past, her collegiate aspirations, and her friendship with Carrie. She regretted her mindless consumption as the evening's wine finally took its toll. Childhood memories dissolved her into a crying baby until she passed out from exhaustion.

There wasn't any conflict about going. She spent the day contemplating possible destinations and then drove to the airport. She wasn't excited or curious because she had again sunk into her apathy, resigned to her fate with this man and his beautiful women. When she arrived, she went to the center of the building, where he was waiting.

His demeanor, warm blue eyes, and caring smile put her at ease. Whatever he was, she wished he could always be like this. There he stood, just as he was on the night she first met him, all in black, with a quiet dignity about him—a power.

"My lord," she said, bowing her head.

"Here's your ticket. The women are already at the gate."

She opened the envelope and felt a mild shock course through her body.

"Rome?"

"On the autumn equinox. What do you think?"

"I've never been there."

"You're going to love it."

"Will I? I doubt it if I am to be tortured and raped again."

"Not this time," he said, cupping her face and kissing her.

It was a kiss she would never forget—slow, sensual, and timeless. She felt her body grow weak. He stopped and backed away. Her eyes slowly opened, and she was immediately warmed and secure. Only a few inches from her face, he smiled at her. There was no sign of wickedness or the demon she greatly feared. His eyes pulled her in, and she could only think of a calm blue sea. As usual, time had stopped entirely; the airport had vanished, and only the two of them were there. A spontaneous and unknown question then escaped her lips.

"Why did you do it?"

He paused for a moment and replied softly.

"I had to. Long ago, I was betrayed. I've never recovered from it, and I need to educate the women entering the coven. They must understand that rebellion will be met with harsh retribution. I don't expect you to understand right now. You will remember soon enough."

She broke out of her trance and immediately forgot what was said. Celsus looped his arm through hers, and they proceeded through airport security.

When the two arrived at the departure gate, she could not believe how beautiful the women looked. It was strange for her to be in such company, yet she knew she belonged and had an inner sense that she fit in perfectly. They were her sisters and her lovers. They all greeted her like a long-lost friend.

Teary-eyed Megan was first. She looked absolutely ravishing. Her long red hair was tied into a tight bun atop her head, and she wore a beautiful green skirt and matching jacket over a deep yellow silk blouse. Her five-inch green heels made her an Amazon woman, but then again, Tara, Nona, and Sanem were of the same intimidating stature. Megan kissed Elizabeth on the cheek and lingered long enough to whisper.

"I missed you."

Then Linzie and Nona kissed her on each cheek simultaneously. Linzie, as usual, looked like a rebellious teen. Her blond curls bounced as she stepped back to let the other women in. Nona looked dignified in her dark slacks and suit jacket. It was similar to what Elizabeth was wearing.

Elizabeth donned a grey pinstriped business suit. She had tied her hair up with several curls hanging down, and she wore only a white camisole with no bra underneath. She appeared professional and alluring at the same time. The other women flocked around her, and she could see that everyone within visual range was glued to the scene, men and women alike.

The plane was a massive Boeing 777, and the first-class seats were more like office spaces than airline seats. They could be electronically rolled back flat into beds. She could pick her own movies and had a basic desk to work on. It made her slightly uncomfortable because she had never traveled in such luxury. Celsus quickly read her thoughts.

"Oh please, Elizabeth. I could have chartered a jet, but I like traveling with the public."

She could only stare at him in disbelief. She noticed the first-class cabin contained the coven and no one else. She looked back at Celsus, who grinned at her. He was already sipping a glass of wine.

As the plane soared into the early evening, she felt a powerful contentedness. She felt everything was finally alright and drifted off into a deep sleep. The nightmares came to her, the unknown language, the young boy, and little triangular shapes carved into drying clay. A voice in her dream brought her close to consciousness.

Come next to me.

She batted her long eyelashes and noticed Celsus prone on his seat-bed. He was smiling at her from under a blanket. She looked around the cabin and saw all the women wide awake and occupied with some activity. Megan was writing intensely while Sakura and Linzie cuddled together, watching a movie. Nona and Tara were engaged in a friendly game of chess. At the same time, Sanem conversed with one of the flight attendants. Elizabeth heard his voice in her mind again.

Come next to me.

Megan put her pen down and leaned over to Elizabeth. "Will you go to him already?"

Celsus held the edge of his blanket up as an invitation. It was the first time she had seen him look so innocent—a man of a thousand faces. At this particular moment, he looked boyish and mischievous. She tilted her head, genuinely perplexed by the stranger before her. He then let his index finger curl into a hook, signaling her to him.

She slid beside him and immediately noticed the intense heat rising under the blanket. The chair, now completely horizontal as a bed, comfortably held them. She let him spoon her as he dropped the blanket around her shoulder like a giant wing. Never before in her life had she felt so safe. He whispered to her, his lips softly touching her ear.

"I love you so much."

She swooned, and goosebumps covered her entire body. She loved the heat and the hardness that nuzzled at her backside. He continued to tickle her ear with his sensual voice.

"I will continue to speak as I greatly enjoy the effect it has on you, but *you* will ask and respond in silence within your mind. This conversation is for us alone, so don't worry about your sisters' thoughts. As always, I expect truthfulness at all times. This is your time now, precious. Ask what you will."

She understood and fell into her familiarity with this eccentric and powerful man.

I finally get the opportunity and can't think of a thing to ask.

As he curled his hand around her right breast, pinching and pulling at her nipple, she remembered the disturbing shield.

There is a coat of arms above the entrance to your house. What do the symbols mean?

She was becoming aroused and agitated at his mischief as he responded.

"Those symbols are over a thousand years old. They represent our history, our disposition, and our curse. The black background symbolizes our misfortune and subsequent evil. It represents the abyss from which we were born.

The wolf's head is you, isn't it? Why a wolf?

"The wolf's head comes from pagan Scandinavia. It represents the outcome of a vicious betrayal. It also represents strength and intelligence along with a fundamental vindictive nature. The horror of being eaten alive should always be considered when contemplating the wolf. The wolf further signifies insatiable hunger, gluttony, and excess, the three most important being sex, food, and knowledge through hedonistic practice."

Apparently.

"Be careful, Elizabeth. I told you it was your time, but you will treat this moment respectfully. You've only tasted what punishment could be."

I am sorry, my lord. What does the white line with the blood drop mean?

"When a line runs through a coat of arms from the upper right to the lower left, it is known as a bend sinister. The color white represents the white chokers, the bend sinister represents the murderous infamy of our family, and the blood drop in the center represents the sanguinary element of the house."

Sanguinary element? Do you mean like vampires?

He stopped his groping.

"I wouldn't say that we are vampires as defined by popular culture. Rather, we are the source of inspiration perpetuating the vampire and werewolf legends."

But how can that be? I was a child once. I was born in this day and age and never had such cravings until I crossed your path. How can you give such an answer if I have had an everyday life up to this point?

He kissed the back of her neck. She moaned as a powerful chill traveled down her spine and found its home in the growing wetness of her sex. He tried to redirect her.

"You digress from your line of questioning."

She squirmed and looped her thumbs along the hem of her waistline to pull her pants down. He stopped her and continued.

"The color red also represents the undying and extreme lust of the house. Red also reveals that this coven has a natural aversion toward pettiness and jealousy and displays a noble generosity to all its members."

I don't see that based on what I have seen. It appears that people can be treated horribly while in your and your women's company.

"Do not mistake your trials for meaningless sadistic pleasures."

What about the winged she-demon?

"It's a harpy. It represents our creator, our mother. You will understand the harpy better than anyone when you come into your full self, my love. It symbolizes the timeless moment of our birth—the start of the nine-fold abomination—wicked, beautiful, deadly, and eternal."

The words seemed incomprehensible to her, almost as if she had lost focus during that particular part of the explanation. Her thoughts went momentarily blank before she thought of concrete childhood fairy tales.

You said the coven perpetuated the vampire and werewolf legends. How is that possible?

"A few thousand years ago, we were together as we are now. An unfortunate event took place that bound us together for all time. Except for Nona, we all died on the same night. Exactly 234 years from that night—*The Event*, as we call it, we were all born again. We age only until we reach the age of our initial demise, and then the physical aging stops. We live 117 years and look ever-so-young when we die. When you return, obscure memories of previous lives will float around in your dreams until I release them. We travel through time like this, 117 years among the living and 117 years haunting the living. We are also responsible for inspiring the incubus and succubus myths."

How is this possible biologically?

"I don't understand how it works. Megan has been digging into the science of genetics to find the answer. As to the non-aging after maturity, she believes something from our spirit-selves combines with our DNA at conception."

What happens when you die?

"It is the same in every life. When Nona doesn't answer our call, we have only 18 hours left—it happens every time."

So Nona is one of us?

"Yes and no."

I don't understand your way, my lord. If you are really that old, I would think you would be wise and considerate of how others feel.

"That is the rationality of the once-born. Do you seriously believe someone could live for thousands of years without thinking and acting differently than everyone else? I cannot say whether or not this is intellectual evolution or sadism born out of eternal boredom. I stopped contemplating such nonsense during the second incarnation. When your memory is finally released, you will find your real self. The floodgates of every single incarnation will embrace you, and the conversation we are having now will be moot. The evolution that occurs throughout lifetimes does not stop with just the intellect. In this, words are difficult—useless. You may very well find yourself to be cruel."

What happened with your eyes—Linzie and Sakura drinking Abdul's blood? Me drinking and craving blood? It's horrific. What is this thing with needing blood?

"It is the blood that feeds our spirits. Blood makes us *feel* things again, like the once-born. All of us manifest our hunger in different ways. The longer it takes for us to feed, the more vicious and monstrous we become. Once in Paris during the last incarnation, I watched Megan rip the cock and balls from a man in one bite, swallowing the parts whole. She clamped her mouth on the open wound and drank the man dry. It was my doing. I did not allow her to feed for months as punishment for some insubordination that I can't even recollect now. I gave her a handsome young man when she found my favor again. She tore him to pieces, and then we fucked on his corpse, drenched in his blood."

Elizabeth ultimately rejected this graphic horror and continued her inquiry.

You keep referring to everyone else as once-born. What do you mean?

"Of all the belief systems, only the Buddhists and animists of the world know what's happening. Imagine we're on a boat in the middle of the ocean. Imagine that I'm holding a dropper containing one drop of water. When that drop falls into the ocean, it's like a departing soul returning to the eternal collective. Some call this collective heaven, some call it god—Valhalla, and so on, depending on the culture. That is the normal progression for the once-born. The soul does survive, but it survives within the collective. There are so many idiots walking around today who find this belief offensive. I believe it is the most beautiful truth of all things."

I am familiar with Buddhist beliefs, but if that is so, where does it leave the coven?

There was a long pause before the master responded.

"We are abominations. It is a terrible thing that we cannot return to the collective. When our time is up, we do not go anywhere. We stay and haunt the living, seducing, raping, and stealing the life force from their bodies while they sleep. The hunger never stops for us. For us, it is 117 years living, 117 years dead, and so on. We are just as bad in death, for we cause madness to those we visit. We are bound to earth for all time. It is horrific—all we have is each other."

My lord, what happened?

"It is time for you to sleep, my angel."

It was late in the morning when they finally arrived. As they walked out of Rome's Fiumicino Airport, the rays of sunshine irritated them. They were anxious to sleep the day away.

A long black limousine pulled up to the curb just as the coven walked outside. No one spoke as they were taken to a two-bedroom chateau along the Fiume Tevere. The ruins of the old Roman Forum and the famous coliseum were not far from the quiet river.

Each of the coven members stepped out of the limo donning sunglasses, and each was furious at the morning sun except Nona, who seemed unaffected by it. Upon entering, Elizabeth noticed that each massive bedroom had two king-sized beds and an oversized claw-footed tub, which stood out in the open, not more than ten feet from the beds.

Celsus, Sanem, and Nona entered one room while Megan, Sakura, Linzie, and Tara entered the other. Elizabeth stood dumbfounded in the hallway until the master noticed her dilemma.

"You're staying in our room," he said, gesturing her.

Sanem embraced Nona, and the two fell asleep immediately. Celsus continued to hoard Elizabeth, while in the next room, the beds held Linzie and Tara and Sakura and Megan, respectively. The rooms' shutters were already drawn tight and blocked out the daylight. Sleep came immediately. Elizabeth correctly assessed that the chateau was designed specifically for the coven.

Late in the afternoon, she opened her eyes to something very peculiar. Celsus was wrapped tightly around her back. She tried hard to detect his breathing but heard nothing and felt nothing. And while she could not see the faces of Sanem and Nona, she couldn't hear their breathing either. It was as if she were the only living being in the room. Her anxiety proliferated until the master's seductive voice gripped her soul.

"You were always my favorite, you know."

She was instantly aroused as he worked his middle finger inside her swelling sex from behind while softly biting her neck. For a moment, she gazed into the darkness and listened. Not a sound.

Masterfully, he took her mind off the eerie silence by working two fingers inside her. She had no idea when it happened, but he had opened a small wound along her neck and drank from her. It wasn't painful or draining but relatively light and sensual.

She moaned as he placed the head of his thick shaft against her lubricated slit. He stayed his thirst for a moment to taste another as he licked her nectar from his fingers. She knew not to take control but could not stop pushing back into him. The head of his manhood popped in, impaling her, and she moaned as he began drinking from her again.

"I am dying, my lord," she said.

Obscure memories and emotions started to overwhelm her. There was an undeniable truth to what she was experiencing. He loved her and wanted so much to trust her. Love was certainly in his nature, but she knew that *trust* was a concept utterly broken in him. Somewhere inside her, she knew she was somehow partly responsible. Her internal dialogue stopped, and she lost all sense of time and space.

They stayed this way for a few hours, resting in a transcendent place between the conscious and subconscious. There were extraordinary moments during their intercourse when they did not move externally. She tightened and released while he throbbed within the depths of her womb. This was not the rape she had endured at Sophia's party. This was lovemaking at the highest level.

The powerful sensations obliterated her thoughts entirely, and in the end, she met his thrusts with her own. Feeling the oncoming climax, she pushed herself back into him and, bringing him in as deep as possible, had a shuddering orgasm that went on and on. She knew he controlled and sustained her climax so that he could erupt within her simultaneously. It was then that she wished for death. She wanted to die simply because nothing in her life had ever compared to the nirvana she experienced at that moment.

She thought she might have heard the echo of her own moans and the sound—the bizarre growling of a wolf—and then there was nothing.

You will befriend him. You will earn his trust, and we shall live as we should in the king's palace.

Elizabeth opened her eyes and knew the night had come. A dozen candles illuminated the room, and the chateau was alive as the coven got ready for a night out in Rome. She sat up and noticed Celsus sitting quietly by the window, deep in thought. Steam rose slowly from the tub, where Nona gently washed Sanem's toned arms and shoulders.

Once again, Elizabeth's reality was altered as she rose out of bed with unusual detachment. Walking out of the bedroom and across the hall, she was unsure of her surroundings and reality. Then she felt the master's semen making its way down the inside of her thigh. *I am home,* she thought. The other bedroom was also lit by candles. Upon stepping through the doorway, she felt like she was hit by an electrical current. She froze with fascination as she saw Sakura and Megan kissing each other in the bathtub. The water was so hot that she could feel the heat from across the room. The two women were enveloped in each other's arms, and their kissing cast Elizabeth into a trance merely from witnessing it.

The sound of moaning quickly broke her fixation. She followed the sound to her left and saw the back of Tara's beautiful body, her arm pumping long, deep thrusts into Linzie. One of Linzie's creamy white calves was wrapped around Tara's taut back, and the contrast of their skin excited Elizabeth greatly.

Tara had Linzie against the wall and was fucking her with a vibrator. There was a light thudding sound as Linzie's head hit the wall behind her with each of Tara's thrusts. That sound drove Elizabeth to the brink of insanity.

Linzie looked at Elizabeth with half-opened blissful eyes. The glimmer reached Elizabeth in full strength, and she felt immediately faint. Just as she was about to lose consciousness, Celsus grabbed her hand and pulled her out of the room.

"They are hungry, Elizabeth, and they will take your world away if you're not careful," he said as he led her into the dining room.

"Tonight, we are taking in the power of Rome, and you will witness each of us feeding."

She felt highly submissive and said nothing. Instead, she knelt down and kissed him, first his hand and then his crotch. When she reached up to pull his pants down, he stopped her. He curled a finger under her chin and lifted her to her feet.

"Tonight, you will watch and learn. Nona will clean you up and dress you in something black and seductive."

It was 10:00 p.m. when the coven emerged from the chateau. They walked along the crowded streets to the lawn in front of the ancient coliseum. Standing quietly in a circle, eyes closed and holding hands, they basked in the warm Mediterranean night. Elizabeth felt great reverence and power among them.

They were all dressed in black as if attending a formal dinner. Celsus wore a fresh rose in his black Armani Suit, the only splash of color amongst the coven's foreboding yet alluring black wardrobe. At the direction of Megan, the chokers were not worn this night.

Elizabeth knew they were killers, and she was suddenly afraid. She also knew she was cut off from their thoughts as she looked around at her surroundings. Beautifully lit by ground lights, the coliseum looked ominous and sent a chill through her body. She saw shapes, couples, an old man walking his dog and wondered why they were not looking at them. The master read her thoughts and addressed her curiosity.

"As conventional as these modern Romans are, some still believe in Strega."

Elizabeth cocked her head.

"Italian witches," he clarified.

He then parted from the coven with two final words.

"Good hunting."

He grabbed Elizabeth's hand and led her toward the coliseum. She turned around to see the women, but they were already gone. It seemed strange that she couldn't see any of them. The distance they covered to get out of sight within such a short period seemed impossible.

When they arrived at the entrance, a man was waiting for them. Nothing was said. She tried to see his face, but he was wearing a fedora, tilted forward, which hid his eyes completely. Celsus handed him a wad of euros, and the mysterious man opened the iron gate. She wanted desperately to ask questions but knew better. Celsus held her hand tightly, and she noticed his hand was getting colder by the second.

After walking through the haunted dark hallways, they ascended the ancient stone stairs and took their seats in what she felt was once the pavilion. In this place, emperors and senators observed bloody spectacles. The dead silence frightened her, and the master's hand was now as cold as the stone beneath their feet.

A light breeze moved through her curls as she gazed at the old battleground. Celsus turned toward her—the glow from his eyes overpowering—the present, instantly destroyed. He kissed her—and she remembered.

She remembered the frenzy of the crowd and the bloodlust. The two of them had sat on this very spot, holding hands, watching the barbarity, barely able to contain their hunger, so many lifetimes ago. They were there, watching gladiators hack each other's limbs, vicious maulings, and the seemingly never-ending parade of slaughter. They were all there, under the hot mid-day sun—seething and drooling, hunting the crowd for quarry. They were all there.

"I have always loved you and always shall," he said.

She felt the ground melt away under her. She could feel his sorrow as she responded—her words sounding much like the language she had been dreaming about.

"Are we to remain here forever?"

"I'm afraid so," he said softly.

She recognized this despair and hopelessness. She let it filter through her body as his voice became one with the wind.

"It is always like this—so devastating—so unforgettable."

There was silence again as the two sat in the cool autumn breeze, waiting for the haunting to pass. She found it amusing when they both stood up at the same time. His hand was getting warmer.

They left the coliseum without speaking. He walked briskly toward the ancient forum, still clutching her hand. It was nearly too much for her. She felt dizzy and faint with each turn of the old Roman paths. Suddenly, he stopped, smelled the air, and slowly turned toward the old Senate house. His hand was hot now.

Quietly, he led her to the edge of the building. She carefully looked around the corner, focused her eyes on the darkness, and saw an old man sitting on the ground kissing a girl. She took a deep breath when she recognized Sakura. Celsus then overtook her thoughts.

Sakura takes her prey delicately and reverently, yet she is the most devastating. Her hunger is by far the worst concerning quantity. She may kill 10, 15, or even 20 in a single night. Sometimes, it seems there is no end to her gluttony.

Elizabeth was spellbound by the scene unfolding before her. She could *feel* the old man's heartbreak for Sakura, though he had met her only moments earlier. One of his calloused, withered hands clutched the inside of her silky thigh. She gently nuzzled his neck below the ear. It was so subtle, sad, and haunting all at once.

Elizabeth must have had some power because she knew the old man had been lonely for many years. As his head tilted to one side, she could feel his heart slowing, his life draining. Although she could only see the back of his head, she knew he was smiling. Sakura gently laid the old man's lifeless body on the ground at the moment of truth.

The hypnotic slowness of what Elizabeth witnessed was shattered when Sakura disappeared within a tenth of a second. No living creature on earth could have moved that fast, which scared her greatly. Celsus burst out laughing.

"What the fuck?" Elizabeth cried out.

"Shhhh. We're standing next to a kill. It's time to go."

He grabbed her hand and resumed the hurried death march. She struggled to keep up, but the master had no sympathy for her.

"The night goes by so quickly. We've much to see and a lot of ground to cover."

The next stop was a nightclub just over a mile away. She was not surprised when the doorman allowed them in without paying cover. Celsus smiled and entered as though he owned the place, and she noticed his hand was hot again.

The scene inside was a riotous rave. The droning pounding of the bass drum, the swirling lights from above, and the mindless robotic melody did nothing for her. She watched the crowd in its fury and wondered only for a moment.

Which woman graces this establishment?

She looked up at Celsus and stated with certainty, "Linzie."

"Yes, and there seems to be a small barrier between us. Not a problem."

He led her to the opposite corner of the dance floor, where a large bouncer stood guarding a door. Before Celsus addressed him, he spoke inside her mind.

The power grows stronger with each incarnation. Sometimes, I wonder if there are any limitations.

Before she could respond, he commanded the man.

"Apri la porta."

Elizabeth perfectly understood, though she had never spoken a word of Italian. Not in this life, anyway.

The man stepped aside and opened the door. As they descended the stairwell, she realized his hand was uncomfortably hot.

"My apologies. It's just too much for me sometimes," he said as he grinned and released her hand.

One lone light bulb hung from the hallway's ceiling at the bottom of the stairs. She found this very creepy until her attention was taken by the sounds of moaning coming from the other side of a door to her left, which was slightly opened.

Celsus looked first and then invited her to take a peek. An oversized janitorial closet revealed Linzie suspended midair between two young Italian men. They held her between them, penetrating both orifices below the waist. The man sodomizing her had not even bothered to remove his pants. Linzie immediately locked eyes with Elizabeth, revealing a wicked smile, indicating that extreme violence was close.

Linzie's eyes were red with blood, and her cravings were out of control. At the moment of her climax, tears of blood streamed down her cheeks. She locked her legs around the man before her and jerked him in with her heels. A sickening crack was heard, and as the man was about to scream, she clamped her mouth over the front of his throat. She had broken his back and choked off his windpipe with her teeth.

The other man pumped away from behind, oblivious to the horror in front of him. She again smiled at Elizabeth and clenched her glutes, sending the young sodomizer into an orgasmic bliss he had never known nor would ever know again. She then unlocked her legs, letting the corpse in front of her fall to the floor. The other man, eyes closed in sheer delight, was oblivious and unprepared for the vicious attack. She spun around with lightning speed and side-kicked the man's right kneecap so hard that his leg broke and bent hideously the wrong way. She punched him square in the throat before he could scream. He fell to the floor, convulsing and choking. The thudding bass drum of the same song droned on as the Roman ravers danced the night away. Elizabeth was in shock. Her "little girl" was a vicious, sadistic killer.

Linzie grabbed a wooden broom and, with superhuman strength, broke it over her thigh. She rammed the jagged edge into the side of the quivering man's neck and then tore it out. Blood jetted out everywhere as Linzie knelt down and feasted, her blond ringlets soaking up some of his blood. Brutal beyond belief, it was the exact opposite of Sakura's killing.

Celsus grabbed Elizabeth's hand, ascended the staircase, and immediately left the club. She could feel his pride and enjoyment and became morbidly curious.

"How can you possibly get off on this? You have explained the need, but why not do it like Sakura? Why must it be so horrific and merciless?"

As they hurried out of the club and down the street, Celsus responded.

"I explained to you that we are all different, and it is not for us to judge each other. Linzie is done for the night. Who knows how many Sakura will kill before sunrise? Which is worse? There is no reason to make judgments or even comparisons. Soon, you too shall feed, and no matter how it goes, we will never judge you."

They ran down a residential side street at an impossible speed. Celsus stopped, smelled the air, and showed obvious disappointment.

"We are too late for the kill, but I want you to see something extraordinary anyway."

He led her around the corner to a dimly lit alley where her reason and reality were utterly destroyed. A large female lion chewed on a woman's arm between two carports. She knew immediately that she was in the presence of Lady Tara.

The big cat was crunching the bone and had already eaten the guts, heart, and one leg. Elizabeth looked inquisitively at Celsus. Reading her thoughts, he responded silently.

Tara feeds on one victim once a month. She is quick, indiscriminate, and devours everything. It is the same every time.

The sound of the crunching bone and the sight of the dismembered corpse made her nauseous. She turned around and vomited. The lion stopped chewing, looked at the master, and growled. Tara was displeased at the interruption.

Celsus approached the big cat without reservation and stroked her head. The animal stretched out, picked up the arm, and began chewing again as he sat beside her and scratched her back. Elizabeth was sick to her stomach and felt as if she would vomit a second time.

After a few minutes, they left the animal in peace. The two walked forever, it seemed, as time and distance lost all relevance and rationality. As they walked along the Via Portuense, Elizabeth noticed a growing throng of street hookers. In perfect Italian, Celsus hailed a taxi and told the driver to drive slowly so they could get a good look at the girls. At one point, he told the driver to stop, looked across the street, and made an observation.

"See that dark-haired queen of the street? Look how regal, how powerful, how beautiful she is."

Elizabeth looked toward the master's gaze and spied Sanem as he continued his adoration.

"Sanem has her own sense of justice. She hates bullies with such passion. Tonight, she will pick up some brutal customer and leave him impotent and afraid of everything for the rest of his life. She tries her best to leave them alive so they can experience this unimaginable fear, but sometimes they don't make it. Her father left her with this legacy."

Sanem's black high heels accentuated her muscular calves. She had obviously ripped her dress up one side nearly to her hip bone, further revealing the magnificence and promise of her powerful legs. From the waist up, her nipples were clearly visible through the sheerness of the garment. With bright red lips and black spiked hair, she looked like some ancient goddess of lust. Elizabeth found her absolutely ravishing.

They didn't have to wait long as a black Ferrari pulled beside Sanem. She momentarily leaned into the passenger window, conversed briefly, and entered the car. When the car sped away, Celsus commanded the cab driver to follow.

Through twists and turns, they followed until he told the driver to cut his headlights. The driver complied, and both vehicles stopped about 50 yards from one another. The street was dark and desolate. He gave the driver 500 euros for the fare and the driver's silence. After they got out, the cab backed away, turned around, and left.

The two approached with great stealth. Elizabeth listened carefully when they were within earshot. The car was slightly bouncing up and down, and they could hear a man groaning inside. Within a few minutes, the groaning turned into rhythmic grunts of pain. After less than a minute of this, the sound of protesting stopped and was replaced by the steady, methodical bounce of the car. Finally, there was no sound at all. Elizabeth stayed focused on the passenger's side as Sanem stepped out, straightened her dress, wiped the blood off her mouth, and approached the two voyeurs.

Elizabeth felt a shock of power course through her body when their eyes met. Sanem's eyes glowed like the sun, and Elizabeth started quivering uncontrollably as she approached. Sanem gently traced her bloody finger along Elizabeth's cheek, casually turned around, and walked away. Elizabeth was awestruck, and Celsus seemed just as captivated.

"Magnificent," he whispered.

Elizabeth was possessed by Sanem's power. How a single street lamp silhouetted her departing goddess-like form was absolutely maddening. She felt an incredible urge to run to her. Celsus sensed her desire and jerked her alongside him.

"Let us have a look at the lucky customer."

She noticed the man's hand slightly trembling as they approached the open passenger door. The scene was only slightly disturbing compared to the others she had witnessed earlier. The car's interior lights revealed his misfortune.

An Italian gentleman, middle-aged and of apparent wealth, was sitting in a compromised position. His suit pants were down to his ankles, and he looked as white as a sheet, with numerous bite marks, bruises, and contusions tattooing his flesh. There was a single slit along his carotid artery about half an inch long. The wound had been crudely stitched shut. A slow trickle of dark blood seeped from it. Celsus checked his pulse.

"He's actually alive. Can you believe it? I'll never understand why she does this, but as I have said, it is not for us to judge the other. See how there is little blood anywhere. To be sure, she has drained his balls, blood, and wallet."

Elizabeth studied the man as though she were analyzing the forensics of a crime scene.

"What are these four wounds along his thigh? See how they're evenly spaced and form a perfect arch?"

"Those are claw punctures, courtesy of our Lady Sanem. There are four like it on his other thigh as well. She straddled and jerked his body into her while feeding on him. Notice the deepening bruises on his cock. What an artist!"

"What did you mean when you said the ones who live will be impotent and afraid of everything for the rest of their lives?"

"I mean, he might as well cut it off now. That shriveled bloody noodle will never have another erection—and he will now know fear in a profound, debilitating way. He is henceforth fucked."

"What's the story here? Who is he?"

"I don't know, and I have no desire to find out. He's a bully of some sort, of that I have no doubt. Probably beats his wife, or maybe he's a mobster. He will now be afraid of his own shadow. He will have to be cared for like an invalid, and sleep will offer no respite. The rest of his life will be a constant nightmare, whether he is sleeping or not. The expression is *no rest for the wicked*—quite literally, in this case. We must hurry now. The XO is close to feeding."

They departed at breakneck speed. Elizabeth was dragged through the dark streets of Rome with total disregard for her fashionable footwear.

"My lord, I cannot keep pace. Soon, you'll be dragging me on my belly."

"Nonsense, you can fly and don't even know it."

"No, my lord. This is impossible!"

"You may cease your complaining now. We are here."

She looked up at a narrow brick building with walls completely covered in ivy. As the master led her up the stone staircase, she wondered what time it was because the activity around them had slowed considerably. They ascended two flights of stairs before entering a musty hallway with eight doors lining each side. It was no surprise to her when they stopped in front of apartment 306.

$3 + 0 + 6 = 9$, she thought.

Celsus looked pleased.

"You are learning, darling," he said as he slowly turned the door lever.

They entered a candlelit room, and Celsus quietly closed the door. From an adjacent room, they could hear a man praying in Latin. The door was open enough for them to get a clear view inside.

They approached with silent stealth like two great predatory animals. The room contained many religious artifacts, including crucifixes, rosaries, portraits of Christ and the Virgin Mary, a bible, and, hanging on the very door they were approaching, the robe of a Roman Catholic priest.

When they fully viewed the spectacle, Celsus overtook Elizabeth's thoughts as she processed the scene.

This is why she is my second. Bravo, Megan. Bravo.

The priest was naked before an altar, and his hands were bound behind his back with black velvet rope. Upon this altar sat Megan, her legs wide open, masturbating before him. She was flanked by two black candles. The priest had just finished praying, only a few inches from her exposed womanhood. Her response to the prayer was to cram a rubber ball in his mouth and secure it with a Velcro strap around the back of his head. She looked like some queen of bondage. She was naked except for black leather boots that ended above her knees and matching gloves that covered her arms just below her biceps. She gracefully stepped off the altar, walked behind the priest, and picked up a cat o'nine whip with hooked metal ends.

Elizabeth felt a chill when she saw the ends of that whip. They looked like nine dental exploration hooks dangling from nine leather straps. Megan sensed her fear and turned toward her with dark red eyes that glowed like hot lava. Elizabeth felt she was in the presence of an unimaginable, inhuman power, yet the familiarity was inescapable.

Megan briefly kept her fixation on Elizabeth as she grabbed a handful of the priest's hair and rammed his torso upon the altar. He moaned as she took two steps back, turned toward her target, and unleashed the first vicious lash. It was precise. He dropped to his knees, screaming behind the rubber ball, his back sliced open in six long cuts with three more complimentary welts.

Megan reached down and picked him up by his hair, stepped back, contemplated her victim for a moment, and then delivered a wicked uppercut between his legs. One of his testicles landed on the floor beneath him, and he passed out from the resulting trauma. Megan picked up the bloody, olive-shaped organ and ate it. She tried to lift him to his feet again but only succeeded in pulling out some of his hair.

Celsus and Elizabeth watched in fascination as she picked the priest up by the velvet ropes that bound his wrists and slammed him face-first back on the altar. A steady flow of blood ran down the inside of his legs from his shredded genitals. She picked up the whip and flogged him on the back thrice. After the third strike, the priest regained consciousness.

He was screaming and crying, though these sounds were still muffled by the rubber ball. When Megan noticed his legs were entirely unscathed, she ripped them open with the cruel device. The whipping was so fierce that a few ribbons of skin fell to the floor, and some were flung against the wall. His natural reaction was to fall to the floor to protect himself, but she held him down on the altar with her free hand and freakish strength.

Just as the priest was about to receive an overhand lash to the back, he desperately attempted to back away. This did nothing to deter Megan as her blow sliced through the air with tremendous velocity. He could not avoid it. The metal hooks descended over the man's head and stuck home. His forehead was torn open at once, and his left eye perforated. He fell to the floor, and again, Megan picked him up by his wrists and slammed him back on the altar. His toes were barely touching the floor.

At this point, she stopped to survey the damage. After a quick assessment, she walked over to the bed, dropped the cat o'nine, and picked up what Elizabeth thought was a sword. Celsus mentally intervened for a history lesson.

It is known as an estock. Notice the blade is triangular and has no cutting edge. It was used to penetrate armor back in the days of the knights. You wrap your hands around the handle and ram it into the intended victim for the finishing blow. Kind of sexual, don't you think? It's pretty effective when your opponent is protected by breastplates and a helmet.

Megan licked her lips, sucked on the tip of the medieval weapon, and slid two bloody fingers into her slit. She controlled everything. It was a timeless scene, drenched in horror and dark sexuality.

She took the weapon from her mouth and carefully placed the sharp tip into the priest's anus. She grabbed a chair, slid it under the priest, and wedged the guard into the edge of the seat. With great care, she sat in the chair and inserted the weapon's handle into her vagina.

From Elizabeth's point of view, it looked as though Megan was sitting in a chair with a giant, sword-like penis stuck in the ass of this priest. He was bound and bent over his altar, unable to move and shaking involuntarily—a sacrifice to the XO's raging hunger. Celsus and Elizabeth could only watch as their captivation and anticipation were too much for words or thoughts.

Megan softly caressed her victim's rear while gently grinding her hips. The wounded priest, showing obvious discomfort, tried to move his body away from the sharp intrusion. She would have none of it and stayed the priest by the ropes. She reached under his mangled genitals, felt around, tore off the remaining testicle, and ate it. The priest sobbed uncontrollably as she scooped blood and flesh from the holy man's wounded back and ate that as well. He made a weak and useless effort to evade the feeding by slightly turning on one shoulder. Megan responded by clenching her glutes, which speared the man's insides by a couple of inches. He screamed. She stroked the weapon to collect fresh blood and licked her hands again. She then turned toward Elizabeth with an icy demonic look, released the Velcro strap that held the ball in the priest's mouth, grabbed the velvet ropes, and pulled the priest down to the hilt with unnatural human strength, impaling him. Elizabeth could feel Megan's otherworldly orgasm, her blissful and total release. This was all about the kill. Feeding was of secondary importance.

The point of the estock protruded from his mouth. The rubber ball and three of his teeth bounced on the hardwood floor beneath them. As his body shook with the spasms of death, Megan lovingly wrapped her arms and legs around him and leaned back into the chair. She slowly opened her mouth as if taking communion to let his blood drip into her.

Elizabeth next remembered walking down the stone steps in front of the priest's building. Celsus ushered her into the exact black limousine that had picked them up from the airport. Nona was sitting in the back, waiting for them.

"My lord," she said, bowing her head with reverence.

"Nona."

"Everything is prepared. They are waiting for you at the chateau."

"Thank you, Nona. Elizabeth, you have one more feeding to witness, and tonight's voyeurisms have left me in a dreadful state. I thought I could restrain myself, but my mouth waters for blood, and I desire your lips."

The master slipped his pants down, grabbed a handful of Elizabeth's hair, and forced her mouth around his engorged shaft. Elizabeth complied with her own hunger, a hunger to please him. Her sucking was loud and obscene, just as he liked. Nona sipped wine and took in the sights of a quiet Rome at night—very late in the night.

After entering the chateau, Elizabeth noticed that most of the tapers had burned down, and a giant plastic tarp now covered the entire living room floor. Two young Italian women stood in the center of the tarp. They were both well endowed, impish, with pigtails, thigh-high white stockings, pleated short black skirts, black patent shoes, and heavy whorish make-up. Nona introduced them.

"My Lord and Lady, the two girls you see before you are Carmela and Giovanna. They are best friends, both 18, and quite the duo at a famous goth club here called "La Banca del Sangue." Carmela and Giovanna, this is Lord Celsus and Lady

Elizabeth of the House of Celsus. He is the genuine article, I assure you."

The two girls approached without hesitation and knelt before him. Celsus turned to Elizabeth, and what she saw startled her greatly. At first, she had no idea what she was looking at. Then, as best as she could process things, the eyes of the master looked as though they contained the stars at night, receding backward slowly. She was stunned and transfixed by the two black holes that appeared to devour the universe. Nona put her arm around Elizabeth and led her to the couch before addressing the two young women.

"Remember, heads down until he tells you otherwise."

As Celsus started to change physically, he inquired about the women.

"These two delicious girls, are they most desired and sought after by men and women alike, yes?"

"Yes, my lord. They are quite popular and very elitist. They believe themselves better than everyone," Nona replied.

"Yet here they are, kneeling before me. Who am I to you, Carmela?"

Carmela attempted to look up to see the master, but he growled at her and placed his hand on her head in disapproval. Elizabeth noticed how his long, razor-sharp claws wrapped perfectly around the young woman's skull. His voice became raspy.

"You two have trusted Nona, a total stranger, with a fantastic tale of immortality."

He smiled at Nona and Elizabeth, his canine teeth now dreadfully long.

"Do not look up, but nod if you wish to be immortal, if you wish to be vampires, if you wish to feed on your subordinates," he said.

The two girls nodded, and the master stepped behind them. He lifted Giovanna to her feet.

"I can do whatever I want, and you would be compliant because you believe, right?"

Giovanna nodded as Celsus lifted her skirt and groped her bottom.

"No underwear. What a naughty girl you are. I know you've made the boys cry over this peach."

He gave her a good swat on her naked butt, and she wiggled from the sting. He looked back at Elizabeth and smiled again. He seemed somewhere between human and beast. Standing behind Carmela, he lifted her to her feet similarly.

"And look at this! Your fruit is even rounder than your friend's and covered by white cotton. Ti adoro, mio delizioso piccolo Venere."

The master knelt behind Carmela, slipped a long claw through the bottom of her panties, and pulled them to one side. Elizabeth watched in fascination as his tongue slithered beneath the woman's rear into her wetness. His tongue seemed impossibly long, perhaps close to nine inches in length. Saliva dripped from his chin as his mouth watered uncontrollably.

Carmela cooed in ecstasy as he tongued her and fingered her friend Giovanna from behind. Both women were obedient, and neither turned to see what monster held them in the grip of their ecstasy.

Suddenly, he stood up, placed a hand on each head, and made them bend over. He proceeded to fuck the two girls from behind, alternating after about five minutes each. He then sodomized them slowly and deeply, with great reverence, in the same manner, alternating at appropriate intervals. The girls moaned and yelped in bliss, totally oblivious to their fate. Nona held Elizabeth tight, no doubt knowing what would eventually transpire.

At last, he unleashed his seed deep in Carmela's ass. The two girls had countless orgasms during the onslaught, and Carmela expressed her gratitude in colorful Italian.

"My lord, your girth has torn me blissfully. Are we now made?"

He could hardly respond, and his voice sounded grotesque when he did.

"There is one small problem. While it is true that I am a genuine article, the idea that I can make others like myself is a myth. I'm not even sure how that whole thing got started. To my knowledge, it can't be done. If I could do it, my beloved sister would have been the only one to receive such a curse—for I cannot stomach the thought of losing her."

Elizabeth heard him in her mind.

I lose the world. I lose myself and find myself, my true self. I hunger. I die. If you are horrified, you can blame yourself. You are responsible. You did this to me. I trusted and loved all of you more than anything, and you all betrayed me and killed my body but failed to kill my spirit. Yes, blame yourselves, including you, Nona. You could have stopped them. Instead, you stood by and allowed them to tear me to pieces. Witness now, Elizabeth, what you did to me.

What followed was a bloodbath of unimaginable horror. Frozen in terror, she watched as Celsus viciously ripped the young women apart limb by limb. When the destruction was over, the beast rolled in the carcasses, blood, and guts, just as any wolf would do. He savored and licked up tremendous amounts of blood, but the natural objects of his desire were the hearts. He suckled and chewed on one for nearly an hour before devouring it. The other he squeezed above his face. Lying on his back in the bones, flesh, and entrails, he drank the blood from the second heart and ate that as well. Then, with incomprehensible speed, he burst through the front door, his fur drenched and matted with blood. Moments later, a howl was heard in the distance.

Elizabeth woke inside the limousine. It was daylight outside, and the reoccurring blackouts were starting to frustrate and annoy her. They had just pulled up in front of the airport with only Nona accompanying her.

"What's going on? Where is everyone?"

"They're all gone, my lady. You're in my care until we arrive back in the States."

"Where are they?"

"In the skies over the Mediterranean. They are on their way to Turkey."

"Turkey?"

"My lady, I will try to answer your questions as soon as we leave. The hunger from the coven went a bit overboard last night. The polizia are very busy today trying to sort it all out. Apparently, there are a few witnesses who are talking. Are you ready?"

"I think so."

"Then it's time to say goodbye to Rome."

On the long flight home, Nona explained how Sanem was very attached to her disabled mother in Turkey. She further explained that the coven had other tasks to complete overseas. When Elizabeth inquired about these tasks, Nona replied that it was the master's place to inform her.

When they arrived back in the States, another black limousine was waiting. During the trip back to her apartment complex, Elizabeth could not get her world right. Everything seemed unreal, and she kept thinking that returning to her drab apartment and old life was meaningless at this point. It actually frightened her. She laughed a little. With every horror she witnessed in Rome, it seemed absurd that she should be afraid of her little apartment. But she was worried. In fact, she was terrified.

She wrapped her arms around Nona's neck and did not want to let go. Nona gently removed her hands and tried to calm her.

"My lady, you are past the halfway point. Your old life only frightens you because you know it is without meaning. You'll be alright, I promise."

"But when will I see you again?"

"I see why they love your desperation so much, my lady. It truly is beautiful."

Elizabeth knew better than to ask again. She hugged and kissed Nona and reluctantly left the car, thus ending her fifth official visit.

Randy V

TRUTH OR DARE

Elizabeth woke as the autumn sun was setting. She felt like she was still in Rome, at the coliseum, at the forum—at the feedings. Her awareness was divided. It had been three weeks since her return from Italy. She didn't feel hollow or apathetic. She wasn't afraid or hungry. She was patiently waiting for them with no real emotions. There were no dreams to haunt her, no thirst to tear at her, and no telepathic messages to drive her mad.

She rose from her couch and stretched like a big feline, aware of her curves and the tremendous power that would soon be hers. She had flashbacks of the terrors she had witnessed and wondered how soon it would be before she would be reacquainted with the hunger.

Her focus was drawn to the countertop in the kitchen, to a single white paper, folded twice and held shut by the crimson wax seal of a wolf's head. It sent a shiver up her spine when she broke it open.

For years I have searched for you
Cried for you, died for you
Terrible, my longing to possess you
To love you again

Nine long nights possessed by need
The curse, the worst desire to feed
Discipline and control are the key
Or kill your friend and lover in need

You'll come as three
But appear as two
The next new moon
An owl and a fool

She smiled and thought of him, the way he looked at her, the way he held her effortlessly, the way he drank from her, made love to her, and even the way he controlled her. She became wet with desire.

The poem was not easy for her to discern, as it was before. Intuitively, she felt the next visit would involve a whipping, which excited her terribly. She smirked at the oncoming mania and spoke aloud.

"Am I to be your marionette forever?"

Yes.

The soft voice of the master drove deep into the depths of her soul. Standing in the middle of her kitchen, she felt the wave of a spontaneous and powerful orgasm. She let her fingers slide down into her panties and could hear his silky voice again.

For you, precious, everything must occur by my count, sweetly, with trepidation but assured. Great care and caution must be exercised when it comes to you. The night hag knows when you are coming back to us. I release the hunger upon you—nine nights to feel its full rage before I welcome you to my table again. I'm dying to see how you handle it.

She moaned out loud and could feel the love flowing over her fingers. Her knees buckled, and she grabbed the countertop for support. His soft laughter faded like a dream as her body quivered from the climax.

Throughout the following nine nights, Elizabeth would suffer severe cramping, strange cravings, and a maddening hunger that would become an ever-escalating obsession. As the nights progressed, her behavior became increasingly bizarre. At one point, during the fourth night, she drove to a local grocery store and bought fresh, unfrozen slabs of ribs. Returning to her apartment, she tore open the brown wax paper wrappings and ate the raw meat. She gnawed on the bones, blissfully sucking herself into an unusual state of nirvana.

The seventh night placed her in a state of madness, pain, and severe hunger. She contemplated eating her neighbor, Carrie. Crawling on her hands and knees to the West wall of her apartment, she put her ear against it and listened.

She could *feel* Carrie as she slept. She could hear her heartbeat—almost taste her flesh—and desired her blood more than anything in the world at that moment. The pain ripped at her like waves breaking upon the ocean, and the cramping was so intense that she curled up into the fetal position and wept. Tears streamed down her face as she thought of the coven, thought of the master, and addressed him out loud, sobbing.

"My lord, of all the harsh things I have endured since our first meeting, this is by far the worst. Why are you doing this to me?"

She didn't expect an answer, and none followed. She had to endure two more nights before he would do anything, and even then, she felt he would not help her just for the sheer pleasure of watching her suffer. She rolled over on her other side, away from the wall, and endured another night of torture. At sunrise, she fell peacefully into a deep sleep. She dreamt of a night long ago in a language long forgotten.

Merchant: *Can you really do this?*
Somro: *Nine nights from this night, he will be dead.*
Merchant: *And no one will know?*
Somro: *It will appear as an accident. Maybe he'll choke on his food, or perhaps he will drown. All you have to do is stay far away from him until you are notified. Ensure you keep plenty of company, trusted friends who swear you have been in their company the whole time.*
Merchant: *What is your price?*
Somro: *One hundred silver shekels.*
Merchant: *Done.*
Somro: *I'll take the girl, too.*

Merchant: *You ask too much.*
Somro: *Take it or leave it.*
Merchant: *But she is my greatest possession.*
Somro: *I am not in the mood to haggle with you. Goodbye.*
Merchant: *All right. You're a hard man.*
Somro: *You have no idea. What's her name?*
Merchant: *Cala.*

The eighth night found Elizabeth teetering on the edge of total insanity. She fought hard against her starvation. It was a raging demon inside her, and she knew if she stayed in her apartment that night, Carrie would die. She liked Carrie and was not about to allow any harm to come to her, no matter what.

She threw on her coat and left her apartment with great urgency. Looking to the night sky, she begged the universe to keep Carrie away from her. Moving down the street, she noticed that walking alleviated her condition. She also noticed something different about her vision. This blessed distraction from her gnawing hunger was fascinating, to say the least. She stopped momentarily, looked down the street into the darkness, and realized she was reading a car's license plate nearly a half mile away.

"Impossible," she said out loud.

No human could have done this in the daylight, let alone at night. Slowly, she turned a full 360 degrees and realized, barring any obstructions, she had new visual skills that were humanly impossible. Not only could she see things focused at unbelievable distances, but she could also see right through the blackest of nights. She could see creatures as insignificant as mice in the darkness with a clarity that defied reason.

Elizabeth walked for nearly ten miles before returning to her apartment. And while the agony of her hunger never left, she found she could tolerate it as long as she kept moving and focused on her newly acquired ability.

As the sky revealed the presence of the oncoming day, she opened the door to her apartment. The last remnant of the night was the stabbing pain she felt when she saw the lights on in Carrie's apartment. She quietly entered her abode, tiptoed to her bedroom, collapsed face down on her bed, and slept as if dead. A great fear surrounded her uneasy sleep as she subconsciously recalled the day she met the master so long ago.

Somro: *You will speak only when spoken to, and you will respond with 'Yes, my lord' or 'No, my lord.' You will obey every command, no matter how insignificant to you. In return, you will never be hungry, and you will never want. I will accommodate most of your wishes. You will have your own room, and a certain prestige will be attached to belonging to me. You'll be free to attend the market and always be protected. Do you understand everything I have said?*
Cala: *Yes, my lord.*
Somro: *Very good. There's just one more item. If you cross me, disobey, or defy me in any way, your punishment will be most severe. Is that understood?*
Cala: *Yes, my lord.*
Somro: *If I see, hear, or even feel the slightest disrespect, I will lash your backside until blood flows. Understand?*
Cala: *Yes, my lord.*

Elizabeth woke on the ninth night with great apprehension. The light of the sun was gone. She sat up in bed, and for a moment, everything was alright. Suddenly, as if punched in the stomach, she moaned in pain and could barely catch her breath.

Hunger was everything and everywhere. She fell to the floor convulsing, and just as suddenly as it had started, it stopped. Looking up at the ceiling, she felt an unusual calm, yet she was certainly not herself.

I thought you might need some help.

"Linzie! Where are you?"

I'm right here inside you.

"I can't take it anymore. Get me out of this!"

Why would I do that?

"Please! This is too cruel! It's so unnecessary!"

First of all, he loves you as much as any of us. Secondly, who are you to decide what is necessary?

"What have I done to deserve any punishment?"

What makes you think you are being punished?

She realized her conversation with Linzie was more than telepathy. Linzie had possessed her, carried on an exchange within her, and performed the physical actions of getting ready for a night out. Elizabeth was not interested in protesting because the terrible pain of her hunger was now blessedly gone.

Yes, I can put that on hold for now. Would you like to see me?

"How is it that I am not in an asylum?"

You are so dramatic. What I am doing takes a lot of practice. I want you to be proud of me. See?

Elizabeth had cleaned her apartment and now found herself taking a nice hot bath. She had no idea how she did it. Everything was involuntary, and there was no sense of time's passing. Linzie was doing everything. Elizabeth's hand slipped between her legs, which was unintentional. She didn't mind.

Follow my voice. See me. My body is here, but I am with you.

Elizabeth saw the coven room as clearly as her toes at the end of her bathtub. She was seeing two completely different scenes simultaneously. She examined the coven room and noticed Nona setting the table. By the fireplace, Linzie sat on the floor naked, facing the flames, still as ice. She looked like she was meditating, legs crossed, hands on her knees, and eyes closed. An iPod was lying beside her, connected to her, and Elizabeth could hear the song.

"That's pretty heavy. What is it?"

Suicide Messiah by Black Label Society. I think of you every time I hear it.

With no will or control, Elizabeth pulled her fingers from her womanhood and stuck them in her mouth.

I love the way you taste. We'll come back to this soon, I promise.

"You are a devil."

So are you, Elizabeth—you'll see.

Elizabeth suddenly found herself standing in her bedroom. Her hair was dry, and she was completely dressed for a night out. Her confusion over her immediate short-term memory loss was replaced by the wonderment of her beauty. Standing in front of her full-length mirror, she was awestruck. Dangling rubies encased within platinum earrings, her scarlet choker, matching blood-red strapless gown, and four-inch red pumps stopped her thoughts entirely.

Goddess.

She was about to respond when a knock on the door startled her. She opened the door, half expecting it to be Celsus. A smiling Carrie greeted her instead.

"Trash Bar tonight," Carrie said with enough fortitude to let Elizabeth know she wouldn't take no for an answer.

She tried to respond, fear gripping her soul, but nothing would come out. Linzie, however, had an immediate response.

"Damn, girl! Look at you!"

"My god, Liz, look at you! Where are *you* going tonight?"

"Carrie, you're coming with me. Fuck the Trash Bar. Some friends up north know how to throw a serious party."

"I'm game. What's the plan?"

"A limo will be here in a few minutes. All we need to do when it gets here is get in."

"Who are these friends of yours?"

"Hang on, Carrie. I'm just going to grab my coat, and we'll walk down together."

Elizabeth walked about ten steps to one of the chairs in her kitchen, grabbed her coat, and had a brief moment of free speech.

"Please don't bring her."

Relax. We're just having some fun.

As the two women were taken away into the night, Linzie continued her deception. At the same time, Elizabeth was reduced to nothing more than a human costume. Carrie admired her.

"You look gorgeous."

"Thanks. You look good too. That catsuit looks tight as hell."

"It's not so bad. It's stretchy, see? Are you going to tell me about this party or what?"

"It's a surprise. I'm sick of the Trash Bar anyway."

"What do you mean? You never go there anymore. As far as I know, you never go anywhere anymore."

Two hours later, Elizabeth rang the great bell to alert the coven. Nona answered the door, looking as beautiful as ever. The entire coven—all but Linzie in attendance—looked striking, and they were all by the front door to greet them. Celsus approached the two women with indelible grace.

"Ladies, welcome to my home. Elizabeth, who do we have here?"

"This is my neighbor, Carrie. Carrie, this is Lord Celsus. I hope I did not inconvenience you, my lord."

"Nonsense. Carrie, you are enchanting, and you are certainly welcome to join us for dinner."

Celsus looked Carrie straight in the eyes, kissed her hand, and continued his introductions.

"This is Megan, Sakura, Sanem, Tara, Heather, and Nona. Linzie is sitting at the table already. She isn't feeling well, but she wouldn't miss dinner with Elizabeth for anything in the world."

Nona grabbed their coats as Celsus led the women into the great coven room. Everyone took a seat, and Carrie felt clearly out of place. Elizabeth sat to Carrie's right, and Sakura took the chair to Carrie's left. Linzie was sitting up but appeared sound asleep at the great round table.

Linzie refused to relinquish control of Elizabeth's body while the real Elizabeth screamed hopelessly within her mind. After the master and the women took their seats, the master raised his silver chalice.

"A toast, our entire family is present for the second time in this lifetime. Cheers!"

"Cheers," the women said in unison.

Carrie said nothing. She felt dazed and wondered where she was, what day it was, and why she was sitting there. She wasn't even sure if she was awake. Celsus acknowledged her confusion and addressed her directly.

"You should feel privileged. It is rare for someone such as you to sit at this table. I believe the women sitting around you are a little jealous of the way Elizabeth tries to protect you. Some of these women hate my eccentricities, my adherence to rituals of my creation—and especially my correction methods."

"I really don't understand any of this, and I feel funny," Carrie replied.

For her, the room was spinning, and she was becoming nauseated. She looked to Elizabeth for answers, but her friend gave no comfort. The look on Elizabeth's face was one of pure contempt, bordering on hatred.

"Elizabeth?" Carrie inquired, completely confused as Celsus tried to comfort her.

"We will try not to hurt you, not tonight anyway. Nona, secure Elizabeth's wrists and ankles. Make sure the ropes are good and tight."

Elizabeth made no effort to resist but continued to stare at Carrie with silent rage. If looks could kill, Carrie would have been dead ten times over. The rest of the women sat sipping their wine indifferently, seemingly detached. Celsus continued speaking to Carrie.

"Birth is a wicked and violent affair. Everyone talks about how beautiful it is, yet it isn't that nice. We all know this from deep within our subconscious memories, but few know the horror as we do. The women in this room must endure it twice in every lifetime. Imagine going through the terror of birth twice."

"I really don't understand," Carrie said with apparent fear.

Celsus looked at Elizabeth and frowned.

"I see our Lady Linzie has intentionally not taught you the customs of this house. Permit me to help you, Carrie. Do not look directly at me or speak to me unless I ask you to. When you speak, you must follow your words with "my lord.""

Carrie finally found a moment of clarity.

"Address you as *my lord*? I don't think so."

He glanced at Sakura, who looked as innocent and delicate as ever. The Japanese flower of natural beauty nodded in affirmation, turned toward Carrie, and viciously slapped her. Carrie shot back at her verbally.

"You fucking cunt! Elizabeth, are you kidding me? I'm out of here!"

As Carrie attempted to stand up, Sakura grabbed her by the shoulder and slammed her back into the chair. Carrie then tried to punch Sakura in the face. Sakura simply caught her fist and started to crush it. Carrie cried out and fell off the chair to her knees. At this point, Celsus intervened.

"Sakura."

Sakura released her devastating grip on Carrie's fist, lifted her by her arms, and gently set her back in the chair. He continued.

"Do you understand now, Carrie?"

"No! I understand that my so-called *friend* has dragged me into some fucked up shit!"

Celsus again glanced at Sakura, and again, Sakura slapped Carrie hard in the face. The blow split open Carrie's lip.

"Fucking bitch! What do you want from me?"

Celsus answered, "A little respect. This is my house, and you will address me as *my lord*."

"Fuck you!" she screamed back.

This time, Sakura slapped Carrie so hard that she was knocked out momentarily. Sakura lifted Carrie off the floor by her arms and gently set her back in the chair. Carrie was dazed, and blood trickled down her chin. Megan took notice of the wound, and the master took notice of Megan.

"Did I not tell everyone to nourish themselves before this night?"

Megan bowed and explained herself.

"You know my situation. I am saving my appetite for our next trip, my lord."

"How forgetful of me. I apologize, my lady."

Megan bowed her head respectfully.

Carrie felt compelled to protest again but thought better of it. She glanced at Sakura, who appeared to be waiting for an excuse to beat her again. She looked down at the table and wondered what would happen next. As tears welled in her eyes, she picked up a cloth napkin and held it to her lip.

Celsus slowly got up from his chair and gracefully walked behind Elizabeth. He placed the index and middle fingers of his hands on her temples, wrapped his thumbs around the back of her head, and addressed the two women within.

"Lady Linzie, you are such a wicked little thing. I am missing you in your proper place. Return now."

Linzie had remained silent as if sleeping. At the master's command, she awakened immediately with a direct and malicious stare at Carrie. Celsus continued.

"My sweet Elizabeth, the hunger that has tormented you for the last nine nights shall remain suspended. When you hear the crack of leather upon flesh, your hunger shall return short of causing a full transformation."

He seemed to float as he returned to his seat and addressed everyone.

"Everything is as it should be. Elizabeth, this dinner has a dual purpose. It is Heather's second chance at the scarlet choker. A few months have passed since her blatant disregard for my rules got her into trouble. Normally, she would wait nine months, but I would like to have my family together as soon as possible, and I am tired of waiting. This is a simple test to see if she can control herself. This dinner is also in your honor, for your benefit and for your knowledge, Elizabeth. Remember how we spoke when we flew to Rome?"

"Yes, my lord," she replied softly.

"You may ask any of us questions tonight. And you may ask plainly without all the formalities. Ask without fear. Ask until you can no longer think of anything or until I get bored. As always, some questions may go unanswered because sometimes there are no words to answer the inquiry. That's just the way it is. When we finish that, you and your neighbor Carrie shall be included in a grand game of truth or dare that will entertain even the most jaded souls. You may begin."

She looked around the room. There was a friendly fire, and Nona stood by the service entrance, ready to accommodate the coven's wishes. The women seemed a little more interested, and something seemed to trouble Megan, but it was subtle. Elizabeth took a deep breath, looked at the master, and began questioning him.

"Why am I bound to this chair?"

"I am accommodating your wish for your friend not to be harmed."

"She is already bleeding."

"Are you going to waste your questions? The little wound on her lip is nothing compared to what she would endure were you set free with the full weight of your ravenous hunger."

"I see. And while we are on the subject of Carrie, why is she here?"

"That was all Linzie's doing. You'd have to ask her."

"Linzie?"

Linzie first addressed the master before answering.

"My lord, you will not take offense this night if I speak my peace?"

"By all means, darling. It matters little. I already know the answer."

"Elizabeth, the master is set in his ways. We have no other course but to follow his direction. It is not worth it to challenge or question him. That said, I am exercising my right as a woman of this coven to take liberties wherever I may and express my displeasure over you being kept from us for so long. The moments you spend with Carrie drive me insane with jealousy. I hate her for no other reason than she lives next door to you, is a friend of yours, and has unparalleled access to you. There is nothing I can do about that. It is our master's way. Tonight, I tried to sabotage your friendship with her. I only wish that it was me instead of Sakura who dealt those blows, although I probably would have broken her neck on the first strike."

Carrie was now terrified and didn't dare look up. She figured she was dealing with some kind of cult and began calculating how fast she could get up and out the front door. Elizabeth addressed the master again.

"You told me the red color in your coat of arms means a natural aversion toward pettiness and jealousy. Is Linzie then a hypocrite, or is she a blasphemer of your house, or perhaps both?"

Linzie looked at her with undeniable sadness. Elizabeth was empathetic enough to feel it and immediately regretted her question. Celsus replied.

"How cruel, Elizabeth. You are correct about the color, but it applies to us and only us. However, jealousy toward the once-born can reach the pinnacle of absurdities within this family."

For some reason, Celsus stared directly at Heather when he made this clarification. Elizabeth redirected the master's focus.

"What is a lesser house?"

"When this coven is at full strength, there are nine members, including me. Those nine members are the heads of nine lesser covens, each containing nine total members, one convener from this house, and eight once-born members. So when my *house* is completely full, there are 81 total members. Of course, only *my* coven lives here. Each white choker in this room has a house within two hours of this place. Each has a single once-born male or female appointed as the executive officer of that lesser house. They are known as the XOs. Megan is my XO, and my sister Sophia is the XO of my lesser house. I really don't care about my lesser house. It is hers to do whatever she wants with it. I am only concerned with the women in this room. I allow them to run their houses as they see fit, without interference. I have only two laws regarding the lesser houses. First, those who would wear the black choker must be approved by me before they enter the houses of their new mistresses. Second, none of the other coveners may feed on or interfere with the members of another's lesser house, including me."

Elizabeth voiced her intrigue.

"So if I survive my trials and end up wearing the white choker, I will have my own lesser house?"

"Of course."

"Very well. Sanem, why do you try to leave your victims alive?"

"My lady Elizabeth, we are monsters, to be sure. But there are others, once-borns, who make life miserable for those who cannot defend themselves and those who can't escape. I have taken a personal interest in these people. It is a never-ending obsession with my past and the only way to any satisfaction. The feedings are justified and taste ever-so-sweet. Sometimes, they die, especially when I am too hungry."

"And your grief when they don't make it?"

"There is none. Sometimes, the hunger is too great to control."

"Sakura, what about your monstrous gluttony?"

"My lady, I cannot help myself. My curse is never-ending hunger. Though I may feed twenty times in a single night, I am never satisfied. I try to find those who beg for release. They are the old, the sick, the lonely, and the heartbroken."

"Is your hunger problematic for the coven?"

"It is. Rome was nearly a disaster for us. I was careless, and for that, I am sorry."

Elizabeth then redirected to Linzie.

"Linzie, I am sorry for what I said. Why are you so cruel when you feed? Why all the brutality? Is it really necessary?"

"No apology needed, my lady. It is not your fault. You are still coming into your own. As to the way I feed, I have no qualms. The once-born are necessary to my survival, and as such, I see them only as food. None are safe from my hunger unless the master himself designates otherwise. For that reason alone, Carrie continues to live. As to my methods, it makes dining so much better. It makes the blood succulent."

Carrie suddenly made a move for the front door. Oblivious to the coven's telepathy, she thought she had a chance. Sakura merely moved her foot to trip her. Carrie landed face-first on the floor. Elizabeth attempted to help her but was bound too tightly to do anything. She looked to the master for help.

"My lord, please release her. There is no reason for her to be here."

"It is Linzie's wish that Carrie be here."

"She knows too much. I don't want her harmed," she protested in response.

"Carrie won't remember anything, I guarantee it. In the morning, she will wake and believe she simply went to bed early."

"Promise me, my lord."

"How dare you! When I said you may speak plainly, I did not mean for you to insult me. I have given you my word, and that is enough," he said, eyes blazing over his cup, followed by a healthy gulp of wine. He then commanded Nona with calm reserve.

"Our guest seems a bit tense. Take her downstairs and let her ride the machine for a while. When she is sufficiently broken, bring her back and secure her the same as Elizabeth."

"As you wish, my lord."

Nona gently helped Carrie to her feet. Carrie was beyond resisting and accepted her fate. The coven had a way of doing that to the once-born. Nona seemed careful and empathetic as she led her into the dark hallway and down the spiral staircase.

Elizabeth felt the shock in her body as she remembered the machine. She laughed at her envy despite the seriousness of her sixth visit. Celsus read her thoughts and spoke enthusiastically.

"You see, my princess, you realize your true self—envy over your friend's appointment with the machine. Do you feel better now?"

"A little, my lord."

"Good. Anything else you would like to ask?"

"Yes. You and Lady Tara are different than the others."

"We are all different. What is your question?"

"Tara, I witnessed your feeding. How did it happen that you feed this way?"

"My lady, moments in our many lives define who we are. During the third incarnation, in the wilds of Africa, a tribal shaman recognized me for what I was. He quickly impressed the council that I was demonic and should be left in the desert to die. I was an infant. They executed my mother by stoning her to death. The shaman said my mother had copulated with a demon and bore me. They took me far out in the desert at night and left me for dead. A female lion was the first to find me. Her fangs pierced my heart as she picked me up from the ground by my torso. It was our Mother who possessed the beast. She traveled far to the East and left me in the care of one who wanted me more than anything. The big cat changed me, so I feed like you witnessed in Rome. I have fed this way ever since."

"Do you feed like this as a child?"

"The feeding never starts until the master finds us."

"What if he doesn't find you?"

"He always finds us—all of us—always."

"My lord, in one respect, you are the same as Lady Tara, but then again, you are different. I believe I saw a wolf in Rome. Correct me if I am wrong, but how did this come to be?"

"My story is similar to Tara's. I was a Norse shaman living in what is known today as Gamla Uppsala, the great pagan stronghold of Sweden. After an incredible slaughter of humans and animals at the summer solstice, I suddenly became intolerant of my infinite boredom. Nine nights after the solstice, I ascended the great center mound to end my life. I drove a dagger into my heart with great determination. I welcomed death, falling on my back and gazing at the night sky. The Mother heard me and obliged. Six wolves and a lioness ascended the mound. One solitary woman of magic watched as the beasts tore flesh from my bones. It was the ultimate betrayal. I was devoured. During the following incarnation, I found out what I had become. I am the origin of the lycanthrope myths and legends of Europe. That is all I want to say about it."

"And the two girls you murdered in Rome?"

"I'm good with all of it."

"Why must it be so horrific with you?"

"Haven't we covered this already? Why do birds fly South for the winter? Why does the sun rise in the East? You will find out soon enough that you are not that different from us."

"What about these nine visits? Why must I endure this if I am already a part of the coven? What's that all about?"

"Well, I doubt anyone sitting here would say I was ever normal, not even the first time around. I will admit I am eccentric, and it does appear that with each passing incarnation, I get worse. But my position, and the short answer to your question, is that you'll just have to deal with it. I will always be your master. My reason or my insanity is irrelevant."

"I see, and who is the Mother?"

"Off-limits."

"Fine. Lady Megan, why did you so viciously feed upon a priest?"

"My lady, a word with the master first."

"Of course."

Megan looked at Celsus, and the two conversed silently. Just as Elizabeth was about to protest, she realized the room had been gently vibrating for some time. A sudden awareness of Carrie screaming in ecstasy made Elizabeth smile. She longed for the machine, and Megan's voice broke her fantasy.

"I had the misfortune of being an orphan. Despite the belief that we choose our parents when we come into this world, I can tell you this is not true, at least not for me."

Celsus interrupted.

"Megan will answer your question at your next visit. You'll have to be content with that for now."

"As you wish, my lord. But Megan, can you tell me what happens to your eyes while feeding?"

"It happens to all of us and will happen to you. I don't really know how to answer with words. The eyes show our soul's age and power. I have no literal answer for you "

Elizabeth contemplated everything for a moment and then looked at Heather.

"Heather, how are you so comfortable with all this? This is only your second official visit, yet you act and seem like you've been wearing the white choker for years. What is your story?"

Heather did not respond right away but instead looked toward Celsus for approval. He was already glaring at Heather, daring her to speak the wrong words.

"My Lady Elizabeth, I come into the world with some abilities and some memories, but I assure you I am far from complete."

Elizabeth suddenly realized that Heather was the one who hated the master's sister, Sophia. It was Heather's telepathy that invaded her thoughts during the night of Sophia's party. Knowing how dangerous this knowledge was, she quickly devised a question for Heather that distracted and dispelled her thought patterns. Elizabeth was starting to gain some control over her mind.

"Do you know how you feed?"

"I do."

Celsus looked annoyed and glared at Heather again as she continued.

"Though I have not fed in this life and will not feed until the master fully releases me, I know that my feeding is the same as when I am without a body—the same as all of us when we are bodiless spirits. Except for Nona, you all have blood lust. When I feed, it is the life force I am after. If I kiss a once-born, they will be lethargic and physically weakened. If I cause an orgasm with my hands, it takes months to recover from. If I use my mouth, they will not recover. For the remainder of their lives, they will waste away. They will not have the strength to take their own lives, though they will desire to die more than anything. What I have said applies to both male and female once-borns. However, if I have intercourse with a once-born male, to the point where he has an orgasm inside of me, he will be dead within minutes. I do not take blood, only the life force. Only coven members are immune."

"Is the hunger as terrible for you as it is for the rest of us?" Elizabeth inquired.

"Absolutely," Heather replied.

Celsus intervened and looked at Heather disapprovingly.

"Are you quite through?"

"Yes, my lord," Heather replied.

Elizabeth suddenly felt sad and expressed her final thoughts to the master.

"My mind goes blank. I can think of nothing else, although I know there are more questions, my lord."

"Soon, you will not ask at all. It's all for *my* entertainment anyway," he said as he lifted his drink. "Let us drink to our beautiful Elizabeth. May you find happiness in this life and the infinite more to come. So be it."

The coven responded in unison, "So be it."

As they drank to the master's toast, Nona walked in with an unconscious Carrie over her shoulder. She set her down carefully and tied her up like she had bound Elizabeth. Celsus continued.

"Elizabeth, your time is up. You've had several turns all spent on truth. It's my turn now. Heather, I dare you to make your best effort at arousing me. You are not allowed to touch me. You must figure out another way."

"As you wish, my lord," Heather replied with cocky self-confidence.

The last time Elizabeth saw Heather, she was dressed up as a nun and brutally raped her former boyfriend. That night, her attire was what she considered school-girl naughty. She knew the master was inclined to this look, especially when it was time for him to feed. However, as Heather stepped up on the great table again, his face was cold and expressionless. His dare was a challenge, and Heather appeared to have no doubt about her abilities. With her braided pig-tails, cherry-red lipstick, white button-down school shirt, no bra, tartan pleated skirt, thigh-high white stockings, black patent Mary Janes, and her assertive, seductive demeanor, any ordinary man would have caved before she even tried. This was a sexual intensity in the extreme, topped off with a lollipop and an attitude that stated, *I get whatever I want.*

Heather sat in the middle of the great round table and opened her beautiful legs before the master. Elizabeth looked to the mirror to get a profile view of the action because Heather was facing away from her and blocking her view of him.

The room quickly filled with Heather's energy and power. With her right hand, she slowly and provocatively moved the lollipop in and out of her mouth, rotating it in the process. She slid her left hand down the front of her white cotton panties and locked eyes with the master.

Elizabeth sensed that this was a serious battle of wills. She knew that no matter what Heather did, the master would not succumb.

No one spoke a word as Heather masturbated in front of him for nearly an hour, moaning out loud in ecstasy when she finally caused her release. Her cooing gave Elizabeth a chill, but Celsus was unimpressed and voiced his discontentment.

"I'm bored with you, but for your efforts, you may pick a truth or dare for me."

"Most certainly a truth, my lord," she said as she put the lollipop back in her mouth and slowly crawled back to her chair, exaggerating the sway of her cotton-covered rear.

"What would you like to know?" he asked.

Heather sat, looked around the table at everyone, and posed her question.

"My lord, isn't it true you'd rather fuck your sister than us? Isn't it true you'd kill all of us if you could *make* her like us? Isn't it true that you are submissive to her behind closed doors?"

Elizabeth was in shock, and judging by everyone else's expression at the table, she was not alone. Nona closed her eyes in resignation, knowing full well that Heather would suffer intensely for her provocative questions. Celsus stood from his throne and walked behind the brazen Heather.

He grabbed her by the pigtails and pulled her backward to the floor. He then dragged her toward the kitchen by her hair, commanding Nona to follow. The other women sat in horror as they waited for Heather's fate. As Carrie started coming to, Sakura broke the silence.

"What is her problem?"

"She's a masochist and likes attention," Linzie answered, sipping wine.

"That's not the kind of attention she should look for," Tara said.

"She can't help it. It's definitely her way of keeping his focus on her, but it brings out the worst in him," Linzie said.

Megan said, "That is not the issue, Linzie, and you know it. She's got a problem with Sophia. She doesn't think Sophia should have this status with us, especially him."

"What do you suggest? I can't change the way she feels. None of us can," Linzie retorted.

"She really needs to get over it," Sanem added.

"Yes, she does," said Celsus, entering the room. "Would anyone else like to try my patience tonight?"

No one answered as he carefully examined each woman's expression and demeanor. He went on.

"I love every one of you, and you all know that. You also know I despise disobedience and rebellion. Once again, I must teach you that crossing me, no matter how insignificant you think the offense is, shall result in severe punishment. The punishment given to members of this coven would easily kill a once-born, like your friend Carrie here. With each lifetime, we all become more resilient. This leads me to take more innovative and drastic measures in getting my point across."

The service door opened as if on cue, and Nona wheeled in a metal serving table. Elizabeth looked at it with curiosity. On top, something significant was veiled by a royal purple satin sheet. As Celsus walked forward, Nona backed away. Approaching the table, he looked at Elizabeth, who immediately recoiled at what she saw—receding stars in his eyes.

"I asked our little princess to show respect at all times, and she deliberately challenges me at every turn. Do any of you disagree?"

The women looked down without responding, and he continued.

"Now she cries to sleep every night, cursing me for keeping her away. After tonight, she will start over again, but first, there is the matter of her audacity. I absolutely cannot let this go unpunished."

He yanked off the satin sheet dramatically. A naked Heather was bound to the tabletop like a roasted pig. She was bound so completely that no movement was possible. Her chin was pressed hard on the table, an apple forced impossibly in her mouth, and her wrists bound to her ankles by a purple velvet rope. She was bound by the back of her neck and her lower back. She was also roped by the back of her knees to the table legs below her face, forcing her into an arch, her meaty butt high in the air.

Elizabeth was shocked and aroused at the same time. She thought Heather's body was perfect, beautiful, thick, and hard. Her porcelain skin was flawless, and her soft, auburn hair had grown longer since their last meeting. A thick lock in front covered her left eye. Her beauty and captivity had such an effect that Elizabeth became immediately aroused. The master started his rant.

"Heather has disrespected me. How sad is this? I who would kill for her, and she has decided to challenge me again."

Elizabeth watched in silent agony, lusting after Heather as Celsus walked around her. The rest of the coven remained quiet as he continued to chastise her.

"Rebel! Disobedient! Insolent! This is how you thank me when Abdul Ghaazi was served up to you on a silver plate? I wanted you with us, and you challenged me on the first visit and then again tonight! This is not Gamla Uppsala, you little bitch. If your intention was to find out what would happen, you succeeded. I doubt this time you will say it was worth it."

He pulled a belt from his waist, a thin leather strip about half an inch in width and a yard in length. He wrapped the buckled end with one loop tightly around his left hand and spoke directly to Elizabeth.

"This has a dual purpose, as you will understand in a moment. Please obey me, Elizabeth. I can no more stop myself from punishing any of you than I could stop myself from feeding."

He then took two steps back and delivered a vicious lash to Heather's hindquarters. Heather screamed from behind the apple but couldn't move in the slightest. He then turned to examine Elizabeth as Carrie regained consciousness.

Elizabeth felt a crack in her nose and thought she had been punched in the face. Blood began pouring out. With the deep scent of iron came a hunger that tore fiercely at her soul with more pain than anything she had experienced. Carrie turned to look at her and started screaming hysterically. She saw something unnatural and monstrous.

Now seemingly satisfied with Elizabeth, Celsus turned his full attention back to Heather. He stood back and let loose another angry lash. The coven sat motionless as the belt hissed through the air to find its mark on her perfect flesh. Two welts rose to the surface as Celsus roughly kneaded her butt with his hands.

"By the Gods, I love this girl's ass!"

Elizabeth could not catch her breath as the pain and hunger tore at her insides. The smell of Carrie's fear, the sound of her screaming, and Heather's punishment were maddening to her and seemed to escalate the pain within. She could feel her toes breaking through her pumps. She tried to scream, but the sound that emerged was more like a screech.

It was a sickening sound, and Carrie responded by crying hysterically, jerking her head, and trying to loosen her bonds.

Celsus knelt down before Heather's rear and spoke to her exposed sex.

"What pleasures you have missed."

He clamped his hands on her ass cheeks, still holding the belt, and drove his tongue deep into Heather's slit. The coven sat still, obediently watching, while the screaming and screeching continued from Carrie and Elizabeth, respectively. He worked his tongue until Heather's sobs turned into moans of pleasure. He backed away, her love juice glistening on his lips, and delivered a prognosis.

"Look how swollen she gets. Her cunt is filled with desire and divine blood. My little brat, you don't think you can get off that easy, do you?"

He surveyed his work thus far and lashed her again. This blow was strategically placed to induce the maximum amount of pain. Only the last inch of his belt found the mark, her swollen clit. She screamed in agony, and the women of the coven began to get visibly agitated. None dared to move because they knew the master was in no mood for any distractions.

Meanwhile, Carrie had achieved a state of catatonia, eyes wide open and completely silent. Elizabeth had partially turned, and Carrie had witnessed it. All reason and internal dialogue within Carrie disappeared.

Elizabeth's world was now hunger, severe pain, and pure instinct. This was not the instinct of a predator in control but of a wild animal starving to death.

Celsus committed 36 total lashes upon Heather's feet, thighs, ass, back, and arms. He gave no quarter, and Heather's skin had split open in several spots. She cried and sobbed uncontrollably as the master taunted her.

"Oh, stop it. I could flay the flesh from your body if I really wanted to. Be grateful I'm holding my belt and not a bullwhip. I'm going easy on you. Wouldn't you agree, Linzie?"

Linzie was hurting inside about Heather and Elizabeth, and the master knew it. She looked up and responded truthfully.

"Yes, my lord."

"Since you are so keen on exercising your rights, and you feel so sorry for your sisters in need of relief, present one of your arms before Lady Elizabeth."

Linzie sighed deeply, stood up from the table, and obeyed the master's command.

"Yes, my lord."

As Linzie rounded the table, she briefly glanced at Carrie with great contempt. Carrie was breathing, but her eyes were blank and lifeless.

Once-born bitch. You'll be dead soon enough, Linzie thought.

The only thing coursing through Elizabeth was the smell of Carrie's blood. Still, as soon as Linzie presented the inside of her arm, she feasted without hesitation. The sound of crunching tendons and muscles could be heard throughout the room as Linzie dropped to her knees. Elizabeth managed to sever some large veins in her arm and fed through them like straws. Linzie protested.

"My lord, her thirst is too great. I am dying."

"Nonsense. But perhaps next time, you may ask my permission before inviting a stranger into this house."

Linzie finally dropped to the floor, white as a sheet and lifeless. Carrie did not respond at all. She was mentally gone, and Linzie appeared dead. Celsus merely laughed at them and turned his wicked intentions entirely upon Heather.

"My goddess, what a state you are in! Megan, Tara, Sakura, and Sanem stand to the four corners of this blessed serving tray."

The women immediately complied as Heather started to hyperventilate. He continued to tease her.

"What's your problem?"

Heather begged with an apple stuffed in her mouth as best as she could. Celsus ignored her and issued an order.

"Nona, get me a dildo. The apple is a nice garnish, but I no longer want to hear her begging for mercy. It's embarrassing. The dimensions should be three inches in diameter and nine inches long."

"As you wish, my lord."

Elizabeth continued to hunger for Carrie's body. She was uninterested in the bizarre scene with Heather, and Linzie's blood did nothing to alleviate her agony. She craved more blood and meat. Upon Nona's return, Celsus orchestrated new levels of torture.

"My dear Megan, would you do the honors and replace the apple with that thing. And make sure to cram it far down her throat so we may not hear her."

"As you wish, my lord."

The XO reluctantly performed the operation. Heather was now breathing hard through her nose and could no longer produce verbal sounds. The colossal dildo was crammed well past her voice box. Celsus leaned in close to her.

"You will learn to accept my sister, or you will suffer endlessly."

He held out his hands and produced razor-sharp claws. Surveying the room momentarily, he spoke with sincere love and adoration.

"You will never know what you all mean to me. To look at any of you shatters my heart to pieces. I love all of you so much that I die in your presence every moment of my cursed life. That goes for you as well, Heather. Though you find yourself on the dark side of my passions tonight, I love you as much as anyone here. Doing what I do now gives me great pain and pleasure."

He placed his claws upon Heather's shoulder blades and slowly raked them down her wounded back. The blood ran freely through the cleaved flesh as he took off his pants and frantically sucked and licked the blood dripping from the table to the floor. Then he lubricated his steely erection with her blood while addressing the coven.

"Ladies, indulge."

Megan, Sanem, Sakura, and Tara feasted on her wounds as he proceeded to sodomize her. There was nothing subtle about his entrance. Once the tip found its mark, he drove to the hilt of his weapon. She closed her eyes as she was painfully torn and violated by the monster.

After several minutes, he growled and snarled at the four women feasting. They backed off—all but Megan. He expressed his displeasure by snapping at her hand. She cried out and backed off, blood dripping from her fingers.

Elizabeth looked at the scene before her, unable to move, starving while her family fed. Celsus was now the monster she recognized from Rome, a wolf standing upright like a human and fucking gregariously. She could sense that he was about to climax.

He held his arms straight out, curled his claws inward toward the target, and brought them down hard upon Heather's rear. Each thumb and every finger penetrated both globes of tattered flesh. He threw his head back and howled. The sound was demonic and signaled his release.

The wolf nodded to the four women to continue feeding. Without hesitation, they fell upon Heather and feasted once more. Tara dropped to the floor on her hands and knees to lap Heather's blood but still maintained her human form. Celsus then moved menacingly toward Elizabeth, clutched the back of her chair, and walked back toward Heather, dragging Elizabeth in the chair.

As the chair scraped the floor, Elizabeth's backward view permitted her to see Linzie in a small pool of blood on the floor and her friend Carrie staring off into space. Elizabeth was indifferent except for the continued want of Carrie's flesh and blood.

Celsus growled and spun the chair around so she was inches from Heather's bloodied womanhood. Elizabeth stretched her neck as far as she could but could not reach the goal. He growled again, grabbed her by the back of her head, and rammed her face into Heather's sex.

Elizabeth fed hard and longed to have her hands. Still, when she attempted to tear off one of Heather's vaginal lips, the master interceded. With his right hand, he clamped down on Elizabeth's face, allowing only her darting tongue to drink from the great wound she had just inflicted. Elizabeth took as much as she could and found Heather's blood to be a little more satisfying than Linzie's. For a brief moment, she found rationality.

Her mind linked with her sight, and the first object to come into focus was the great mirror that adorned the West wall. The mirror revealed the entire scene of unnatural horror. She first caught sight of the master, which sent a chill through her body. She was shocked when she saw Heather's sad and tortured state and horrified by her four sisters who fed on her. Elizabeth cocked her head in amazement when she spied Nona standing in the corner, calm and reflective. Then came the moment of truth when she tried to see herself.

Her rationality was departing as fast as she could process what she had become. Her pumps were dangling from her ankles. Where her feet should have been, there were large talons—three forward and one thumb upon each foot, still securely tied to the chair. Everything else looked normal until she looked into her own eyes. She saw an inhuman face—half owl, half woman. Her hair was comingled with feathers, her ears were pointed, her piercing eyes were abnormally large and orange, and she had a bloody, hooked beak in place of a nose and mouth.

The master took her attention with a terrible roar. One by one, he threw the women off Heather. Such was the force that each landed on the floor and cowered, even the mighty Sanem. With his razor-sharp claws, he sliced off the ropes that held Heather bound and removed the giant dildo from her mouth. Heather seemed like a rag doll as he pulled her head back awkwardly and looked into her eyes.

The last thing Elizabeth witnessed was a large, bipedal wolf dragging Heather by the hair across the floor and up to the second floor, her heels thudding against the wooden steps as he made his ascent. The howling continued as darkness, deafness, and blindness completely enveloped her.

The banging on her door was relentless. Elizabeth got out of bed with the mindset of punching someone for waking her. When she swung open the door, the noonday sun seemed to burn her retinas out. Unable to see, she blurted out angrily.

"Can I fucking help you?"

Carrie was taken aback, but she could clearly see her error.

"I'm so sorry. Come over whenever you get up. Sorry, I woke you."

"I'm up now. Come in."

"Are you sure?"

"Yeah, come in before the sun blinds me permanently."

Carrie stepped in and closed the door behind her. The living room of Elizabeth's apartment was pitch black. After Elizabeth turned on the weak 40-watt bulb over her stove,

Carrie noticed that Elizabeth had stapled heavy black drapes to her window frames, sealing out any potential light. Elizabeth started a pot of coffee.

"What's up with this?" Carrie pointed at the drapes.

"I like sleeping late sometimes, and the sun annoys me."

"Speaking of sleep, the weirdest thing just happened to me. I wanted to come over last night to drag you to the Trash Bar, but then I felt a little tired and just went to bed."

"What's so weird about that?"

"I must have slept for 14 hours. I have never slept more than nine hours in my whole life. And there's something else..."

"Yeah?"

"I feel like I had sex last night. It's the weirdest thing."

Suddenly, the events from the previous night came rushing back into Elizabeth's mind. For several moments, she contemplated and fought for her reality. Carrie brought her back.

"Elizabeth?"

"You probably needed to catch up on your sleep and just had some good dreams."

"I don't know. I feel good, but it's just kind of weird. Want to get some lunch? I'll buy."

"No thanks, Carrie. Unlike you, I didn't sleep that well last night. I think I will go back to bed for a while."

"Will you call me when you get up? I'm worried about you."

"Stop worrying. I'll call you when I get up."

As soon as Carrie left, Elizabeth replayed the previous night's events in her mind. She had immediate concerns for both Linzie and Heather. The attacks upon these two women were as vicious as anything she had witnessed up to this point. While she didn't know Heather well, she shuddered when considering the brutality inflicted upon her. She thought of

Heather's troubles and felt genuine sympathy for her. Then she thought of Linzie and felt awful about the terrible feeding she couldn't control.

My lord, tell me they live. Tell me they live, please, I beg you.

Her guilty thoughts led her to the worst memory—the hunger, the devastating, cruel curse that tore her soul to shreds. She had a new understanding of this. The hunger was never to be taken lightly. Nothing could compete with it, not even love. As she now understood it, the hunger was to be taken care of as soon as it reared up. Attempting to suppress it could lead to the awful death of anyone within striking range.

Elizabeth continued to beg the coven for a response, but none came. Then, it occurred to her that the hunger was not present. She thought about the master and wondered why she was subjected to this. Her thoughts were interrupted when Megan's haunting voice entered her mind.

Don't you ever tire of asking the same questions over and over?

Elizabeth, no longer surprised by the abrupt telepathy, responded with a whisper.

"How are they?"

They will be alright.

Elizabeth paused momentarily, feeling great relief at the knowledge of their well-being. This feeling was quickly replaced by a severe annoyance concerning the master's schemes and punishments. She informed Megan of her dilemmas.

"You must admit this all seems a bit pointless."

Why do you tempt him? You must have learned something by now?

"I've learned that I can't be with you or him or the rest of my sisters because of some insane rules and rituals that will soon be moot."

Be careful, Elizabeth—or I will punish you myself.

"Promises."

You have three more visits, my love. Try not to blow it. I need you with us soon.

"What's next?"

I will come for you myself—very soon.

"Promises."

MEGAN'S REVENGE

Elizabeth sat with her legs dangling through the bars of her balcony, swinging them like a little girl. It was three in the morning, annoyingly cold, and she was bored out of her mind. She contemplated her life as she lightly pounded her head on the iron bars.

The rationality behind everything seemed right there at the edge of her mind. It was similar to remembering a song but not remembering the name of the band that played it. She knew trying to remember the coven's history would eventually drive her mad. She kept telling herself to be content as the truth would come sooner or later.

"You're going to get brain damage doing that."

The soft voice behind her broke the still of the night.

"Megan. What are you doing here?"

"I told you I would come for you."

Elizabeth rose to her feet, but Megan grabbed her before she could say anything and kissed her. It was a hot, desperate kiss full of such power that Elizabeth's curiosity dissolved.

The two women fell upon Elizabeth's bed in a flurry of passion. Megan showered her face with kisses and love bites on her neck and ear lobes. She stopped momentarily to slip out of her clothes while Elizabeth swiftly removed her long cotton nightshirt.

Megan carefully planted kisses down Elizabeth's neck and chest until she found her erect nipples. Elizabeth moaned in response as Megan kneaded her breasts and bit at the little towers. Those bites stung with pleasure, and she was quickly lost in bliss. Megan held each nipple, pinching them between her thumbs and forefingers as she kissed Elizabeth's womanhood. This play evoked a verbal response.

"Mouth of a goddess—my goddess—my goddess, Megan!"

Megan did not respond but instead sucked Elizabeth's clitoris between her teeth while rapidly flicking at it with her tongue, which elicited more colorful blasphemes through clenched teeth.

"Goddess fuck—oh fuck—goddess fucking Christ!"

She was coming with the force of an erupting volcano. Rather than let up, Megan continued her oral assault as she slid three fingers inside her and pumped fiercely. Elizabeth thrashed wildly as Megan gripped her hips to maintain her mouth lock.

The final release was an explosion. Elizabeth clenched the sheets, blacked out, and separated from her body. Below, she could see Megan sucking on her convulsing body. With a touch of mischief, she quickly entered through the top of Megan's head. It was a mistake she would regret forever.

A boy's screams echo throughout the orphanage's dark corridors, but his screams are muffled because he is gagged. What horror do you commit, Father O'Mallin? Are you not this boy's spiritual guide and guardian? What heinous crime is this? I peek around the corner and see that our Holy Father is a monster. He violates my friend. He sees me and shows no remorse. "Join us, Megan," he says. I shake my head. I am trembling, small, and scared. Then there is Timmy. I am too small to help. I am petrified of this demon. He comes for me.

Elizabeth immediately returned to her body and was panic-stricken. Megan grabbed her, held her tight, and tried to comfort her.

"It's okay. It's okay."

"You were there! You're the little girl! Oh no, Megan, what did he do to you?"

"Elizabeth, what possessed you to possess me?"

Megan had a single tear rolling down her cheek, but she laughed a little at her silly inquiry. Elizabeth was traumatized and hysterical.

"It was real, wasn't it? You were there! It was real."

"You have to calm down, Elizabeth."

Elizabeth jumped out of bed and began pacing the floor while holding her hands to her cheeks.

"Oh fuck!"

Megan jumped out of bed and placed her right hand over Elizabeth's heart. With this subtle gesture, Elizabeth calmed down.

Elizabeth backed up and sat down on her bed. Megan approached behind her, wrapped her arms and legs around her, and spoke softly in her ear.

"Better?"

"Yes."

"I could have kept you out, but I had no idea you could do it."

"What do you mean?"

"You aren't supposed to be able to do those things right now, not before the second birth."

"I'm not sure how I did it, but what I saw really happened, didn't it?"

"Yes."

"You only feed on them, don't you?"

"Yes, all holy hypocrites, no matter what their religion."

"And the priests?"

"They are at the top of the list, along with the bishops who move and protect them."

Elizabeth felt a pure, empathetic link with Megan and spoke with compassion in her heart. Without any evidence or knowledge in this lifetime, she knew the walls of defense had fallen. Megan was totally vulnerable. Elizabeth spoke with sadness, tears streaming down her face.

"The Executive Officer, second-in-command, powerful beyond belief—yet feeds less than anyone else. But when she does, it is vindication, personal justice."

"I don't think it is justice. I took so many innocent lives before my destiny with this awful man. Perhaps every time I come into the world of the living, I am being punished for those lives. But it is justice for others. It certainly is vindication in that respect. It's an ugly circle. The slaughters committed in the name of Christianity make our coven's existence about as significant as a grain of sand. All would judge us as evil abominations, yet this religion must be accountable for its history."

"Is it only the Christians?"

"All religions have committed atrocities against innocents, but quantitatively, the Christians are by far the worst, with radical Islam in the wings waiting and wishing to shatter the record. Both religions are hypocritical beyond belief. I believe some of the followers are good people with good intentions. Still, they've all been duped about their religion's hypocritical history."

"What happened to you?"

"My mother gave me up for adoption when I was born. My father pressured her into it. She was underage, and my presence in the world would have created a major scandal for both of them."

"How do you feel about it?"

"I have no ill will towards either of them. It was my destiny this time around. I believe myself to be a living manifestation of karma for those in trusted holy positions."

"I can't stand the knowledge of your abuse. You were an innocent child."

"No, Elizabeth. For as long as I can remember, I have been a murdering monster. It's not the abuse inflicted upon me. That is not the issue. The issue is with the other children."

"Is he still alive?"

"That's why I'm here. You're coming with me to witness his execution."

Elizabeth was speechless and apprehensive. Though she had witnessed the killings in Rome and many other bouts of cruelty within the coven, Megan's resolve made her uneasy. She diverted.

"What was it like feeding on the priest in Rome?"

"He was most delicious and satisfying."

"Who was he?"

"Father Sandino, another disgusting pedophile."

"Have you fed since?"

"Only on Heather at your last visit, but now I shall feed on Father O'Mallin himself."

"What's going on?"

"We're taking another trip. The car is downstairs. Grab your passport."

"Where are we going?"

"Ireland."

Megan Callaghan was born in Stockton, California, during the summer of 1980. She was immediately placed in a Catholic orphanage run by the infamous Father Virgil O'Mallin. At seven, she was adopted by the Callaghans, a young couple who lived in Eureka, just South of the giant redwoods. The Callaghans chose her solely because of her flaming red hair. They were of Irish descent, and Megan's history revealed that her biological parents were Irish. For her new parents, it was a perfect fit.

She never talked about the unbelievable and horrific suffering she endured at the hands of the monster known as Father O'Mallin. Every moment of her life, she tried to forget. In the 1998 highly publicized trial, which the Church frantically tried to suppress, O'Mallin was finally convicted and sent to prison. However, he only served four years of his seven-year sentence. Considering the atrocious crimes he had committed, it was an incredible travesty of justice. Megan's parents suspected their daughter had been sexually abused by this priest but could not bring themselves to ask her about it. Deep down, they didn't want to know. It was too much for them to bear. Instead, they celebrated her graduation from high school.

Megan was the ideal daughter: outstanding grades, polite, sweet disposition, always helping those in need—an all-around "good girl." Her parents only encountered friction when they attempted to take her to Sunday Mass. They always noticed a look of absolute hatred in her usually loving green eyes. They only saw that look on Sunday mornings, and she insisted it was nothing. When she turned 11, she politely asked her parents to allow her to seek her own truths and find her own faith. She asked with unusual wisdom, absolute conviction, and total love. Her parents conceded, and Megan never walked into a church again.

At age 15, she joined a pen pal club that encouraged students from different states and countries worldwide to write to one another. The first letter she received was from a 15-year-old boy from Portland, Oregon, less than eight hours north of her. She found the letter humble, the photograph charming, and the name 'Celsus' strangely familiar. Most interesting was the postscript, which bluntly stated, *"There is no reason to answer any other letter. I have found you, and I will see you soon. You will write to me, and you will wait for me."*

Megan's disposition is loving and sweet, but she is not someone you can approach. On the contrary, she is pretty unapproachable. Many men have tried, but all have failed. Yet, when it comes to Celsus, she expresses absolute love, loyalty, and servitude. Five years after the initial contact, and much to the sadness of her parents, she got into a car with Celsus, Nona, and Sophia. She was never seen by her family again.

Elizabeth and Megan slept through most of the flight over the North Atlantic. When they arrived in Dublin, cleared customs and immigration, and exited the airport, the sun had set in the dreary overcast Irish sky. Megan winked at Elizabeth.

"Look for a smiley face," she said.

"Huh?"

"You know what a smiley face looks like, right?"

"Yes."

"Like that one."

Elizabeth turned in the direction Megan was pointing and saw a handsome young man with curly brown hair holding up a yellow cardboard smiley face on the end of a stick. They approached him, and he spoke first.

"Lady Megan and Lady Elizabeth, I presume."

"That's correct," Megan replied.

"I'm Tim. Right this way."

"You're an American," Elizabeth said, surprised at his West Coast accent.

"It's true. You're not going to hold it against me, are you?"

The driver was obviously flirting with Elizabeth, and Megan put him in his place playfully with a warm smile.

"Your employer, who is also my boss, did not explain the protocol you must use when dealing with us?"

"My apologies. It will not happen again, my ladies."

Like a scolded dog, Tim turned and led the two women to a black Rolls Royce. He opened the door for them, threw their luggage in the trunk, and held his tongue for the entire trip. The two women could sense his frustration but were content to let him struggle silently. They barely conversed during the drive deep into the Irish countryside.

Elizabeth was a little distracted when they left Dublin. She secretly wished she could explore the city. Megan read her thoughts and spoke gently to her.

"There will be plenty of time to see the whole world, Elizabeth. Believe me. Anyway, Ireland is miserable this time of year. This is coven business, and you must stay focused. It is also a gift for you."

"What gift?"

"Your seventh visit is one of simply witnessing this man's reckoning. All you have to do is watch. I arranged that with the master, and he agreed to it."

"These visits have all been very challenging for me. How will this test me?"

"Only the master knows what will happen tonight, and he has said that your presence during this event will test your constitution."

Elizabeth believed her. A shiver traveled up her back as she remembered what happened to Father Sandino. Megan responded verbally to her memory.

"That was nothing. I have something truly unique for O'Mallin."

They traveled west for nearly two hours. It was early November, and the weather was fitting as they traveled up a narrow, twisting road. A chilly mist saturated the air, and it seemed unusually black outside. No lights indicated they were not close to any residential areas.

The car began bouncing around as the potholes increased. Megan seemed lost in a trance, and Elizabeth had no desire to disturb her. She thought about the rest of the coven and knew they were waiting in some remote location.

Sure enough, the car's headlights illuminated a large, old barn straight in front of them. *End of the road, end of reality,* she thought. The car's wheels began to spin out as Tim tried to ascend the muddy hill leading up to the barn. He got about halfway up the hill before he quit. After the car slid back a few feet, he explained the futility of continuing.

"Sorry, ladies. Looks like we'll have to abandon the car and walk up there."

Megan seemed irritated and addressed him curtly.

"I see no need for you to escort us any further. We are quite capable."

"I'm sure of it, Lady Megan, but Lord Celsus gave me strict instructions to bring you both directly to him."

Megan raised an eyebrow and conceded, "Well then, lead the way."

Surprisingly, no one slipped as they walked up the hill toward the ominous grey barn. The cold, moist air slid around Elizabeth's neck like a snake, chilling her to shiver. When they finally reached the large sliding door, the flicker of a fire could be seen radiating beneath. Tim pulled the door back, and Elizabeth's sense of reality returned to dark, fleeting memories.

There, they stood in a circle once more. Sanem, Tara, Linzie, and Sakura stood by torches in the four cardinal directions; Sakura in the East, Tara in the South, Sanem in the West, and Linzie in the North. They were all fully dressed in black, their white chokers strangely absent. Nona tended to a fire not too far from Tara. She smiled as Tim locked the door.

Celsus occupied the center of the circle with an older man sitting in a wooden chair beside him. Elizabeth noticed the master wore the same long wool trench coat he had worn when they first met. He smiled warmly as he addressed them.

"Elizabeth, Megan. How was the trip?"

Both women bowed before him. Accordingly, only Megan responded.

"My lord, the trip was easy. We slept through most of it. May I ask why *Tim* is present, my lord?"

"You may, but first, I want you to look in his eyes and see if you can figure it out yourself."

Megan moved in front of Tim and looked deep into his soul. Her eyes widened when she realized what she was seeing, and she softly verbalized her shock.

"Oh no, this cannot be. You can't be here."

Tim was just as shocked. His eyes welled with tears as he realized who he was looking at, a face from long ago.

"I don't believe it. Megan?"

The two hugged each other tightly.

"My lord," Megan said, still looking into Tim's eyes, "why have you done this? This is supposed to be my night."

"It *is* your night. Tim has been accommodating with this operation. I thought he might get some satisfaction from tonight's proceedings."

"My lord, he has suffered enough in this life. He must not see this."

The old man stood up and interrupted the conversation with an Americanized Irish accent.

"Will someone explain to me what this is all about?"

Celsus placed a hand on his shoulder, forcing him back in the chair. He revealed his impatience.

"My dearest Megan, the coven is here, Tim is here, Father O'Mallin is here, and now you are here. I have refrained from ending this lecher's life, and my patience is taxed. It is time for you to take charge now."

"Yes, my lord."

Elizabeth and Tim remained by the door while Megan approached the old man. Elizabeth could sense heat rising from Megan's body, but she wasn't sure how. It was a new, unfamiliar ability. Megan knelt down close to the old man and spoke.

"Father O'Mallin, I have waited two decades for this night."

O'Mallin was clueless about his predicament and became belligerent.

"Who are you people?"

Megan straddled him and drove her tongue in his mouth while grabbing his crotch. When she stopped kissing him, she petted his bald head with her free hand and spoke with seething hatred inches from his face.

"What's the matter, Father? Not young enough for you anymore?"

O'Mallin tried to push Megan off, but she would have none of it. She gripped his genitals hard and spoke through clenched teeth while O'Mallin moaned in pain.

"Father, I am going to get up now, and if you attempt to get out of this chair again, my sister Sanem will break one of your legs. If you speak without being asked to speak, she will slap you. If you speak to me, you will end every utterance with 'my goddess.' If you do not, I will kick you in the face. Do you understand everything I said?"

"I don't understand any of this. Someone will look for me, and you'll all be in serious trouble."

Megan took a few steps back and delivered a vicious sidekick to O'Mallin's face. His head snapped back from the force of the blow, which broke out three of his front bottom teeth and split his lip wide open. Blood slowly trickled down his chin. He was stunned, but not enough to keep him from attempting to escape.

As he rushed for the door, Sanem tripped him with her foot and sent him crashing down on the dirt floor. She grabbed him by the ankle as he struggled to get up, pulled his leg out straight, and smashed his right shin with a metal pipe. O'Mallin screamed as Tim slid down against the door and started to weep.

"That's good, Sanem," Megan said. "No one is going to be looking for you, Father. The people in your village know who you are and despise you. Who do you think helped us get you here? They have wanted you dead since they learned of your sordid past. I understand you tried to seduce a young boy since your arrival here."

Megan lifted O'Mallin by his arms and dragged him back to the chair. She then sensuously licked the blood off his chin and neck. O'Mallin started to cry as Megan closed her eyes and transported her memories into O'Mallin. He responded.

"Please, I couldn't help it. The church knew. I told them, and they knew. I couldn't stop. Please don't hurt me, please!"

Sanem marched up to Father O'Mallin and slapped him so hard he fell off the chair. She quickly set him back up, though he was clearly too stunned to know it. Megan laughed.

"How about that, my lord? He broke all three rules in less than a minute."

Celsus chuckled as he lit up a clove cigarette, his favorite. After contemplating for a moment, he exhaled the sweet smoke in O'Mallin's face and began a sarcastic discourse.

"Well, if he asks forgiveness from his god, he will be forgiven, and then he gets to do it all over again. Such is the way with you Christians. You can do whatever the fuck you want, ask for forgiveness, be forgiven, and then do it all over again. It's actually quite convenient. If I were a Christian, I would spend my entire life killing, raping, maiming, and robbing, not to mention war and genocide. I would ask for forgiveness once a week on Sunday, be forgiven, and start again on Monday. When I die, I could sit in heaven with God, Jesus, and the saints, even if I killed and tortured millions of innocent people. I don't know—seems like a pretty good deal to me."

Megan was turning. Despite all the horror and hate surrounding her, she made one last telepathic and empathetic link to Elizabeth.

I want you with me, sister.

Elizabeth inhaled sharply as Megan walked toward her and kissed her passionately. Elizabeth felt her body on fire, and she shook uncontrollably. Tim held his arms around his knees and cried next to her.

Megan turned around, walked past the master without looking at him, and approached O'Mallin. She picked up a meat hook with a rope secured around the handle. Blood poured from her eyes, and O'Mallin cried out.

"Oh God, please! Please!"

Again, Sanem was there with lightning speed, and again, she slapped him off the chair. She sat him back on the chair, his head tilted to one side. Celsus took a drag from his clove and began his taunts again.

"Oh God, please! Please! What a coward."

Megan stared at O'Mallin with bloody eyes and addressed the coven.

"Undress him. I want him to feel as a child would feel—completely vulnerable."

Linzie and Sakura rapidly undressed the old man. He screamed in agony when they removed the shoe from his broken leg. They took his pants off and placed him back in the chair. Two bones were sticking out the side of his calf. Megan looked hideous, and her bloody eyes began to glow deep orange, like raging hot lava. She addressed the coven again after they took their places.

"Keep him conscious. That's all I ask. Keep him conscious."

No one responded, but Elizabeth knew they would use their powers to keep him as aware as possible, no matter what Megan did. Megan fixed her hideous stare on O'Mallin while throwing the rope over a crossbeam directly above him. She handed the end of the rope to Sanem and approached O'Mallin, hook in hand.

"Father Virgil O'Mallin, I sentence you to physical death this night for the raping and molestation of hundreds of innocent children. Some were given to you by trusting but ignorant parents for education in the ways of your religion. Others, like Tim and I, had the misfortune of ending up in your orphanage, in your care. You are the result of your religion's rules against nature. However, this is no excuse for your appalling actions, and you will not be shown an ounce of mercy this night. I sentence your soul to Lili for the spiritual killings of innocent children, some of whom have since taken their own lives. You will suffer a second death, a death of finality. Do you have any words before I carry out your execution? Don't forget to end your lies with 'my goddess.'"

His voice quivered as he responded, "I am guilty of the crimes you spoke of. But God has forgiven me a long time ago. I have made amends for my soul, and I know I will reside in the kingdom of our heavenly Father. As to ending my response, I will end it as such—may God forgive all of you."

Megan, true to her word, kicked him square in the face again, knocking out two more teeth and flipping his chair over backward. O'Mallin was unconscious. The master laughed and addressed her.

"My dear Megan, before you begin, may I speak with him briefly?"

"Of course, my lord," she replied, looking quite demonic at this point as she knelt down and placed her hand gently upon the old man's forehead. "Wake, Father O'Mallin, wake."

The priest coughed and spit up blood. He was obviously terrified but still belligerent and utterly ignorant of his fate.

"You are all monsters!" he said with a lisp, as one would expect from someone now missing his front teeth.

Celsus began pacing around him counterclockwise. He contemplated for a moment before responding.

"Yes, it is true. We are monsters, but we do not pretend to be spiritual leaders as you do. Look at you—liar—hypocrite—destroyer—monster—both Catholic priest and pedophile, in charge of children—a living nightmare. Megan has waited for this moment for over 20 years. Her wrath has become its own living entity. We shall witness a unique act of revenge I have desired to see for quite some time. Father O'Mallin, you sure picked the wrong girl to fuck with," he said with a mock Irish accent.

Megan allowed Celsus to finish and gripped the back of O'Mallin's neck for leverage as she slowly inserted the meat hook into his anus. He screamed in agony as she twisted the hook inward until it would move no more. The master taunted him again.

"What a baby. Imagine what your Christ went through. Imagine what your victims went through. Have you no dignity?"

Tim had reached the breaking point and cried out.

"My lord, Celsus, may I please wait in the car?"

"Of course. Don't worry—we'll take care of everything."

Tim hurriedly unlocked the door and ran out into the night. Before shutting the door and locking it again, Elizabeth noticed a cold rain had started to fall. Megan held O'Mallin down and asked Nona to bring her a mallet.

Nona walked gracefully toward Megan and presented a large rubber mallet as if she were presenting a scepter to a queen. With great ferocity and determination, Megan gripped the mallet and swung down hard on the handle of the meat hook. The resulting blow sent the hook's point crashing through the right side of his hip, shattering the bone. It protruded grotesquely, and O'Mallin again passed out from the trauma.

Megan threw the mallet across the room and began stroking his head. She was petting him as one would pet a cat. She then bent over and licked the blood off the hook's point. She savored the taste as she commanded her family.

"Make him conscious."

Celsus and the rest of the women concentrated on him. He moaned in agony as Megan stood up and turned toward Sanem. No words were spoken as Sanem grabbed the rope and, in a fantastic feat of strength, with no pulleys to assist her, pulled O'Mallin five feet off the ground until he swung freely over the center of the room. She secured the rope to a support beam, and for a few silent moments, they all watched the naked old man swinging from his asshole by a large meat hook.

Megan steadied him as he cried out in misery. His body twitched and convulsed as he pleaded again.

"Please. Please."

She lifted the old man's head by his chin and licked the blood off his face, ensuring he could see her demonic eyes up close.

"Deliver me from Lucifer! God forgive me!" he pleaded.

Celsus interjected.

"You see, this is what I'm talking about. Didn't you say that your God has already forgiven you? Having second thoughts on that, are we? Indeed, *Lugh* was a hero to the ancient Irish. He was once worshipped here as a benevolent force in life. Your religion eventually demonized him and called him Lucifer. But then again, your religion does that to everyone. Your brainwashed zombie missionaries always tell people how wrong they are. Look at yourself, Father. You are a *real* evil in this world."

The former priest somehow found the strength to argue, though he could not look up at the master.

"The missionaries provided food, clothing, shelter, education, and deliverance from ignorance and darkness!"

Celsus knelt down and spoke condescendingly.

"Yes, and in return, they gave up their traditions, language, land, and of course—their souls. You know what amazes me? In the last 55 years, I know over 4,400 of your fellow priests have committed the same disgusting crimes. Over 10,000 allegations, only 250 convictions, and a little over 100 prison sentences, including yours—and that's just in the United States and only in the last 55 years! Imagine how many got away with it! What are the *true* numbers in this country, worldwide, and throughout history? Hundreds of thousands, if not millions, I imagine. It's a monumental evil. How does your organization keep going? How do you keep it out of the press? Any other corporation with those kinds of criminal statistics would have been crushed years ago."

O'Mallin, hanging from the hook and bleeding from his wounds, managed a challenging reply.

"I remember studying the writings of a man named Celsus back in the seminary. He also hated Christianity. Such a lofty title you have given yourself, *Lord Celsus*."

Megan grabbed the priest by the ear and turned his head to face Celsus as she admonished him.

"You will treat him with respect!"

"I will not," he replied defiantly.

Megan held his head steady as she brought her fist crashing down on his nose, breaking it. She repeated herself as blood spurted out from the new wound.

"You will respect him!"

Celsus intervened as more blood departed from the priest.

"It's alright, Megan. I just need to vent for a moment. Father O'Mallin—unlike you, I am not pretending to be anyone. I am the same Celsus you studied in the seminary.

Believing or not believing doesn't matter. Will you choose to live your last moments protecting your corrupt and hypocritical religion, desperately and illogically refuting the truth of nature? Or will you admit to your religion's awesome atrocities—of which there are so many, they are uncountable?"

O'Mallin barely managed to reply.

"There are good people, good Christians. I am not one, but there are good Christians."

Celsus looked up momentarily, took a drag from his clove, and nodded.

"Yes, we have a point of agreement. There are good Christians. I will not argue this. My problem is that your religious leaders have never really acknowledged the suffering, torture, and executions of so *many* innocent people. I have a problem with this. The list is very long, Father. Hundreds of thousands were killed during your witch hunts in Europe, the Inquisition, the St. Bartholomew's Day Massacres, the treatment of non-Christian populations the world over, not to mention the unspeakable horror of your institutionalized pedophilia, and on and on. Your magnanimous religion's mandated killing and destruction are rivaled only by the Islamic jihads mandated by the Koran. Please forgive me, Megan. This is your moment and your stage."

Megan nodded to Celsus in acknowledgment, let the priest's head fall, and walked to the fire. From it, she produced a long red hot ice pick with a wooden handle. Carrying it back to O'Mallin with great purpose, she spun him around like a side of beef, grabbed his flaccid penis in her hand, and inserted the pick about two inches through the opening.

A wisp of smoke rose up in the air as O'Mallin screamed and flopped around hysterically. She left it in for a few seconds and then pulled it back out with burning tissue attached. Then, as if it were a roasted marshmallow, she pulled the substance off with her fingers, burning them in the process, and ate it. O'Mallin's body convulsed and contorted.

Megan returned the ice pick to the fire and looked to Nona, who responded by handing her a four-foot strand of barbed wire. Megan turned and approached O'Mallin while winding the end of the wire around her right hand She circled the wretched priest, who continued to twitch and convulse from the mutilation of his penis. She seemed to be analyzing the best angle of attack, and her disposition was like that of the abyss—cold, black, unending, and ominous.

She stopped directly behind O'Mallin and delivered nine vicious blows to O'Mallin's legs and back. He screamed in agony as his flesh was torn to ribbons. O'Mallin passed out on the third strike, his body swinging in the air like a dead fish on a hook. When she finished, she wrapped the wire around his head, a sarcastic tribute to Christ's crown of thorns. She then commanded Sakura without emotion.

"Cauterize the wounds."

Sakura went to the fire pit and pulled out the red-hot ice pick. Before setting to work, she stopped as the coven bowed their heads and concentrated. O'Mallin screamed out in agony.

"Stop! For God's sake, please stop!"

The master's antagonistic dialogue continued.

"The third commandment: Thou shall not take the name of the Lord thy God in vain. I think you did just that— blasphemer—hypocrite."

Before O'Mallin could respond, Sakura began rolling the burning pick over his fresh wounds. He screamed and thrashed about until Megan held his body steady. Sakura was thorough and seemed to enjoy the task immensely. Again, O'Mallin passed out, and Megan was clearly agitated.

"You *will* stay with us!"

O'Mallin came to but was delirious. Megan reached down and picked up his right hand. She looked at it for a few seconds before addressing him.

"I remember what you did to me with these fingers."

With that said, she began chewing off and eating his fingers individually. She did the same thing with his other hand. He stayed conscious and screamed hysterically the entire time. When Megan was finished, she looked at Sakura. Sakura grabbed the pick from the fire once more and cauterized the stumps on O'Mallin's hands.

O'Mallin prayed. He was delirious. Saliva and blood dribbled from his damaged mouth and nose as he weakly tried to recite the Lord's Prayer. Celsus was not pleased.

"Megan, I adore you, but I cannot tolerate this. I have the one instrument you asked me to bring. I'm not telling you to expedite your ritual in any way, but could you please stop his verbal pollution. I am having difficulty contributing to his staying alert because of it, and I certainly don't enjoy it."

O'Mallin yelled out as best as he could.

"I will be a martyr. You are doing God's work and don't even know it. I shall be redeemed, and my soul restored."

At this proclamation, Megan and Celsus laughed with abandon. Elizabeth noticed that her eyes had not changed, nor had her disposition, yet she laughed like a young woman in love. The sound of her beautiful laughter and the visual of her demonic eyes were utterly incomprehensible. Elizabeth started to grow faint. When Celsus finally stopped laughing and coughing, he spoke to O'Mallin about the cold reality of the future.

"No one will ever know what happened to you. You will simply disappear, and no one will know or care, for that matter. As to redemption and restitution, you lost all that the first time you destroyed an innocent child's spirit. No, sir, the only thing waiting for you in the afterlife is Lili's stomach. I think she will enjoy you very much."

Celsus then reached into his coat pocket and produced a small metal object. Elizabeth initially thought it was a pen until he removed the protective cap from the end. It was a scalpel. Megan took it and addressed her master.

"I will not cut out his tongue, for his screaming is the most beautiful music I have ever heard. However, I will ease your suffering, my lord."

Megan found the large rubber mallet she had thrown away earlier, walked up to the mangled O'Mallin, and smashed him square on the chin with a swift, perfectly placed uppercut. It broke his jaw. He could not finish the prayer but could clearly still voice his agonies.

Elizabeth became detached and noticed the tone of his scream had changed considerably from before. She watched as Megan knelt beneath O'Mallin's head and opened her mouth to drink the blood from his new wounds. After a few minutes, she rose to her feet. She approached Elizabeth, blood dripping from her chin, her eyes glowing with savage revenge.

Megan kissed her and gently probed her mouth in the process. As Elizabeth tasted the blood of O'Mallin, she feared the hunger would come upon her again. She dreaded the unforgiving pain and hoped it would not return. Celsus interrupted.

"Repressing Elizabeth's hunger and contributing to O'Mallin's awareness is more than I can handle. Carry on, Megan—it is time."

Elizabeth found Megan exceptionally beautiful, even in her terrible state of being. Sensing her thoughts and feelings, Megan spoke silently.

Elizabeth, I do this for the children whose lives were destroyed by this wretched monster.

Megan then turned her attention back to O'Mallin. He hung from the beam, severely mutilated but alive, as she issued another command.

"Sanem, lower him to the ground and then secure the rope again."

"As you wish, my lady."

Sanem gently lowered the battered man to the ground. The stumps of O'Mallin's hands touched first as he fell over on his left side, the point of the meat hook sticking out grotesquely from his right hip.

Elizabeth understood why Megan was the XO. Megan stood perfectly still, like a statue, her unbroken gaze a magic vice further crushing O'Mallin's already shattered reality. He began to choke as dark streams of blood slowly oozed from her hateful eyes. Linzie placed her knee on the side of his head so that he couldn't move as Sakura returned with the red-hot ice pick.

With bloody eyes, Megan knelt down, grabbed O'Mallin by the base of his shriveled, mutilated penis and scrotum, and sliced them off with the scalpel.

O'Mallin cried hopelessly, now wishing for death. Megan ignored him, took the hot pick from Sakura, and skewered the old man's detached bloody parts. For Elizabeth, the smell of burning flesh finally overpowered her, and she vomited. Megan devoured the priest's former instruments of evil with no more emotion than if she were sliding food off a shish kebab.

The coven was held captive by Megan's tremendous power as she cauterized the fresh wound between his legs, which caused O'Mallin to vomit violently. Celsus was filled with pride and affection.

"I love you, Megan."

She turned toward her master and smiled, responding without words.

I love you, my lord—forever.

Celsus looked at Elizabeth in curiosity and asked her nonchalantly, "How do you feel?"

"I am nauseated, my lord."

"Yes, I imagine you are. This is without question a very intense operation."

Commanded in silence by the XO, Linzie released O'Mallin's head. As he tried pathetically to prop up his weakened body on one elbow, Megan gripped his knee with one hand and the protruding tibia and fibula bones with the other. She tore the foot free from his leg with demonic strength and flung it across the room.

O'Mallin immediately passed out. A large flap of skin, exposed tendons, and most of the calf muscle remained attached to his bleeding leg. Linzie reached down quickly and cinched off the bleeding with her hands while the coven tried desperately to revive him.

Linzie yelled, "You're not dead. Wake up, Father! Wake!"

As he regained consciousness, he shuddered at the sickening sound of Megan's lower jaw unlocking from her skull. He was frozen in terror at the monstrous sight as she opened her mouth to an impossible circumference and deep-throated the entire end of his mutilated leg. She fed gregariously.

This was the grotesque end for Father O'Mallin. He tried desperately to drag himself away, but Sanem jumped to the rope and pulled with all her might. The result was a mutilated old pedophile, impaled and swinging from a meat hook. Megan was attached below his knee sucking profusely.

Nona walked toward this visual abomination with a can of gasoline in one hand and a small shale rock in the other. She dumped the fuel over O'Mallin's head and shoulders.

Megan continued to feed and shifted her bloody eyes toward the master—a signal for the grand finale. Celsus grinned, took one last hit from his clove, and flicked it on O'Mallin's head. His body flopped around as he burned while Megan continued to suck away every possible drop of blood.

Elizabeth watched in awe as Megan completed her feeding, unlocked the barn door, and walked off into the cold, rainy night. Elizabeth found her more beautiful than anything she had ever seen. It made her think of an old Irish mythological creature.

Leanhaun Shee.

Nona knelt down directly beneath O'Mallin's body and chanted. She held the little shale rock in her left hand and made downward waving motions with her right hand as if fanning something into the rock. For a moment, Elizabeth forgot everything and was hypnotized by Nona's strange actions.

Suddenly, Elizabeth found herself connected with Megan. She could feel herself in the cold, muddy field, yet something was very different—the XO had utterly lost her mind.

The next thing Elizabeth experienced was flying home from Ireland. She had no recollection of leaving the barn, getting to the airport, or boarding the plane. This lapse of memory frightened her greatly. She looked around and could see both Sakura and Linzie sound asleep. She knew they were the only coven members who made the trip back. She was in the first-class cabin and, looking over at Sakura's little movie screen, could see by the airplane's GPS system that they were just West of the southern tip of Greenland.

Sakura opened her eyes and looked at Elizabeth without moving a muscle. Telepathy seemed to be the primary method of communication on this trip.

Yes, my lady?

Where is everyone?

Linzie and I are tasked to escort you home. The rest are immersed in helping Megan. She has tried to kill herself twice since she left the barn. She will surely try again.

Elizabeth felt as if someone had stabbed her in the heart. She spoke aloud, forgetting herself.

"Are you telling me she might die?"

Elizabeth, you must calm yourself and be disciplined to speak without words.

I cannot fathom losing her. I love her so much.

We all love her. They are doing everything in their power. Nona is with her. I believe she will be alright.

How can you be so sure? She might die.

It is accurate, and the loss would devastate us all. But you would still see her. She would still be with us.

Elizabeth did not respond. Her thoughts went blank, forcing her away from the memories of the barn and the possibility of Megan's death. Within minutes, she was sound asleep...the seventh visit concluded.

FAMILY HISTORY

A whole year had passed since her first meeting with him. This cold December night, she stood on the curb waiting. A brisk wind carried tiny crystalline flakes of snow through the trees. The moon was voluptuous, and her body knew the significance of this night.

She closed her eyes and let the cold wind caress her face as she listened to the dead leaves stirring on the street. She felt a small measure of happiness as she saw her child dive into a pile of leaves, her faithful beagle nipping at her feet. Before the haunting could truly blossom, the long black car dispelled it.

The house was dark except for a flickering light inside the great coven room. This was a warm fire, to be sure, and Elizabeth knew he was waiting for her.

Nona opened the door, kissed her on the cheek, and took her coat.

"He is in the coven room, my lady."

"Thank you, Nona. Where is everyone?"

"It's just the three of us. Everyone else is spending time at their own houses tonight. You can stop worrying about Megan. She is her perfect self again."

The room seemed alive from the illumination of a steady fire in the great hearth. The master sat motionless, just as he had the night of her first visit. From his high-backed throne, he motioned her to him with two lazy fingers. She complied and knelt on her knees before him, eyes cast downward, waiting for his commands.

He stood before her, and his royal blue robe fell open. For a moment, he did nothing but gaze into the flames. The atmosphere was peaceful and quiet. Then he slid his hand behind Elizabeth's head and gently pulled her toward him. He was engorged entirely, and she devoured him with great hunger. His calves were tense with pleasure, and he undulated to her rhythms.

"Such talent, such love—I've missed you so much," he said.

She responded by sucking harder, losing all sense of things, the room, and time itself. At the moment of truth, he whispered to her.

"Yes, lover, that's it. Take it—and all the memories that go with it."

He ejaculated so hard that she gagged from the force of his semen. He did not release his grip on her hair but pulled her to her feet. When she opened her eyes, she saw the familiar stars retreating into his black eyes. Fear gripped her soul with the monstrous memories of Rome and the brutality unleashed on Heather. As always, he knew her thoughts and soothed her.

"My beautiful Elizabeth, I will not hurt you this night."

He sat on his throne before the fire and pulled her down on his lap like a little girl.

"I have a bedtime story for you. Quiet now and listen."

On cue, Nona handed him a silver chalice containing wine and blood. Elizabeth curled her hands around his neck and snuggled with him. She could feel his strong heartbeat thudding as he took a deep drink and offered the chalice to her. The iron-scented brew filled her body and soul.

He gently took the cup from her hands, placed it on the floor, and held her very tight for a moment. When his arms finally relaxed, he told of the great curse that had plagued them for thousands of years.

Δ

Celsus speaks

The city-state of Babylon in all its glory during the reign of Hammurabi—can you believe, nearly 3,800 years ago? We were all there. Of course, we were known by different names then, but for the sake of simplicity, I'll use everyone's current name when telling the story except ours. I was called Somro back then, and you were known as Cala.

I had nearly everything—wealth, power, eight beautiful slave wives, and the respect of Babylon's greatest king, Hammurabi. But I wanted more. I was a greedy, young, enterprising sorcerer with much talent and corruption.

I can still smell it and hear it. Can you, Cala? Babylon was so beautiful and seductive, a goddess unto herself. According to modern calculations, the year was 1764 BC, three days before the end of the Akitu, the New Year festival. King Hammurabi was occupied with a war against a formidable coalition of enemies. I was dead serious about taking Ulla's position as high counselor to the King. In three days, if everything went right, I would have been the new high counselor of my beloved city, or so I thought.

The night before the conclusion of the Akitu, I performed an extremely dangerous ritual to complete a monumental goal. I had discovered the most sought-after power of all, physical immortality. How I made this discovery is another story for another time.

There was no way my operation could work unless I possessed one last magical ingredient: the blood and semen of a virgin male mixed with an indefinable substance within the womb of our soul-devouring Mother, Lili.

The boy's name was Abu, and he had finally come to trust me. I almost felt sorry for him, but knowing his life would end horribly in a few nights was of little consequence to me. My lust for power overcame any such ridiculous feelings. I kept him happy and healthy for Lili for two years.

I purchased him two years before The Event. A poor single woman in the central marketplace did not have the means to raise him. At nine years old and severely undernourished, he was useless, certainly not worth the five shekels of silver I paid out for him. To the mother, it was a fortune. She left without saying a word.

As the boy cried, I could read the mother's thoughts. I had the ability even back then, though it was nowhere near as honed as today. The mother was sad, but it was a simple matter of survival. Such were the ways of this great city, and it seems not much has changed since then. It mattered not as I grabbed the boy by his frail little wrist and led him to his destiny, my home.

Frightened and hungry, he was perfect for my needs. It would be at least 20 months before he would start showing signs of puberty. By then, I would have him as fit as an 11-year-old boy could possibly be, prime for Lili.

That first night, I lined up all eight of my delicious wives and asked him which one he liked best. He chose you, Cala. You were a goddess. You had long, silky black hair, playful brown almond-shaped eyes, soft, voluptuous flesh, and large, beautiful breasts. You were worth more than your weight in gold. How I loved the nights I spent with you. I digress.

You were part of a payment from a wealthy merchant living in the city's north. I killed this merchant's older brother, giving this man firstborn inheritance rights. I used simple sorcery and received a hundred shekels of silver and you for payment. Not bad for one night of work.

I told you to befriend Abu and instructed you never to have sex with him. I told you that if you did, I would cut off your arms. You knew this was no idle threat. Since you knew I could read thoughts, you would not dare. The rest of the girls were warned as well. All obeyed, and he was never left alone.

I remember you asked me about Lili. You reasoned that she would sense the boy's frustrations and mount him as we slept. I was annoyed at your brazen insolence and intelligence but explained that Abu's bed would be encased in a protective circle.

You persisted with your informality and actually asked me what my plans were. Do you remember me losing control? Do you remember me grabbing you by the throat? I screamed at you not to inquire about my goals and told you that if you opened your mouth again without my permission, I would sew it shut. You trembled with fear. Even then, your vulnerability excited me greatly. I remember kissing you, telling you to obey me, and telling you that Abu would worship you as if you were Inanna herself. How I relished your uncontrollable quivering.

It took two years of preparation for that one special night that would change us forever. You will remember, Cala.

It was then that Elizabeth and Celsus held a perfect psychic link. Vocalized reminiscing became unnecessary as they gazed into the fire. She closed her eyes and embraced the full memory as he continued.

Three nights, and it would all be over. There I sat, contemplating, gloating. The boy slept peacefully while you stroked his hair. Your room was next to mine, allowing me to monitor everything. I laughed out loud, and you looked up at me.

"My lord?" you asked.

"Nothing," I said, grinning.

I had the world in my hand, and I would control the destiny of many with what I knew. Evil consumed me. I planned to submit the elixir of life to Hammurabi in return for the position as his high counselor. It would have changed the course of history. The King would give me the position, and we would rule the world forever.

As the appointed time drew near, I began to feel paranoid. An older man by the name of Ulla was the current high counselor. He was my competition and a powerful sorcerer in his own right. He knew I would challenge him before the King during the Akitu celebrations. I was surprised that nothing had happened yet. I dismissed my fear with logic. After all, I was the only one who knew what would happen. My house was surrounded by powerful protective magic I had learned as a child. Not even Ulla could penetrate this wall. If he was going to do something, it would have to be in the realm of the physical. Tara and Sanem, my two bodyguards, always protected me. They were vigilant and dangerous.

I could have had male brutes for guards, but there was something incredibly enticing about owning female warriors. I knew how to use a sword, but Sanem was an expert, and Tara was brutal. Both women were physically equal in strength. They were stronger than most men, and most men feared and desired them for how they looked. I never left the house without having either of them with me. They were like sisters to each other even back then.

A blacksmith had purchased Tara from an Egyptian trader. She had many of the same features she has today: tall, muscular, black hair, black eyes, black skin, thick, sensuous lips, and a perfect ass. I watched her kill a soldier the night she came to be mine.

This soldier purchased weapons from the smith when he noticed Tara cleaning some blades. He cracked some lewd joke about her lips. The soldier and the smith began to argue about her strength and a wager was struck. If the soldier could pin Tara against her will, the smith would hand over his finest swords. If she could fend off or pin the soldier, then the soldier would pay the smith five extra shekels of silver.

The bet was made, and a meeting was arranged by a field near my home at sunset. I happened to be enjoying the evening when I heard the fight.

It was fierce, and Tara was out of her mind. She went into some kind of crazy battle rage, overpowered the soldier, and began choking him with her bare hands, shrieking madly. It sounded hideous. Sanem ran outside and asked me if everything was all right. I told her to follow me to the commotion.

Through the tall brush, we watched as the smith, terrified at how things were going, whipped Tara with a rope, but it was too late. The soldier was dead. Tara had crawled under the table like a guilty dog, hoping its master would forgive it for whatever wrongdoings it had incurred. She was bleeding from the fight, and her master was hysterical.

You see, the penalty for murder was death. If a slave committed the murder, not only would the slave be put to death, but the slave's owner would suffer significant material loss to the victim's family and public humiliation. In this case, his name and business would have been finished.

Judging by the smith's disposition, I saw he was versed in the law. He was crying and babbling like an idiot when we approached. Tara came out from under the table to appease him. The smith smacked her face with an open hand and whipped her again. She just stood there and took it. She could have killed him much quicker than the soldier. Still, she was loyal to this pathetic waste and took his blows without any protest.

I ordered him to stop and look around. By some strange fortune, Sanem and I were the only ones who had witnessed the killing. I told him I would care for the body for a small fee. He looked at his weaponry and said I could have anything I wanted. I told him that Tara was the only price for my silence. He was greatly relieved and accepted my terms. His exact words were, "Take the bitch."

We wrapped the soldier's body in blankets and headed for the Euphrates. Sanem carried the body on her back for nearly two miles before we reached the river's edge. It was a feat of superhuman strength, and she wasn't even made yet. She tied some heavy rocks to the corpse and, before delivering the body to the Great Serpent, sliced off the index finger from his right hand and gave it to Tara. Later, the petrified finger would hang from a gold chain around Tara's neck. Their friendship was born that very night.

As we walked home, I told Tara that her sole purpose was to serve, protect, and please me. When we arrived at my home, our joining was as fierce as her fight. It took me an entire day to recover from her gratitude.

Sanem, in contrast, was a slave of the palace yet certainly looked and exuded high-born status. There was never a rivalry between the two women. In fact, there has never been a rivalry between any of you, ever.

Sanem was from Assur in the North. She was educated in Hammurabi's court, skilled in combat, and a perfect warrior. Even back then, her arms were ripped from the daily lifting and transportation of materials used in my experiments. She had incredible eyes, intimidating to those who did not know her. She could excite a man sexually with a glance or make him shrink in fear. Her eyes, body, skill, intellect, and power were, and still are, her greatest gifts.

She was a gift from Hammurabi. I received her for accurately predicting his enemies' strategic intentions during a critical time in the war. Ulla wildly protested Sanem's departure from the palace, but his protests fell on deaf ears. She was mine for keeps. Ulla hated me because she was now my property. Having the king's favor and attention incensed him even more.

Sanem confessed that he had taken her against her will—an impossible task, to be sure. To do it, he slipped powerful herbs into her food while the King held court. She could not move while he performed the lewdest of humiliations upon her face and body. She spoke candidly about the ordeal, saying he could not achieve an erection. She said he sweated, grunted, and beat her about the face and body with his small, impotent penis. The insult to her dignity was so grave that she told no one during her stay at the royal palace. She told me her greatest wish was to see me usurp the disgusting counselor and bring her back to her rightful station in life.

Every woman in the King's palace either idolized or envied her. Hammurabi let go of her in a most honorable way. He did it because of her intimidating nature and the jealousy of the highest-ranking wife within his harem

My eight slave wives, including you, Cala, were extraordinary in their ways and loyal to no one but me. It was an immensely hedonistic life, but I was never satisfied. I had to have it all, no matter whom I stepped on or killed. It was Babylon. It was *her* growing within me. I burned for power and was possessed by never-ending want.

One night, as we neared The Event, I fell asleep when I heard Megan's voice.

"There is a woman here to see you, my lord."

"Who is it?" I asked.

"I do not recognize her. She says she has traveled from Nippur to see you."

"Bring her."

I was curious because this woman had come from my birth city. I hadn't seen the city in years, and there were plenty of sorcerers there to handle the darkest needs of both Babylon and Nippur. Sanem opened the hide of my bed chamber and introduced her.

"Lord Somro, Lady Siraba of Nippur."

She was robbed and veiled in black. The only things visible were a pair of striking blue eyes and a silver amulet that hung from her neck, which revealed my personal seal for reasons unknown to me at the time. She was small and appeared to glide across the room as she walked toward me.

Sanem was understandably apprehensive and followed close behind. Lady Siraba stopped about five feet before me and unveiled her face. I completely lost my senses for a moment. Her eyes told of an ancient secret that I could feel at the core of my being. I tried to read her thoughts but came up against a powerful mental barrier. She was a first-rate sorceress, and I had no clue what was happening.

"It is pointless to try and read my thoughts," she said in a soft melodic voice. "I have come from Nippur to save you from disaster."

"Who are you?" I asked, with no authority in my voice.

"When the time is right, you will know who I am."

I gazed at the amulet around her neck. I thought this seal was one of a kind, and I wanted to ask her about it, but my ego would not allow it. I was mesmerized and clearly losing my grip on reality. She continued.

"If you proceed with this ritual, it will be the end of your life and perhaps the death of your soul."

"What are you talking about?" I asked, regaining my composure.

"You do not have to pretend with me. I have seen your evil. You are a powerful magician, of that there is no doubt, but you do not respect the laws of the universe. This false sense of invulnerability shall take you into the abyss where the waiting Lili will devour you."

Then I noticed Sanem's curious look.

"Leave us, Sanem," I said. "Make sure no one gets near my chamber."

"As you wish, my lord," she said obediently.

I gave her a nod, assuring her I was in no danger. There was something familiar about this strange woman that made me feel unexplainably safe. It was like knowing without reason.

"What do you want?" I asked.

"I want to show you Inanna's love," she said, looking right through me with her sky-blue eyes. I replied with condescending resolve.

"That is a nice gesture coming from a lady of the magic arts, but as you can see, I am surrounded by girls who keep my spear clean daily. I am quite tired now and would like to get some sleep. I will have Sakura prepare a bed for you. We can speak more tomorrow. Since you are so clever with my business, Lady Siraba, you must also know there is nothing you can say or do to stop me."

"You are right. There is nothing I can do to stop you, but perhaps I can open your eyes a little. Perhaps you will change your mind before your spirit is swallowed by eternal darkness."

"I don't even know you. You should have stayed in Nippur. I believe you have made a mistake," I said to her candidly.

Then she opened both of her palms before me and started chanting. I tried to yell for Sanem, but my sound was muffled and cut off. I could not move. Her eyes were glowing like blinding white lights. I was initially afraid, but suddenly, the fear left my body and was replaced by the sensation of being kissed. I felt immense, overwhelming contentment and couldn't see anything but a soft white brilliance before me. It was beautiful.

I realized I was making love, and although I did not know what it was, I could feel tears streaming down my face. Then I felt a deep pain in my chest, for I knew it would not last. I couldn't tell you how long the experience lasted. Time itself had stopped.

Through the white light, the familiar surroundings of my bed chamber began to materialize. Sanem must have heard my cry. There she was, lying on the floor a few feet from my bed, masturbating. Watching Sanem make love to herself is one of the world's great wonders. Everything was so beautiful in the soft white light, and my body shook from the most powerful orgasm I had ever experienced.

I could not move or speak. I just closed my eyes and let the effects of the diminishing warmness put me to sleep. I always believed I had made love to the goddess Inanna herself. It took over 270 years to understand what happened to me that night. Had Siraba's legacy survived, we would not be here today.

When I woke, the morning sun was streaming into my room. The rays fell upon Sanem's body like a supernatural golden gown. She was still lying in the same spot.

"What happened last night?" I inquired.

Sanem stirred a little, opened her eyes, and began stretching her taut body in the morning sun. She seemed confused when she realized she had been lying on the floor in my bed chamber. We looked at each other with questions in our eyes, unable to speak. It was you, Cala, who broke the silence.

"My lord, may we go outside and play?"

"Wait here a moment," I said, finally getting something out of my mouth.

I let down all three hides, one covering the entrance to your room, one covering the access to the ritual room, and the other covering the entry into the hallway. I looked at Sanem again.

"What happened last night?"

"My lord, I heard you cry out to me. I ran as fast as I could. When I came into your room, I saw …"

I grabbed Sanem by the shoulders, looked into her eyes, and commanded.

"What? What did you see?"

"I'm not sure, my lord, but it was intense. I thought I was dreaming. I saw you and something. It made me wet—like when I take you in my mouth."

She knew as much as I did. So I asked if you had seen a strange woman that morning, to which you replied you had not. I was getting impatient.

"Sanem, get the rest of the girls in here now."

When they were all before me, I put the same question to them.

"Did you see our guest leave the house this morning or last night?"

The answer was the same. Frustrated, I dismissed all eight of you, but you returned to annoy me.

"My lord, may we go outside and play?"

"It is two days before the Akitu. I want Abu inside. If you want to play, play in the house."

You had this gorgeous, disappointed look on your face. I loved that look. Some things never change.

I had been lying, telling you both that he would perform the rite of manhood in private on the last night of the Akitu. By this time, Abu was so horny he was walking around with a constant erection. Whenever he tried to touch himself, you or one of the other girls would beat his hand with a stick. I found this to be very cruel as it went on for months. The girls could barely restrain themselves, and your affection for him had grown considerably.

I had to find out what had happened the night before, so I went into the ritual room and took down a clay bowl used for divination. This room was off-limits to anyone unless I brought them in myself. This is where I would perform the operation, now only two nights away.

I filled the bowl with water and cut my hand to allow nine drops of blood to fall into it. I cleared my mind and began to see shapes in the water. I saw Tara, Nona, and Sanem. Sanem was crying, and Nona was dead. Then I saw Ulla's face. He was laughing. As anger stirred my spirit, the picture began to fade. You must be completely blank in the mind and free of emotions to divine this way. Once any feelings occur, the vision will fade.

I cleared my mind and again saw Ulla's ugly face. But this time, it was different. This second vision did not follow the usual patterns of water divination.

When I used divination this way, I viewed visions of the past, present, and future. By gently focusing on the question, my mind materialized the event as it happened—much like the remote control of today's digital media: fast-forward, review, and play. I have had no need for such devices since that first life. Everything is done with the mind alone now. Back then, the diving bowl was simply a screen to view a vision. It is always the mind that really produces the images. You can see anything you want but can't communicate through the water, which is why this second vision was so unusual.

Ulla's eyes stared back at me. When I moved my eyes, his eyes followed. I thought that he must be divining at the same time I was and that some sort of window phenomenon must have come about. Then something strange happened.

Ulla's face began to melt. Not once did his eyes leave mine, nor did they blink. His face began to drip off his head. This was not Ulla. This was not human. The face was in a horrid state. Muscles and tendons started to hang from the partly exposed skull when slowly the face began to reconstruct itself. The eyes closed, and I was compelled by an unknown force to watch the transformation.

I could not speak or move for the second time in 12 hours. However, this was quite different from the night before. I was not feeling any comfort or warmth, only terror. As the face began to take shape, the anxiety grew stronger in me. Because I was a magician of the highest order, I refused to let fear overtake me. I came to my senses and was about to scream a banishing when suddenly the transformation was complete.

I held my tongue because the divination bowl held the most alluring woman I had ever seen. Her eyes were still closed, her naked voluptuous body covered in oil. She began caressing her large, slippery breasts, pinching her nipples. I could hear her breathing, and she moaned in a deep voice when she exhaled. My cock was so hard it was painful.

With her eyes still closed, she began caressing her thighs. I could smell the sweet-scented oil as she smeared it around her legs. It was maddening. Her beauty transfixed me as she slid a long, slender finger within herself. The room was getting hot. Beads of sweat dripped down my face, stinging my eyes, but I would not dare wipe them or blink for fear of losing the ominous vision.

First, her glistening lips parted, and then her eyes opened. They were glowing red and staring right through me. I came instantly. My semen shot into the diving bowl as if magnetically drawn in. I couldn't stop the orgasm; it felt like I was being ripped apart.

I repeatedly screamed a banishing until the pulling and ripping between my legs stopped. On the water's surface, a smile came slowly across her lips, now dripping with saliva. The vision clouded over, and the image disappeared. I collapsed on the floor, unconscious. It was my first encounter with Lili.

I was unconscious for hours. You were taught never to disturb me while I was in the ritual room. When I woke up, it was already dark. I felt my way to the entrance, lifted the hide, and saw torches lit in my bed chamber. Food and water had been placed on the table next to my bed. My strength was sapped. I called for Megan, my first slave.

"Yes, my lord," she said as she entered the room.

"What happened today?"

"Nothing unusual, my lord. Cala, Abu, and the other girls took care of their daily chores and played inside all day. I sent Linzie to the market for food, my lord."

"That's it? Nobody heard anything strange coming from the ritual room?"

"No, my lord."

"Alright, Megan, tell Linzie and Nona to sleep with me tonight and tell Tara and Sanem to be especially vigilant. There is evil around us."

"As you wish, my lord," she said, leaving the room.

About five minutes later, the two girls climbed into bed with me. Their bodies were warm from standing next to the fire pit. This was and still is a common rule for all of you; come to bed clean and warm.

Within minutes, we were sound asleep. I simply didn't have the strength to go over the events of the last couple of days. As I slept, I dreamt of Lili. She had almost wrenched my soul from my body—yet I still wanted her. Even back then, it was believed that an encounter with Lili left a man cursed and unsatisfied for the remainder of his life.

I knew it was her, but I wanted that face, that body—most of all, I wanted the evil within her. There seemed to be chemistry between us, but that was delusional thinking on my part, arrogance in the extreme. For me to feel this way, even for a moment during the ritual, would be suicide. She had a hook in me, and I would be intentionally calling her into my home the following night. I knew I had to keep my wits about me. I was not about to let her seduce me again. If I did, it would mean death.

I was awakened abruptly by a loud crash and the distinct clash of metal a split second later. Jumping out of bed, I quickly grabbed my sword. As I turned to look back, I noticed Nona was not there. I screamed.

"Where is she?!"

As I ran down the hall, I screamed at the girls.

"Get back in your rooms!"

When I arrived at the entrance, I saw a man about to split Sanem's skull. He was standing behind her as she fought with another man. I lunged forward and ran the man through his lower back. When I pulled the sword out, some of his insides came out. He dropped dead on the spot. Sanem parried a slash almost simultaneously and decapitated her assailant with one mighty blow.

It ended as quickly as it had started. There were six bodies on the floor; three dead men, a fourth who was choking on his own blood, Tara, who had suffered a horrific leg wound, and Nona—innocent Nona, lying in a crimson puddle of her own blood, her eyes open and lifeless, a sizeable gaping slash across her throat.

Sanem fell to her knees, put her head on Nona's lap, and wept. It was the only time in 3,800 years that I had seen this woman cry. I spoke urgently to her.

"Ulla did this. Get Tara into the ritual room. Get a clean cloth, keep pressure on the wound, and have the girls help you."

Sanem did not protest. She picked Tara off the floor like a baby and followed my commands, a single tear falling on my forearm as she passed.

The assassin was hanging on by a thread. He had a deep slash on the shoulder of his right arm. This wound would have killed him slowly, but the second wound was far worse. His right lung had been punctured by a thrust to the chest. He was lying on his back, immobilized, coughing up blood. Sanem had cut him up pretty good.

"How much did Ulla pay you?" I demanded.

The man simply turned away. You know I hate to be ignored. I stuck about three inches of my blade into the wound on his shoulder.

"Please, please," he managed to say while coughing up blood.

"Your life isn't worth excrement right now. I may be able to save you, but I want some information first. I was the object of your desire, yes? Is Ulla that frightened?"

No response. I poked around in the wound some more.

"Please don't," he begged.

I looked down at Nona's lifeless form and churned the point into the man's arm. I already knew the answers and didn't give a damn. I wanted satisfaction, yet somehow, I knew I wouldn't get it, no matter how I dealt with him.

The sounds coming from that entrance room were sickening. It was the first time I had ever tortured someone. This poor bastard couldn't even scream with his whole heart because he only had one lung. It sounded like half crying, half drowning. Those hideous screams mixed with the sound of my sword point sloshing around in this man's shoulder were unique to my ears. It was as if a demon took hold of me. It was blissful.

The torture became too much for him, and he died, drowning in his blood and convulsing. I stayed for a moment to savor his death, even taking some of his blood from my sword to taste it—perhaps a prelude of things to come.

The room was a mess, and there was blood everywhere. Amidst the shards of wood from the front door was the carnage of a short but fierce battle. I could not stop looking at Nona. It was devastating, and I could hear the wailing in my house as the rest of the women found out about their sister's fate. Sanem walked back in to give me a report.

"My lord, we stopped the bleeding, but the wound is deep. We'll have to keep an eye on her. I fear she may be taken from us as well."

"What happened?" I asked.

"We were asleep in here, my lord, Tara and I, as always, when the front door exploded. Nona had just walked in. Tara grabbed a spear, and I drew my sword, but I couldn't get to Nona fast enough. The first man cut her throat before we could do anything. I am so sorry, my lord. I should have saved her."

Sanem's tears flowed, but she maintained her warrior posture.

"Permission to speak freely, my lord?"

I nodded.

"Tell me there will be retribution. Tell me I will savor the rot of his dead body. Tell me why this happened."

"I can assure you, there will be retribution. I cannot tell you why, but the reasons will be clear after the Akitu. What happened after Nona?"

"Tara engaged the man who killed Nona. She ran him through the heart immediately. The second man who entered was quick enough to lay open Tara's leg, taking her out of the fight. My lord, I never felt such murderous rage. The other two came at me. I thought I had killed the one you tortured. As you see, he had little skill, and I laid him out with a cut and thrust. I cut the head off the last man, but the second man, who injured Tara, had maneuvered behind me. You saved my life, my lord."

"Yes, and you and Tara saved ours."

I looked down at Nona's body and felt an overwhelming sadness as Sanem expressed her deepest wish.

"I want him to burn for this, my lord," she sobbed.

"He will pay, Sanem. I promise. How do you know it was him?"

Sanem reached down and pointed at the back of one of the assassin's hands. It was the brand of a crescent moon, the mark of Ulla. I can't explain what I felt. It was the first actual loss our fine house had suffered. Still, I was undeterred by the ritual and my upcoming negotiations with Hammurabi. I was thinking about Ulla's torture, sanctioned by the King himself. He would have suffered greatly.

The girls spent the rest of the night tending to Tara, cleaning up all the blood and debris, while Megan and I wrapped the bodies and moved them outside. Sanem stood guard at the front of the house, sword drawn, arms crossed, a clear warning for everyone to stay away. She was a stone of vigilance.

By sunrise, the grueling task of cleaning the entrance room was finished. Four bodies had been stacked, one on top of the other, against the wall at the back of my home. Nona's body was kept inside, in the ritual room, along the west wall, until she could have an appropriate funeral. After I made the rank of high counselor, she would have a burial fit for a queen.

Everyone was exhausted. We all sat at the long table to eat our morning food, which Linzie had prepared. No one spoke, and the mood was depressing. The silence was attributed to an empty space at the table, usually occupied by Nona. Tara's space was also open, and she seemed to be taking a turn for the worse. The wound had developed an infection. She had a terrible fever, and the prognosis was grim.

How selfish I was, sitting at the head of this table. I was sad about Nona and Tara, but at this point, all I could think about was immortality and the ritual that would bring it to me in less than 14 hours. This ritual would bring everything I desired. Deep down, I was thoughtless. I was rotten to the core and getting worse. That night, I would reach the pinnacle of my evil.

I was stuffing my face, immersed in my obsession, when I noticed Abu staring at me. He knew, and I felt sorry for him for one timeless moment. Then, it was back to business as usual.

"What are you looking at?" I asked loudly, startling him.

"Nothing, my lord," he said as he looked down at his food and began eating again.

"You should be happy, boy. You are going to be a man tonight. You are going to lay your first seed between Cala's silky thighs. What do you think of that?"

The boy looked up and replied sadly.

"I miss Nona, my lord."

I slammed my fist down on the table and gritted my teeth angrily, but then relaxed when I realized I had frightened everyone.

"I know, boy. I miss her too."

Linzie and Sakura cried silently as I tried to lift their spirits.

"I know the past couple of nights have been strange, and the loss of Nona is terrible, but tomorrow, after the Akitu, vengeance shall be ours. I will take my place as the new high counselor to Hammurabi. Ulla is responsible for all of this. He knows I possess the power to take his seat. Last night, he sent his men to kill me. He underestimated us. I need you all to stay strong. Tara needs you, I need you, and you need each other. I have all the proof I need linking Ulla to the crime. He was dumb enough not to send mercenaries but his own men. We will see him publicly executed. I promise. Tomorrow, by the Gods, we shall move our belongings to Hammurabi's palace. The day after that, Nona shall have a glorious funeral, and soon after that, Ulla shall burn to death. You will not speak of these matters. After tonight, our fortunes shall change."

I had given them a little light. Sanem looked at me with hopeful eyes. She believed, and I continued.

"We have been awake for a long while, yet things still need to be done. Linzie, go to Nasser, the builder, and tell him to make me a new door. Tell him it must be done today. After that, you may retire."

"Yes, my lord," she said with overwhelming sadness.

"Sanem, I know you are tired, but you must stand the watch until my work is done."

"My lord, I dare this man to try again. Fear not, for all who try to thwart you this night will suffer my wrath. I am wide awake, my lord."

"Good. Sakura, I need you to stay close to Tara. Make sure she gets everything she needs. Clean the wound, change the dressing, and do what you can. If she can just hang on for a few more hours, I might be able to save her."

"My lord, you need not ask."

Then I touched you on the shoulder.

"Nothing goes wrong now, Cala. I am too close to success."

"Always, my lord," you said, with half-open teary eyes.

You and the boy heard me torturing that man. I knew Abu had never experienced such violence, even though it was purely auditory for him. After it was done, he spent the entire night shaking and crying. You stayed with him, but you were unable to pacify him. It was of little consequence in the light of what was about to happen, leagues beyond the shock of the previous night. I didn't care. I just smiled at Heather and led her to my bed.

It must have been midday when I heard pounding coming from the entrance room. Heather was sound asleep, her arms and legs wrapped tightly around me. I figured it was Nasser, and I began to drift back into sleep when I heard your familiar trembling voice.

"My lord, may I sleep with you and Heather? The noise frightened me, and my only wish is for you to hold me until Nasser is done. Please."

When you sounded so vulnerable and scared, it always did something to me. To this day, it still does. I could never figure it out, though I know it has something to do with your innocence. I looked in your room and saw Abu sound asleep, his arms bound, despite Nasser's annoying work.

"Yes, you may stay with me, but do not disturb me. I need this sleep more than ever. I must be rested for tonight."

"Yes, my lord."

You gently climbed into bed so as not to disturb Heather. I put my arms around you, cupped one of your breasts in my hand, and fell into a deep sleep.

I dreamt of Lili. She was naked in the darkness, eyes glowing at me, exciting me, her body perfect and voluptuous. It was all a figment of my imagination. Lili has one proper form beyond human comprehension.

She came to me as a wild fantasy—Lili, Great Mother, predator, vampire, serpent, owl, night hag. Was I dreaming? I could smell the sweet-scented oil. Her long and wet jet-black hair framed a perfect face, set off by beautiful thick lips and eyes like an abyss. She sat down in the darkness, a darkness that seemed to radiate from her, and stretched her long, shapely legs wide before me.

Come, Somro.

Her lips never moved. I was bound and compelled. There was nothing I could do, no banishing I could voice. Clearly, she had me this time. I was possessed by her shapely feet, the curves of her beautiful legs, and the black tuft of mystery between them. I was being drawn in like a lamb to the slaughter, and I loved it. She crawled toward me on her hands and knees. When she was close enough, she grabbed me by the back of my legs, pulled me forward, and started to suck me slowly, deeply. It was mindless bliss. At that moment, her lips became my universe. Nothing mattered anymore. I wanted this—forever.

Just as I was about to come, she stopped, pushed me down, and straddled me. Her eyes looked like burning coals, and a forked red tongue darted from her mouth. I wanted to die right then and there. She gripped me by the cock, which exploded with pain. Blood ruptured from it. She sat upon me, and I could feel my pelvis being crushed. I was screaming. She was killing me at all levels—mentally, emotionally, physically, and spiritually. I managed to clamp my hands around her neck. I squeezed with whatever strength I had. She smiled at me and licked my face with her long serpent tongue. Somehow, I woke up.

Heather screamed my name while trying to pull my hands from your throat. Like the vision, you were on top of me, and I was inside you. Abu was screaming from the adjoining room. It was total chaos. I let Heather take my hands from your throat just as Sanem and Megan burst into the room. I almost killed you, Cala. Lili was there, and the protective circle seemed to be weakening. At that moment, I had real doubts. I wondered if I could really pull it off.

"Get the boy," I said to Sanem as I sat up.

After she untied him, he rushed into my room and threw his arms around you. Typically, this would have warranted a whipping, but he was so distressed that I let it go. You were crying, and he was obviously in love with you. I believe you were falling for him, too. Do you remember how he was when you suffered a slight cut or burn or when I punished you? He would get so jealous whenever you slept with me. He hated me, and I thought nothing of it. To me, he was always part of the plan, no more. He did hate me, but he had come to trust me anyway. I digress.

I remember you looking up at me with those big, innocent eyes. You pleaded with me out of fear.

"My lord, I had no control. A thing came into me and made me climb on you! She made me! She made me!"

You were hysterical. I held you for a moment and told you I understood.

"After tonight, this will never happen again."

Then I turned my attention to Abu.

"You must protect her. Tonight, you will be her husband. You will make love to her. Your love shall drive away all the bad dreams. You do love her, don't you?"

"More than life itself, my lord."

"Interesting choice of words, my young warrior. Tonight, you may prove it."

I was giving the boy a quest for love. It was romantic, at least on the surface, anyway. Lying was a skill I had perfected throughout my life. It started out as a means of survival.

"Megan, sweep out the ritual room and prepare a bed in the center. Light all four torches. I will be in momentarily."

I could see the sun's rays reaching a horizontal line from the West window of my bed chamber. It was time. When I walked into the room, Megan was putting the final touches on a soft grass bed in the center of the well-worn circle, which was cut right into the earth. There were fresh blankets, and the floor was swept. I thanked Megan and dismissed her with two final orders.

"You have the watch outside this room, and Sanem will guard the outside of the house. No one gets in. Send Cala and Abu in here at once."

"As you wish, my lord," she said, bowing her head in servitude.

I looked toward the western wall where Nona's body lay wrapped tightly in wool blankets. It finally got to me. I knelt down on my knees, unwrapped the portion of wool covering Nona's face, and cried—my tears landing upon her lips. I had no time to sort through these emotions as you and the boy walked behind me. You were so bloody innocent.

"My lord?"

I wiped my tears, stood up, turned to you, and commanded.

"I need Abu lying down with his head facing north. You will see four stakes in the earth with twine next to each one. Secure his hands and feet tightly, very tightly."

"Yes, my lord."

This room was different than the others in that it had four high walls but no ceiling. That night, the stars were brilliant, and the air cool. After you tied his wrists and ankles, I knelt down on my knees, back to the eastern wall, facing west. You were less than six feet in front of me.

"Cala, disrobe."

You were a goddess in your own right. No matter how often I had seen you naked, you were never more beautiful than at that moment. The flickering fire traced the curves of your voluptuous body. The site of you vulnerable, naked, and completely submissive was truly angelic.

"Take the dagger from my altar and give him a small cut."

"Where, my lord?" you asked.

"You know where. We've gone over this several times," I replied, annoyed at your predictable trepidation. "After the cut, you will make him hard and straddle him."

You obeyed my commands perfectly, and although Abu was clearly frightened, he could still perform. The preparation had been flawless. I started to sing, slowly at first, but seething, burning, and frenzied until I reached the zenith of my invocation.

Dark goddess of the desert, I call upon you!
Primordial Mother of all things, I call upon you!
You who know everything!
You who see everything!
You who visit the dreams of men!
You who copulate in the desert!
Night hag! Goddess of jackals!
Goddess of dreams, I command you!
Owl-Goddess!
Take this girl's body!
Take this boy's blood and essence!
Take their souls!
I command you, Lili!
I command you!

I screamed at you, "Stab him in the heart!"
Shocked, you looked at me and questioned the order.
"My lord?"
"Stab him now, Cala!"
You could not do it, and I knew you would not. I continued to call upon Lili, for I knew *she* would have no problem delivering the death stroke. I could sense her presence coming into you, and then it happened. You threw your head back in ecstasy, and I knew she had you. You raised the dagger as I continued to chant.

Serpent-goddess, Great Mother, I command you!
You who know everything!
You who see everything!
You who steal the seed of men while they sleep!
Night hag! Goddess of jackals!
Goddess of dreams, I command you!

Owl-goddess!
Take this girl's body!
Take this boy's blood and essence!
Take their souls!
And give me the elixir from your womb!
I command you, Lili!
I command you!

The Present

Suddenly, the fire died out. The flames, hot coals, and smoke instantly and impossibly vanished as a cold, harsh wind blasted against the windows. Instinctively, Elizabeth clutched hard around the master's neck for protection. Her mind refused to accept the abyss that suddenly engulfed the room. But the master's flesh was as cold as ice, and he was so ridged. This was new territory for Elizabeth, and an unknown fear gripped her so hard she thought she would die. Nona's voice cut through the chaos and irrationality of her mind.

"Be gone, Lili! Be gone!"

Nona entered the room with a giant torch. Elizabeth was amazed at Nona's eyes, which glowed like two illuminated sapphires. Elizabeth understood her, loved her, remembered her, and honored her as the spiritual guardian of the coven.

Nona Almeida was born in Fortaleza, Brazil, in early 1980. She was the only child of a 44-year-old father and a 21-year-old mother. He had been an architect for over 20 years at the time of her birth and, knowing a child was on the way, had an unusual impulsive desire to move to North America. His tenacity paid off when he was hired by a design firm in

Texas following Nona's third birthday. The family did immigrate but lived in Houston less than a year before a golden opportunity, analyzing structural stress levels, brought them to Portland, Oregon.

Like Celsus, she was a prodigy in school. She learned English within a few months and had excellent reading, writing, and math skills before kindergarten.

Like Megan's family, hers was devoutly Catholic. Unlike Megan, she had no trouble attending Sunday Mass. She was always polite and respectful, and this was perhaps her most fantastic charade.

Even as a child, she was a secretive but zealous researcher into all things occult and metaphysical. Subjects such as astrology, numerology, divination, telepathy, symbolic magic, necromancy, voodoo, witchcraft, animism, astral projection, and shamanism kept her undivided attention.

The library was the only place the intelligent little Brazilian girl wished to be. Her mother and father could not count the times they found their child looking at what they considered strange esoteric literature. Her father can still recall the three books she had on a reading table during one such visit to the public library: the *Egyptian Book of the Dead,* the *Malleus Maleficarum,* and the *Lesser Key of Solomon.* Her father found himself in temporary shock at the discovery of the books. Still, he concluded that she must have pulled them all randomly from the same shelf and simply wanted to satisfy her curiosity. After all, she was only five when this incident occurred.

When she started kindergarten, she met Celsus, and soon, the two children became inseparable. It was often observed how they would spend time together in lengthy conversations, always careful to ensure no one could hear them. At first, both sets of parents were alarmed by how much time the two spent together. Still, after acknowledging what well-behaved kids they were, their parents allowed their friendship to flourish.

When they reached puberty, their behavior became increasingly bizarre, and they became much more adept at hiding their true natures. By the time the two reached the age of nine, they had progressed into a full-blown adult relationship with each other—and again, no one ever knew.

Nona was relentless concerning her "other studies" during high school. For her, homework was a farce, and the real work entailed creating mistakes to not draw attention to herself—just like Celsus.

Physically, she couldn't help but draw attention. This was and still is unavoidable as she is exotic and supernaturally beautiful. There wasn't a single student in her school who did not turn to look when she walked by. Her olive skin and jet-black hair contrasted intensely with her light blue eyes. She developed her strong, voluptuous body in her mid-teens and was generally considered unapproachable.

Other high school students still reminisce about the strange personalities of Celsus and Nona. The most common remembrance was that they always seemed like they were plotting something. One man remembers courageously asking Nona for a date during their senior year. She simply and coldly told him no. Celsus later approached him and said he would kill him if he ever talked to her again. The man believes to this day that Celsus was not the exaggerating or bluffing type. After that, he avoided Nona like the plague.

In 1998, after Celsus returned from Boston with his fortune, she needed nothing. He lavished trips, gifts, and dinners upon her without reserve, though she kept everything a secret as usual. Two years later, Celsus and his younger sister Sophia picked her up one night and left for California to get Megan. Nona was never seen or heard from again. Some in

Portland still wrongly speculate that Celsus probably killed her.

When Elizabeth looked at the face of the master, she was shocked, for he looked dead and felt dead. She had never seen that look in his eyes, frozen in fear. It was as if he had died from sheer terror, the last moment frozen on his face for all eternity. She shook uncontrollably as Nona unlocked her grip from his neck.

"Lady Elizabeth, please, I need you to sit at the round table for a moment."

Elizabeth tried to respond, but the entire scene was too much for her. Her brain would not function properly. Nona led her to the table and gently sat her down.

Elizabeth then watched with strange detachment as Nona laid down a perfect circle of sea salt around the master. He had not moved nor shown any sign that he was even alive. Nona then lit four torches mounted to iron floor stands surrounding him. Satisfied that he was safe, she went to Elizabeth, took her hand, and led her through the hall.

They ascended three flights of stairs until they reached Nona's room in the attic of the grand mansion. She then carefully undressed Elizabeth and put her to bed.

Elizabeth looked at Nona and pleaded without words, unable to speak. Nona undressed herself and climbed into bed next to her. The two naked women snuggled, and Elizabeth, now warm and safe, fell sound asleep. Surprisingly, no dreams haunted her that night.

The following morning, Nona fed her a magnificent breakfast. The two did not speak, and Elizabeth understood the need for silence. She knew she was fragile and that something heavy had gone down. The entire story was blocked. Her mind was compartmentalized, which seemed appropriate and necessary for her sanity. She was thankful that Nona had pulled down the heavy velvet drapes to block out the sun. After this hearty and grounding meal, Nona helped her get dressed.

When the two women descended to the second level, Nona held a finger to her lips signaling Elizabeth to wait quietly. At the same time, she entered the master's bedroom. She closed the door behind her.

Elizabeth's mind remained safely blank. She had no curiosity whatsoever and stood silently in the hallway, admiring the beautiful woodwork while waiting for Nona. The memory of the master's story and the assault of the supernatural remained close, yet she refused to touch it. She had neither the power nor the constitution to handle it.

Five minutes later, Nona emerged from the master's room, gently grabbed Elizabeth's hand, and descended to the entrance. Elizabeth moaned with displeasure at the frigid wind and blinding morning sun as Nona opened the door of the long black limousine and helped her in. She found the familiar car blessedly warm and dark as the two set off for her apartment.

Two hours later, as they approached the complex, Elizabeth finally spoke.

"Please, don't leave me."

"Sweet angel, only one visit left, and you'll never have to leave us again, not in this life anyway," Nona assured her.

"I can't be alone. Please, Nona. I'm begging you. Please don't leave me."

Nona clicked on the driver intercom.

"I need you to wait. I'm walking up with her."

Elizabeth became more desperate.

"I can't go up there. I can't go there. Please, Nona."

Nona held her tightly as they pulled up next to the complex. Elizabeth found her old living space to be alienating and terribly frightening. Nona got out and gently tugged her hand.

"My Lady Elizabeth, you know how much I love you. Do you trust me?"

"Yes, of course. I trust you more than anyone because you have been kind to me. Do you know why I am scared?"

"You are frightened because your old life is hollow and meaningless, and you are so close to the end of your trials."

Elizabeth finally relented, and the two women ascended the stairwell to her apartment. As Elizabeth searched for her key, reluctantly obeying Nona's subtle commands, Carrie emerged from her apartment and made eye contact.

Elizabeth could see Carrie's confusion as Nona's eyes became the brilliantly illuminated sapphires from the previous night. Loaded with magic, Nona willed Carrie to forget everything. Carrie simply walked past them as if they were not there.

Elizabeth looked at Nona's eyes again, and the burning blue disappeared. After they entered the apartment, Nona gave her a kiss—the kiss of the guardian. That kiss gave Elizabeth the strength to endure her final separation. Nona backed away a few inches and spoke softly.

"My beautiful sister, I adore you so much. I promise everything will be fine. You do this every time, my angel."

"Why am I blocked, Nona?"

"You are so close. Not long now—not long at all."

Before Elizabeth could protest any further, Nona was gone. The longing and loneliness she felt at that moment were more profound than anything she could have imagined. She stood facing the door of her apartment for nearly an hour before she could curl up in a fetal position on her couch. Sanity, reason, and everything she ever knew were questioned.

She vomited. A war raged in her mind and body as her spirit slept.

THE WHITE CHOKER

Elizabeth found her way through the winter and spring of 2009. She returned to school, taking only night classes, as the daylight had become intolerable. She knew they were out there, watching her, listening to her thoughts, and waiting for the final visit. She knew this and was torn apart inside. The scarlet choker lay buried in the bottom drawer of her dresser, and it haunted her. She wanted so much to burn it, as if she could destroy her fate with them by doing so.

She tried hard to forget, especially at night when alone, but an intense desire would gnaw at her. It made her sex throb and filled her entire body with lust. She missed Megan's tongue, Sakura's divine kiss, Linzie's obsessive love, Sanem's strength, Tara's goddess-like presence, Nona's empathy, Heather's rebellious spirit, and the master's absolute domination and power over her. It seemed so superficial, a simple way of rationalizing the impossible. She lived doing what ordinary people do, yet all the while, she felt as if there was a veil over her eyes.

She had just enough strength to operate in the world of the once-born but felt the truth was an altogether different matter. She knew it was the master who kept the blindfold wrapped tightly around her reality. She also knew that her current understanding of life was rapidly ending. It was the summer solstice when the inevitable contact came. This time, it was Sanem who invaded her mind.

It is time. Your second birth is now. It's just as well. None of us can stand it any longer. At night, when you are soaking wet for us, we feel your terrible hunger. The master keeps us bound. Our torment for you is his pleasure. But make no mistake—he loves you with the strength of a hurricane. He loves you as much as any of us. Nona is coming for you now.

"What should I bring? What should I wear?"

White with the red choker.
Elizabeth looked at her clock and frowned.
"9:00 p.m. and still light out. Fuck."
The veil was wrapped tight.

She instinctively knew to prepare a purification bath. The knowledge of creating it had nothing to do with learning or memory. It was a direct connection with the master's grand fetishes. She prepared the nylon satchel with great reverence, adding equal parts of fresh hyssop, lavender, and mint. The hot water took on a deep green hue as she lit the four candles gracing each corner of the tub. She added fresh rose petals to the surface of the steaming, emerald water. Before she entered the sacred space, she filled an enormous douche with the sacred water and hung it on the shower head. She then let her entire body submerge into the near-scalding water, holding her breath as fragments of ancient Babylon began to flood her memory. Every time she tried to focus on this, her vision would blur. The veil was about to disintegrate.

Sensing the coven's presence, she stood up in a cloud of scented steam. Sex and power accumulated throughout her body as she placed her right foot on the tub's rim. She pulled down the plastic tube, inserted it into her vagina, and let the burn take away all doubts. After allowing half the bag to pass through her womanhood, she shoved the tube into her anus. As if on cue, the master's voice embraced her.

My beautiful dripping goddess—your foot upon the rim—powerful, clean, and sweet—who would have thought I could be envious of a simple tube?

Elizabeth, flush with power, responded verbally.

"My lord, were it only your steely spear that impales me. I want nothing else. Rip me. Tear me with your weapon, my lord."

Oh, I will, Cala. I absolutely will.

She dried off and wandered naked throughout her darkening apartment. She looked at the wall at portraits of her family and felt nostalgic when she thought of the time before the coven. Life was simple—lonely but straightforward. At that moment, she understood that her parents were just the means to enter this life. She was grateful to them, but this was goodbye. Her real family had always been the coven—always.

Her feelings subsided as she entered her bedroom and grabbed handfuls of baby powder from a glass bowl. It had been sitting on her dresser for nine days, though she couldn't recall placing it there. She threw it haphazardly upon her body and massaged it into her flesh. She pinched her nipples and spread the white powder all over her body with an air of sexual confidence.

"My lord approves?"

My beloved, you tempt the beast before you are even within range.

"As it should be, my lord—you fucking devil."

It is time to sever this link. Already, you find your power, and I am tempted beyond understanding.

"Yes, my lord."

She felt the softness of her freshly shaven mound by running her fingers over it. Her womanhood was filled with blood and desire, especially the little love knob on top. She knew the master was gone, and she knew why. He had not fed, and the perfection of her obedience to his ways drove him insane. In a way, it was the first time she felt she had the upper hand. Controlling from the bottom. It was a fantasy that made her slick with desire.

She smiled as she slipped into her white one-piece sundress. It was shoulderless, and a thin strip of elastic held the dress in place by the top of her cleavage. It did nothing to hide her stout nipples nor the subtle valley of her engorged cleft. The final touch was the infamous scarlet choker.

She looked into her mirror, her own eyes, and the glimmer, which matched the color of her choker. She laughed, pirouetted, donned her sunglasses, and walked out barefoot and beautiful. It was 10:00 p.m., and time was irrelevant.

The familiar black limo was already waiting on the street with its rear passenger door open. She walked toward it with regal pride and entered. A waiting Nona grabbed her and kissed her passionately.

"My lady, I have missed you so much."

Elizabeth acted coy with her response.

"My dear, I thought I was supposed to be the drama queen."

Elizabeth embraced her as the car headed toward the Northern wilderness. As the forest grew thicker, she remembered the story of Cala. With great detachment and increasing power, she made her inquiry.

"What's the rest of the story?"

Nona looked lovingly at her profile and responded as if she knew she would ask.

"I had not departed but lingered, unsure of what happened. I didn't comprehend that I was dead, but I did witness everything after my death. When *she* came, it was like a red flood. She was formless, and the room filled with her energy and power. It was heavy, crushing. I was nothing but a speck in the corner, a witness. She knew I was there, but the master's plan worked so well that she didn't care about me. The red flood condensed. She came through the top of your skull. Your heart stopped. You were dead but trapped inside your body. She trapped you. The master screamed at her to kill the boy and give up the substance. She hissed like a snake, cut the boy's restraints, and tossed the dagger aside. The boy launched himself up the altar and over the wall. I don't know what happened to him after that."

"Why did she let the boy go?"

"The master wanted more than immortality. He wanted Lili to submit to his will. She let the boy go because it was the only means of immediate defiance until she could kill the master and everyone associated with him for his audacity."

"What happened next?"

"Your body fell over on the ground, and you looked dead. The master stuck his fingers inside you, and I could see your spirit struggling. He then walked to my dead body and inserted the substance into my mouth. At that moment, I felt something change which is impossible to describe with words.

I can only say that I was *made* at that moment into what I have always been since. Then, your body came to life, and stood up. The moment Lili fixed her attention on the master, your spirit escaped to me. Your essence was red…changed from your contact with Lili. Our spirits were together. We watched as she walked toward the master. He tried to escape but could not. She stuck her fingers in her sex and then forced them into his mouth. That is when he joined us, his great fear freeing his soul from his body. Your dead body held the primordial Mother. The red flood killed five other women through that same touch of blood and terror. Heather was the last. She picked up a dagger and tried to run but found herself trapped in a corner and plunged the dagger into her own heart before Lili could reach her. The night hag knelt down and stuck her bloody fingers into Heather's mouth, but she was already gone. I did notice a red tint encompassing everyone but Heather. The hue of her energy seemed lighter, almost pinkish."

There was a momentary pause before Nona continued.

"Lili was angry at us. The red flood was everywhere. I believe that the master's magic kept us from the wrath of the Mother, kept us from dissipating, and turned us into monsters. There is nothing natural about staying intact. We were different from that point on. Lili pursued the nine of us through the cosmos for 234 years, years that seemed like the same night. When we came back, we lived again for 117 years. The master and I are always born first, and the rest of you follow within weeks—a few months at the most. Heather is always last. It is always 117 years with a body and 117 years without one. We come into the world of the living much like the rain, random as to where we are born. It is the master who collects us up again. We go on and on."

"I remember Lili. She is always close."

"That's correct."

"How were you spared the bloodlust?"

"I'm sure it's because I was already dead. That's the only reason it could be. I did not suffer my spirit torn from her touch as you all did. I think the way Heather died has something to do with how she feeds."

"Lady Nona, you have helped us kill countless people in every incarnation."

"I am your sister and guardian, Elizabeth. There is no other way."

"Have you no regret over the lives you help us take?"

"First of all, you do not need my assistance to feed. Secondly, if I assist, it's because I love you."

"It's all coming back to me now. Your death is the signal. We know the year, but we never know the day. You leave exactly 18 hours before we do."

"Yes."

"We don't age a day beyond the age when we died the first time, do we?"

Nona looked at her and responded with a smile.

"You will look like you do now for nearly 90 more years, and you will outlive everyone you know—except us, of course."

"Did Lili make us?"

"I believe the master's alchemy worked. He is our Father, and Lili is our Mother. She made us indirectly, without any intention of creating us. The master wanted immortality, and he got it. It just wasn't quite what he expected, and the eight of us were the unfortunate casualties of his sorcery. I have made it a point to study the laws of the universe ever since—every detail, to avoid compounding the curse any further. As of yet, nothing has worked. Things get worse with each incarnation."

"What are we?"

"I do not know. Megan is trying to sort it out from a scientific angle. I have always tried to understand it at a spiritual level. The rest of you simply don't care anymore. I don't think there's an answer to your question. Goddess knows we have tried to understand it forever."

"Are there other gods and goddesses?"

"To be sure, they are the collective energies and awareness of all the people who have ever lived. They are all around us, all the time, but Lili is something different."

"What do you mean?"

"She is before humanity. She is not energy per se, but rather a true separate intelligence far beyond our understanding."

"The coven seems like it has grown beyond understanding. Why all the sadism, rituals, and such? It all seems useless and unnecessary."

"We are evolving, Elizabeth. You are bound to think differently when you live for thousands of years. There is a reason he is called the master. It is pointless to question him and even more so to challenge him."

"Has anyone ever really challenged him?"

"Rarely, and the retribution is not worth it."

"Do tell."

"You'll remember soon enough."

"Nona, I want to give you something."

Elizabeth gently broke her embrace, knelt down on the floor of the limo, and proceeded to kiss Nona's shapely calves. She then pushed Nona's black silk dress up to her hips, spreading her legs apart to get closer. She knew Nona wasn't wearing any panties. Kissing the inside of her thighs, she savored the effect she was having. Her gentle love bites sent shivers up Nona's spine.

"My goddess, Elizabeth, it's been so long."

Elizabeth closed her eyes and inhaled deeply, taking in Nona's scent. She paused, inches from her womanhood, mouth-watering, then opened her eyes and looked up at her. She found Nona's ancient power, leaned forward, and kissed her silky, moistened slit. The sensations Nona experienced were otherworldly as Elizabeth drank deeply, filling herself with Nona's essence. For her, it was a higher form of feeding. When the car finally arrived at the house, Nona ended it.

"You must stop. We have plenty of time for this, and I have had countless orgasms. What a wicked mouth you have."

"All the better to eat you with," she replied with a grin as she sucked Nona's love from her fingers. "My sweet Nona, you taste so good I could devour you."

"No, no! You should be careful what you say. You have an appetite every bit as ferocious as the master's!"

"Really?"

"Yes. I believe you could really eat me, given half the chance. Look what you did to poor Linzie."

"Nona, how can you talk so? It was no fault of mine."

"I'm sorry. It's just that you have no idea what it's like to witness your feeding."

"I'm ready, Nona. Let's see what these devils have planned for me."

Elizabeth ascended the stone stairs and remembered her first visit. She felt much wiser now. After they entered the entrance hall, Nona turned and gave her a soft, lingering kiss on the lips, a hint of her own scent causing her to smile.

"Stay here while I get changed. I'll be back in a minute."

Elizabeth giggled as Nona raced up the winding staircase. The house was strangely absent of any lights or candles. The sun had finally set, and she wondered why the place looked so dead. She tried to summon Lord Celsus and Lady Megan but to no avail. She thought about trying the others but intuitively figured it would be a waste of time.

Suddenly, she realized the glimmer was gone. She wasn't afraid, for she knew the coven was down the path behind the house. She knew they were working on her, forcing the veil over the truth until the last moment. She laughed again when she heard Nona racing down the stairs. Nona was always so composed, and Elizabeth found great entertainment in her excitement.

Nona was a vision of beauty. She wore a simple white silk dress that draped down over her curvaceous body and lightly touched her calves. Her nipples poked out of the silk fabric prominently, and Elizabeth immediately craved to suck on them. Only two little straps held the dress on. Elizabeth asked the obvious.

"Do you have any clue how beautiful you are?"

"Come, they are waiting for you," Nona said, ignoring the compliment.

She grabbed Elizabeth by the hand and led her through the kitchen and out the back door. The two women appeared innocent and naive as they walked down the cobblestone path toward the tree line.

The sky had turned black because the moon was dead. Everything seemed disconnected, but clearly, she knew the coven created the confusion. The strange thoughts racing through her head seemed inappropriate. She knew the second birth was always like this. Pieces of past lives were flickering in and out of her memory. She knew that Celsus was getting worse with each incarnation, but she felt great pain when she thought of him. She loved him so much.

Nona slowed as they approached the torches that illuminated the path. Suddenly, the memory of this path overwhelmed her. *Raymond.* She remembered sucking the master's blood, Sakura's, plunging a dagger into Raymond's leg, the riding crop, and the hot welts.

The two women emerged into the familiar circular clearing. All was silent except for the fire that crackled under the dark solstice night. There, the coven stood like ancient stone sculptures. The master knelt before the fire in a long, hooded blue velvet cape while the five other women stood evenly spaced in a circle around him. They were naked except for their white chokers. They were goddesses, and they were waiting for her.

Nona gently pulled Elizabeth's dress off. The elastic caught her nipples, and they sprang free to attention as the dress came down. Though Celsus had his back to her, he made a verbal observation as if he had eyes in the back of his head.

"Glorious."

As she stepped free from the dress that now formed a white cotton circle in the earth, she felt an unusual power rising. This power was indefinable. It was undoubtedly the whole of what she had experienced up to this point, yet it was repressed and contained, barely.

Celsus rose from his place before the fire and approached her, the hood drawn over his face. She was curious about what lurked beneath as he walked up behind her and placed his hands on her shoulders. His hands were hot, and she could feel the sharp points of his claws as they gently rested along the top of her cleavage. His left thumbnail slid under her scarlet choker and sliced it apart. It fell down the front of her chest, causing goosebumps to cover her body. Then he spoke.

"We have waited for so long. Elizabeth is your given name in this life, but we all know you by your first given name, 'Cala'—who took on the raging owl. My sweet Cala, you are the eighth of the 17th incarnation. Can you feel my desire?"

He kicked her right foot out to the side a few inches, knelt down, and rose up again, letting his ridged cock spring up between her legs. It pulsed and parted her vaginal lips.

"Yes, my lord. I feel you. I need you."

"What do you see before you, Cala?"

"The most beautiful women on earth, my lord."

"Yes, but what graces the center of the circle?"

"A stone marble table, the height of my knees, my lord."

"Anything else?"

"Four chains with shackles emerging from the ground. Two on one side and two on the other, my lord."

"Put the shackles on your ankles as you face the table. When you are done, lie face down along its length."

"Yes, my lord."

Elizabeth walked as graciously as possible to the base of the table. The five women surrounding it were gorgeous, alluring, predatory, and goddess-like, and their smiles were warm. When she arrived at the appointed spot, she glanced over her shoulder at Nona, who was now holding hands with the master. Nona nodded, signaling her to complete the task.

The shackles seemed absurdly heavy. The crude-looking rusted iron was an inch thick, making her wonder. The veil was nearly off now. Only a corner hid the reason for such massive restraints. They were self-locking and made an unmistakable sound when they latched. The links of the chains were equally out of proportion with her. With great effort, she dragged the heavy chains with her feet as she crawled on the table. She met the cold stone, first with her erect nipples and then the rest of her body. Random historical thoughts picked up incredible speed within her mind.

I remember the last life when we lived in France and supported American independence. I remember when we moved here, debating the repercussions of the Civil War before we died halfway through it. I drank de Sade's blood before we sailed across the Atlantic.

The master did not walk. He floated toward the marble table, and his long blue cape concealed the truth of the matter. It dragged behind him, and there was no discernible cadence to his movement. She watched the hooded, wraith-like Celsus pick up one of the remaining shackles and clamp it to her right wrist.

She noticed his claws and inhaled deeply, allowing herself to follow his preternatural movement as he went around the table and clamped the last remaining shackle on her left wrist. There seemed to be plenty of play in the arm restraints but almost none with her legs. The master broke the serenity of the forest with unnatural strength and volume.

"Tonight, we welcome our sister back among us! We will stay with her inside this protective circle until the sun rises! When the sun rises, we will sleep together, as we have done for 16 past lives. You all know how this night will go. The night hag will come, and we must be strong. Resistance without disrespect, protection without anger, magic with strength, and most of all, Cala in our lives again! So be it!"

"So be it!" the women responded in unison.

He moved to the head of the table, knelt down at eye level with Elizabeth, and pulled his cape off. The wolf needed her blood and would wait no longer. His eyes were black, and stars quickly receded within. There was hunger, terrible hunger in those eyes. His teeth were gleaming, long, and sharp. Her time had come. She closed her eyes, exhaled, and let go. The master would feed first, as always.

He grabbed her skull with one hand. His claws tore into her scalp as he turned her head to fully expose her neck. The monster studied her pulse for a moment and then sniffed the air as if reading the blood within her. Then, with little care for what she felt, he bit down savagely. He was unreserved, and she quickly lost consciousness.

After a few minutes of deep drinking, the wolf-man stopped, licked his palm, and slapped it over the wound. He growled at Megan to take her place at the front of the altar. He growled again, signaling his approval for her to feed. Megan knelt down and took over where the master had left off. Little blood trails ran down Elizabeth's face from the scalp wounds.

He maneuvered behind her and crawled up on the altar between her legs. He threw his head back and howled. Elizabeth woke and knew she was dying, filling the belly of the XO. Then, a new pain overtook her senses. The wolf punctured both femoral arteries along the inside of her thighs with his thumb claws. As her life spurted out, the master lubricated his steely manhood with her blood and sodomized her. She could feel him tearing her. No longer able to speak, her thoughts revealed her state of mind.

Blissful death I ask of you, my lord and master, my wolf, so divine, so cruel—I love you. Let me die. No more lives. Let me die upon your stake.

Celsus clamped his claws into Elizabeth's hips with such force that Megan lost her balance and fell off the table. A look of surprise crossed Megan's face as blood oozed down her chin. Celsus growled and signaled Sanem to partake of their sister's blood.

Sanem ran to Elizabeth and began drinking deeply from the original wound. Megan walked behind the wolf, kissed his back, and massaged his scrotum from behind as he continued his assault. He shook his head and growled at the other three women to join in. Tara, now a mighty lion, clamped onto Elizabeth's left forearm and punctured an artery. At the same time, Sakura and Linzie worked their way under the master, each locking onto a femoral blood fountain. The wolf pumped away until his orgasm exploded. He let out another horrific howl, but she did not regain consciousness this time. She appeared dead.

One by one, the master separated the women from Elizabeth's body. He knelt down and licked each wound. His saliva formed a seal, preventing further blood loss. The five female monsters and their angelic sister, Nona, waited for further instructions. None of them knew what would follow, as with each life, the master increased his seemingly mindless requirements for rejoining the coven. He spied Nona by the fire, calm and peaceful as ever. There was communication between them. Everyone could hear his voice in their minds.

Nona, the silver cup. It's time to bring her home.

Yes, my lord.

Nona walked to the stone altar on the east side of the circle. She picked up a large, ornate silver chalice, which she obediently delivered to Celsus.

I require only a drop of your blood.

Nona held out her hand, and Celsus barely sliced the end of her index finger with a claw. She turned her hand over the chalice and let a single drop fall. Then he moved to Lady Megan. He grabbed Megan's right arm with lightning speed and slit her wrist. Megan winced and smiled at the master seductively as her blood poured into the chalice. He did the same thing to the other women until the goblet was full and stood before Elizabeth.

She was white as a ghost with trails of drying blood caked on her face. For her, there was only darkness—

peaceful, safe darkness. Celsus, half-man, half-wolf, reached down with a callous grip and picked her up by the neck. Her arms swung lifelessly in front of her. He got close to her face and gently whispered.

"Awaken, Cala."

Her eyes opened wide instantly. A breeze stirred through the trees surrounding the circle, yet her arms hung, unmoving beneath her. He brought the chalice to her lips and whispered again.

"Drink the elixir of your sisters. Drink and return to us."

Her eyes stayed open and corpselike, and she did not move. He dipped the chalice into her mouth. It was then that her hands slowly moved. She cupped the master's clawed hands in her own, and the wind picked up around them. The only other sound was that of Elizabeth gulping down the mixture of powerful blood. She released her hands and rocked back on her knees when she finished. She was devoid of thought, seemingly in some kind of purgatory. The master addressed the coven.

"Prepare yourselves. The time has come. Nona, get Cala's dinner."

"As you wish, my lord."

"Cala, you will now receive my blood. When the binding spell is broken, you will feel the full weight of your soul. You will experience hunger as you never have in this incarnation or any other, for it grows more terrible with each life. You will remember everything from the beginning to the present. You will take your place in this coven once again, and you will see the Mother. Do not allow her to control you. We are here for you, and we will protect you. The red flood will surround us, but do not let it in. You have always belonged with us, and you always will. Take my blood, Cala."

Celsus hopped on the table and knelt down on his knees. He reached around her head and pulled her face into his neck.

At first, there was nothing, but then everyone heard a crunching sound. The wolf growled as her body came to life. The five women backed up as Elizabeth fell on top of him.

At this point, Nona emerged from the path with two wretched men and a young woman, all chained together in a single-file line. She silently led the three captives, who looked like they were in a trance.

As Elizabeth drank the master's blood, her wounds rapidly healed, and her body transformed. Her ankles quickly filled out the remaining space in the iron shackles, and her feet turned into large talons—the same talons one would find on a great horned owl, only much more prominent. Two massive wings sprouted from her back and grew to a monstrous 18-foot wingspan. Those wings began to flap, blowing everyone's hair around and fanning the fire into a furnace. The master was fighting for his life.

He punched Elizabeth on her right side, but it had no effect. No one dared help him because they knew the punishment for interference would entail having the skin flayed from their bodies.

When the situation seemed hopeless, he finally managed to maneuver his knees under her and kick her off. He let the momentum of his kick roll him off the table in a backward summersault right onto his feet. He growled at Elizabeth with such ferocity that everyone took several steps back. The wolf huffed loudly from the struggle, and blood flowed freely from his neck. Elizabeth's disposition was no better.

She screeched at the wolf, and the sound was ear-shattering. Everyone except the captives covered their ears. Her head was monstrous, half human, half owl. Her beak was coated in blood, and her tongue darted like a spear. Her glowing red eyes penetrated everything. Like a great predator, she quickly assessed her surroundings by turning her head 180 degrees in both directions. Her body stayed suspended in the air by her gigantic flapping wings. Still, she could not turn or rise more than four feet from the ground due to the massive restraints. An impressive cloak of feathers cascaded down her shoulders. She noticed the wind that now gathered strength from an emerging terrible storm. The sky had changed from black to red. Celsus sniffed the air as if he sensed another more dangerous predator than himself. He glared at Nona.

Nona turned and handed the lead chain of the first captive to Lady Megan. The XO wound the chain once around her hand and waited for instructions as Nona approached the altar and chanted in the old language. Everyone but the captives knew precisely what she was saying.

"The circle keeps you at bay. The circle is our family. We feel your intentions, Lili. You are not welcome here. Be gone, Lili! Be gone!"

Celsus approached Megan and separated the chains holding the first captive. He grabbed the man by his neck and threw him at the winged beast. She caught him and ceased her flapping. As she softly descended on the marble table, she kept her wings outstretched as a warning for everyone to keep away. Then she started tearing chunks out of the man she recognized but had no remorse for devouring.

Raymond.

He screamed as she clamped down on his left forearm with her talons while simultaneously tearing off his left bicep with her beak. The screaming seemed to irritate her, and she quieted him by ripping his throat out after gulping down the bicep.

All stood silent while she methodically eviscerated, dismembered, and cannibalized Raymond. Within 10 minutes, his body was reduced to a bloody, tattered skeleton as she pecked through the eye sockets, retrieving parts of his brain.

Celsus was still irritated by her attack on him and turned to the next victim. He growled fiercely and waved his hand before the man's face. The man became aware of his situation as if he were released from his trance into a nightmare. The pasty-looking man would have been much better off not knowing his fate. It was the master's sadistic bent, even in the form of a monstrous beast, which took precedence over everything.

The unfortunate man rubbed his eyes and thought he had fallen into hell. His mind could not process the reality. He looked beyond, trying to find something tangible to process, but only madness and horror existed. The swirling, angry red wind was loud and terrifying. His thoughts could only process a forest fire at night in a windstorm. He heard a clarification in his mind from Celsus.

Lili is the storm.

The young man screamed out with all his heart and soul. "In the name of Allah the Merciful, forgive my sins!"

Celsus stayed in his mind, an evil intruder.

Look around you, Abdul. Does it look like your god is listening?

Abdul realized he was chained to a woman he didn't recognize. She looked like she had brain damage, though she seemed healthy. It didn't make any sense. Then he noticed Nona's back and could faintly hear her chanting at the red menace. Her arms were outstretched, and she appeared strong and determined, like some ancient priestess. Then he saw Linzie. There was no warmth to her, only the hideous red glow of her eyes and cold indifference to his plight. One by one, he looked at the naked women, beautiful and terrifying with their glowing red eyes, until his eyes rested upon Lady Tara. The original spell had kept its charge, and even in the middle of this horrific nightmare, he still wanted her, even as a lioness. Celsus growled.

Abdul froze in terror when he looked to see what had produced the demonic sound. Covered in grey fur and revealing a set of monstrous canines, stood Lord Celsus, a living lycanthrope. Another monster stood on the table next to the wolf, beyond what Abdul's imagination could produce in the worst of nightmares.

The owl-woman sat, still pecking at Raymond's skull, hungry beyond reason. Her body was that of a woman, while her feet and head were those of a massive owl hybrid. Draped along the sides of the stone table, two gigantic wings defied all rationality. Abdul's last shred of sanity disappeared. After separating him from the female victim, Celsus sank his claws into his shoulder. Abdul screamed in agony, and the owl monster took notice. Celsus brought Abdul's face close to his own. Abdul shit himself as the wolf licked at the trails of blood running down his chest. Everyone in the circle was now privy to the wolf's thoughts.

Heather, I know you can see. This was supposed to be your sacrifice. I now give him to Cala. With it goes the remainder of your punishment. The worst of your deprivation is over. A lesson to you and everyone here—do not challenge me. I will hurt you. I may even kill you.

Abdul whimpered as the beast lifted him off his feet and hurled him forcefully at Elizabeth. Pure of instinct and reflex, she caught him by the leg with her right foot. Abdul screamed out loud as the other set of talons sank through the meat of his left hamstring. She flung the ravaged carcass of Raymond upon the ground, grabbed Abdul by the wrists, and pulled him close to her bloody beak.

She went right for the carotid artery. Quickly severing it, she drank to her heart's content while the rest of the coven watched. She drained all the blood from his body, and her head slowly turned back into its beautiful human form while the wings and talons remained. She let Abdul's lifeless body drop down on the stone table, and it was then that everyone could plainly see her large owl-like eyes. She spoke in the ancient Babylonian tongue, and her voice was inhuman.

"My precious beast, my lord and master, my wolf who is angry at me, I apologize to you from the bottom of my dark heart. My hunger overtakes my servitude. Please do not be angry with me, my lord. I have missed you so much. I have missed you all so much, my sweet sisters."

Cala stopped her dialog when she sensed the red wind swirling around the circle. She spoke with profound respect.

"Lili, I see you have come to join us."

Celsus reconstituted into his familiar human self and addressed his long-lost slave and lover.

"Welcome, Cala. If you wish the night hag gone, you must sacrifice a human to her. As with every second birth, Lili always waits, especially when it concerns you."

"My lord, I will always do as you wish, but my arms and legs are shackled, and my memory returns slowly with thoughts from thousands of years. What will you have me do?"

"Megan, free her!"

"Yes, my lord."

Megan undid the massive shackles that had cut deep into her wrists and ankles from her struggles. One by one, the four heavy chains slid off the stone altar. They hit the ground, each with a definitive resonance as if something forbidden was being released into the world. When finally free, she grabbed Megan and kissed her deeply, running the length of her inhuman tongue down Megan's throat. Her wings closed around the XO, making the scene both hideous and beautiful. The red wind roared louder, as did Nona's binding chant. The master yelled.

"The sacrifice, Cala!"

"My lord, who would you have me sacrifice?"

He grabbed the final captive and presented her. Cala immediately recognized the young woman, her next-door neighbor, Carrie.

"Your cruelty knows no bounds, my lord. Why th_s one?"

"You dare question me?"

She thought for a moment—an eternal moment. She thought of her tremendous power and the fact that she was no longer restrained. He moved within inches of her face and spoke candidly.

"It is folly, and you know it. Now is not the time, but you know well I welcome any challenge."

She smiled, threw her arms around him, and showered him with kisses.

"Master, may I ask you one small favor?"

"You may."

"Please keep her spellbound. She is truly innocent and I do not wish her to have any knowledge of her fate. No terror for this one, please, my lord."

Her voice was seductively sweet. She reached between his legs and groped him while he responded in a manner that surprised no one.

"As you wish, but your request comes with a price to be determined later. You will swear to receive whatever I determine a fair price for the deprivation I suffer now."

"I swear, my lord."

"So be it. Lili is upon us. Appease the hag before she smashes us!"

She turned to Carrie, who appeared to have no thoughts as if lobotomized. Satisfied with her condition, she picked her up like a groom crossing the threshold with his bride. As she was about to ascend, Nona rushed up to her.

"My lady, take this with you. It contains the soul of O'Mallin. This should do it."

She took the little stone and marveled for a moment at the prospect of permanently killing the spirit of Megan's childhood nightmare. Her wings then flared out, and she ascended straight up. The sheer volume of air blew Nona and Celsus back a step.

As she entered the top of the cone of protection, she became acutely aware of Nona's tremendous power. She looked down at Nona from a height of 90 feet and shouted.

"You are no monster! You are the greatest sorceress that walks the earth!"

Then she looked straight into the violent, swirling, red wind.

"Lili, Great Mother, I offer you the blood of an innocent and the soul of a monster. Will you accept these sacrifices? Will you take the pure blood of an innocent over the blood of your children? Will you take the soul of a monster over the souls of your children?"

All at once, the swirling stopped, and the red wind concentrated into the outline of a flying serpent. The coven witnessed two monsters flying above them, psychically linked—the red serpent precisely mimicking Cala's wing movements.

Nona stopped chanting, the protection cone diminished, and Cala handed Carrie and the stone to Lili. For a brief moment, there was calm, and then the grotesque sound of Carrie's bones cracking loudly echoed throughout the woods. Blood splattered on the coven below. Celsus and the women licked at the droplets like children playing in the rain. Not a single drop landed on Nona.

Suddenly, the entire coven froze because they could feel the consumption of Father O'Mallin's soul. It was a unique sensation, terribly final, with no literal description. Then there was nothing—no red serpent, no more blood, no more bones cracking, nothing, not even a body.

Cala softly descended until her feet touched the ground. She fell forward on her knees and then curled into a fetal position on the blood-soaked grass. The fire had died down considerably, and she cried. She knew they were all staring at her. She knew they loved her, but she just wanted peace. She welcomed the darkness and one particular memory.

I loved playing along the banks of the Euphrates with the other children. I was like them once. Once, I enjoyed the sun. Every day seemed to last for an eternity. What a miserable curse—eternity.

She woke to a warm fire and found herself between Sanem and Tara. She recognized the room from her first visit after waking from her experience on the machine. Sanem spoke first, obviously having read her thoughts.

"This is your room now."

She did not respond but instead sat up and looked around. Tara slid a hand up her thigh, and Cala found her touch energizing. The sheets were dark purple satin, and against them, her milky flesh was the only contrasting color between the two dark goddesses. Tara spoke next.

"We've been watching you all day," she said, kissing Cala's shoulder.

Sanem ran her hand through Cala's hair and curled up to her back. Cala could feel the heat rising from Sanem's womanhood on the back of her thighs, but something deep within was nagging at her.

I am hungry, she thought to herself.

"You may take our blood," Tara replied.

"I love you both so much. You know that. But I do not want your blood this first night. I want the blood of a brute."

Tara smiled and replied, "You haven't changed a bit. Have at it, sister."

"What does the master say?"

Sanem answered while kissing the back of Cala's neck.

"He is hunting alone tonight. Who knows, you may even see him at some point."

Cala jumped over Tara and stretched. Two giant wings sprouted from her back as she balled her hands into fists high above her head. Then, she curled her talons across the ancient Persian rug beneath her. She looked down and saw other triple slices across its surface.

"You kept my old rug."

Sanem laughed.

"Of course. How long have you had it?"

"I can't remember anymore."

The breeze from the open balcony took Cala's attention completely. As she stepped out, the gentle wind caressed her face. Her wings opened wide, and just as she was about to take off, Tara stopped her.

"Wait! There is something the master left for you. It's on top of your dresser."

Cala turned and walked back in. As she approached her dresser, she spied a rolled parchment bound by a white choker, a beautiful ornate vase holding several roses, and an old book. The vase was in the shape of an owl's head. In the vase, nine roses stood proud and in full bloom—seven red, one white, and one black.

She opened the ancient-looking book and remembered it as her old diary from France. The pages regarding her night with de Sade had been returned, carefully and expertly rebound to their rightful place.

Cala then slipped off the choker and read the elegant handwriting of the master, written with a fountain pen in his own blood.

My dearest Cala

Drink to your heart's content and return to me by daybreak

Lord Celsus

She looked up into the mirror and noticed her eyes, more prominent than expected, powerful beyond the understanding of the once-born. She smiled at the two women on the bed behind her. They smiled back, and Sanem addressed her in the mirror's reflection.

"Don't forget the choker. You earned it."

She dropped the parchment as a flood of harsh memories possessed her. Donning the white choker, she remembered the Coven of Siraba and their descendants: how they had prevented the first incarnation, how they had tried so hard to destroy them, and their ultimate failure and destruction by the soul of the master. She remembered when she and the other women killed and devoured Celsus in the wilds of Sweden, creating the beast he has been ever since. She also remembered the consequences of their actions, the horrific suffering of deprivation in both life and death for their rebellion against him. She stopped to admire the new choker and her two sisters in bed. Still looking through the reflection in the mirror, the two women were captivated and glowing at her memories. Tara spoke first.

"Why do you think only of the horrendous? Our moments of happiness and bliss far outweigh the bad."

She turned around and faced the two women.

"What about all the lives we have taken? Can you seriously make such a statement without considering that?"

Sanem laughed playfully and responded.

"As I sit here reading your thoughts and feeling your emotions, I see you have no remorse whatsoever for any lives taken. We are what we are, and you are toying with us."

She walked back to the balcony and giggled.

"Just checking, my ladies."

She hooked her talons around the balcony rail and took a deep breath. A clear night, a new moon, a new beginning, and trillions of stars intensified her hunger.

A brute—he must be a brute.

Cala licked her lips and soared off into the night—naked, monstrous, and beautiful.

HOME FREE

A cool autumn breeze surrounded the two immortals as they left the University of Toledo's Center for Performing Arts. Celsus and Cala walked arm-in-arm to the waiting limousine in the parking lot. The master seemed to be at peace, and Cala spoke to him telepathically, not wanting to disturb the quiet of the night.

Home Free—a play about two incestuous siblings all grown up and seriously dysfunctional, with Heather playing the part of Joanna. Quite a stretch for her, wouldn't you say, my lord?

Cala, must you always be so sarcastic?

When is her first visit, my lord? I can barely stand it anymore; she is suffering worse than I did.

Do you think it is any easier on me? Do you have any idea how terrible this is for me? Samhain is only two weeks away. She will have her first visit this Samhain.

What do you have in store for her?

She will play the flip side of her original visit.

Heather as a submissive? I can't see it, my lord.

She must. It is the only way back for her.

Who will run her, my lord?

We all will. I expect no mercy.

As they approached the limousine, Cala noticed the door was already open. Two glasses of vintage Chardonnay were waiting for them. She finally asked the question that had plagued her for almost two years.

"My lord, permission to speak candidly?"

"Yes."

"Who is driving this god-forsaken car?"

He let his hand fall casually upon the privacy window switch.

"You don't know?"

"No."

When the window dropped, Cala was shocked to see a smiling Sophia wearing a typical limousine driver's hat, suit coat, and black choker.

"Your sister? Your sister has been driving this car all along?"

She remembered Sophia's attempt at intimidating her the night she was nearly whipped to death. The master put his hand on her thigh to break her thoughts.

"Sophia is my sister. She is the XO of my lesser house and my lover. You will never hurt her. You will protect her and love her as I do. She did nothing to you that night except make you blush. Her blood is off-limits. Do you understand what I am saying?"

"Yes, my lord."

As the privacy window returned to its up position, Cala knew precisely what would happen next. The long black car drove to the far corner of the parking lot. As she unbuttoned her blouse, Sophia opened the door and sat between them.

Celsus and Cala undressed completely while Sophia stripped off everything but her black hat, suit coat, and black choker. The master stretched out on the limo floor and beckoned the two women.

Heather approached the car cautiously. She knew exactly who was in it and what they were doing. She rolled her eyes in disgust when she heard Sophia's voice.

"Devils! Sweet devils! Your tongue, my brother! Oh my fucking god, I love you!"

Just as Sophia was about to orgasm, there was a knock on the window. It was Heather trying to steal a peek. Cala rolled down the window while Celsus pushed his sister up by the hips to raise his head.

"You know better, Heather. You are not following protocol."

"My lord, please forgive me. I couldn't help but notice the car on my way out."

Still holding Sophia's glistening sex only inches from his face, he replied.

"Stand there and watch then, but you may only watch."

"Thank you, my lord," she replied softly.

Sophia's eyes closed in ecstasy as her brother resumed his oral assault. If her eyes had opened, she would not have been able to detect what Cala clearly could—a subtle demonic pinkish light in Heather's eyes—eyes fixed upon Sophia—eyes filled with eternal hatred and murderous desire.

$$\Delta$$

Elsewhere in the Great Lakes region, people were dying in unnatural ways. The other women of the Coven fed gregariously, and the sky over those cursed cities held an eerie red hue. The 17th coven was nearly complete.

Randy V

CHRONOLOGY
(non-inclusive)

1764 BC – Year of the first death, known as the Event.

1764 BC to 1530 BC – The sorceress Siraba and her descendants bind the spirits of Somro and his eight slave wives for several generations. They succeed in delaying the second incarnation for one entire cycle. Still, ultimately, the nine evil beings reenter the world of the living.

1530 BC to 1413 BC – (2nd incarnation) - Somro and Nona enter the world with their full memories. After tracking them across the globe, he learns he can will the memories to the other seven women. After 117 years of life, they believe they are immortal until one night when Nona abruptly dies. He and the other seven women die precisely 18 hours later. This exact sequence of events happens in every subsequent incarnation.

1296 BC to 1179 BC – (3rd incarnation)

1062 BC to 946 BC – (4th incarnation)

828 BC to 711 BC – (5th incarnation)

594 BC to 477 BC – (6th incarnation)

360 BC to 243 BC – (7th incarnation)

126 BC to 9 BC – (8th incarnation)

108 to 225 – (9th incarnation) - The spirit of Somro takes the name Celsus. This is the same historical Celsus of the Roman Empire. Around 178 AD, he writes *The True Word*, a philosophical discourse against Judeo-Christian beliefs.

342 to 459 – (10th incarnation) – In 459 AD, Celsus attempts to end his curse at Gamla Uppsala in Sweden. Lili simultaneously possesses seven of his coven's eight women, and they eat him alive. Nona witnesses the act but does nothing to prevent it.

576 to 693 – (11th incarnation) - Celsus now feeds as a wolf due to his previous death. He punishes the women by making them live in absolute madness for the entire incarnation by not releasing their memories. Nona is punished indirectly as she is forced to witness a century of her sisters' mental suffering but can do nothing to help them.

810 to 927 – (12th incarnation)

1044 to 1161 – (13th incarnation)

1278 to 1395 – (14th incarnation)

1512 to 1629 – (15th incarnation) – Celsus murders Cala in early 1560 for the killing of a political ally. She immediately possesses the unborn fetus of Báthory Erzsébet of Hungary but was born without her true memories. Incensed, Celsus refuses to acknowledge her for the remaining incarnation and forbids the coven from helping her. On August 21, 1614, she suffered a second death.

1746 to 1863 – (16th incarnation)

1980 to 2097 – (17th incarnation)

ABOUT THE AUTHOR

Photo by Morgan LeFay © 2008

Randy is a U.S. Army intelligence veteran, former fede-al air marshal, and graduate of the University of Toledo. He h⊃lds a Bachelor of Arts in Anthropology with departmental honor: and a Master of Arts in Sociology, specializing in social psychology. He is currently pursuing a Ph.D. in Communication and resides in Sturgis, South Dakota.